PLUNDER

PLUNDER

Thriller

Jürgen Dallüge

To order additional copies of this book, contact:
Xlibris Corporation
1-888-795-4274
www.Xlibris.com
Orders@Xlibris.com
37799

Dorothy, Betty and Margarete

To Jan

"... that drains the Empire of its wealth and sent, in exchange for baubles, our money to foreign nations and even to the enemies of Rome."

Warning by Tiberius to the Senate of Rome

Preface

From the office of the Chief of Council for War Crimes in Nuremberg on 28 December 1948, Dr. Robert M.W. Kemper wrote a letter of pivotal importance to Mr. Perry Lankhuff of the Political Division, Office of Military Government, United States (OMGUS) in Berlin.

The words, expression and Grammatik of this letter are the identical text of Dr. Kemper's written words and grammar and can therefore not be altered. Here, the excerpt of the letter:

"In the course of our trial against . . . diplomats which has just been concluded, it brought to light that the German Foreign Office had a special Ribbentrop gold fund, in gold bullion, weighing approximately fifteen tons.

Out of the fifteen tons, about eleven tons of Ribbentrop's Foreign Office gold was hurriedly removed from Berlin in 1945:

1. *6.5 tons to Ribbentrop's castle Fuschle in Austria (now American Zone of Austria). The larger part of this consignment was allegedly turned over to American troops in the neighborhood of Fuschle.*
2. *2 tons to Schleswig-Holstein in the British Zone, allegedly turned over to the British.*
3. *3 tons to the South of Germany on the shores of Lake Konstanze, an area at this time in American hands. Out of the last amount, two-third of a ton was brought over to Bern, Switzerland, in the closing days of the war. This was done in the presence of the son of the former German Minister of Foreign Affairs, von Neurath who, according to newspaper reports, arrived a short time ago in Argentina. About four tons were sent between 1943 and 1945 to German embassies, notable to Madrid, Spain (one ton), to Stockholm, Sweden (one-half ton), to Ankara, Turkey (about one ton), to Lisbon, Portugal (an unknown quantity). Since I interviewed several*

hundred German diplomats, including ambassadors, ministers, and fiscal and personnel administrators, I know that the summation which I made above is highly reliable. But so far as I know there was never any check made whether gold of this amount was ever recovered or whether Foreign Office gold turned over by German foreign service people to allied authorities at the end of the war was identical with sums indicated by my investigation."

Dr. Robert Kemper's query had been forwarded to the FED (Foreign Exchange Depository), and on 3 May 1949 the Acting Chief of the FED, Frank J. Roberts, responded with a statement about the German Foreign Office gold as reflected in the records of the FED. It was more expansive than any other fine metal. Six-and-a-half tons of the precious metal, gold, platinum and iridium from Castle Fuschle vanished in the last day of World War Two.

This is the story of what might have happened to it.

The greatest robberies on record by the end of World War II:

1. Jewels, securities, foreign currency taken at gun point from the Berlin Reichsbank by SS General Joseph Spacil, April 22, 1945.

   $ 47,190,786.-

2. Eleven boxes weighing 330 pounds, believed to contain gold stolen by persons unknown, sometimes after burial near Mittenwalde, Bavaria, on April 27, 1945.

   $ 26,922,229.-

3. Gold currency bonds taken from the Reichsbank in Berlin by major Fedor Novikow of Red Army intelligence, May 15, 1945.

   $ 2,200,000,000.-

4. 6.5 tons of gold of the Ribbentrop gold. Last seen at Castle Fuschle, Austria, March/April 1945.

   $ 107,759,550.-

5. Ninety bars of gold and $ 4,580,378 in gold coins. Taken from the Reichsbank in Berlin by the Red Army in May 1945.

   $ 49,801,990.-

6. Seventeen bags of foreign currency, taken from the Reichsbank in Berlin and hidden; stolen again in May 1945. Probably by a Colonel Fritz Rauch, Helmut Gröger. Recovered in parts by the U.S. Army, which then disappeared.

$ 10,332,910.-

7. One truckload of foreign currency, a portion of which was last seen on the desk of U.S. Major Kenneth Asa McIntryre in Garmisch, Bavaria.

$ 44,000,000.-

8. One hundred gold bars from the Reichsbank in Berlin, which were recovered by U.S. Sergeant Albert Singleton near Mittenwalde in June 1945 and subsequently disappeared in the hands of the CIC.

$ 20,395,627.-

9. Unspecified amount of gems and gold with an estimated value of $ 38,000,000.—from Hungarian Jews handed over by SS-General Kurt Becher to the U.S. Military Government in Salzburg, Austria. Disappeared.

$ 38,000,000.-

$ 2,544,403,922

Prologue

Ephraim Katz.

His lower arm still hurt. Somebody had tattooed a six-digit number into his flesh. He was only fourteen years old and he could not cry. Ephraim had inherited the fine skill of an engraver from his father. Both had been separated when they came into the camp.

Young Ephraim had just melted 72 pounds of gold in a special furnace. Before the gold was melted the metals had been tooth fillings. Fillings broken from the living and the dead. When Ephraim took the warm gold bar it was still warm, like the former owner's body temperature. Ephraim began to engrave a statement into the soft surface of the gold:

> *I, Ephraim Katz have melted today 72 pounds*
> *Of gold teeth fillings into bars. It was*
> *broken from the mouth of the living and the dead.*
> *May Yahweh forgive. I can not.*

Ephraim was a prisoner of the camp in Sachsenhausen. An inmate of barrack 18/19. This particular barrack was under the strict control of the SS secret service. Here the SS secret service printed the counterfeit money and melted gold of any form and purpose into bars. Ephraim also witnessed seven trucks hauling away the gold bars carefully stacked and secured on pallets. With the haul went the engraved gold piece. He had done his work. He survived.

Ephraim Katz.

1

How it all started

In July 1944, the SS Secret Service's monthly *Egmont Report* made it very clear what all in that organization already suspected. Germany was going to lose the war. On August 10, 1944, in the Hotel Maison Rouge in Strasbourg, France, a secret conference was called that was attended by representatives of German industry, the military, especially the Navy and the SS. At that meeting plans were discussed for safely moving the blueprints of new weapon systems, which could not be completed in time, out of the country. Minutes from this meeting also suggested how and where the fortunes should be distributed. For example—precious metals.

*

San Nazaire, France, February 1945

Under the cover of a raging winter night, a huge black water war machine, U-boat 2345, slipped from its base in San Nazaire, unknown and unseen, into the penumbra of the Atlantic Ocean. The U-boat was a class IXD2. During World War II, this U-boat had once been assigned to a group, Monsoon II, a thirty-U-boat Wolfpack.

She had set sail to reach the Island of Penang in Malaysia by the end of 1943. From there this German U-boat would cooperate with Japanese submarines into Singapore and Surabaya under the code name "Operation Siegfried", to fight the American Navy. While the first group of U-boats set sail on this lengthy and precarious journey to South-East Asia, the commander of U-boat 2345 had received a last-minute order *not* to sail. Since then, U-boat

2345 had never been taken out on an assignment. She just disappeared from the war scene.

But sixteen months later, in February 1945 and much closer to the end of the lost war, on this stormy winter night, U-boat 2345 began its very long and extended mission. The order of the highest priority for U-boat Commander Helbig was to avoid contact with any ship and to stay out of sight and trouble. Therefore, he was not to give any details of their location or direction. The 2345 IXD2 U-boat, the largest U-boat ever built during World War II, headed south, carrying a crew of forty-eight.

With a range of 30,000 miles, she was a long-range ocean-going craft, planned for ultimate performance. With an innovative snorkel system, fitted with an underwater coating, this perfect ocean-going boat could travel for three months without surfacing. Her double hull was covered with a special rubber skin to deflect radar. She had soundless hydrogen-peroxide engines, moving her by a belt drive, completely noiseless at a speed of five knots.

The submarine could hold up to 800 tons of freight, and with her sleek hull, she could cruise at a maximum speed of 18 knots, enough to outrun any destroyer at that time. The huge, advanced battery system made her the first truly electric underwater boat. Her new anti-radar device was highly sensitive and would help to ensure her safety on this hazardous voyage. Although it could be considered an act of lunacy at this stage of World War II, to drive a submarine through the Gulf of Biscay and around the Cape of Hope, this immense boat was prepared.

Now the freight. The cargo gave the U-boat 2345 its purpose.

Before the journey began, some major modifications had taken place to make the boat ready for the special mission and its secret cargo. Her interior was adjusted to carry bulk cargo, such as dismantled V2 rockets and prototypes of new weapons technology. Modification included four torpedo tubes with specially crafted container that would hold blueprints for new weapons technologies, armaments, and precious metals to be used in the years to come. Preparation for the defeat. And after.

The loading of such vast amounts of precious metal freight required the detachment of the U-boat's outer keel plates. That had been overseen by a hand selected task force, the *Marine Sonder Dienst Ausland*[1]. The payload included thirty-six tons of mercury, 105 tons of silver in its purest form,

---

[1]   Navy Special Foreign Service

forty-five tons of gold from the *Reichsbank* and 198 tons of Uranium-235 from the mines in Aue, Germany. The order was to transport the booty of the Reich, which had lost the war, to safety.

*

A stiff wind blew from north-northwest. The clouds were hanging low, like dirty laundry over the choppy grey salty water. The commander of U-boat 2345 left the hatch open for a long time so his men could breathe fresh air. His crew was young and none of them were married. They had been very carefully selected over a period of twelve months. Selected from a good race of former Hitler Youth, well trained and educated. With their waxen faces and assumed indifference, what they would need most was luck. If such a thing existed.

Thirty miles out to sea, the water became increasingly rough. As far as the commander could see, white caps danced on the crests of the waves. Not wanting to press any luck he might have, the commander issued his command.

"Prepare to dive," he said quietly, "and take her down to sixty-five feet."

The hatch closed, and the crew could hear the soft gurgling sound of the sea's embrace, an illusion of safety they did not have. Never would. But for the moment, safe.

*

For the next three days the boat cut through the ocean undetected and, after the Gulf of Biscay, they were clear, heading south. Death approached the U-boat for the first time on the sixth day. They were located. The allies had developed a new system of detecting submarines with the Code name Huff-Duff. It was a high-frequency-direction-finding system where U-boat contact signals could be detected and its definite bearing displayed on a cathode-ray tube. First a submarine was located by a plane, normally a Catalina flying boat, and in that short moment, its destruction was set in motion. U-boat 2345 had been detected this way, without knowing it.

Unexpectedly and suddenly the lights flickered with peculiar lingering roars. A series of depth charges exploded. Commander *(KL)* Helbig rushed into the sonar room. Abruptly everything grew quiet. The petty officer sat in front of the sonar, chewing on his lower lip. In the dim light his head seemed to be squeezed between his earphones.

"They're going crazy up there," he whispered depressed, not daring to look up. "They're on listen-and-attack maneuvers. They must have something new. Definitely being guided by a plane. They will throw a pattern now. It's going to be noisy in here."

And it was. Every two minutes, a new series of well-aimed depth charges whipped, growled and exploded around the boat with echoing ugly roars. Death rumbling howls that screamed—*hey, you young little morons, what are you doing down there. I'll shred your steel tube to bits and pieces, stupid juveniles, and I'll fill your lungs with cold black salt water.'*

The commander let the boat sink deeper. Behind him he could hear a sailor crying. He smelled the vomit of another sailor hunched in the corner. After forty depth charges, there seemed to be a pause. Death was a patient creature, it could wait for eternity. The crew could hear the silence. Pure quietness not containing serenity. It was as if all at once they were shut in a steel jar, floating in nothingness. The commander could not figure out if they were hit. Made a dismissing motion with his left hand to the three officers. They knew time for damage control had come. Still floating. No one said anything. What was there to say?

"Oh, it is so great to be here, for the Fuehrer and the Homeland in this round steel trap, 200 fucking meters below daylight."

The men stared with dim expressionless faces at the ceiling of steel and waited for the next series to be dropped. They did not look at each other.

"Two hundred and ten meters," the helmsman whispered at the barometer.

The commander still directed him thumbs down. There was a soft cracking sound of stressed metal. It was picked up by the destroyer above and hell began again. Now the charges fell regularly once more. Every ten seconds, the U-boat jolted in a short violent shudder.

"Damage control," Helbig whispered.

"No leaks—everything okay," the watch mumbled, staring with glazed eyes at his gauges.

"Remain at this depth," Helbig responded quietly, "and everyone lie down."

He wanted to save oxygen. Another hour went by. He knew they were waiting for him to make a move. Finally a pale, twisting sizzle broke the silence before the next detonation. It was a single depth charge without any patterns. Just one single deep charge. It had fallen overboard by accident. Its blast threw the entire U-boat to one side and the steel seemed to buckle for a moment when the wave of the discharge impacted with the outer skin of the double hull, just eight feet away from the boat's sail. A long hollow echo rumbled across the underworld of night-like cold water. Ironically, it was this close brush with death that actually saved the men and their submarine. Tied up to a single manila rope to the conning tower, in that dark icy water, was a forty gallon drum of heavy 40HP synthetic engine oil, produced in the Buna Chemical plant in Germany. Under the impact of that last single charge, the drum's thin metal broke and began to nonchalantly release its contents. Hurrying, the oil began to rise to the surface of the Atlantic Ocean, like it couldn't't wait to show its different colors in the dazzling daylight above. On the surface of the ocean it began to spread in wide and constantly changing colorful circles.

The British captain of the destroyer claimed a kill. But instead of leaving, he stayed and waited. Perhaps to pick up some survivors, which was not likely from his experiences. U-boat? Submarine? It was not like a battlefield where humans would die one after another over a certain period of time. No. As a matter of fact, in the steel tube, once hit, they would all die at once. With that last single depth charge, time began to slow down in the U-boat. Minutes went by in silence. Commander Helbig looked up at the steel ceiling, seeing nothing. His mind was somewhere—outside—trying to fathom why this unknown captain desisted from further attack. Somehow he felt he knew his foe was still there. Helbig waited eight more hours in silence. One of the men went insane.

Finally Helbig switched to electric power and began a silent escape. A *Schleichfahrt,* soft and slow. The next charges they heard came from very far off, like fading thunders, widely scattered and without pattern. Four hours later the sonar man, still whispering, announced: "Everything quiet. We are clear, Herr Kaleu."

"Blow tanks," the commander called.

Air whistled and hissed as the boat rose to the surface. The conning tower jutted out of the water.

"Free," the watch announced. Helbig opened the tower hatch and jumped onto the bridge. Fresh air rushed into the boat. It was a milky, moonlit night and they were alone. After this it took U-boat 2345 sixty days to move in silence along the West African coast of Sierra Leone, Liberia and around Cape of Hope to Gwadar. West Pakistan. They arrived three days ahead of schedule. U-2345 settled down and remained on the bottom in the shallow water of only thirty feet. The shore. No life. It was a wild, lonesome, sunburned stretch of a coast with nothing on it. The crew had to wait another seventy-two hours for the next phase of their mission: an additional six tons of cargo from Hungary.

Gold and Platinum.

2

Castle Fuschle, Austria, March 1945

The frosty wind blew fine but steadily from the high peaks of the Alps. Dark clouds were pregnant with snow again. Men in SS uniforms were loading canopied trucks in hasty silence. There was certain urgency because the first two trucks had to leave the estate before dawn to avoid the low flying Spitfires, which these days, chased and shot at anything moving on the ground. The Americans had, without a doubt, completed air superiority.

German Foreign Minister Joachim von Ribbentrop walked into the courtyard and had a last look at the treasure. He still could not grasp the fact that they had lost the war. It was an enormous stash of precious metal, fifteen tons of it. Six and a half tons of gold were supposed to be turned over to U.S. troops in Austria, two and a half more tons were on their way to Schleswig-Hollstein, allegedly to be handed over to British troops. Most of the "hand-over" gold would just disappear after the hand-over.

By 0100 the first two trucks with two and a half tons of precious metals, platinum, palladium, iridium, osmium, rhodium and gold left Castle Fuschle. The truck drivers would hide in the forests with their precious cargo during the day and wait for night to travel with blue-colored headlights.

Two hours before Budapest, the trucks were detected by a squadron of eighteen P-51 Mustang fighter aircraft, with its three divisions split in two three-plane sections, cruising in its full strength in at an altitude of 19,000 feet. Squadron leader Colonel Richard B. Cooper spotted the two trucks and decided it was not worth to launch a full attack in three needed sequences. By radio, Cooper advised his left wingman to take care of the trucks. Just shoot the hell out of them. Finish them off. The wing man Lt. Frank Boens from Idaho had seen the two trucks earlier and wondered whether they would do away with them. He received the radio order and banked his plane immediately over the left wing tip, beginning the peel-off from his squadron.

He advanced to fifteen-thousand feet and positioned his plane for the attack with the setting sun behind. He throttled back and lifted the nose of his P-51 somewhat above the horizon, increasing his stall position. With the movement of his right thumb he operated the dive and landing flaps, checked the peel-off direction one more time and let the Mustang plane literally fall over its left wing. Boens dove at an almost ninety degree angle toward the two racing trucks. The P-51 accelerated fast to 425kmp.

Boens opened the throttle and pulled the stick. It was the first low-level run. The four 53-2 Browning machine guns hailed an initial round as an opener, so to speak. Boens pulled the stick further. A five-G tortured his body when he climbed again to roll over for the next dive. He had flown some difficult missions during the battle over England, had shot down six Japanese Aichi dive bombers of the Naguma force over the Pacific in 1942. Had participated in the conquest of Midway and all the other little pathetic islands where young blood was spilled and bodies maimed for the sake of a few square miles of useless empty islands.

And now in the spring of 1945, by the end of this war, Boens assumed these two fast moving trucks were just a sort of bonus after all the years of demolition he had lived through. Pilot Boens was young. So marvelous and handsomely immature, with the mix of the arrogance of youth *and* experience. He was just twenty-three-years old. He dropped his guard. The sun greeted his smiling face when he pushed the stick and rolled over onto the next attack. He loved flying. Approached in a seventy degree angle.

On the second truck's platform, installed on a tripod, was a machinegun, an MG42. The German teenager gunner had been wounded in the first hail of the P-51's thundershower of bullets. Under the impact of the bullets he had been thrown off the truck and down the embankment. There he broke his neck in a water-filled ditch. His body would be found some days later by farmers. But at the moment the barrel of the machine-gun gazed without aim into the air.

Also on the second truck was the officer responsible for the transport of the loot. His name was Kurt Becher, Colonel Kurt Becher. He had seen the war from its first day on and Becher was no coward. The second truck's sergeant-driver stopped abruptly to let the P-51 overrun the target by its own speed. The Colonel jumped out, hurried at the platform and took in a cool attempt the gun. Having the approaching plane in the cross-hairs, he pulled the trigger. The MG42 released one-thousand two-hundred-rounds-per-minute, pursuing the incoming Mustang plane.

It was like the plane flew into a chain saw. Young life-loving Lt. Frank Boens had joyously thrown his P-51 into the second dive. Coming down from 13,000 feet ready to activate the trigger, he never thought about an obstacle. By three-thousand feet he wondered for a moment why suddenly the propeller took off on its own, taking the airbrake with it. With amazement and strange curiosity, he noticed that the tailgate separated from the plane and soared in a different direction. The wings and fuselage were still in a diving mood when the last bullet hit the carburetor. Spilling high octane fuel was ignited by a spark. Frank wondered for a moment what the name of his unborn child in Idaho would be. Wondered whether it was really fair being shot down after all these years of war and why he could not open his seat belt to bail out. Mercifully his consciousness did not function anymore or he would have realized that his arms were on fire, like the whole plane. The existence of young and handsome Frank Boens disintegrated in his P-51 when it collided, still at a 70-degree diving angle, with the frozen ground.

Three hours later the two trucks rolled onto the airfield of Budapest.

3

Budapest, Hungary, March 1945

The rumbling of far-away exploding grenades created the illusion of a thunderstorm. Actually it was a thunderstorm. But one created by humans.

The uniform looked good on him. Colonel of the *Luftwaffe*. He wore a Knight's Cross with diamond, oak leaves and the swords. It promised to be a bright and sunny day. Ideal weather to fly. He looked into the mirror and saw the face of a handsome stranger.

*

Colonel Claus von Hadik had no family and was alone. Alone as a soldier could be in a war. He did not have a place to turn to. Even after this war, he would not have a place to go. Sometimes he wondered how he had survived the slaughters in the air. Today there was something inside him that told him he would not survive this war. The airfield, with its grey concrete strips, was molded into the long valley twenty miles outside Budapest. His eyes took in the tight security, the SS soldiers with their Schmeisser machine guns over their shoulders. He wondered what kind of death this day would bring.

She was beautiful and sat on the end of the runway. She was a well guarded secret of World War II and the most advanced in her class. Her skin was smooth and made from a strong aluminum-titanium alloy. In the entire field of aircraft design, few had ever seen her. Except the brilliant minds that had brought her to life on drawing boards, and the highly skilled mechanics that had brought her to real life. He was chosen to be a part of her world. Nobody in the field of aviation could ever imagine that something of her technical beauty and advance by 1942 would exist. She was a state-of-the-art ultra-long-range bomber.

She sat under a camouflage net at the end of the runway, and the Colonel had recognized her covered sumptuousness immediately. Like a gentle cat waiting to be petted. There was something lascivious about her. Her form was so smooth and gentle. From his first experiences with her three years back, he knew he would be able to handle her again. She had spirit and he knew that if he treated her right, she would take him, under any conditions, to wherever he wanted to go with her. He wondered for a moment who piloted her to Hungary. What von Hadik did not know was that she had never been tested to her breaking point. Her weak spot was the super-charger. The intake did not have a filter that would have perfectly suited her. She certainly had his loyalty, because he was the first in her life to have her. When he was with her the first time she had spread her wings to let him know the secrets of how she could respond to him. From the moment he entered her, she accepted him and responded to him as her master.

And this was her story.

She was a Messerschmidt 264 with four V3 one-thousand seven-hundred horse power each of her BMW 801D cylinder, radial engines. Her span was 141 feet and her length sixty-eight feet and seven inches. Her height was only fourteen feet and two inches. This was the reason she looked like a crouched cat on the airfield ready to purr or pounce. With her weight and a maximum load of 123,460 pounds, she could fly at a optimum speed of 351-miles-per-hour. Her most comfortable speed was 217 miles per hour. At this comfortable rate of cruising, she could sail for an *incredible 9,312 miles without refueling.*

The High Command planned to use her for a propaganda trip to the east coast of the United States where they would drop leaflets and counterfeit dollars over New York. Then she would return to Europe and would ditch—short of fuel—offshore near a U-boat, which would bring back the crew. Only three of the 264's were built, then the program was scrapped.

However the *SS-Reichssicherheits Hauptamt,* took over the program. But for unspecified purposes, she simply disappeared. She was almost forgotten when she got this first and only assignment at the end of World War II. For this last mission an experienced flyer was needed to handle her. Hours earlier two trucks arrived from Austria and the cargo was loaded immediately onto the plane. That gave the plane a payload of six and a half tons.

He walked around the aircraft for a last visual checkup under the suspicious eyes of the SS guards. Then he climbed up the short aluminum ladder and moved into the cockpit. The flight engineer and the navigator looked nervous and almost frightened. He knew them from their work together on the first flight. They were civilians, highly skilled engineers who did not understand the game of war.

"*Ist alles in Ordnung?*" he asked them.

"*Ja, Herr Oberst,*" one of them replied, "where are we going?"

"I don't know." was his honest answer. He got up, went back into the cargo bay, and checked the cargo. Inspected the payload of the pallets, symmetrically piled and tightly covered, was carefully tied precisely in the center of the 264. The cargo attracted his curiosity. He took his pocket knife and cut a short gash through the heavy tarp. Metal. Lustrous silvery-gleaming. Only then he saw the sign—*Warnung*—OSMIUM. Osmium oxide would release a toxic gas. He backed off.

He checked the next pallet. A sign informed him about what was on it. PLATINUM in its purest form of bars of standard weights and measures. Two-thousand pounds. Piled up on the next pallet was the world's hardest, most corrosion-resistant metal, able to withstand heat of 2.000EC-Iridium. The 5000 pounds gold on the next pallets looked almost lost. However, the value of all the concentrated precious metals was beyond comprehension. He whistled and moved back into the cockpit and strapped himself into the seat. Waited.

Artillery fire of incoming rounds was now perhaps two miles away. He was in no hurry. Looked at his watch. It was 15:47. As he began to go over the pre-flight checklist, he saw a *Kübelwagen* racing across the airfield. It stopped close to the plane. An SS officer jumped out and walked in fast elastic, long strides to the Messerschmitt.

"Colonel von Hadik," he heard the sharp voice behind him pronounce, "here are your flight orders."

The impact of two grenades exploding at the end of the runway shook the plane slightly. Chain-like bursts of machine gun fire interrupted the strange heavy silence between the explosions. The Colonel took the envelope and broke the red seal. He pulled out a map, unfolded it and began to study the instructions. The flight order was unreal, absurd. Still, he was a soldier by profession and did not question an order.

He turned around and looked at the *Sturmbannführer*.

Calm and relaxed he pointed to the map.

"And . . . then what?"

"After you have reached the Gwadar, a group of our agents will take the cargo to a submarine."

"They are already in a covered stand-by and waiting for your arrival. The plane will be blown up and you will be on a submarine on your way to Uruguay. You have no other choice."

"Heil Hitler and good luck."

Two SS-Staffelführer came on board and made themselves comfortable in front of the cargo. Security guards. The doors were locked.

"Everybody on board?" he asked, realizing the uselessness of his question.

"It's all clear, Herr Oberst," the flight engineer said. As von Hadik took the checklist his feet shuffled for the control pedals. Found them.

"Weight and balance?" he began.

"Check."

"Fuel transfer valves and switches?"

"Right, all of them."

"Intercooler?"

"Clear."

"Fuel shut-off switches?"

"Check."

"Autopilot?"

"Off."

It went on for another five minutes.

"Start engines," the colonel said.

He heard the whining as the generator began to pull and the hum of the starter engine as it engaged. The number one, right outboard engine came to life with a short stuttering and the air screw began to rotate, at first hesitatingly, while black smoke escaped from the exhaust stubs. Then it roared to life with all of its 1,340 horsepower. The second engine followed. The third and then the fourth.

Von Hadik looked outside the glass cabin every time and watched the propellers begin to rotate until the revolutions of each engine made the blades look like silver whirls in the twilight of this spring afternoon of 1945. He adjusted the four engines until each had reached the same gyration, increased the power and held her back with the brakes.

"Tower, this is flight Steiermark-seven-five ready for take-off," the colonel announced over the microphone.

"Steiermark-seven-five. You are clear for take-off. Wind is three-two-one at thirty kilometers," an anonymous voice said.

Claus von Hadik gave more power to the engines, let the brakes go and left the parking pad. Taxied east, and when he came to the end of the runway he turned her into the wind. Increasing the power, he moved into the main runway and let her go. A grenade exploded behind the racing Messerschmidt 264, making the runway useless behind him. The plane raced down the concrete strip with the fat, rich sound of the roaring engines. He felt the beginning lift, gently pulled the control wheel and lifted her nose. With this small motion of his arms, he knew that his last flight had begun.

At first he kept her at an extremely low altitude. The swastika had been, for whatever reason, taken off of the rudder. His intuition told him it had something to do with the cargo. The Colonel crossed the Second Ukrainian Front of the Red Army of General Malinowski. An army that had pounded Budapest and its surrounding area with thousands of 122 mm Howitzers. The effect was devastating.

The plane's camouflage was perfect. Its colors blended perfectly into the environment of both sky and earth. The light of the hazy sunset was at his back when he turned the plane into a southwest course. During the first hours, the mills of his mind began to revolve, undecided how and where to die.

But the Gods of War had already granted his wish to discontinue his life. Miles away they began to create the circumstances that would lead to the disappearance of the plane and its crew.

The monotonous, redundant heavy humming of the four airscrews let his mind drift into the past, but without losing the ability to observe the hostile sky. Six years of flying, six years of war had taught him this. Subconsciously his mind had manifested death. His head went up mechanically and his eyes carefully scanned the sky above him. There was still a soft light far above the horizon. He could see a squadron of RAF Lancasters surrounded by three Wickers Wellingtons 6000 feet above him. The long contrails gave away the course of northwest. They now owned the sky and did not have to worry about being attacked. He lit a cigarette, inhaled deeply and allowed the smoke to escape through his nose. His memory pulled him back, back to the past. It was a short sharp exchange of words between him and his father. No, Claus von Hadik couldn't choose the conservatory, a life in war and not in music. When he was eight, young Claus had learned the piano and at the age of fourteen he played Chopin, Liszt, and Handel better than he had done anything else in his life. But still he ended up in the Luftwaffe, at the *Fliegerschule.*

He thought about the dreary numbness of war. He thought about the long reconnaissance flights across the Atlantic Ocean, close to the shores of the United States. He thought about the long distance flights far behind the Ural Mountains into the Soviet Union in 1940. He thought about the attack on the Island of Crete where his squadron had spilled out the finest men ever trained. paratroopers. Only they died in three senseless waves of attack over Maleme, Iraklion and Khania. Men killed before they even touched the ground or could disengage their parachutes.

"Herr Oberst, two more minutes to changing course to 0237 east. We are in reach of Ankara."

The voice brought him back to present. Ankara had to be avoided. The British were there. He forwarded his command to his plane via the swivel mounted control stick. Smoothly the Messerschmitt dipped her right wing and the compass showed straight south east to Circus.

His eyes searched the sky above and below him before his thoughts trailed off again. He had loved his parents despite them calling him a dreamer when he explained about the music he wanted to compose. His dream was to conduct an orchestra with 1500 musicians and make Beethoven worth listening to. In his purity of mind as a growing and gifted child, he had all the spiritual knowledge that there was a range of beauty unrecognized by the human sense of hearing. He wanted to talk about the melodies he had in his mind and wanted to compose. Wanted to talk with adults about his music, but he only saw smirking smiles around him and with shortsightedness, they patted his shoulder in sarcastic forgiveness. He felt so alone among them that he could not express to anybody that the melodies he heard were not sound waves but pulsations received from the spirit of a celestial personality, an expression of the soul, when the harmony of sound creates color at the same time. It would not have made sense to them. So, he had to give in to the long tradition of a military family.

And then, there were the more agonizing memories. The recollection of horror. By 1941 he was assigned to the Eastern Front. Russia. He was just twenty-seven and had already reached the rank of captain with shiny new medals on his chest. There was the first chill of what war really meant. He flew a Junkers 52/3m to rescue wounded men. While the injured human cargo was loaded, he met the field doctor.

"These are the worst cases," the overworked tired doctor said. Maybe better off dead, than alive." The shrill screams of men without arms (plural), without legs (plural), or the shredded-away faces were as surreal to him like a Hieronymus Bosch painting. Men with shot-off jaws would ask with a gesture to smoke a cigarette. A face shot-off for a piece of metal. Dear God, what a hell of a price to pay. And between the agony of blood and bodily destruction, he saw her. The nurse.

She moved between the wounded men like an angel. Giving them water, a friendly word, or an opium injection to the gruesomely dismembered. She flew back with him. They married four weeks later. But did he really love her? He liked her. But love—no. He did not know what it was. War. She was a good comrade and accepted him since men were rare in time of war. He respected her individuality and was good to her. She got pregnant and did not have to return to the front. The day she moved into her parents house in Hamburg, July 24, 1943, 740 RAF bombers dropped 2,396 tons of bombs on the city. The air raid was completed in two hours of destruction. She perished in the firestorm with her unborn child along with forty-one thousand beings. His bitterness was the perfect fusion for grasping the meaninglessness of the killing. Now he flew this remarkable plane on his last mission of a lost war, knowing it was a flight into eternity. Thousand miles away, conditions for his death took on their final form.

4

Four thousand feet above the Jambai Hamrin, three hundred miles north from Baghdad, a cold front of many days was on its way to collide with a warm front, which was moving in rapidly from the southwest of Saudi Arabia. A *Shamal*, a sandstorm. It would be the first of the new season.

*

Jabal Hamrin, Iraq, March 1945

His eyes were open although he was deeply asleep. His tendons were tightly locked with muscles on the edge of rock. It kept him balanced. With the first light of the new young day he woke up and his heart trembled in joy and anticipation. He was a Gypaetus barbatus, a bearded vulture, a *Lämmergeier*. He and his kind would appear as single or in pairs in this particular area of northern Mesopotamia. He was single. Mostly he had been seen circling around mountaintops or leisurely patrolling a mountain side. His appearance was majestic and overwhelming when he sailed along in slow motion high above the desert. The sailing creature hardly moved its immense wings. He was a seasoned flier and hunter. He had been allover the area. Had made it even South, over the blue sea humans called the Mediterranean, to be a sort of a visitor over the southern deserts of Turkey and northern Iraq. There he was a powerful guest. In the northern part of the Middle East and Africa the Bedouins called him a *kabmudsen*, a power bird.

In the cold of this new morning he shook his strong body twice, as his powerful legs, blessed with lethally long, knife-blade sharp talons tightly locked their grips to the rim of a rock. Over seven-thousand feet below was the desert. He looked down from his high stony perch. It *was* his empire. A region hardly supporting vegetation throughout its surface.

Where plants were not able to form a close cover, but were widely spaced with bare patches between them, and where life might largely depend on growing daily depressions. The valley on which he was looking down at was sparsely covered with shrub vegetation. Shrubs used by the Bedouins only as firewood. It was a land of uncultivated ground. The land below him supported nothing. It was the highest aridity in an absolute desert area, an area that supported little or nothing. A wild land over which wandering men of the desert and their animals had scratched out a daily survival scheme for the next thousands of years to outlast the rest of the world. The lack of water in this region and the dry harshness of this rangeland only allowed a stunt, low growing woody vegetation.

The Gypaetus barbatus was hungry and is was time for the hunt. Yes, he could easily catch a small injured goat, a deer. Today, he wanted real meat. Real nourishment. Fresh blood. He could effortlessly snatch a lamb with his enormous talons. A lamb. That is what he wanted today. Not only because of the meat. But because of the large bones. The bones were an even more important link in his chain of food supply. The bird needed the marrow of the bones. He would take the big bones one by one and drop them from the air to shatter them to get to the important nourishment. That was what he was looking for on this promising cold morning.

He turned his elegant feathered head around in staccato motions. His cold emerald-colored eyes searched the still dark deadly land, the dunes below. He opened his beak and stretched his jaws and neck several times, as if making certain that his body, in its perfect creation, would function flawlessly while hunting for his prey. He became restless. The air was hot and moist and he could sense the build-up of a sandstorm, somewhere. Out there. A force that could mill around hundreds of thousands of tons of sand for days.

He stretched his wings like a skipper making his boat sail with the right wind. The bearded vulture loosened the grip of his talons, pushed his body away from the rim and began to sail. Welcomed the wind of the still navy-blue sky around his powerful breast and used the rising pocket of warmer air to soar to greater heights. The thermal air on this morning was undercut by the leftovers of the cold night and was therefore so strong that the vulture rose in big looping circles. He lengthened his huge but delicate white and black wings and rose motionlessly into the updraft. His exquisite and sensitive eyes searched for the prey somewhere thousands of meters below. The time of his hunt began. With his supreme aerodynamic design he was a lord of the air, an ultimate efficient flyer. The power bird corrected his course and sailed northwest. It was 07:30.

*

Hazy sun broke down the last left-over of the night. The vulture knew where he would get his food as he cruised into another valley. His target was Arbil, a small village of Kurds living there since the beginning of time, when men of culture began to write down the occurrences of history. It was a village blessed with many chickens and lambs. He had sailed over it many times in the past.

For him, the bird with its 2.72 meter (7.5 feet) wingspan, the business of stalking, while motivated by impulse and instinct, was also a skill for him. His body shuddered as he voyaged. His feathers appeared like a lustrous blue-black gleaming hull in the morning light. The thermal brought him to the air where the day was still fresh and young. He liked to sail on outstretched wings. No motion.

Far below him, what looked like mountains were dunes. The bird adjusted by instinct some tint feathers on his outer wings. This reduced the wind drag and developed a dissimilar vortex, so he could rise with the thermal. Oh, he was such a perfect flyer. He let himself float upward again with the cool air stream from the top of the high elevation. His sailing frame fell into the next valley and he screamed in delight and joy while adjusting his course slightly *too much* north-northwest.

*

The slight alteration created the kismet for the Messerschmitt 264 on its way to Gwadar. Twenty minutes before the bird decided to glide full speed into the valley, just 100 miles away at an altitude of 6,000 feet; Colonel Claus von Hadik corrected the course of his plane three degrees further south-southeast.

*

Through the rags of dark clouds drifting below him the pilot observed the wide and never-ending guts of the desert, when the first unexpected hard wave of hot wind hit the plane. At first it came in handfuls, drumming on the metal skin of the plane like hail. There was the rushing sound of sand for a moment as the first gushing wind threw almost playfully sand over the Messerschmitt. It was the beginning of the sandstorm. The Shamal had arrived. The Colonel tried to bring the plane up to a higher altitude. The

Me-264 responded too slowly. He leveled the plane out and flew it ahead in a straight path trying to figure out what happened. There was a heavy roar when he changed the propeller pitch to adjust the plane to the lower altitude. After three seconds the pitch-change mechanism on engine one and three was stuck and did not allow the twelve propeller-blades of the four engines to adjust properly. The sunlight was suddenly hazy and sweat began to run down between his shoulders. Ahead he saw the brownish-yellow curtain of dust and sand. When it struck the plane, it almost blotted the daylight out. The scattered rugs of clouds changed to a solid wall of yellow and visibility began to drop. He knew he had no chance of avoiding the chaos of the wailing sand and dust. The impact of wind grabbed the plane in its jaws and shook it, like a lion mauling its prey. Again the sharp clatter of sand. It was also the first wave of dancing winds from different directions tossing sand into the oil cooler inlet and the dust began to build up a fine thin wall of powder on the filter of the air-inlet. The same happened to the carburetor-supercharger air-inlet.

The Colonel flew on for another twenty minutes, surrounded by the screeching sound of sandstorm. A half dozen crazy bolts flashed from the same point across the sky, scattering the Messerschmitt with their intense power, like anti-aircraft fire. Half of the air inlet to the oil cooler was now closed by dust. Visibility was zero. Below him, somewhere was the desert. He attempted one more time to pull up to a higher altitude. She shuddered under the impact of the increasing storm. What concerned him was the raising oil temperature. It had reached its technical and chemical optimum where the viscosity of its molecular structure would break down any moment. When another impact of hot wind shook the plane violently, his mind flirted the first time with the possibility of death.

Unknown and invisible to the pilot, ahead was death with its black wings spread, as he began his cotillion across the wind-torn sky. Sometimes, in the whirlpool of screaming heat outside, von Hadik could see for a fraction of a second the scars of the dry wadis[2] in the deadly land below.

*

The vulture was taken by surprise with the first shock of the unexpected wind. It confused the huge bird for a moment. Again, with short staccato

---

[2]   Arabic. A dry riverbed.

motions, his head moved and he began to search through the sudden turbulence for an edge to land on and to wait. He was a real and true creation of the mountains and blessed with patience.

And then the Gyaetus barbatus heard a very thunderous aggressive roaring. It caught the angle of his sharp eyes. He noticed the shadow of a huge bird much larger than he. Survival instinct told him to escape because he might have entered strange territory. He shot to the left to elude a confrontation. His life came to an instant standstill when his powerful torso was sucked into the air-inlet of engine number two of the airplane. The destruction of his perfect body was utter and absolute. The temperature in the engine rose and within an instant the Colonel could hear the first ignition failure. Yet it disappeared, only to return seconds later with a whole salvo of misfiring. Engine number two died. The additional workload for engines one, three and four came unexpected and the colonel felt the power decrease. It slowed the plane and the slipstream around the wing's profile broke up. The time to die had come.

The metal bird lost altitude fast in the outside inferno. The silence of fear amongst the men began to be palpable in the plane. The Colonel scrutinized below for the ground and still hoped, somehow, for a wind change.

But they were cut off from time and space in the deadly yellow curtain of fast-moving hot sand bouncing against the fuselage. He watched the altimeter. They had a thousand feet left and visibility was nonexistent. The colonel was calm and quiet, even though he knew that the yellow cloud of sand outside was his ghost-like nemesis. Still, there was no ground to see. The racing drapes of sand outside were even thicker now as their elevation dropped. Blinding dust whipped along the windshield. A few more seconds, he knew, and the last safety margin to lift the plane would be gone. It was already over and too late.

Milling propeller blades threw tons of sand and wet soil into the air, hit stones and dragged the plane down. The Colonel heard the metallic screeching. The last engine flamed out. There were moaning cracking sounds of metal combined with the muffling clatter of the fuselage. They were scraping along the ground and digging deeper into the sand. He expected the explosion of several thousands of gallons of fuel any second and was almost correct in his thinking. A fuel line broke and the highly combustible fluid spilled over the hot engine block, but tons of whirling sand stopped the fire, cutting it off from the necessary oxygen, even before it started. Somewhere a hatch burst open. Fine sand poured through the sudden opening. The movement of the crashed plane got slower and the doomed metal brute dug deeper and deeper into the ground. The plane was covered with sand, inviting the darkness from where they would never escape.

Silence. An absolute and impeccable silence followed.

A force has a physical effect that creates or tends to produce a change in the motion of an object. The motion of an object will change in proportion to the magnitude of the force applied.

When the Messerschmitt 264 came to an abrupt standstill under the desert sand, the law of force became reality. Every action produced by a force creates a reaction equal in magnitude but opposite in direction. And that's what happened to the pallets of the precious metals. The two pallets of the platinum retaliated immediately to the sudden halt by continuing its forward movement. The anchoring system of the pallets broke loose and two tons of platinum bars, each four inches wide and two inches high, rushed forward with their own weight with almost the speed of the crashed airplane. The second bar of the freed platinum bars shattered the occipital bone of one of the SS guards and killed him instantly. The second guard was thrown against the wall during the impact and the following ton of the metal crushed his legs and the two ilium of his pelvis. He screamed in pain for a minute and then fainted, buried beneath the platinum. The weight of the priceless metal had also shattered his azygous veins, and the internal bleeding killed him two minutes later. It was like some spirit had decided the end. The darkness of the plane and the sudden paralyzing silence was serene. Death had walked in. The flight engineer beside the Colonel was thrown forward in his seat and when the plane came to a standstill; his head snapped back and broke his neck.

The Colonel's safety belt detached as he was hurled against some hard thing on the dashboard. The skin of his forehead burst open, and he could feel the blood running down his face. It was not serious, but the pain was excruciating. He passed out. Did not know how long he had been unconscious. He heard the sound of a rattling moan. Got up on unsteady feet and grabbed the flashlight that was strapped against his seat. He followed the moaning. What he saw made his blood curl. The second flight engineer had been smashed against the frame of the fuselage and some sharp metal edge had cut through his body. His ribs had snapped out of his sternum and were protruding through his flesh. Blood bubbled from the huge cut, exposing pulsating organs beneath it. The engineer had not lost consciousness and stared into the beam of the flashlight. The lethally wounded human creature rasped in pain:

"I know what it is. I have an open body. Colonel, please shoot me."

The Colonel pulled out his Beretta and pressed the pistol behind the man's ear. Went mentally through the Lord's Prayer and pulled the trigger. The sound of the shot was muffled. The Colonel's mouth was dry and his lips felt as if they were glued together. The merciful cancellation of the man's life drained most of the energy that was left in the Colonel. He made it back to his seat and sat down. His intuition and instinct told him that the plane was covered with tons of sand and was doomed.

The storm might still be raging outside. Escape had become impossible and his will to live began to diminish further. He leaned back, comfortable in his seat. As he closed his eyes, a deep peace crept into his mind and inner being. He drifted off to spheres where he could hear all the melodies and sounds he had always wanted to compose. Melodies beyond human comprehension. And as the hours in the darkness of the buried plane became timeless to him, his consciousness slipped into a state of ecstasy where he fathomed that someday human beings would grasp the great appreciation of harmonic sound. Harmonic sounds that would once and forever change the course of a whole nation or even the entire civilized world. And with the thought that harmonious music, in equilibrium with space and time, would one day be a universal language of men and spirit, he died.

The Shamil raged for six days and the plane was covered with eleven feet of sand. A grave for unknown soldiers.

The sand of Jabal Hamrin, Iraq.

*

U-boat 2345, Gwadar, India

Commander Helbig woke up in his bunk with some very bad vibes. He did not have an explanation for it but he sensed that something had gone terribly wrong with the Messerschmitt. The U-boat laid still on the bottom in the shallow waters of Gwadar, just one mile off the town, as it had for three nights and days. When the sun rose into the brilliance of the third morning, filling the lead-grey sky with misty coldness, the commander decided to sail. The Messerschmitt was now three days overdue. The commander understood war and he knew from his well-developed combat experience that the bomber and its pilot were lost. They would now sail.

Late that morning they surfaced to periscope depth. The boat rose twenty-five feet. Slowly and carefully.

"Up Scope," the commander said as he stood with his white hat on the back of his head. His eyes glued to the periscope, his arms hung casually over the handles while he spun the periscope around. The area was clear. No sign of the plane on the beach. He still held the childish hope that somehow the plane would show up.

"Take her to the bottom," Helbig commanded. They would sail that night. When the day was gone, U-boat 2345 turned 270 degrees southwest and began its final mission. The boat would travel across and below the Arabian Sea again, around Cape Aghuros and along the South African coast. During those days of travel the crew had to get used to it again.

To the whispering.

To the awesome powers of the sea above and below.

To the loneliness.

They would navigate undetected beneath the Atlantic to reach the Rio de la Plata twenty-eight days later in Buenos Aires to deliver. At the instant the boat left the waters of the Gwadar, Colonel Claus von Hadik's symphony of a brave life faded out in his crashed plane. His grave was under mountains of sand.

Six tons of the most inestimable metals mankind ever had discovered perished only to be discovered during another war.

The Gulf War.

Desert Storm.

5

Ephraim Katz

Island of Cyprus, Summer 1946

    The war was over. The sun of an early summer shone from an immaculate blue sky reflecting her radiation from the Mediterranean Sea with more shimmering light. The island was surrounded by the blue of the sea. A strange island, beautifully done by its creator with the soft lapping waves, hissing their lost passion onto the white beaches. The quality of the beaches was outstanding. They were named for their beauty years later in catalogs of various travel agencies all around the world. But now, at this moment, there were 1,400 children on the island with no parents. Children in strictly watched quarters. The visibly old military tents could not be considered as comfortable housing for these orphans and near orphans. The tykes had come from all over the war-torn Europe and from the camp for children, Theresian Stadt. This crowd of human critters was split into ten different groups of 140 hungry little human beings. Each group had a leader. They had come from all over war-torn Europe and brought to the island of Crete in the Mediterranean by the International Red Cross. Collected little human critters, human left-over of a war justified by all involved. Now only half-heartily wanted. They would go to Palestine perhaps with their parents (if they had still been alive.) To the Promised Land. So it was said.

    He was just sixteen years old. Ephraim Katz was worried. It was the worry of an overly-mature child who had seen too much in the course of his short path of life.

    It concerned him gravely that the children on this island did not have enough food in this camp. To him, the neonates acted like little animals. Disturbed (he could see they felt displaced) and greedy for food. Ephraim Katz was a group leader and had been provided with a pistol by the Britons for the sake of discipline among the 1,400 diminutives.

One year earlier, at the end of April 1945, Ephraim Katz had escaped from Sachsenhausen. He had nothing to lose when Block 18/19 was evacuated and brought on SS trucks to southern Germany, to Bavaria. It was one-o'-clock in the morning and life had granted him a new birthday. His sixteenth birthday was just one hour old, when he jumped from the fast moving truck and fled into the night. Senseless salvos were fired after him into the darkness. He went westward and only at night like a hunted animal and slept during the day in bushes or wherever he could hide. An American soldier captured him, and he landed in a camp for displaced children. Worried about the mentality of camps he broke out on a summer night in August 1945 and made it farther south toward Italy. Was caught again. The man whose words young Ephraim bore in mind was a Lieutenant Colonel, Isser Beeri. Beeri had immense practice in covert operations—smuggling, sleuthing and gathering information in the struggle of a new upcoming state—Israel. Isser Berii was the commander of Shai which was the acronym for Sherud Yediot—known as Haganah, the forerunner of Israel's intelligence. Berii still wore the uniform of the British army because he had fought on their side in Italy. Colonel Berii noticed that young Ephraim Katz was obviously sick of the camps, but smart and streetwise. He had potential for more. Much more than watching hungry children. This time Ephraim listened very carefully and understood. Now he could barely wait to get to Palestine. The homeland, his father had talked a lot about it. Young Ephraim Katz could not get his mind off the gold he had once handled. Not that he was selfish. Visualized it during silent minutes (which were rare)and from where it had come (the teeth fillings). Promised himself to return it to his people—the rightful owners. Regardless of where it was. Regardless of how long it would take.

It would take over fifty years.

The rest of his life.

Ephraim Katz.

The Creation of a Plot

6

Air Force Base Cukurca, Turkey, Border to Iraq, February 1991

Over the last weeks the crew had repeatedly rehearsed the assignment with a sand table, all of the "in" knowing at this point what the tangible objective would be. An observation post deep inside Iraq. The first step of the rehearsal was to learn the particulars of the terrain. It was a team of five highly trained men from Special Forces, men experienced in high value and high risk missions. They would live totally on their own for days behind enemy lines, where they would move into sneak-and-peek operations of a long-range surveillance detachment. All five were also experienced and skilled at jumping from altitudes of thirty thousand feet (HALO). Coordinates for the site were selected. They were to dig themselves in, camouflage the position, and then observe any enemy's activities. The selected observation post was a soft hill just six hundred yard east of the new highway from Chech and was still a blank spot for intelligence. It needed immediate cover and surveillance. Constant clouds of dust over the area made it impossible for satellite reconnaissance to transmit what was taking place in this section of Iraq. The five men were the last team that had to be brought from the North into position before the air attacks would begin.

The team initiated a new technology. Their uniforms would instantly imitate the surroundings and would instantly blend into the changing colors of the day or night, aided by a computer built into their camouflage. Incorporated into the textile were some light-sensitive sensors that would calibrate the light reflection of the fabric and change its pigment to the color of the environment. The uniforms were also impregnated with an infrared-absorbing solution that made it impossible for an enemy infrared detecting device to get any reading at all. This important new war toy from the Army's Natick Research and Development Center outside Boston was just waiting for a bona fide.

All the men wore a backpack computer connected to a monochrome display. The system contained the battlefield maps with details of bushes or trees, if any, here in the middle of nowhere. They wore insulating jump suits with an oxygen system. The mission they were assigned to was an operation of significance. Cukurca Air Force Base is split into four predominant sections. The most important, with silent activities at this late evening was the east side of the base. There were the runway and alert hangars for the fighter squadron are located. This area of the Cukurca base is molded into stretching wooded area, enclosed by eight feet barbed-wire-topped fences and tightly guarded around the clock by mounted surveillance cameras and guards. At the end of the runway stood a single HC-130 Hercules in dark camouflage, positioned into the wind and ready for take-off. Five men and their gear were standing at the rear, observing almost mindlessly as the pilot had a final walk around the plane for a last visual check-up with a strong flashlight.

Then the pilot came over to the leader of the group, took the flying helmet off and removed the gloves. Combed the hair back with the right hand, slung the arms around the Major's neck and gave him a long warm kiss with all the ingredients of French and everything else included. Tongues released the message about closeness.

Rachel. Captain Rachel Peters. She was Major Thomas Peter's wife and one of the finest flyers the Special Forces ever had for a mission like this. Since the end of the Cold War she had flown two hundred assignment of high altitude reconnaissance over the Balkans and the Middle East. Amongst the flyers she had the professional reputation to fly the C-130 like a stunt jet, if necessary.

She moved her mouth slightly away from his and mumbled,

"Promise me you will be back home in one piece, paramour."

They held each other for a moment and then she let him go.

*

Rachel and the co-pilot ran down the pre-flight checklist one more time.

"Tower, this four-seven-one-one request permission for take-off. Ready for take-off."

"Four-seven-one-one, you're clear for take-off. Wind is two-five-four at thirty kilometers."

"Roger and out," Rachel said, increased the power and headed for the taxiway. Brought the plane in a slow right turn around and into the runway. She let the plane go. Had to blink her eyes several times. There was no such material like dust or a bug in her eyes to provoke it. Just some stupid little burning moisture. It wasn't that easy to transport your own husband into a war.

Airborne, she turned the plane immediately south south-east and went into a sharp rate of climb. It did not take much time to reach the altitude of thirty-four thousand feet. On the western horizon was a small string of blue lights left. It was a leftover from the past day. Here Rachel carefully turned the plane into a smooth left turn and flew straight east for ten minutes. A red light in the cargo bay began to flash. The plane began its first and only circle. Rachel was on the jump run and reduced the power of the plane from cruising speed to almost a landing approach velocity. In this kind of speed the plane just might stall when the men heard and felt the sudden slow down and drop. The whining sound of a hydraulic system initiated the opening of the rear clamshell door. The bitter cold of the dark night slapped the men in their faces. They pulled their 2Viper infra-red head gear over their eyes.

The Major looked over to his men and nodded. He jumped first. Four more men hurled into the icy night of twenty-seven thousand feet altitude. They would reach the ground in absolute silence and invisibility.

Rachel banged the heavy plane over the right wing and wondered honestly for a moment whether this kind of flying had ever been a part of the plane's test program.

*

Dark cold winds. They would reach the ground and the target like a whisper in the night. The parachutes offered them a magnificent means of clandestine entry into the hostile country and the mountains below. Rachel with the plane stayed 47 miles away from the drop zone and there would be no noise of the approaching plane where the men would land.

In a free-fall the five men reached the last safe elevation of 2,500 feet before they opened their parachutes. Or even lower. Their chutes were unusual, consisting of double-layer canopies shaped like airfoils, generating the lift and extending the dive.

The Major and his men had already reached an unfettered speed of 200 feet per second. The velocity of the free fall became unreal to Tom. To reduce the speed and to gather control, he bent his arms and legs slightly. With an elusive adjustment of his hand positions, he did not turn over or spin anymore. Tom screamed, when a turbulence whirled him away, driving him into a pirouette. For a fraction of a second he could see stars revolving around him, like a spiral tunnel. It made him sick when his body gyrated like a leaf in a tornado through the night over the desert. But out of the high-speed confusion, in extremely fast downward movement for which the human mind was not normally meant to be made for, he remembered that he was in control. He placed his arms against his side and the drag of his angled feet caused him to fall now head-first into the unknown darkness. It stopped the spin and he resumed his free-fall position.

Had a look at his wrist altimeter. Another 4,600-foot plunge before he would pull the ripcord and steer to the landing point. He fell through another two-thousand feet and now it seemed to him like the speed of light. Common sense had been lost. The radio indicator began to chirp. He was just three hundred feet west from the drop point 47. Pulling the ripcord he heard the rush of the released and expanding canopy above him. The lunacy race of 200 feet per second came almost abruptly to a standstill. He moaned and jerked his head back, and could suddenly see the stars above in an orderly way while he listened to the heartbeat in his ears.

He noticed he was off course and had to turn. Tom sailed at 30mph when he pulled down the steering toggle at the rear. The left side of the canopy curled slightly and bent the flow of air. Made two turns to search the land below for the smallest token of light. Nothing to see. Only the dark silence of the desert. Released the toggles and the turning stopped. Now he was right on course, a sort of cross-country ride. He paid out a twenty-foot line that secured a medium-sized bundle, containing his weapon, food and equipment. Utensils of a deadly trade. Only 12.8 inches long, the diminutive Heckler and Koch MP5K submachine gun could shred nine-hundred rounds per minute in full-automatic mode.

He searched for the men through his night vision goggles. Three had already reached the ground. He steered ahead while getting closer to the dark ground. It was time to separate from his gear so he would not injure himself during the landing. He started to pull on both toggles simultaneously. The final approach. He was two hundred yards off target. Pulled the cords very carefully so the parachute would not loose too much lift too soon and drop him too hard. The last thing he needed would be a broken ankle in the middle of this desert.

Touchdown at walking speed. The chute followed with a gentle hiss, faltering on the ground. Wrapped it up and after the last final mobility he got motionless. He curled up in the soil and listened into the soundlessness of the night for hostility. The tension of the free-fall began to withdraw from his body. He threw up.

As he lay on his back for a moment he could see the stars sparkling in their eternal appearance against the dark space behind them, which was the background of all the other universes. At least that's what Rachel had told him. For a moment he was lost in the beauty. Got up to his knees. His senses began to function again accordingly with the factor of time and the surroundings he was confronted with. The night vision goggles gave him a clear direction to the bulge of the mountain, the final target, sitting there in pattern like a star. He made out the four moving shadows on their way to the visible hunk on the gradient. Then they were together. Tom Peters, Dean Rosco, Mark Berret, John Duskin and Garry Kessler. They had to disappear fast into the smooth hill by digging in and camouflaging.

The drop point. A huge hill-like dune.

"Sergeant Duskin, Sergeant Rosco. It is now 01100. Have the post ready by 02200. Sergeant Berret, you take the first watch. Sergeant Kessler, prepare radio contact."

The communication would be sent by microwave and could not be intercepted by the Iraqis. So as not to disturb the silence of the night, all wore whisper-com headphones in their ears. One hundred feet away on the gentle slope the two sergeants started to dig into the sand. After the first three shovels of earth the dirt was moving under their feet and began to drag them downward, like deadly quicksand. There was nothing to hold on to.

Duskin wanted to reach for his transmitter. It was too late. Both men were sucked into a hole and a sudden downward movement like a maelstrom. By instinct, Rosco moved his body to keep his feet first. His body hit a sort of metal frame and was tossed through a door-like opening. He had no idea what it was when he landed in a compartment. Felt the metal structure and rolled away, knowing Duskin followed. His instinct told him there was no immediate danger and that something unique had happened. He pulled his gun and froze, listening with wide-open mouth to inhale more air under stress. It was also breathing without noise. He heard Duskin's voice from the opening.

"You okay?"

"Sure. What the hell is this?"

"Dunno. Let's check and report back."

The flashlight threw a strong beam into the dark space. First the beam was zipping along in the dark. Unfocused. Then slowly, more centered and collected. The air was cool and stale. The light beam hit the first damaged metal structure. A sure thing. It was human-made, but still they did not know what it was. As their adrenaline flowed, both moved their bodies slowly with their guns in their hands. Neither would miss a fly's eye fifty feet away.

Then they saw it. A cockpit. In the two chairs were the shadows of two humans, obviously dead. Duskin turned around slowly, with his gun in both hands.

Rosco had seen dead bodies of pilots crashed in some dubious missions he had completed in Peru and the Far East. One of those kinds of missions where family members would get the message that the beloved son or husband had died in a training accident, for example, in Arizona.

What he saw made him choke.

He moved closer and tumbled over some bricks on the floor, but did not pay attention to them. He hesitated and moved the light beam downward along the wall. A skeleton on the floor appeared. The ribs were popped out from the sternum. A bullet-hole behind the ear with a huge outlet in the forehead. Rosco stepped closer, holding back his consternation, as he neared the cockpit with smooth and soft steps. Now realizing the absurdity of the place, he saw something in the left chair of the cockpit. A mummified body dressed in a uniform. What caught his attention was a cross around the neck of the bony man, a tiny swastika in the center. His eyes followed the beam of the flashlight. The shaft of light moved cautiously over the shoulder of the well-preserved dead man. His heart hammered against his chest and he fathomed that his breath became short.

"What is it?" he heard the whisper in his intercom.

"Duskin," he heard himself saying, "come over here. You won't believe this. This is like a bad dream."

The second light beam flashed around.

"Dear Lord," Duskin mumbled behind him, "we better call the Major. This is a dead German flyer from World War II. A colonel with a Knight's Cross."

It was Sergeant Duskin's hobby to know everything about uniforms and the wars over the last thousand years, and he wondered for a moment how this German had ended up here. Major Peters heard the crackle in his intercom. Rosco's voice sounded strange and distracted.

"Major," he heard. "you'd better get up here and see this right away."

Moving carefully up the hill fifty yards away from where both his men should be, he used his night binoculars to relocate from his original path and searched the area below. He could only see a crater in the ground. It did not look like a bunker.

"Rosco, Duskin. Are you clear?" he whispered.

"Yes. All clear. Where are you now?"

"I'm coming in from the top."

Seconds later he slid into the hole and through the frame of a door. A crashed plane. He got the feeling of suddenly being in a grave chamber somewhere far way—a lost place in ancient times. There were metal bricks all over the plane. A third skeleton in a well-preserved SS-uniform was discovered under a pile of the bricks, with a lot of broken bones, a machine pistol beside the mummy. The Major moved to the cockpit.

"I'll be darned," he mumbled. "It's a German. A Luftwaffe colonel." He paused for a moment.

"Men, let's get moving. We have a place to stay. Duskin, get the men in here. Rosco, you stay with me."

The Major began an intense search around the skeleton. There must be a flight order, a log book. Instructions, targets, whatever. Something. The Germans would not have sent a plane away without proper orders. Not the Germans. He searched under the seat and found a leather map case. The quality was evident. Fine black calf. It had several compartments. The lack of moisture and fresh air had preserved the leather and its contents. It was as if the mummified colonel smiled at him with his exposed flawless teeth. Major Tom Peters opened the case carefully. The first thing he pulled out was a map. Then he looked at his watch. The hour of the ghosts. Thirty minutes after midnight. Was it the chilly air of this very early morning hour that made him shiver? He put the map back into the case.

*

Morning arrived. They all felt like they were in a grave. At 1300 hours the Major playfully picked up one of the bricks in the crashed plane. His mind had been mulling about this place since they had entered it. He was surprised how heavy the metal brick was. Even without being an expert, he realized it was gold. Soft, smooth and very heavy. Gold of twenty-four carats. The labels read *Deutsche Reichsbank.* Platinum, Iridium, Osmium. All over the floor. Whatever the Germans had in mind, something had gone wrong. Deadly wrong.

The Major sensed that the men wanted to get out of this metal tube. He stared at the floor and his eyes caught some of the metal bricks again and attempted to refocus, when he heard Rosco.

"It's gold, Major. Isn't it? You don't have to answer, Major. I know minerals. I took a semester geology."

The dim light in the crashed plane came through the broken hatch, as if hesitating to deliver the right brightness. The light was out of focus.

The Major turned around.

"Who else knows?"

"No one, I think" Rosco said.

"Let's keep it that way for the moment, Sergeant."

"I understand, Major. We don't need trouble here."

It was a team trained to trust each other under the most difficult circumstances. Their lives depended on this kind of unconditional trust. There were no secrets between men on a mission like this, but this was different. The gold could change it.

On the third day the Major noticed that Duskin had gotten restless over the last day and milled around him a lot.

"What is it Duskin?" asked the Major, taking the initiative.

"You know, Major . . . uh . . . I, well, how should I say it? You know, when we cleaned this place three nights ago . . . you know, I was wondering why these bricks were so heavy . . . and, you know . . . ." his voice lost its hesitation, "I believe it is gold."

"You're right. Who else knows?"

"Sergeant Kessler and Sergeant Berret."

The word was out. Now it was time to coordinate things.

For three more days and nights the relationship amongst the men was somehow tense. Nobody talked about it, but the Major could feel the men's minds were on the metal.

Quietly Sergeant Duskin was the first one who spoke.

"I think," he said simply and in a tone too loud, "when this war is over we should pick it up. It doesn't belong to anybody." Confirming silence hung in the air.

"How?" the Major asked.

"Well, we wait a year or two. Maybe three," he laughed, "then we buy a nice truck to pick it up. And we just don't talk about this whole thing. We leave the Force. Retire, if I might say so."

It did not belong to anybody. It was all their's.

7

CIA Headquarters, Langley Virginia

Deputy Director for Intelligence David Meyers had another hour before the P.B. (President's Daily Brief). He had now been with the department for twenty-eight years and had seen a lot of men come and go, including presidents. It had never been the director's desire to go higher in the ranks. It was enough reward for him to see his eminence recognized by his ability to report to the President directly when dealing with uncomfortable topics, and demanding solutions for problems nobody wanted to take responsibility for, like a second turn of war with Yugoslavia. He was ready to retire. He had served a country and not opinions. For him opinions were just some cheap commodities. In all the years of his career, Meyers had made an art out of dodging press conferences and by never showing an ego, that human calamity. He had none. To express written half-truths to the buffoons and mandarins of the media was not his business. Meyers liked his status quo of anonymity. It was a ravishing Indian summer day with all the gentleness of soft winds and sun. Not a cloud. Thought it over what the President might want. Normally these most sensitive intelligence details would be summarized and sent to the President. But Meyers had the gut feeling that the President wanted to know something more about the nuclear material smuggled from Russia into Europe. And the danger relative to the United States.

The biggest haul of nuclear material had come 10 days ago when a Lufthansa flight from Moscow landed in Frankfurt with 350 grams of atomic fuel on board. It was a MAX-mixed-oxide fuel for reactors but perfectly usable in a bomb. The material had such a startling purity that it only could have come from, the experts said, a top-of-the-line Russian nuclear lab. The Russians were miffed and called it a "provocation", once again using the language of the Cold War.

Having materials of mass destruction available on the black market was like buying lettuce in a grocery store in La Jolla's Safeway. It had become a historical and nightmarish challenge for the world. The appearance of the nuclear samples on the European black market was a red alert and began to raise the "question" in the agency; when would the first freelancer build a bomb? Meyer was convinced it wouldn't happen because it was still too complicated.

He was well prepared for the grilling and decided, having some spare minutes left, to dutifully read through what he called the 'etc. file'. Minor info he normally wouldn't't be bothered with but had to know. Opened it. Blessed God. Only one report in it today. Five members of the Special Forces after their tour of duty in Iraq and fifteen years in the service, had resigned. The group quit after a covert operation in northern Iraq. Area of operation: twenty-five miles northeast from Chech. Meyers shook his head. He really did not want to be harassed with this kind of reports. After years in *this kind* of service it should be enough. Give them their pension and let them go. DDCI glanced at the pictures. He had a good memory for faces and men. Major Peters. A brilliant strategist when it came to action. Always calm. Sergeant Dean Rosco. Meyers smiled and shook his head. Very talented. Never wanted to attend the academy. Meyers remembered vaguely that Rosco once was sent to Israel to train and to be trained. And then there were Duskin, Berret and Kessler. Meyers wished them mentally all the best. Oh yes, and the woman, Lieutenant Rachel Peters. He initialed the folder, followed by date, and had already forgotten the whole file when he left for DPB. Soon the five men and the woman would bring unexpected stress into his professional routine.

*

Israel, Tel Aviv, June 30, 1948

Ephraim Katz

There was another war again in the world. A war of independence. Israel's war. The day was humid and contained, an impeccable blue sky, flaring heat reflected back from the white painted walls of the apartment buildings on Ben Yehuda Street. It was just another one of those average hot summer days in Tel Aviv. A person with a fine sense for surveillance would have noticed that within a short period of time, six men had arrived in separate cars, taxis and bicycles along this ordinary residential vicinity with its blaring music from vegetable stands and shops. The men were in their mid-twenties, strong, with faces of no-nonsense. They had the ability to blend, blasé dressed, into the areas where vendors sold their still fresh-looking vegetables. Individually, they vanished into building number sixty-five, which was identical to the others along the boring, sun-white burned street.

Among the arriving men, entering alone was a 'youngster'. He looked mature and serious. Nobody would have understood his motives for walking into this building. Nobody would have understood his motives even if he would have talked about it in public, what cruelty he had seen in his young life. And all in the name of money and gold. He was alone with his soul. His name was Ephraim Katz and he had just returned from the Island of Crete.

His heart pounded. Up two flights of stairs behind a door with a seasoned brass sign and black letters, saying CONSULTANCY ASSISTANCE, was the headquarter of SHAI (acronym for Sherut Yediot—Information Services). The men who gathered in Tel Aviv on this last day of June 1948 would be the substance and fiber of four major secret agencies that would later become Israel's intelligence community.

The congregated men brought along astounding backgrounds in covert operations like spying, smuggling, gathering information and execution. They were skills the men had brought along from their time with Haganah (defense). They had served as teenagers since 1937 to make the new state Israel happened and survive.

This historical meeting in building number eighty-five resulted in the future creation of three agencies of Israel. Military intelligence (Aman—the acronym for Intelligence Wing), a domestic secret service (Shin-Bet the acronym for General Security Service), Foreign intelligence (operatives with diplomatic cover) resulting later in the 'Institute for Intelligence and Special Tasks'—better known as Mossad.

A promising career in the intelligence community began for the youngest member, Ephraim Katz. He had never dreamed in his young life, that he would be counted among the toughest and most dedicated men of Israel's struggle for survival. He only had precious metals on his mind. Six and a half tons.

*

Napa, California, June 2003

Rachel had watched him for some time and she knew that he had often been distracted during the past months. She felt left out. He was her soul mate. Their life was like a graceful movement, a sparkling dance through the seasons of life, together on the merry-go-round of creation. She loved him and that was the reason she left him alone with his thoughts.

Tom's mind was always somewhere else. He was hiding something. But what? The strain in the mornings was the worst, when the coffee was like black bitter syrup and the morning sun seemed to shine through a grey filter. She promised herself to get to the bottom of the matter. Delayed. Day after day. Week after week.

Then one evening . . . .

She made a huge fire in the bedroom fireplace. Her hair was still damp from the shower and dressed in her pale-blue fluffy bathrobe; she curled up on the fat cushions of her favorite chair and looked at him.

"Paramour," she said, a word she used not quite often, and only when she wanted to express how close she felt to him, "what is it?"

She looked at him with her soft gentle grey eyes, staring at him like a cat, "come here," she almost whispered, "talk."

The deep silence was only interrupted by the faraway sound of the foghorns from the Bay and the warm cracking of the burning wood. He looked at her and tried a sort of smile and failed miserably, because it was out of symmetry. He walked over to her, sat down on the edge of the chair and felt uncomfortable. Sat down on the floor and looked up at her.

"So, what is it?" she cheered him up.

"Well," he said, stretching the word as long and as far as he could. Then silence.

"What?" she said. "Talk."

She slid down from the chair and lay beside him. Took his head and placed it on her stomach. Tom was grateful that he could talk without looking at her. He gazed at the ceiling.

"Do you remember, when you flew us to point 47 in Iraq?"

A thoughtful silence lingered through the room. "Yes," she said, slightly hesitating while her fingers moved playfully through his hair. He began to talk.

About the mission in Iraq. Talked about the desert. Talked about the huge dune. Talked about the crashed plane in the sand, giving them all shelter and protection. The dead German Luftwaffe colonel. The tons of precious metals and the gold they had found. Six tons of it. The worth, mind staggering. The mutual understanding of the five men not to talk about the treasure. The millions still sitting in this dune, so hard to approach.

He changed his position and looked at her while he spilled out what had occupied his mind for the past years. He was grateful that he had found a good listener. She listened carefully while gazing at him. As he went on, her chin started to drop slightly, her face looked longer somehow. Then her mouth opened while she listened. When he stopped talking, the silence seemed to echo.

"You don't look as smart with your mouth open," he said wearily. A bright beaming smile appeared on her face.

"What do you think?" he asked.

"Let's get it. That's what you want. Right?"

"Let's what?"

"Let's get the stuff, I said."

He heard the firmness in her voice.

"You must be out of ?"

"No, I am not."

"Out of the question."

"It's not out of the question. We can pull it off."

She moved away from him for a moment, embraced him and changed the subject completely by giving him one of these slow burning kisses, sucking gently the tip of his tongue.

"Let me seduce you," she muttered between it as she slid out of her bathrobe, "that's what you also need."

He wanted her to understand that it was just a fantasy about the precious metals in those Iraqi dunes, while she began to unbutton his shirt. She had already transferred his mind to the niche of lovemaking. She knew how to get him out of his clothes and enjoyed that he was looking down at her. Her dark hair went beautifully with her tanned skin over a body lean and flawless. "Do we have a deal?" she whispered on her way to another orgasm. Actually, he did not expect her to come back to the treasure, and thought it was over by telling her his fantasy.

"What deal?" he muttered on her lips.

"It's too dangerous for you. Isn't it?"

This was a provocation.

He just wanted to make love and gave in.

"No," he said.

"Would you do it?"

"Sure I would," while his mouth wandered along her left temple. One of her prime spots.

"You know," she said dreamily, but interrupted suddenly as she released a hissing sound.

She changed back to the subject: "Sometimes it's meaningful to put the dear life on the line. H'bout you?"

She kissed while holding his face, then wound her arms around his neck and legs around his hips. Her mouth was a living appendage to him, and he could not stop moving his hands all over her.

"I love you," he said with a hoarsely whispering voice.

"Let's do it together. Yes?" The last "yes" sounded like a question.

He whispered seven "yes's."

And while the moon began to wander across the San Francisco Bay, reflecting its silver light on top of the milky pocket of fog, sitting like a huge soft cotton ball on top of the water, they exhausted their bodies into comfortable weariness. She rolled to her left side and he pulled her closer. He kissed her temple and ear "Good Night, precious."

She chuckled: "Feels good, word-inventor," and pulled his arm around her. Moved her rump against him. Then she made a sound like a cat half-asleep, and the big close hugs liquefied them into a deep sleep.

*

Morning had come. He woke up and felt the burning pain on both of his knees. It was from the carpet. Went to the bathroom. He put on his bathrobe and followed the coffee smell to the kitchen. There was Rachel. All dressed up. All personality. A hand-tailored Florence Cramer business suit. His wedding present sparkled on her left wrist. An Ebel Beluga watch sprinkled with 22 karat diamonds dust. She wore a decent silver necklace from Judith Leiber around her neck and a modest smell of Safari for Men.

'Why she always uses my aftershave,' he thought and felt totally displaced in his outfit.

"What are you up to?" he asked.

"Rosco wants to meet us in two hours. I talked to him this morning."

"Wait a minute. Why?"

"You promised me last night we would pick up the treasure."

As always, she came straight to the point. No pretense.

"Seven times," she added with a soft knowing smile, "and you better hurry up now. Be ready by 1200, Major."

He got angry.

"Tell you what. You meet Rosco. I'll go down to the club and clean the boat. Okay?"

"Your suit is on the bed. Now get moving," she said stubbornly, "you know why you're gonna come with me? Because you love me."

She hit a raw nerve. He adored her and admitted it every day to himself. Nevertheless, the thing with all the precious metals was too much, and he suddenly wished he had not told her about it.

"Look, I've been wanting to clean the boat for two weeks and the beds have to be taken out, because"

"Get moving," she said and threw him a kiss.

"Okay," he said, giving in, "I'll come. But don't even think about this stuff anymore."

She poured herself another cup of hazelnut coffee, and vanished into the living room with the New York Times under her arm.

Shower. Shave. Rubbed some good smelling fluids from Rachel's one-hundred dollar bottle *Lair du Temps* into his face. Moved to the bedroom. She had it all ready for him. The twelve hundred dollar rayon three-button single-breasted with the ribbed railroad stripes from Joseph About. The two hundred and twenty-dollar cotton Talbot shirt with the silk jacquard pin-dot Boss tie. In front of the bed was the leather wingtip Kenneth Cole shoes. Now he really yearned to be in his worn-out jeans, cleaning the head on the boat. Anyway, he hadn't seen Rosco for quite some time. Had a look in the mirror. Not bad. They both agreed once that whenever they bought something it should be expensive and classy. No junk. Buy less. Quality and timeless.

"Paramour," Rachel said when he came into the living room thirty minutes later, "you used my perfume."

Half amused.

Hell, didn't he has to buy a bottle of Ralph Lauren every three weeks for fifty bucks?

But then a warm, bright grin wavered over her face.

"You look like a real ladies man. Let's go."

She tiptoed and gave him a butterfly-like kiss on his cheek.

Outside sat the golden Volvo 740, sparkling as if it had just been delivered from a dealership. There were grey clouds over the North Bay, and it looked like rain. They drove in silence for the first ten miles. They could be in silence for hours without any need for conversation. Just being together was enough for both of them. But very big thoughts lingered around. About a six tons treasure in the desert of Iraq. He would not even admit to himself that he was already hooked.

The sign for Highway 29 East came up. It was time to talk. Casual of course. He was man enough to handle it.

"Why are we dressed up like this, if I may take the liberty of asking you?"

"Yes. You may."

"So, why?"

"Look, Tom, if you want to talk about big money, you have to be dressed like big money."

The sound of her voice was filled with impatience. Silence again. He could feel she was pissed. Traffic light. Red. He was in the wrong lane. Green came and he had to cut two lanes to make a left onto 121. They drove in silence again for twenty minutes. Rachel and Tom. Married and profoundly in love for years.

*

They had met at Vandenberg Air Force Base in Nevada where some officers of the Special Forces took a unique course. She was one of the best flight instructors and specialized in two fields, flying the Hercules C-130 transport plane like a stunt jet when necessary, but her specialty was helicopters. All sorts. Rachel was one of the few helicopter pilots that could fly the Russian MIL Mi. The MIL Mi was the heaviest choppers in the world.

The course covered areas like aerial navigation, setting up landing or drop zones and radio communications. The day Rachel walked into the classroom she was confronted by twenty-eight men who had to learn the basic skills of flying some chopper in case of an emergency. Just the basics. Nothing else. Just get the damn thing from point A to point B or as far as you can.

She was slim. Sort of a sporty type with dark short hair in a pageboy cut. Grey-yellow eyes. More yellow than grey. High round cheekbones. Her Indian ancestry was evident in her mouth and eyes. Some Irish and Belgian were there too. There was strength and vitality around her when she moved. An energetic movement without fear. She almost got married once and bailed out at the last minute. He dealt in real estate and did quite well, in spite of his preference for partying. His pale eyes got this watery look after his second Bourbon, and he was a lousy lover on top. His touches were rough and he had no sensitivity. Living with this man who had nothing to say even when talking for hours, was the hardest part. She told him one day that she was tired of his alcohol-soaked absent mind. She was tired of a man who fell asleep when she wanted to talk about a book. She was tired of his resentments and constant disapprovals. In short, they had nothing in common. He refused to change his drug and drinking habits, no matter how often she had asked him to. And one day, in his stoned rostrum, he accused her of ignoring him because he was not rich enough. She thought it over for one day, and then just walked out. When she looked back, she wondered why for Christ's sake she had stayed in this relationship so long. He called once and asked she to come back to him. He never picked up the phone again after she told him to take hike.

*

Her very essence commanded respect. The men in the classroom had taken a course at Air Traffic Control school and trained to act as mobile aircraft controllers on their own missions or behind enemy lines. Now they would get the final touch of flying. Initially she had the feeling of talking to herself while explaining to the men about radar warning receivers, infrared-countermeasures jamming device, detachable fuel tanks and hostage-taking. She discussed the possibility of shot pilots and injured pilots while the chopper was completely intact. Who would take them back from hundreds of miles inside hostile territory? She had read a study once about *gegenseitige Ersetzbarkeit* from the East German Army, a confidential paper confiscated during the uprising in East Germany in 1989. Any soldier should be able to take over the role of leader in case of an emergency. She liked the idea that men and machines could still be brought back, if only one or two men on the team were able to handle the simplest operations of the chopper. Just enough to get away. First there was hesitation in the disciplined, well-organized male body of military bureaucrats. It made sense. When she raised her head the first time to actually face the men, she saw him.

Last row. Major Tom Peters.

That's what she read on his uniform. She could see that he was a hard man and had certainly gone through some significant experiences. There was also something around and in his eyes. Somehow gentle. He was a seasoned man. Not by age, but by experience. She could sense his strength and his confidence, and felt she wanted to be close to him. He looked at her thoughtfully. She could read him immediately. A man with enormous self-discipline. A man who would respect the identity of others. She saw he took her seriously and she suddenly had an urge to know. As an equal. He sensed it and she had a difficult time taking her eyes off his gentle, handsome face. Over the next days they had the unspoken mutual understanding of liking each other very much while reading each other's eyes. Despite the unromantic environment, they began to feel the increase of their exceptional fusion. The first three days they did not talk. The third day he walked into her office. Mumbled an apology and walked to her desk. While he moved for the sake of symmetries some of the files on the desk to have something to do, he said without looking at her: "You know, I am in love with you and we should talk about this sometimes. I found a spot for dinner where we could talk this over."

She liked the idea and said yes, and that was the beginning. They never had to create an artificial gaiety when they saw each other. They just were.

"I love you," he said simply.

"I know," she answered. It was so uncomplicated.

He told her about his parents being killed in a car crash when he had reached the delicate age of eight and his growing up in his uncle's household. Two weeks later they were married.

*

Tom and Rachel.

He made a sharp right as he left the Silverado Trail and turned into the mountains. It was a winding road to the place where they would meet Rosco. Wearing an elegant town and country outfit, a Calvin Klein version of classic three-button nubby wool single-breasted, Rosco was already waiting on the outside deck with the magnificent view over the valley, when they entered the *Auberge Du Soleil*. Flap pockets and double-pleated trousers. White turtle neck. Good-looking contrast with his dark curly hair and bright blue eyes. He unfolded his six-foot-four frame from behind the table, toppled the glass of water with a twist of lemon in it all over the white cotton tablecloth and made it to the middle of the deck. Seriously delighted to see them both, his face cracked into a wide grin, shaking hands, slapping each other's backs, kiss on Rachel's cheek. They went back to the table. There was a moment of joyful and hesitating silence. The usual "how're you doin' and the "fine" answer" followed. The burgundy-red umbrella gave a sort of engaging protection against the blazing but cold sunlight. Silently Rachel stared over into the colorful beauty of the valley. She counted six falcons cruising in circles, artfully balancing on the up draft of the afternoon air. There was a wedding on the lower deck and a band played Glenn Miller. The waiter came and announced the specialties of the day, raised his right eyebrow when he saw the wet spot. Left, came back and changed the tablecloth. Dropped the menus, but was sensitive enough not to call them "folks." Expensively dressed people, expensive smell. The soup of the day would be a Lobster-Kuri Squash. Specialty of the day was a rosemary grilled Sterling Salmon with horseradish potato hash, wild mushroom sauce and beet oil. For seventeen twenty-eight, each. And would they like to have something from the bar? A cocktail? Rachel nodded her head. Yes, just a large bottle of Calistoga. And a glass. Please. Tom had a discreet look at his watch. 1430. Yeah, a glass of Mum would do it. Rosco went for the same. Small talk about the weather followed. Yes, San Francisco was fogged in. All three waited for each other. The Mums came. Sips. Silence.

"Should I start?" Rachel asked.

Her voice was a half-pitch too high. It always happened when Rachel got exited.

"Okay," Rosco asked, "what's up?"

*

Dean Rosco. Thirty-eight. Something radiated from him that kept the weaklings of life at three arm's-length distance. He chose the people he wanted to be with. One day, when he had reached the tender wild age of seventeen, he took his baseball club, smashed the glass door of the artfully-carved antique display cabinet, an grabbed a double-barreled Chatsworth sporting shotgun, with its delicate fine engravings, which confirmed the superb quality of English craftsmanship, and loaded it. Calm and filled with anger, he walked into his father's studio. His father, Dr. Peter Rosco, psychiatrist and darling of San Francisco, Marin, and to a certain extent Los Angeles' high-society, had just returned from his office on Montgomery Street, where he treated with empty words and Gestaltungs Therapy the self-pitying and over inflated egos of artists, actors with a small write-up in *Vanity Fair,* CEO's and burned out stockbrokers for eight hours on a daily basis. Consequently, he felt like a mental garbage-can for the outpourings of the haughty self-assumed elite, and his own frustration had reached the level of disgust. His job became to him a masquerade in a thousand-dollar suit. In truth, there was never a necessity for him to work at all, since he had inherited substantial wealth from his father, controlling real estate holdings in New York, Connecticut, New Jersey and Nevada.

The doctor had just beaten up his wife again and felt somehow relaxed. He was in the middle of filling his one-hundred-and twenty-five-dollar Bohemian crystal tumbler to the rim with Chivas. Just five inches away from his head the bullet ripped through the hand-woven silk wall covering next to Dr. Peter Rosco. This manipulator of the mind, with his thinning grayish hair, looked into the ice-cold, motionless face of his seventeen-year-old. He listened to the well-articulated message of his son with a face with fear. For the first time in his dominating existence—he experienced fear. And the message was:

"If you ever beat my mother again, I will kill you. I will kill you with this rifle. I did not miss when I pulled the trigger."

For many years, the juvenile Dean Rosco had noticed the bruises and black spots on his mother's arms and legs. Sometimes her sunglasses were too big, covering a black eye and couldn't't justify a laser face lifting. Young Rosco had to watch this last beating of his mother and it was beyond his understanding. Her left upper incisor tooth, the one and two, was split with the last blow to her face. When she sank to the white fluffy Dupont *Stone Master* master, the spilling blood from her mouth ruined the carpet. What the boy did not understand was the yelling of his father, accusing the woman of spoiling the carpet which he had worked so hard for. As a three-year-old, little Dean Rosco first witnessed the beating of his mother. He had crawled over to her when his mother cried in pain with a swollen face, to nurture her with the gentleness of a child's innocence. She held him, and he felt that he was the one giving her the energy to survive. Through the years of the marriage, living under these conditions, she had become a classic case of an abused woman with all the symptoms of co-dependency ? hoping, after each beating that things would change. Or hanging in for the sake of a three million-dollar house, the property, her child.

This last beating and the blow to her head were different. Not only were her twenty-thousand dollar dental crowns were crushed. No, something else happened with the last impact. The arachnoid, the delicate membrane of the brain and spinal cord could not absorb the impact of the final blow and cracked under his father's fist, creating an almost invisible bleeding between the parietal lobe and the temporal lobe inside her brain.

The cruel paralysis of his mother's face occurred two days later, after he pulled the trigger to warn his father. A day later she went into a coma, which lasted four weeks. The Gods were sympathetic, and she died a death of mercy in her sleep. The funeral took place at Saint Hilary's Church, halfway up the hills in Tiburon. Two hundred and ten people appeared at this holy location. Among the attending crowd, only two people knew about the manslaughter, Dean Rosco and his celebrity father. Doctor Peter Rosco was the hub of the gathering throng and returned the handshakes with a tearful face. Counterfeit tears. Dean Rosco stared at his father. The doctor ? a man's man, he was called ? glanced at his son uncomfortably and saw the deadly sadness in the teenager's eyes. With such a profusion of white and red roses on top of her casket, nobody could doubt how much Dr. Peter Rosco suffered over the loss of his beloved wife, who had slipped on the moist brick steps, so the story went, and had fallen down the ten sharp-edged stairs. After the ritual of the funeral, when the liturgy of handshakes ended, the doctor walked over to Dean. He came up in front of him and reached out to put his hand on his son's shoulder in a show of unity. The seventeen-year-old sprang back as his hand swept his father's hand away with an angry motion that could not be misread by the crowd. Young Dean walked away. This event was registered by the congregation and discussed over the kitchen counters of this small town, where nobody could bring a shirt to the cleaners without feeling obliged to make an announcement to the whole world. Six weeks later Dean Rosco was in San Luis Rey. United States Marine Corps. He never saw his father again.

Two years after his wife's death, on a calm spring morning, Dr. Rosco took his Harley Davidson for a casual ride along Highway 1 North. Cutting a sharp curve somewhere between Sea Ranch and Anchor Bay, he almost hit a huge RV. The motorbike spun out of control and shot straight over the cliff down to the rocky beach two hundred feet below. Because the deadly accident happened during a high tide, the body was washed ashore two days later, twenty miles north.

During *this* funeral, Sergeant Rosco met Francis L. Donovan, attorney for the Boston law firm of Sterling Fox & Donovan, a quiet paunchy man who, after expressing his condolences, filled the young Sergeant in on his sudden wealth. He asked what young Mr. Rosco had in mind to do with the inheritance.

The sergeant thought short and hard. Then ?

"Let it grow. If one of you guys fuck around with my property, I'll skin you alive. Tell this to your people in Boston."

Francis L. Donovan looked into the expressionless young face and knew the wealthy man from the Special Forces was serious. Sergeant Rosco returned to his unit the next day and twenty-four hours later he was on his way to Israel to be lectured in a new academically discipline—the study of terrorism. In the Jaffé Center for Strategical Studies at Tel-Aviv University, they met, Dean Rosco and Fon Yun, a man from Singapore. The *Meluckha*[3] department of Mossad made only one, but successful move, to get them on their list of delegates.

He thought the war in Iraq was not justified anyway. Bought a ranch near Petaluma and settled down. Wealthy and with nothing to do. Now after twenty years of dedicated service to his country, some missions and a war later, they were civilians. And he asked: "So, what's up?"

---

[3]   Recruitment Department of Mossad.

Rachel inhaled deeply.

"Well, remember the drop. Point forty-seven? You know . . . I mean . . . ."

Rachel had become speechless for the first time in her life, the reality of the hidden wealth starting to sink in.

The Major took over.

"Remember all that metal?"

"Yes," Rosco said, "we gonna do it?"

The Major leaned forward, lowered his voice and nodded:

"I think it can be done."

Rosco glanced swiftly at Rachel, while she fussed with her hair.

"She is in, all the way," the major said, "we might need a good flyer anyway. First we need to talk to the rest."

There was a long anticipatory lull under the blue sky as the golden Eagles of Napa danced and the sunlight washed the trees in the valley. The azure sky and the grace of the sailing birds were like the music of a newly composed song. That was the way Rachel saw it. Eventually Rosco broke the silence and put it straight to the Major.

"There is only one chance that the metal can be taken out. Duskin, Berret, you and me."

No word about Rachel.

She had heard the reluctance in his voice. The Major could not blame Rosco's aversion. Contemplating wealth was easy-pondering the possibility of death. Their own government wouldn't even be willing to acknowledge their existence.

"I think it can be done," Rachel chirped.

"What makes you think so?" Rosco asked softly.

"Let's eat first. I am starved."

In an irrevocable tone Rosco challenged the two: "So, you think it can be done?"

"Yes. But like all the missions, anything is imaginable, if you have the right people."

And as a sort of warning he added to his saying: "And everybody might not make it back."

Rachel nodded in agreement and the Major began to wonder whether Rachel knew more than she pretended to know at the moment. The Sterling Salmon came. It was excellent and they ate in silence. Thoughts were flying furiously.

"First, the men," Rosco started.

"Where is Duskin?" the Major asked.

"Well, he called me once before he left for Singapore. Got a job as a bodyguard for some wealthy chap and his brood. I don't know his address. The only contact I have in Singapore is an older Chinese. A private investigator. Fon Yun is his name."

"H'bout Berret?"

Rosco chuckled.

"That is another story. When he came home, his wife was in the middle, pardon my French, of getting laid by a neighbor. Well, you know Berret. He just packed up. He took his van and left. Sells Indian jewelry."

"Where can we find him?"

"At this time of the year, in Arizona. A place called Quartzsite. Along Highway 10. But I'll tell you what, why don't you both stay here for a couple of days, so we really . . ." interrupted by Rachel saying that they had brought along a suitcase with all their needs in it. Tom had no idea about this, but kept a straight face in front of Rosco.

What about Kessler? Garry? Yes. Forget it. In Ankara. Station officer in Turkey. Works closely with David Meyers, the DDCI. Kessler is in charge of Eastern Europe and Middle East there. Plays the game together with the NSA and CIA.

"Do you know some place here where we can get together for few days to work the whole thing out? Some where quiet and out of the way, but not too much?" the Major asked.

"Yes, but first let's find the men."

8

Platinum.

Supposedly the universe ignited and exploded all at once. Or perhaps a convulsive eruption took place. Anyway, the substance was thrown somewhere like from a shovel filled with marbles, and had formed into the circumferential speed of a racing enormous giant meteor at a point in nowhere, where even the distinguished universe could not have begun yet. Space and matters for ranges to go between did not exist.

Nothing.

Absolute nothing could relate or be said about this epoch. One can only speculate. Perhaps the reasoning of time and life had not yet began because the Life Carriers had not considered any existence to *where* the meteor had been ordered to end up. But who knows.

The meteor, by means of unknown tremendous magnetism absorbed other marble-like substances shattering into its surface, at speeds never to be measured. Perhaps by a velocity many times faster than the speed of light. Still, the meteor was comparatively less than a dust particle to the cosmos and the distances this space-lump roamed. It passed the violent energies of hydrogen and helium when propelling through the clouds of gaseous, liquid, and solid matters of atomic-molecular relationship. Passed through the vastness of billions of galaxies with stars of physically gaseous and tremendously dense at the same time. Passed superheated clouds on their brink to be stars of matters. Some of them, unstable, would appear only for a moment with a blink of light and burn out in a momentary tremble of time and collapse under their own weight. On its voyage the meteor also collided often with large matters on their own mission to new and other stars. Their own journeys interrupted by just being absorbed into the matter of this racing giant, which had decelerated to 658,000,000 miles per second. Other stars reached diameters of one billion miles to withstand anything in what they were flowing in. Not all stars the meteorite passed on its way to the target were solid. Some were of the reddish and blue glimmering and had a density in their centers of their gigantic masses that one cubic inch could weigh up to six thousand pounds.

Collisions happened many times and it began to wear down the meteor in size and form.

Into nothing.

The meteor pressed on, shot thought knots of gases and reached sometimes the outer skirt of a spiraling arm, belonging to a new galaxy. Here the meteor swung into a new course, following the direction and the gravity of the helix in spiral. Still, enormous in its size it had reached now an area in space where time and distance began to be a comprehension and took on a meaning. The meteor dashed into an area which had a quite orderly structure of forty-three moons, nine planets and one nebula star. They all did not go to anywhere, because they were bound by the invisible leash of this particular star. All were forced to circle around it in a precise systematic order.

Sucked into the rotating spiral arm of this galaxy, forces altered the course of the meteor and it began its final approach to a planet it was assigned to. In the unfolding of new creations it had traveled for two octillion ($2x10??$) and one-hundred thousand trillion miles. Its close target was a planet later called Earth. The outer layer of Earth was still in an almost molten stage.

It was then, two billion years ago, that the giant meteorite slammed straight one-hundred forty miles deep into this upper crust and into an area later known as the Canadian province of Ontario. The impact not only created the crater called Sudbury Basin; the force of the impact also fractured the earth's hull. The magma, mineral-rich in iron, calcium, chromium, iron, silver platinum, gold and other myriads of the elements, gushed to the surface, or were shoved close to the surface around the planet to cool down.

And there where it would be found and wrestled from mines 3000 feet deep and away from daylight, in mines with names like Thompson in Canada, Noril'sk and Tinakh in Siberia, Pechenga in Norway or the Merensky Reef in the Bophuthatswana of Transvaal in South Africa. Experts measured platinum by a value hard to be understood, since one ton of ore only would yield enough of the metal to cover the nail of a man's index finger. Worldwide daily production was measured only in troy ounces (approx. 35 gram).

Platinum.

For whatever reasons, its value had long been overshadowed by the supremacy of gold. Only for a short period of time it gained prominence in the trade of jewelries. In the earlier swap of the Middle Ages, alchemists theorized that the mystical substance would transmute lead into gold. This was a sure thing. Some lost their heads when they could not deliver the noble metal to the kings, starving for cash.

There were the pre-Columbians. They were the first forging jewels from platinum alloy. And then there were the Spanish Conquistadores. The Spaniards found it mixed with gold extracted from the rivers of what is now known as the Chocó region of Colombia. They cursed the silvery grain in their gold pans. Painstakingly, they removed the patina one by one. They believed patina was gold not buried long enough to turn yellow. So, they threw it back into the river to ripen.

Platinum—little silver—they called it.

Words about the strange new metal reached Europe in the mid-16th century.

"There is a substance," wrote Italian scholar Julius Caesar Salinger, "which it has not hitherto been possible to melt by fire or by any of the Spanish arts."

Not even the hottest furnace could melt it. Two-hundred years later the Europeans did finally learn that platina was not one metal, but five separate elements. And this was palladium, rhodium, iridium and osmium. The Russian Karl Karlovich Klaus extracted in 1804 the final element ruthenium.

During World War Two, the Germans were the first to understand and to master the importance and technical value of platinum to keep electrical systems of planes and vehicles operating effectively. They were the first to be aware of the good mechanical properties. Rhodium with its high reflectivity represented properties to be used in surfacing anti-aircraft searchlights. Palladium would be used in the chemical plants of Buna by Schkopau as catalysts for hydrogenation of the full fledged production of synthetic oil in the building F61. It was just the tip of the iceberg how to technically use these metals in the future.

Most of the platinum producers were at war with the Germans; only Colombia was not. In spite of the best effort of the FBI and British intelligence, the German secret service managed to smuggle almost one ton of platinum out of the remote Colombian jungle.

Each year ten-thousand tons of silver and thousand tons of gold reach the free-world market but only seventy tons of platinum. The significance of platinum appeared to be obvious. Its technical use was unlimited and unexplored. The one ton of platinum in the crashed plane, only with a hundred-atom-thin layer of the metal kept a razor-baled edge sharp and did not corrode.

Aurum. AU. Gold.

In the course of history its color had been identified often with the royalty of the sun. When hammered into thin sheets it would transmit green light. If boiled, the vapor would be green, and when refined, its powder would be chocolate brown. That's what gold was. The great whore of civilization. What was it that made it so important? The prehistoric civilizations of Egypt and Rome were crucified by gold. The metal was brought up from abysses under conditions of unbelievable torment and grieving. In the second century the historian Diodorus wrote that "all are forced to labor at their task until they die, worn out by agony amid their toil."

Why was it that men around the world in wrinkled shirts and the heavy smell of stress under their armpits, pushed buttons on their computers to create a significance that does not truly exist? The grip of gold is insane and ludicrous. A bright sparkling metal, solicitous of emotion and successful throughout history to ruin integrity. No logic could ever explain a more absurd waste of human resources than to dig gold in distant corners of the earth for the sole purpose of transporting it and reburying it immediately afterward in other deep holes, specially excavated to receive it and massively guarded to protect it.

For example, five stories below the streets of New York, an armed sentinel stands before a 90-ton steel door. A door which can only be opened when its huge wheels are turned. Clockwise. Only then one could walk into the room behind, where the gold was. It gave off a butter-yellow flush. Further inside this unique construction, was a booth containing 107,000 bricks. Each weighing 30-33 pounds. Market value $ 153,000 each. Altogether, a frosty $117 billion. It was only one of the 122 impregnable compartments in the vault of the Federal Reserve. It is rumored that some 50 nations hide their gold hoards in New York at this place for safekeeping. The total—10,000 metric tons of gold.

The technical need increased year after year because of gold's unique properties, resisting corrosion and being a superb electrical conductor, combined with its incredible malleability. It can be beaten into a foil less than five-millionths of an inch thin. These properties have given gold its real and only value to serve society. No computer could exist without gold. Laced somewhere between its components, it was. Because of its exceptional conductivity and repellency to corrosion, 47 metric tons are used every year in the electronic industry alone.

Two mining houses, the Charter Consolidated in London the largest producer of gold in the world, and the Consolidated Gold Field in South Africa, once did a study. They found that demand for gold was growing faster than the world production. Not including Russia, Consolidated Field found that approximately 1,412 tons of gold were produced worldwide every year. 1,058 tons for jewelry, 76 tons for dental fillings, 91 tons for electronic equipment and 111 tons in coins and medals. Only a humble 75 tons or so of gold served the purpose of filling teeth each year. The numbers created doubt in South Africa, the true realm of gold. Johannesburg felt that numbers like these would weaken the important role of their yellow stockpile. Gold was too soft to be used in its purest form. That's where often platinum came in. Amalgamated with it. The quantity of gold in items was specified by the carat scale. The Italians called it 'karat', the Arabs named it 'carat', the Greeks would name it 'keratin', relating it the fruit of a carob tree. The tree had hornlike fruits that contained seeds. These used to create the steadiness of a scale in Arabia, the gold souks in Morocco, Beirut, Djedda, Bangkok or Madras. 24 karats was the purest form of gold.

Tom suppressed a yawn and looked at his watch. But obviously it was the world's fuel to run on. Lit a cigarette, inhaled deeply and enjoyed the smell and the relaxation that came along with it. A smooth and gentle breeze danced around his forehead. He closed his eyes and some doubt crept into his senses. Was it worth it? He opened his eyes again. The lights of the stars had something soothing to him. The day had retired hours ago. He took some deep puffs of fresh air and went back into the living room. His gut feeling was that they could pull it off. Scratched his forehead and sat down again. He took out the calculator and a yellow pad. When he sat, the cat jumped from her favorite pillow and moved toward him like silk, her bushy grey tail held straight up. The cat rubbed her head against his leg and looked up at him with her big metallic eyes. Tom bent down and took her on his lap.

"What do you think, Jordan?"

The cat trampled and purred and circled twice before curling up again. The fingers of his left hand thoughtlessly caressed her fluffy fur. He took the calculator. A ton of gold was 32,000 ounces. Multiplied by six would equal 192,000 ounces. The price per ounce would be between $369.67. and $560. He did not feel guilty. Five men had discovered it. It was theirs. They deserved it. He began to work on the layout. A master plan. Two hours later he knew it was a full-scale operation. It was 04:30 in the morning before he crawled silently under the thick, smooth comforter. Rachel moved over.

"I know, we can do it," she mumbled.

They were hooked. And there was still the platinum, palladium, the iridium and rhodium, the osmium. He was not so sure what it was worth and what they should do with it.

9

Singapore

The 747 Big Top of Singapore Airline 001 swung into a westward course and made a final correction over the Straights of Malacca. The graceful left turn straightened the plane out and into the final approach to Changi airport. The 747 whistled with a steady low whining of its four engines through some clouds and bounced playfully against them. Releasing its landing gears, the Boeing got closer to the straight gray ribbon of the runway. Hissing along the runway's blue AIL's, the whining was low and steady. Then rubber screeched and yelped as it touched down. The passenger in row H21 was a female, and according to the boarding list, her name was Rachel Peters. It took Rachel ten minutes to get through customs and two minutes to get a taxi.

"Which hotel?" the Chinese taxi driver asked.

"Shangri-La," she said, pretending to be tired and closed her eyes.

*

The next day. Late morning.

Rachel walked down the soft hill to Orchard Road and took one of those yellow taxis.

"Nee Soon," she said, and added the address to it.

"I know," the driver replied, "I know."

"How far is it?" she asked.

"I know, I know," the driver replied with almost close eyes, still digesting his breakfast *and* driving. He nodded three times with an expression in his face like being insulted about the question. The trip took twenty five minutes. Between palm trees a weather-worn old concrete building appeared. The road began to narrow and turned out to be more winding than she expected.

Rachel ordered the driver to stop. She paid and got out. A wave of hot humid air washed over her face.

The building.

It was an unattractive rundown chunk of concrete with a black painted steel door. Windows like a prison. Paint bubbles on the walls, created over the years by intense humidity, had burst, exposing myriads of prior paint coats. She pressed the knob of the buzzer down. Nothing. No sound. Tried it one more time. Then the steel door gave in to her demand. It opened, allowing her to enter a hallway with a destitute source of light. Her heart added on another beat, and she had a last look back. It was a destitute area between very narrow standing trees and bushes. On both sides, dumped old cars with no tires and broken windshields. Nobody would ever miss her. It had gotten so hot that even the birds were still.

She took a deep breath and wondered for a moment what this brand new white Mercedes 500S was doing here between the older beaten up Toyotas and Nissans. She stepped into the hall. The steel door closed with a soft hollow metallic sound. She felt trapped. She did not like this one bit and stepped into the badly lit hallway and hesitated. She started to set her left foot at the beginning of three upcoming flights of very flimsy wooden staircases. When she made it to the second floor, she saw a sign on the door. It looked like hardwood and had a peephole in it.

Fon Yun, Private Investigator

The sign was made from brass and it had not seen any polisher for quite some years. The little bright center of the hole got dark. Somebody observed her. The door opened.

A Chinese woman in a stage of advanced pregnancy appeared and let her in. Her facial and body behavior signaled mid-thirty, without hiding the discomfort of not honestly representing the real age of twenty something and her physical conditions.

"What do you want?"

It sounded like the hissing of a dragon. Rachel collected her thoughts and smiled.

"Courtesy," she said, "and Mister Fon Yun is expecting me."

It changed the scene. A grinning smile appeared on the lady's face, disclosing that she was no longer in possession of the right half upper part of the I2 incisor.

The reception area had no windows. Some tall and trim Chinese men were lounging around with watchful eyes. Somebody typed away on an antique *Underwood* typewriter that appeared to be at least fifty years of old age. What she was confronted with was striking to her. There were piles of old worn—out and very well thumbed files and the smell of stale Szechwan food. No computer, no fax machine, no phone. At least not visible. It was office disorder at its finest. The 12-less on her side ushered Rachel into the bordering room. There was the man she wanted to talk to.

*

The man arose from behind a huge desk, which was covered with rings from hot tea pots, placed there over long periods of time. The desk of unknown age was cluttered with papers and files. Files inconceivably dirty and in even more fantastic disorder. Some looked so old and worn, like they had been there since Sir Stamford Raffles, an agent for some British trading organization, had set his foot on the jungle-covered island in 1819. This office was a creative mess.

Rachel realized the telephone.

A telephone!

An old black Siemens clunker from 1936 with a rotary dial. No fax. No computer. A small window approximately seven feet high from the floor. The air was hot, thick, and musty, and made the walls sweat. Rachel got the impression that the Casablanca ceiling fan, marked with tons of fly shit, in its slow rotating motions, did its best to slice the thick air into disks. There was a back up unit to cool things off. A loud humming air conditioner blew rotten warm air into this rat hole of an office the size of a chicken cage. Something caught her attention in the set up. The office was decorated, affixing the interior to the Chinese principles of feng shui, with the human being in harmony with its surroundings. The door she had entered was to his left.

Rising from behind his desk Fon Yun faced the rising sun and hence his chi (energy) could not be sucked out. A single huge Arawana with gold-like skin was floating in a three-foot fish tank between plants and toys back and forth, picturing with the cool water the possible accesses to wealth and prosperity. The Arawana moved in very self-assured motion, like he knew about the price he had been purchased for. Perhaps twenty-thousand dollars, perhaps fifty-thousand. The man's lush chair gave off a deep black hue, re-enforcing the element of water.

Rachel liked, by instinct, the set-up without having a resolving thought for it. The man behind the desk noticed her mental approval with a short smile.

What unforeseen pleasure it was, the Chinese said from behind the desk. She guessed, he had to be somewhere in his sixties, no, maybe forties. Her mind did not release a number. Not a single grey hair, combed back straight in Asian fashion, ending in a ponytail. For a Chinese, he was a tall man, six feet-two or so. Good developed shoulders. A pleasant looking face, but not persuasive. She broke away from her observation and listened for the first time to his soft voice. Shook her head for a moment like she had to overcome the feel of only being slightly her.

Rachel could not define it. It was a good sensation to be a sudden refined different being. Senses directed and steered her mind. It was a short-term adjustment, she did not understand. Rachel stared at the man and wanted to fathom were she had seen him before. Nothing came up on her mind-screen.

"Yes?" Fun Yun asked.

Their eyes met as his eyes examined her intense for a long time. Rachel turned her head and concentrated her focus, surpassing everything in this room, onto one spot. Her eyes caught up on a rosewood case, hanging across from her on the wall. A nicely square-shaped box. Artfully carved on the outside and lacquered in deep reddish brown. The case, covered with crystal glass, containing a liner of hand-woven white silk, was the home of four knives. Each was a different size of a kris, the national traditional weapon of the Malaysia.

This kris—the bloodiest of all fighting knives—was a double edged rapier dagger with a wavy blade. The knives on the wall varied from six to twelve inches and were especially designed for thrusting. Those fine pieces of a master craftsman, those bluish blades had been made many seasons ago in a small village in Khota Baru. The tradition stated that the more waves the blade had, the greater the power the owner would have in the fight. The six-inch long kris had marks of rust spots compared with the other knives being sparkling clean.

However, the life story of this man, Fon Yun, was not without interest, to be left unreported. Fon Yun was a Malay-Chinese and had fought with the British Tracker-Killer teams in Malaya and the state of Borneo in the fifties against the Communists. He was a jungle expert and kept pressuring at this time, on enemy guerillas.

The guerillas were Fon Yun's personal foes. The Malay had never favored the Chinese immigrants, since it was said; the Chinese were smarter and controlled most of the important businesses in Malaya (now *Malaysia*) except the military.

Many moons ago, Malay communist guerilla burned down Fon Yun's home by Alar Setar in the state of Kedah, raped his mother to death, hanged his father upside down until he was deceased. They shot his three brothers, and kidnapped his beloved twin sister, Tamar. She was sold like merchandise to a brothel in Bangkok. Selling a virgin meant more money for the gangsters of the jungle (years later romanced by the media as rebels).

On a bright morning she took a Ricksha along Alun Amarin and jumped from the Phra Pinklao Bridge. The river carried her inert body for some miles then spit the dead body out on the edge of *Klon Mon*. As a proud woman, she could no longer take the mental abuse and degradation of womanhood in which she was forced to live. Prostitution.

The only reason young Fon Yun survived the massacre was his absence. He was in Kuala Lumpur on business. When he returned, a friend told him what happened and that they had taken Tamar away. Tamar, his beloved twin sister. Fon saw with stoned face, the ravaged house when he returned. And something perished in the friendly and young heart of Fon Yun forever. Fon wanted to scream. Scream away the pain and agony when he saw the senseless destruction around him. But he only choked, gasping for air. The shriek stopped and sank back deep inside, deep into the abyss of his being where the soul would be, only to be released decades later.

The next day he was gone to Bangkok. First he went to the river were the boats came from the north and left further south. The immense stream had flowed all the way from the mountains of the Himalayas to run through the metropolis of Thailand. There the river was labeled the Chao Phraya, but the locals called it simply Mae Nam. The river.

Fon Yun showed her picture and asked for his sister Tamar. Nobody knew or had seen her and everybody shook their head. He drank and whored his way across Bangkok until, one late evening, he was confronted at the Copper Alley, a small side street in a *soi,* a side water street, filled with little craftsmen shops. A pockmarked face, revealed the sister's fate. Oh, yes he knew about the girl from Malaya.

"Why do you ask about this girl from Malaya? She was a whore. Some men sold her. She killed herself in the river. Who are you? Informer?" he was asked when suddenly somebody put a stiletto blade on Fon Yun's throat from behind. His head was pulled back and he found it very difficult to breath. He wore his kris across his belt. Pulled it and shoved it in a hard motion into the man behind him. He rotated the kris in a swift flux in his hand. All the eight inches of the well-curved kris went into the pimp's soft belly and killed him instantly.

Fon Yun knew enough. After his initial revocation of a stranger's life he returned to his country and went to the British. He offered his service as a fighter. They happily took this ambiguous young man, and when he returned from his seventh tour of duty in the jungles of Terengganu, the masters of running the colonies, the British, gave him his own tracker-killer team. From then on Fon Yun consequently traced the so-called freedom fighters to their hideouts with howling hordes of snarling blood dogs and armed men destroying his enemies. It was a small group of a dozen men he led. The word *mercy* was never on their agenda. Mercenaries from Indonesia and Iban headhunters from Borneo, some Gurkhas from Nepal in between, were his troops. The Ibans and the Gurkhas came from different locations and cultures in this world, yet they had something in common. It was their love for knives.

Once the commando had reached a hideout, the Gurkhas and Ibans would move with a deadly grace and elegance in total silence from tree to tree, to reach the dwells where the enemy, most of the time communist guerillas, rested. The Gurkhas liked this kind of attack. They would even put their guns down to use their *kukri* knives for slashing throats.

The warriors from the Iban tribe, with their wide painted faces, were different. They wanted to have the head when they used their kris. They were headhunters since the beginning of time and it was a question of honor for them to get the enemy's head chopped off as a trophy. It was a sort of an Oscar-winning event so to speak, when slicing off somebody's head.

Soon the word was out that Fon Yun's group never took prisoners. His formula was simple. Interrogate with force, get the information, shoot and apologize to the superiors later, if asked *why* the shooting. The Ibans admired Fon Yun because of all the heads he allowed them to have. Often, the simple appearance of Fon Yun was enough to discourage any further attempt to fight. He always wore black and his appearance was the one of an apparition of death. Even his own men got hot cramped feelings sometimes in their stomach when Fon Yun made certain, in his own way that no prisoners were taken. Then the eternal cycle of bad energy closed in on him.

Two weeks after his wife gave birth to a healthy pair of twins, she was shot by communist guerillas. The babies laid just beside her, soaked with the blood of their dead mother and survived. From then on Fon Yun was like a Leopard—the shrewdest, and most vicious of all great cats. But Fun Yun also acted out another element of this great cat. Restless loneliness, patient, quick and ruthless in the kill. His soul got cold and he began to search for death. But distinction would not come. And so, over the years the combat in the jungle had become his private war.

London, at this time still feeling responsible for the colony, started to feel uneasy about the slaughter when the reports began to pour into the MI5 office on London's St. James Street. They found themselves suddenly working too close with a man and his aptitudes for knifes and actually shared their cutthroat attitude toward intelligence operations. Fon Yun was a hard and brave fighter, whose call came to a sudden end with his last assignment.

Fon Yun and his men had surrounded a small native village near the Guanong Kasan mountain. The informer had been paid with British Pounds and reported that the village harbored guerillas. While the group encircled the village, Fon Yun and his safety man moved silently like two black Pumas through the jungle, nearer and nearer to the lone hut where his enemies rested.

Fifty yards away. In a small clearing. The hut.

With a calm downward motion of his hand Fon Yun ordered his safety man to stop moving and only to back up. Carefully and without a noise he placed his Sterling gun on the ground. Took two hand grenades from his belt and hung them on his strong teeth. He drew his slim kris and ran in long elastic strides to the shed. Vaulted through an open window, somewhere and somehow his right hand got a head by the hair. He jerked the head far back. The unknown man's neck was stretched, and bent up. The blade of his kris slid freely through both Sterno mastid and some other soft pasture. From ear to ear, across the anonymous throat, from just below the kris slit the unknown child soldier's throat from the right ear to the left. Yes, the kris sliced clear through the jugular and esophagus. Blood gushed over his hands when he removed the bloody kris from his enemy's slashed platysma. There was screaming, mixed with commands behind him when he leaped out the far side of the hut and plunged back into the jungle, leaving the activated hand grenades inside.

First, it seemed like the corrugated metal roof lifted some feet and dropped down again with a tremor. A fraction of a second later the walls of the house buckled outside in a fireball and explosion. The survivors, four frightened and very young guerillas, ran away from the flames only to face snarling dogs, headhunters, soldiers and a Chinese man, dressed in black, fluid soaked clothes, showing no emotion. He was the only one who pointed his Sterling gun at them. This time Fon Yun didn't even ask questions, he just pulled the trigger. Oh, it was a cruel war in the highlands of Malaya everybody wished to forget. After that execution, the British High Command in Kuala Lumpur suggested carefully to Fon Yun to leave the service, or things should be done only by the book. That was not for him. Fon spit at the floor and retreated. He never cleaned this particular kris. The blood corroded dark spots into the blade, never to be removed again. But life created a new opportunity for Fon.

*

Since 1819 Great Britain controlled Singapore, until the island became a part of the independent Federation of Malaysia in the second half of the twenty century. Nobody really knew what to do with this piece of rotten jungle island with some sampans, a port, a polo track in front of the parliament building and Gin-slurping Englishmen in the Raffles Hotel. The Malaysians thought it might be a racial and religious trouble spot in the future and soon excluded Singapore from the Federation.

The Singaporeans did it on their own and became an independent country joining the Commonwealth and the United Nations. The new man in South East Asia, to turn things around on this island, was a man called Lee Kuan Yew.

Lee, the son of a rich ship-owner, was a lawyer with a heavy touch of Oxford, became the first prime minister. When Lee took Singapore over it was a haven of smugglers, criminals, and tycoons with dubious businesses in drugs, gold, prostitution, and contract killing, you name it. So, the new man needed a strong hand, somebody to clean up the jungle of a city.

Fon Yun accepted a discreet request and moved to Singapore. When he crossed the Jahore Bridge, connecting Singapore with Malaysia, he looked back into the color orgy of a generous sunset. The soft change of silk colors touched his heart, and after all the years, it was the first time that his eyes filled with tears. So, alone deep down, his mind could not escape the misdeeds his soul was guilty for years. He promised himself that one day he would do good. He would save some lives. Paths of lives in need to be protected. Somewhere, somehow. Gently, he buried this confidence and self-promises under some rose leaves of his soul.

When he entered Singapore he had nobody to be with. Not the soft shoulder of a calm nurturing wife. He was alone. On the east end of Orchard Road Fon Yun opened a tailor shop called Golden Silk. He had four employees, making fine suits and shirts. But this was the "front" office. And with the same intensity and force, Fon Yun formed a team of ruthless and fearless fighters for the jungle of the city. Young men sworn in absolute secrecy and loyalty. Betrayal, the worst form of breaking allegiance and trust, would be punished by death. This was Fon's rule. His eyes, when talking, revealed only little or nothing about his thesis of life—if you are not a part of the answer, then you are a part of the problem.

Again there was no one like Fon Yun with such cold-blooded lethal cunning, outwitting even the best-laid plans of well-organized gangs and tirelessly tracking down the outlaws. Soon, dead bodies of gangsters, chronicled thieves and pimps, were found sometimes in the morning in the trenches along the streets across the island. Bodies of a badly beaten and obviously tortured torso floated; face downward, in the murky waters of the port, reminding Singaporeans that no living Asian mobster was safe. Dead. Puzzling for the investigators of the government. All the dead were on the wanted list, notoriously known for their long lives in crime. Interestingly, police investigations led nowhere.

The clean-up was merciless. No official wanted to have anything to do with it. Only the Prime Minister, getting security reports on his desk, sometimes dared to guess who was behind it. Still, it took Fon ten years to clean up the municipality, until his methods did not find favor with his new masters anymore. By then, the island was almost free of crime. Now, it was an image question for the cleanest and dullest city in the world. The prime minister invited Fon Yun to a private lunch. As he looked at the Prime Minister's cool eyes over sweet-and sour pork chops, Fon knew he was yesterday's man. An epoch had come to an end. He had seen too much not to understand that from now on devotion *and* loyalty would be a virtue that had be come passé. The men in politics needed suddenly clean hands.

"That's it, Prime Minister?" Fon Yun asked ahead.

The Prime Minister of Singapore nodded.

"Well, then . . . you don't mind . . . ," Fon Yun said as he got up, thinking about how many times he had killed with his bare hands for this man and the country. Fon Yun—the private investigator. Again, he was the best. Nobody ever figured out the mysterious systems and channels Fon used for communication to gain and secure intelligence and data. Certainly, Fon knew too well, how the human ingredient and primitive biosphere of the mortal soul could be broken down. Knowledge, pressure, bribe and, if necessary, the admonition of death with the erudition to others.

10

"Yes, what can I do for *you*?" Rachel absorbed his question, "you come from Dean Rosco? He trains my people. Good man."

"Yes. I need information about someone who works in Singapore?"

"What kind information?" he asked with a motionless face.

Rachel realized how poorly the man was dressed. His clothes looked like as if he had slept in them. She got some doubt whether or not this was the right place. Fon stared at her. He had deep, dark, demanding eyes without irises.

"About a man."

"What man? Chinese?"

"No. American. He works here in Singapore."

"Where? What? You have address?"

"No. His name is Peter Duskin."

"I not know," Fon muttered in pigeon English," why you no go to immigration. You his wife?"

"No. I only want to know where he works."

Rachel opened her purse for a moment to pull out a napkin. At the same time she gave Fon a chance to have a quick look at the wad of 100-dollar bills, American dollars. He smoothed out.

Rachel noticed it very carefully and closed the purse.

"Well," Fon said warily, "I have connection in immigration. My cousin work there. But this too expensive for you. Also, when you need it? I assume today."

This was the first time his face showed the indication of a smile.

"I don't care about the money. I want to know where he works . . ."

Rachel stopped talking. Fon said nothing. Nor did he move a muscle. He fixed Rachel in a perforating stare and seemed aiming to gaze her down. He noticed he had met his equivalent. The woman just stared back.

A rush traveled through her mind, generating a memory reconstruction. She felt that Fon's mind withdrew, to read her and strangely, she permitted her mind to follow his. Like jumping into a tunnel of a cloud of swarming stars. The silence was unique. Rachel felt exceptionally close to Fon. She did not have an explanation. There was something from the past. Not her past. His and hers!? Her mind misbehaved by lingering around hazed reflections. Like looking into a crystal mirror from ten different angles the same time. Thoughts, she could not relate to. Something dreadful happened in the past.

Not even in her past, she thought. A mental communication took place. A transmission of a message from the past. Swift.

"I knew, one day I would see you again, Tamar, sister," she heard Fon's voice in her mind."

"How do you know it's me."

"Because you do not have fear. Only pride. Like your brothers had. Your father and mother."

"What happened to them, my brother?"

"Their murders have paid the price for years. They have paid for the grief they inflicted on you in Bangkok."

"What happened to me?"

"You killed yourself."

"Why?"

"It was for the supremacy of your self-respect. You did not want to live in disgrace and pain."

"What do you want from me?"

"Nothing. I am grateful that your soul is alive. Wherever you will go, there will be unknown factors you cannot control. I will be there. You will be safe"

Who's voice was it? A verbalization was whispering inside her. Rachel did not feel vulnerable. She could not move her body. Her vocal cords did not release a sound. It was like the presence of someone inside her.

She looked at her watch and was surprised that only one minute had passed since she met Fon. It took her some seconds to regain her composure. Still, their eyes looked into each other. Finally he broke the quietness, which had become so forbidding that even Fon's hands became clammy. He deeply respected her.

"Which hotel you stay?" he asked abruptly. His face was expressionless.

"Shangri La."

Silence again. Rachel gave him an arched left eyebrow. She felt comfortable with him. Fon looked at his watch. She noticed a diamond—spangled

Tag-Heuer 18-Karat gold watch. Worth three thousand dollars. This son of a bitch, she thought with a gentle smile, with rags as clothes, you would buy him a soup, but wears a gold watch. Now she knew who owned this brand new S500 Mercedes with its 100 percent import tax on top that was parked in the front of the building.

"You are obviously not here for a private reason. Are you?"

The pigeon English had suddenly disappeared, replaced by a very reasonable tone of Oxford. It was a calm and measured question of a man, who in spite of all his inner deficiencies he had created in his life of killing, plotting, and human hunting, still certified himself to be the best investigator and security man in Asia. Even the British MI5, and in the good old days of Cold War, the KGB, draw often life momentous intelligence. All cash business.

A KGB agent paid him once with counterfeit money Fon some vital information that had cost Fon 's best field man's life.

The agent from Moscow could honestly assume he was safe when he was back in London three days later. It took Fon only twenty-hours to find out where the Soviet was. The next day a man by the name Liu Chuang, he was Fon's best henchman and in possession of a real British passport, flew from Hong Kong to London.

And this is what happened in London.

The Soviet Cultural attaché left his apartment at Victoria Grove in the morning around seven. He was well known by the British counter—espionage as KGB colonel Boris Sverdlovsk. Boris was a careful man by profession and nature and always observed his environment before going to his car. And there was nothing out of the ordinary on this clammy London morning. Just a Chinese street sweeper to be seen in an official uniform of a London gardener. Cleaning the parking area from the sticky leaves, this had been released from their duties of coating the trees overnight. The Chinese smiled and nodded a friendly "Good Morning, Sir", while swinging his broom. The KGB man crossed the street and opened the door of his Peugeot. Got in and wanted to close the car door.

He couldn't't.

Looked upwards from his seat to find the obstacle for the sudden obstacle. Noticed in surprisingly slow motion, *a* smiling Chinese street sweeper between the open door and the frame of the car. It looked also very strange somehow that this street sweeper pointed a gun at him. The man from Moscow even observed, in a curious stage of mind, a professional gun. It was a 9mm Mamba automatic with a stubby silencer attached to it. Even noticed in a fraction of time, what was left in his life, the simple and elegant lines of the weapon. Got even a glimpse of a short flame from the barrel. However, he did not have to deal with the fact that the soft lead bullet penetrated his left malar bone and ripped through the Gyrus Fon nicatus of his brain. Departed, without having lost not even a third of its velocity, the Occipital Bone of his skull and left behind a two-inch exit hole.

The Colonel's brain.

All over the car's interior.

From ceiling to floor.

Brain.

The street sweeper emptied an envelope with seventy-five one-hundred counterfeit dollar bills over the now obviously dead body. Dropped the gun in the car and had made sure it did *not* look like a suicide. Before this very profane and appalling event of this daybreak on this small street was discovered and found its way to the desk of the Metropolitan Police, the street sweeper had already crossed into Europe and twelve hours later was in Hong Kong.

Since a Soviet diplomat, so the official recapitulation was killed on British soil, a further delay was inconceivable. This kind of affair was a question of high politics. Nobody knew where the rumor came from. But it was persistent and clear. Even the Russians couldn't fuck around with Fon.

*

Rachel did not answer. She was not going to be netted again in the tranquility.

"Whom do you work for?" was another measured inquiry.

No answer.

"Private?"

"This may be a fair arrogation. But, you might assume, I am not here to be interrogated by you."

His respect grew and he rose from his chair, which also marked the end of the conversation.

"You will have this data by seven this evening. I prefer you pay now. This would be eight hundred dollars. Please be available this evening."

She handed him eight brand-new bills. He pocketed the money. Suddenly the tone was the one of a man who was in charge of giving orders. It was the voice of a man in control. She could hear it. While walking her to the door, Rachel observed the powerful body movement of Fon. The movement of a man whose appearance was ageless. He stopped. A sympathetic smile

appeared on his face and he put his heavy left hand on her shoulder. She felt
it had to be.

"Allow me one question. I mean you gave me the money. What if I don't
deliver and you . . ."

She looked him into the eye and he stopped, allowing some anticipating
silence for her answer.

It was a sort of statement with a blasé forgiving shrug.

"Mister Fon," she said, "you might have noticed I am not afraid of you.
If I don't have the information this evening, I'll be back and you'll be without
a knee cap."

It was precisely what he had hoped to hear. He laughed.

"I like you. I really do. You have what we Chinese call in Mandarin
Li Yia Dan Lan[4]. I like also the belt you wear. Very smart. You remind me
of . . . ," Fon' his face got a soft touch of sadness for a moment, ". . . uh,
never mind."

"Your sister?"

She did not fathom why she said it.

He gazed at her and opened the door.

After she left Fon Yun placed a call. The receiver was the electrician of
the Shangri-La Hotel. Ten minutes later two bugs were positioned in Rachel's
room.

*

When Rachel returned to the Shangri-La Hotel she took a long shower
to wash away the sweat and dirt of the day. Then took a nap, apparently
sleeping away some jet lag. By six she took another hot shower to keep
the pores of her skin open so she would not sweat. She did a makeup of a
decent interpretation. Underlined the beauty of her eyes by darkening her
eyelashes, using the Lancôme Caracoles Excellent brush with the skill of an
artist. Slipped into light blue Versace silk trousers and a simple white cotton
blouse. She tightened the blouse around her hips with a belt. A strange belt.
It was called the Blackie Collin Belt, a double edged dagger, worn as a belt
buckle. By 1972 this particular blade was a hit in a gun show in Kansas City.
What appeared to be the belt buckle was a grayish looking handle made from
extremely strong Corian. The razor sharp Teflon threaded plastic blade was

---

[4]   Chinese Mandarin: means :You have guts.

artfully build into a small flexible pliable sheet at the inner lining of a elegant Brazilian light blue leather belt which now held the blouse in perfect place. And like any good fighting knife it was light enough to be worn at all times, without the feeling of weight. A drop of Jil Sander Number Four behind the ears. She had a last look into the full-length mirror. Very attractive and decent. Her inner voice was sure and strong. She wondered for a moment, what kind of person would deliver the information. She went down into the bar. It was around six fifty. Her appearance was enough to find the interest of a Chinese man. He was superbly dressed. All Hérmes. He came over to her and sat down on the next empty chair.

"Mind if I sit down?"

The Hérmes man sat down without her endorsement.

"I understand you need information about Peter."

Fraction of silence.

"You have to understand we work without anything in writing."

The Hérmes man ordered dinner. Selected some fine Chinese nourishment, prepared in some mysterious way over blue-burning flames by hissing and growling in stainless steel pans, inviting observation. They ate in silence and it was not until after espresso and a brandy on the side that the Hérmes man got around to the real purpose of the meeting. He moved his chair sideways to his left, giving him enough space to cross his right leg over the left knee. With the movement of his chair and the crossing of his legs he had managed to get closer to her without bending over at her. He began to talk.

She listened carefully for fifteen minutes.

At the end he said, "Mister Fon likes you and he wants to let you know he will be around, if you need him. This is done very seldom. But he likes you. What you want to do will not be possible without his help. You know. You remind him of his sister. Tamar was her name."

"And what happened to her?"

"He has not authorized me to talk about this."

"And who are you, to appraise this all?"

"I am his only son," the man said. His face revealed the arduousness of a man who still had some life-accounts payable open: "I had a brother. But somebody's bomb killed him. But this is another story."

He saw Rachel's eyes asking him.

"Mr. Fon did not allow me to talk about it. And I will respect my father's wish."

*

Peter Duskin.

As a youngster he could not wait to get away from his overprotecting, constantly-whining mother in San Diego. His father had left the family for another woman. Peter's mother drank too much and had her first glass of Chardonnay already by noon when she waltzed through her estate, as she called it, in her washed-out blue woolen nightgown. She liked the mindless conversations with her neighbors about the how-are-you and the I-just found-a-new-gardener talk. She always had an excuse to have a full glass in her hand. Young Duskin started to dislike her when she no longer listened to what he wanted to say. He only knew there was a whole world out there.

On his 18th birthday he went to the recruiting office of the Marines. A week later Peter Duskin faced his first drill sergeant at Fort Bragg. He was strong in will and big enough to undergo the hardest training without ever disapproving it. Simple-minded but very practical, with a sharp sense for observation. The part of a personal profile included the superiority of handling knives. He could throw any kitchen knife, or the real thing, more than twenty feet into anybody's throat. His gift was not unnoticed, and a report went to the Special Forces.

His love for knives began when he was twelve. His mother had asked him to sharpen a kitchen knife. She gave him an Arkansas Surgical Black Stone and some oil. This did the trick. When he put the knife on the stone, it was like he had done it a lifetime before. Knew instantly how and why he had to hold the knife in a 20-degree angle and knew when he had to stop with skill. A knife does not get sharper by honing a finer bevel. It will only weaken the blade. While he sharpened the knife, he could see how the structure of the blade began to respond to his stroking demand, sensing that he had to maintain the same angle for the greatest possible effect. Things had to be equal. He found knives fascinating. With his first pocket money he bought a Sykes-Fair bairn knife, considered to be an ultimate killing knife, at a flea market. And like others collecting stamps, Peter Duskin had a handsome collection of knives by the time he was fifteen. There was a Dan Dennehy fighting blade, a collection of the finest knives like a Morseth special with brass-wrapped tang and ivory handle, Jess Horn tiny model with a 3 ?-inch blade, a George Hebron model with an ivory Micarta handle, Recon Special, 6-inch Bucker Gascon, John Smith's sleek Model 5 with brass trim and butt. Knifes in all shapes and forms, with damascened blades and blued double-edged. But his finest possession was a Dennehy triangular-bladed boot knife. He trained himself to throw it over some fifty feet in distance with deadly accuracy and using the saber fighter stance as the foundation for knife fighting of thrust, defense, and attack.

He designed his own cream-like soft leather holster and wore the triangular between his shoulder blades. This was his secret. Pretending to surrender, he would raise his hands, folding them behind his neck. The fingertips of his right hand would reach the top of the handle and pull the knife from behind his back, throw it while his torso turned, with a dancer-like motion into the target. He trained hard until he never failed to hit.

This knowledge was his advantage when he entered the Marines. To the surprise of his superiors he had quit the service immediately after the return from Iraq. He found an ad in a newspaper. Somebody in Singapore needed an impenetrable ring of muscles, of bodyguards. British or American would be preferred. He wrote to the unknown job agency on 54th Street in New York and got the job. He left a note for Rosco to find him in Singapore. Peter Duskin was now a part of a growing army of men and women whose job it was to guard people who did not have the eligibility of kings or diplomats. He had to guard people with extensive amounts of new wealth. His job was to think the unthinkable, to think in terms of the worst happening.

Being a bodyguard, Peter Duskin lived the very fineness of this line between all-quiet and all hell breaking loose. A job where he had to watch out for those who were watching the people around him *and* his boss. He could not rule out anyone because they just looked old or even respectable. Peter's motto was simple—dangerous people come in all configurations and proportions. They had to move their bosses in a choreographed unison to shadow their charge in and out of whatever intricate place he wanted to be. Over the previous three exhausting days Rachel followed Peter in his actions as a security man and realized that his social elegance started to wear thin after eight hours on the job dealing with the constantly changing demands of his client. He was never a prelude to departure and Rachel felt sorry for him being shoved around by having to pay constant attention to some spoiled human beings. She did not understand why a highly trained man with so much dignity and front line experience, had to wait on the caprices of a few paranoid Singaporeans. Rachel remembered that once upon a time, Peter jumped only when his commanding officer told him to. Now he had to take his orders from spoiled ladies.

Rachel had seen enough. It was time to talk.

11

Peter Duskin liked to spent the evenings on his days off in the Raffles Hotel. He had certain rituals at this place. Entering the hotel through the ornate cast iron portico, which led into the lobby with its famous range of Persian rugs, he would go into the ballroom where the Long Bar was. Would say 'hello' to Charles, the Chinese bartender, and have a beer. Go into the Billiard Bar and frolicked two games with his English friends from the High Commissioner's office. Got the "what's-new" chat.

By seven he was leaving the Billiard Bar to sit down at his charming white-painted cast iron table under the high palm trees in the lush garden. Here he had the first real drink. It was a beverage of his taste. Invented by a bar man named Ngiam Tong Boon in 1915. A half-filled tumbler with finely crushed ice and a half lime squeezed over it. Then a 3oz gin, 1 oz cherry brandy and some Benedictine were added to it. It was called a Singapore Sling. When the Sling came he was pleased that a small fortune cookie came with it on the tray. Inhaled deeply and began to relax. Looked up to the stars. After the first sip, he opened the fortune cookie. The writing on the enclosed small paper said—*There will be a lucky change in your life.*

Rachel entered the hotel just one minute after him and stayed out of his sight without losing visual contact of him. She wore a simple white cotton blouse and grey Levi's. Her hair looked a bit tousled. She had purposely picked out the outfit. Nobody would ever remember a magnificent but average-looking female tourist. She observed him for some more minutes from the lobby to get a better feel about him. Was he meeting someone? He had not changed or aged a bit. Trim and fit. Pleasant tan. Then she took a deep breath and moved. Duskin suddenly felt he was not alone and looked up. A woman sat down in the empty chair beside him.

"How do you find Singapore, Peter?" she asked.

Illogically, he noticed that her enamel fingernails and lipstick matched. He positioned his eyes on her and smiled. Any observer would have thought they were a couple just on their first date. She adored him for his flawless self-discipline. She saw the question in his eyes.

"You don't mind?"

"What?" he smiled.

"That I sit here."

"No."

She was almost disappointed how he reacted to her sudden appearance.

"Finding you was not easy, Peter," she said. He decided to wait things out what she had to say. But he just knew the time had come. They talked for two hours. Three weeks later Peter Duskin went on an extended vacation to Mendocino, California.

*

Quartzsite, Arizona

His beard was three days old, *if* this could be considered a beard. It was a no-shave and looked out of place on his handsome face with his melting brown eyes. The dust and sun had gotten to him and he was drunk. On top of this he had squatted on the long bar in the 'Silver Buggle'. He entered the drinker's place, filled with a blaring crowd, just when the second race was on. The mob ejaculating their howls, beseeching their favorite horse to win while staring at a 22-inch Sony TV screen from a distance of twenty feet. Followed by an abrupt muttering of excuses and laments when the horses had crossed the line at the end of their race. Each horse appeared to be a disappointment. Loser animals. But then the horde went back to the cashier. A new bet. A new beer. A new defeat. He had spent almost the whole afternoon between clouds of smoke, stale beer and rubber-like pizza. Had watched the television screen above him for hours and had bet away his money on some horse race event aired from Richmond, California. East Bay. He was hooked to the Sony screen. Every time the gates sprang open he did what the rest did, yell and scream his favorite horse's name repeatedly, bouncing his fist, sometimes containing a bottle of Miller, on the top of the bar, while small pearls of his salvia left his mouth only to arch in a concave course behind the bar between the hot dogs. His acoustical patronage had not been a help at all for the running animals five hundred miles away. All his chosen horses had lost.

Later in the day he felt like a real ass when the other betters were seating in groups and duos around his loneliness, prattling and laughing into their beers while still examining the 'perhapses' why their horse had not been in a winning mood. It had gotten louder. Some hillbilly music was rubbing his nerves. This was the last thing he needed. He had to admit he understood shit about horse racing and was sick of this place.

Leaned another five minutes on the bar counter and downed another bottle of Red Wolf. Put his big black dusty Stetson hat on his greasy shoulder-length hair. Skipped the last sip from the bottle, out of twelve, and staggered across the bar outside. Hot dust inflated wind slapped his face. The worn-down heels of his once brown cowboy boots left the sensation in him of lumbering on ball bearings. This was insane. Surveyed mentally his activities of the last few hours. He had just blown six-hundred dollars on some horses running around in circles. There was even a little man on its back pretending to beat the hell out of the speeding critter. That was the way he saw it in his drunken mind. It was like the stock market for him. No money left. Shit.

He badly needed a new tire for his scrap-metal-looking 74 Chevy van with 223,432 miles on it. No spare tire. Well, he had one, but it was flat too. After the tire blew somewhere along Highway 95 near Lake Havasu he had promised himself, after each 100 miles, to buy a used one. This self-promise went on for four months.

His body argued about the gravity of a badly needed shower. He could actually smell the old dusty heat and sweat of days on his body. Musty. Especially around his jeans, this, once taken off, would stand easily behind a door without his body inserted. Tomorrow he wanted to be in Yuma on business. He would set up his tables in the center of the town. No tire. No go. No flea market. He staggered across the filled up parking lot and then paused. Not quite sure about his destination. The heat and the mild hovering dust, originating in the harsh breakers of the desert wind, bothered him even more now. Felt pressure in his bladder. Too much beer in it. Maneuvered himself into a left turn between some parked cars. Supported his waving body with his left hand against a truck, while the right hand began to fumble with the zipper of his jeans. The relief took a minute and thirty seconds flat. Tightened the buckle of his sweat-stained belt one more notch. Now he felt better and moved on.

*

At precisely the same time, twenty-one miles away, ex-Major Tom Peters crossed the border from California on Highway Ten into Arizona in his white

Dodge Grand Voyager. It was the fourth time in a week. He had three more places to check to find the man they needed.

*

Mark Berret reached Main Street and made a right. A wide radius of a curve. He walked with unsteady feet along the sun-burned embankments. Did his best to focus his eyes on the Flamosa Mountains five miles ahead of him. They went out of focus. He had to navigate his body another two miles to his van and was concerned about Coral for a moment. How she was doing. He looked forward to a solid nap before he would allow life to confront him with decision-making again. The dilemma with the flat tire demanded entrance into his mind for a moment. He brushed it under his mental carpet. No reason to be worried. Worry, the little fucker. Where does it lead to? To nowhere. A waste of time. On top, no help at all. Somehow it would work out. Wouldn't it? He reeled along another mile and reached the bridge, sixteen feet and three inches high, to the interchange crossing over Highway 10 to . . . well, deserts. That is where his van was. And Coral.

He stopped and began to search for his cigarettes. Found them. Had slept on them for two nights. Pulled out the package. Cheap red-brown paper with a black logo. Strawberry Kailas Bids. That's what the package told him. Twenty of them. A goddess with three heads was printed on it. White small typeset on the bottom—Sanlal Bastiram Sarda. Who knows what that meant. Anyway, he even couldn't remember how he got the idea in the first place to smoke this sweet cheap shit from India. Or was it Indonesia? Who cared. Lit one with a red throw-away, inhaled deeply and decided to rest for some minutes. The trashy sweet scent of the exhaled smoke hovered around his head. Noticed the wind was gone. He did not like the taste of the cigarette. His mouth felt dry. He turned around and looked over La Pisa Plain. Heat haze rippled over the exposed pinkish-lavender tinted Dome mountain range of the Pleomastia and Kola. It was his fourth year. And this is what had happened to him.

*

Mark Berret. When he left the force, he had resigned like the rest of the team. The McDonald Douglas C-130 touched down at Travis Airbase. The closest to his hometown of Lodi, California.

After what happened in his house he did not know where to go when he had returned. Actually his second name was Berendovsky and his grandparents had left Russia in the twenties. Sometimes he remembered the beating he had taken from his mother when he refused to speak Russian with her. She beat it into his blood and telling him not to forget the land of his fathers. So, Mark spoke and understood Russian. Fluently. Never used it but liked the guttural aspects of it. Had even read Dostojevsky novels. Anyway. He had not announced his homecoming to Linda, his wife of three years because he had decided to surprise her. It was also a surprise to him. It was an early afternoon when he arrived at his house. He had flowers in his left hand and he opened the door in silence. He stepped into the hallway. Looked into the kitchen. No Linda. The living room. Nothing. As he stood in front of the bedroom door, he could hear her gasping, a sound he knew so well. In an almost amusing, slightly cynical trance, he opened the door. The first thing that he saw was a bare ass. The dropped pants covered the penetrator's feet. Near the right foot was a used condom on the over-a-long-time-tortured beige, once seventy-percent-off-sale Armstrong Stone Master carpet. Son of a gun, he thought without feeling any jealousy, she's getting laid. He was a fair man. Who could blame her? He was the one out of town most of the time, and she even didn't even know where he was or whether or not he was already dead. He watched the lustful afternoon happening for some more seconds and tried to blink it off, thinking that his eyes might have supplied him with a misinterpretation of the circumstances he was witnessing. It would have some impact. He would leave.

Mark Berret did not share the orthodox erudition about domestic violence that the male is the solitary fomentation of physical abuse. Having seen enough his natural humor began to rise again over his mental horizons and he stepped outside. Considered his strategical site and retreated to the kitchen. Kept his breath for a moment and then yelled:

"Hellohhh, I am home. I'll make some coffee."

Now he had to laugh. A little bit too loud with a small grain of acid in it. He envisioned the hurry that was now taking place between the freshly-stained bed sheets. He did not wait. Went into the garage and gathered everything saleable he had there. Plates, pots, a dusty answering machine, (still functioning), two vacuum cleaners (not functioning), and many such things he had stored there for later use, a use which never came, but now they were ready to be thrown into the RV and back into circulation of a special commerce. Some old furniture. A set of old tools. Nevertheless, good steel, good brand names. Brushing the explaining Linda off while collecting his future business assets. The good thing was he did not need counseling to get him moving. They split.

This antique collection of deposed items was the beginning of his new career. Selling in flea markets. He wanted to be as far away as he could. An hour later he was on the road. And drove as far as he could. No roof over his head. Over the last years he had some loose relationships along the highways he drove. Nothing serious. Sometimes he thought that it was the last kind of not commercialized independency. He did not want to work for some manager who was not smarter than he was. It would kill him. Better being on the road and selling goods nobody really wanted to have in their garages anymore. Bought in garages sales the things he would need for the next town's show for a dollar and sold it for ten. He made decent profits and began to set some money aside. Sometimes he drank too much beer in his loneliness and he felt that it (the shake) would catch up with him soon if he would not stop. He did not want to get the booze take over his mind. Now he was stuck in this hot dusty and overcrowded town of Quartzsite. A town with one stoplight and heavy traffic. The sun had gotten serious and blasted down on him. Damn, why did he drink so much? Fuckin' horses. He began to blame the world for the present misery he had inflicted on himself. He no longer traversed his body in the direction of his van. Decided to rest while he got the feel that his Stetson hat had soaked up another gallon of perspiration from his body. Fumbled for another of those Indian cigarettes. He knew already that the taste would forward the message to his brain to, perhaps throw up. Below him, just sixteen feet and three inches, was Highway 10. For a moment he flirted with the idea, how it would be to jump off just before one of those eighteen wheelers racing along the highway below to Phoenix. Imagined how it would crush his body and its pieces spattered all over Ten. Pulled out the throw-away again and lit another Indian one. When he bent down to light it, his attention turned to a white van which stopped beside him. Annoyed, he raised his head. Just checking. It was a white Grand Voyager. Then the window on the driver's side went down with a soft humm.

*

The Major had taken Exit nineteen into Quartzsite. Rolled up the ramp and came to a stop sign, planning to make a left over the bridge. A man with a dark Stetson, dirty jeans and run-down cowboy boots leaned against the bridge's railing.

"Son of a gun. There he is," the Major mumbled to himself.

Stopped the van and pushed down the little lever on his door. With a rich humm, the right window went down. Then the Major bent over and opened the door.

*

He watched with his drunken eyes the door opening. Nothing. Then a man in a white T-shirt and jeans materialized somehow on the right side of the van. He choked for a moment and began to lick his alcohol—dry lips.

"I do not believe this. It's you, Major."

He noticed the short but forceful motion of Tom Peter's head to the white van.

"Get in. You need a shower. You look like a sewer king. Let's talk."

Duskin had never given up the hope on the treasure in the desert. He was ready for it. Forget Lake Havasu tomorrow and the spare tire. The only thing he would take with him would be Coral. They drove over to his van. Picked up his I.D.s. Took off the license plate. He would turn it in to the DMV the next day. No, he would not, the Major said.

"Where are we going, Major?" Berret asked.

"You have to sober up. You are in five-feet-deep-shit with your life. Aren't you? You look like shit and smell like shit. Do you have the shakes?"

Berret shook his head in an "I-don't-think-so" motion and was grateful somebody told him the truth he so vehemently had denied for months. He sensed there was no common ground at the moment between him and the Major for a conversation. They drove in silence to his van. Berret stared out at the Arizona countryside with an unknown feeling of embarrassment. With a new life around the corner, he saw suddenly how far down he had let himself go. It was not the kind of business he was in which had brought him down. He blamed it on himself. It was the booze.

Mark took the small covered basket with Coral in it. His pet.

A rattle snake.

The Major had his man.

The hotel room was the first real roof Mark Berret had over his head in years. He would sweat when he saw the bottles of the Seagrams and Barcadi nicely placed on the fridge, but he didn't touch the booze. With the clean clothes and the showers, taking care of himself again, his awareness and self-mastery began to return. The running and exercise in the morning and long walks in the heat, the weight lifting in the workout room began to get easier for him and contributed to the rising of his spirits. At the beginning of the second week the Major and Berret had increased their running distance to four miles. The fat was gone and he looked lean and trim again.

"We will leave for Mendocino tomorrow."

"And then what? It's a long drive."

"We'll talk on the way."

*

Mendocino, California, October

It was not one of these on and off heavy rains with some broken clouds between, releasing some blue from behind to let the sun have a peek; no, it was streaming and steady. The grey and green of the land and the color of the houses looked over magnified in the constant wetness. Sometimes yesterday it began to rain. Not much at the beginning, just some sprinkles. Now it was just pouring down without any sign in the air for letting up. Streets were slick. There was slippery looking curvy Highway 1. The grey band of it moved along the ocean, and some acreage with houses on it came into sight. The property was called Pullen' Landing. A house had been built there once in 1877 during the Gold Rush, where schooners loaded railroad ties, hand-split, made from giant Redwood corpses, and shipped to San Francisco. And as the years passed, the old house cultivated quite a vibrant history. During Prohibition it was used as a base for rum running and even used by smugglers for bringing in Chinese laborers (nothing new in history) to work in the logging camps and on the railroad. Years later, when the Feds carried on their frenzied investigation for "Baby Face" Nelson, the authorities discovered the deserted farmhouse as his hideout. Oh yes, it was a lively stretch of California in those days. The first real owners arrived on the Mendocino Coast from the coast of Maine in 1947, bringing with them the love and the freedom of the ocean and to build a new and more worthwhile existence. This old house, like so many dwellings along the coast, began to be a mirror-image of those they had left behind in New England. In 'Little River' they had spotted the old house, by then totally abandoned. A decision was made to turn the property into a quiet country inn. The first Bed and Breakfast in the area. The "Heritage House". The estate had grown throughout the years.

Now, on this cool and rainy October day, eight cottages at the Inn were scattered over almost forty acres of lush, charming gardens, spectacular in their design, lengthened along the cliffs of the craggy, ever-dancing Pacific coastline. They had names like Seacliff, Beach House, Carousel, Greenwood, Chart Room, Opera Ice Cream, Pilot House or Same Time Next Year. The scenery was unspoiled and the stride unhurried. Nevertheless, it was wrapped up in the moment, in sheets of water, pouring down from an invisible blanket of clouds of unknown heights where somewhere the sun might be hiding behind. A week earlier, Rachel had made the reservations and had gotten off-season rates. She would stay with Tom in the 'Same Time Next Year Cottage," of course. Two-hundred-ninety-eight dollars.

A week?

No, a night.

Tom winced.

But it would include a full breakfast and dinner for two, she eased Tom's anguish.

He gave in. For the sake of what was planned and what was ahead. They paid cash. Duskin was on his way from Singapore and Rosco had still to wrap up some business in Napa. So he said. Tom had brought Berret along. Actually Tom and Rachel were on their own for the first two days. The first day they had watched the sun illuminating the cliffs in the rosy sunset, a sun surrounded by evening clouds in grey-blue. And then it got wet. They made love to the sound of the rain as the ocean bounced playfully against the low bluff, while unwinding in comfort, both had the unspoken understanding that this might be their last vacation on earth. The final day of being alone together before the men would arrive had ended. A playful, strong wind promenaded from the ocean. The rain had stopped for an hour or so, but with the promising clouds painted on the sky, it would be back with more. In the afternoon Tom, Rachel and Mark Berret walked somewhere long the cliff above the ocean. They crossed over to Highway 1. Here a small swift change in the planned event took place. When it happened, it was unrecognized by all involved. By 14:07 DDCI David Meyers, on vacation, drove his rented Town Car through along the hamlet of Little River. The last curve before Mendocino.

Two men, and a woman stepped out of nowhere. He had to slow down and came to an almost halt not to run them over. Apologetic hand gestures on both sides. Absolving smiles. His wife Patricia sighed annoyingly. Meyers, once in service, always in service, got a full picture of the two men and the woman.

After he had passed them, he wondered for a moment that somehow, and somewhere, he had seen these faces before. The thought faded away. By 1830 hours over dinner in the Heritage House, his mind released to him, suddenly, the fact that the man he had seen this afternoon was the retired

Major Tom Peters. The woman was his wife Rachel. An excellent, as he could recall, helicopter pilot. The second man—a Mark Berret. Wondered for a moment what they were doing here. But it was obvious. It was a vacation. The first mental note sank in his mind.

*

The cottage embraced them with a warm welcome. Huge logs were burning in the fireplace adding heat crackles and a surplus of coziness to the wooden paneled room. Rachel sat on the floor with her back leaning against the end of the couch. Within reach was a huge bowl of fresh popcorn releasing the smell of butter and salt. She had made it for all of them, but noticed there was no esteem in the room for her act of good will to be fed with movie food.

Without saying a word, Rosco opened his briefcase and took out five identical folders each containing copies of maps and two neatly printed pages of legal size and passed the folders to each person. It was reading time. The silence was only interrupted by the sound of shuffling papers and turning pages, the humming of the fire, and the drumming of the rain on the roof. Great particulars had been given to the description of an eighteen-wheeler, a Volvo truck with a reefer attached to it, a map with highlighted roads and highways in Anatolia, Turkey, and how the weather might be. Some confusing calendar dates followed. Among the papers was a drawing created freehand, showing no proportion, but with some estimated appraisal, displaying a road, a point marked with the word 'castle', two crosses explained by the words 'drop' and 'car'.

Berret looked up first, walked to the window, spending some time gazing out through the glass into the serious rain. Rolled his eyes upward without inviting the rest of his face and provided the clouds with an inspector's look. Disapproved their tense color. Poked with his left index finger in his right ear for the sake of complication for a moment. And waited. Duskin moved to the couch like being in trance, laid down on it, crossed his hands behind his head and permitted his eyes to wander aimlessly along the redwood ceiling, like trying to find a crack in it. Tom, with a stiff neck, sat at the edge of the bed and pitched a tense 'I-told-you-so' look at Rachel. She was on the floor, with her back leaning against the couch, examining the fireplace. Flames, reflected in her eyes, created the illusions of sparks in her yellow irises. Only Rosco seemed to be really relaxed by watching the indecisions. His right hand moved around his chin. Some chin rubbing of a twelve hours unshaved could be heard. He obviously had spent a great deal of time and money preparing the information thoroughly describing each one's precise performance to get the six-and-a-half tons of gold. With the sound of the rain in their ears, and the snarling clatter on the roof of 'Next Time Next Year', they all began to fathom what they were up against. A fat log in the fireplace cracked loudly into the hush.

"We still can go home," Rosco said testily, with an unmotivating smile in face.

"No way," Berret mumbled.

"You sure all the bars are still there. I mean, let's face it. It's now a couple of years man, since we have been inside this German plane," Duskin inquired.

A yes-nod from Rosco. Yes, it was still there.

"What makes you so sure, man?" Duskin asked.

"I just know it. Let's leave this way. Okay?"

No change in post-reading position. No motion could really expose their thoughts, besides Rachel fussing with the ends of her hair again. Everybody looked somewhere else but they did not look to one another. Something was missing. They realized the rain had stopped.

"H'bout the weight? You're talking six and a half tons. Tons, man!"

"We'll fly it out," Rachel chipped in. The tone of her voice was faraway, like explaining the art of making grandmother cookies, "everybody has to contribute his best abilities. Okay?"

"You . . . what?" Duskin said, "you have nothing to fly this . . ."

Rosco had patiently listened to every word they had to say, and then he interrupted and talked for ten minutes, taking care to special details about the flying and the chopper, necessary by now, and noticed the receptivity he gained. Then silence set in again. They went back to the Rosco paper for a second reading. Rosco talked about the helicopter and the six and a half tons of metals worth more than a fortune. Their equal shares. Rosco studied Berret and Duskin carefully and thought they would be the first to get up and go to their rooms with the excuse, perhaps to think it over.

By morning dawn, the sun, a bright yellow-silvery-golden disc, had decided to take her turn after the long rain.

They were still together, covering all the grounds and angles in every way, tasks, responsibility, and timing in their human perfection. Nobody had opposed the project all night long. Until dawn, the men and Rachel listened to Rosco, as he went through the entire plan. When Rosco had finished, a numb silence set in. They only had one shot and they knew it. Get it or die. Anyone arrested would be expected to give himself a last gift, the quick and clean way out, which was preferable to a slow and painful death perhaps created by the capturers. They even understood from Rosco's carefully presented layout that they would have a chopper lifting six and a half tons. Rachel got impatient when she noticed how hesitating men's minds can be.

"Let me tell you something. The Soviets boasted with their MIL Mi-26 sixty-two tons to six-thousand feet. This was a record. Why shouldn't I lift 6 tons ten feet with their chopper? You tell me."

Meanwhile it was 0645.

"One more thing," Rosco said, "don't use ATM cards from now on. Every time you use an automated teller, the bank records the time, date and location of your transaction. Don't browse on the web. A lot of sites record what you're looking for and when you have been surfing. And from now on, don't use your cell-phone. You and I know too well, your calls can be intercepted and your access number cribbed by eavesdroppers with a police scanner. Your cordless is just a tracking device. Just use a public phone. If you don't have to call—don't. The phone company doesn't need a court order to note the number you're gonna call. Or who's calling you. Got this? No credit card use. Okay? Everything you charge will be in a database," he smiled, "and don't get the idea to use discount coupons from a super market, they track what you have purchased. To make the long story short, nobody has to know where you are. Cash only. Okay? Now let's run."

*

Somebody else decided to run on this flawless morning. The rest of the rain clouds hung undecided over the western horizons of the Pacific. They were done and empty. David Meyers was already in his second mile along Highway 1 for the sake of increasing his life expectancy. At least that's what his doctors had told him. Reluctantly, he had to admit it felt good to offer his body this kind of motivation. When he slowed down, he saw to his astonishment, a group of four men and a woman dashing along Highway 1 North. Direction Fort Bragg. Even thought they were civilians, it looked strange to Meyers somehow that their body language, while running, communicated some (for Meyers visibly too much) military 'group-background.' And it was the second time he noticed Tom Peters, Rachel, this female pilot and the rest of the people who had resigned after their Iraq assignment. David Meyers had been in the phantom business too long not to recognize a slight abnormality in daily life when it occurred. His mind stored it away in the "check-it-later compartment" of his brain (that's what he named it quite some years ago). Made a mental note to have somebody have discreetly check out the lives of those sprinting people.

12

Moscow, Russia

He was proud to admit to *not* being one of the *reketiry*, the most powerful Russian 'mafiya', a term for the racketeers, mobsters and petty criminals who were increasingly the establishment of this new order of Russia. In prison they had called him 'comrade thief'.

His name was Gaidar. Nicolai Gregoriovich Gaidar. He had grown up in the Republic of Azerbaijan during the last ruling of Communist Party Secretary Gorbatchev.

The advantages Gaidar had over other citizens of the *rodina* was that he also was once in the rank of a young sergeant, a member of a *spetsnatz* commando unit in the Vedeno region in Chechnya and could be considered a highly trained and experienced man in the métier of warfare. Actually he should have been dead by now because of an operation his commando was deeply involved somewhere on the outskirt of Grozny, which had been bungled and a lot of his men had died in a senseless fight against the experienced Chechnian fighters to conquer a city with a population of five thousand souls who had left their land twenty-four hours earlier. He only survived, wounded, because a Colonel by the name of Mirzev of the Soviet Air Force had rescued Gaidar and some crippled left-over of his men in a daring helicopter mission.

Gaidar also had been in a Gulag camp (not far away from Moscow, in Jaroslawl) after his demobilization for selling some stolen AK47 machine guns and Makarov pistols on the black market in Moscow and Kiev. He was aware about the increasing demand for this kind of intimidating toys. Just closing a gap in what the market demanded. That's what capitalism suddenly was for the Russians. Competition was stiff and sometimes deadly. The time ex-sergeant Gaidar spend in the slammer was, by common Russian standards, considerably short. Just two years.

And there he had met his future partner Trutnev. Trutnev was an ethnic Russian and former night club bouncer. Trutnev's luck had run short on a particular evening when he was the victim of an attack, undertaken by a well-dressed drunk, forcing his way into the facilities where the primitive sound of rap music made the walls vibrate. Karma came down on Trutnev like a ton of bricks. He had beaten up the son of a new politician, who strongly believed that his father was a cousin of God, while the father thought he *was* the Almighty. The court and its jurors requested strong punishment. The rumor was, that the judge was on the father's payroll. Guilty. How comfortable, it all was for the judge and the jurors in a closed session. How easy it was to do justice behind shut doors. No defender, no public, no press. His sentence was mapped out ahead of time anyway. The judge even joked that Trutnev should not be embittered. See, the court routine proceeded quite pleasantly. Much more pleasant than in the past. Well, so, all right. Citizen Trutnev was going to the penitentiary. Pjotor did four years, and from the first day, never mingled with the rest of his inmates. Until he met the man from the republic of Georgia.

Pjotor and Gaidar.

They both liked each other. It was the realization that they both had the same ability to be merchants in a common sense and would create the product which made the world turn around:

Money.

Gaidar and Pjotor fell, for whatever unknown reasons, under a general amnesty. They both had made their way into the world of new entrepreneurs in Moscow. To be more explicit, into the underworld where now every marketable resource in the country, suddenly available, was en route, illegally and in staggering numbers, to the nearest international border. Timber, coal, precious metals, weapons, and nuclear material.

Both saw how everybody, being rude enough, grew rich. At first, both men needed cash. They decided to rob a bank. Gaidar had gotten a tip from a buddy in his hometown of Astara, just a mile away from the border of Iran. Something would happen in Moscow. Gaidar and Pjotor could not believe their luck and timing. It was the day when a powerful bomb went off in a busy tunnel underpass beneath Tverskaya Ulitsa in Moscow. During this time of turmoil, security forces did not have the time nor the manpower to protect state assets, or what was left of it. There was a street in western Moscow by the name of Uliza Semaxko. The chosen bank they had in mind was just sitting there in form of a poison-green-painted 18th century brick building. Or even earlier. It was a short and very impressive bank visit with an old Zil truck they had stolen. The truck didn't have to be hot-wired. The owner,

Gaidar's cousin, who just happened to be visiting his 107-year-old aunt in Georgia, a state with a reputation for high age, had, of course, no idea what was going on in the capital at the time.

It was around lunch when they stopped the truck in front of the bank building. Gaidar donated, as a necessary tool for this particular performance from his small inventory, a Kalashnikov, an AK47. Pjotor, carrying the weapon did not hesitate to open fire. Just a salvo. Only one. Six intense rounds over the heads. As the wall received the bullets, it released, in return, long chiseled splinters of plaster, spreading it around like dusty fireworks. Nobody should be harmed. A shooting in a bank building, and over lunch, for God's sake, was by all respect for the great leader of the motherland, new to the just politically liberated crowd. Something unthinkable, something unimaginable just happened. Pjotor jumped over the counter and pointed the AK47 at the ashen teller who, having also served as a private in the Caucasus mountains, understood in the nick of time, the reason of both men's visit, without further need of any interpretation.

Pjotor ripped the phone cords out of the wall and smashed the only radio transmitter with the butt of his weapon. Their haul, amassed with the forced help of the bank employee, was in the range of just one-hundred-sixty-five thousand dollars and thirty million Rubles. Not to be considered serious start-up capital in a new Russia. But at least it was something.

Their upcoming business was the one nobody ever thought about in this new class of entrepreneurs. The commerce of oil merchants. With the help of some larcenists they stole two almost brand-new tank trucks, filled to the rim with good fuel, from the third armored division stationed outside Moscow. The commander of the division, a Colonel Shurov, close to retirement after thirty years serving the *rodina,* and short of cash, because he had not been paid a single kopek over the last months salary, was more than happy to accept some U.S. dollars for not seeing the announced thievery (Gaidar and the Colonel knew each other from Chechnya). The General was also a honorable member of the defense council of Moscow and knew how to write off the two trucks with cool established accounting arguments.

First they did it on their own. Their enterprise operated breathtakingly uncomplicated. An enterprise which worked at the beginning at gunpoint.

*

And this was the way it worked. In the western part of Europe, the gas is heavily taxed. For example, a gallon of regular costs $5.25. But the fuel in a Russian gas station was sold for approximately some skimpy sixty cent per gallon. As a matter of fact, if the Russian price would not be that low, the rest of the country would have already economically collapsed.

What did Gaidar and Pjotor do? Well, they filled their tankers up from state tank farms at gunpoint and re-sold the gasoline to some pals in Poland and Germany. Wealth almost outran them immediately. They prospered fast, which, for a moment, raised the eyebrows of some bosses in the tightly-structured control system among the rival new gangs around and in Moscow. The news was whispered from one privileged ear to another about the greasy swap. An eye might be kept on it. So the comrades thieves decided. But the relaxed state of mind of the boss of the bosses, the rukvodstvo[5] corroded quite a bit and in just a very short time.

By the end of 1999 Moscow had reached the fame of being the most expensive city on earth. The *reketiry* now controlled myriads of the city's major institutions. This began with Sheremetevo International Airport, carefully divided between gangs into a sort of mafia 'zones.' Each of Moscow's half-dozen leading gangs controlled now a portion of the very lucrative transportation system in and out of the city. This kind of arrangement defined why a 20-mile ride into the capital cost $50 for a foreigner and $32 for Russians. If somebody broke the rules, death was perhaps inevitable. Harsh punishment would wait for drivers serving the airport car rental, if they would not shell out every month $ 1000.—protection money to the residing *Dolgoprudnaja* gang who drove around in Volvos to collect. The *Lyubertsy* controlled the hookers, and it was quite an impressive large number of women and men being in the commerce of arousal and timed coitus, the *Solntsevo* cashed in on slot machines, the *Azerbaijani* handled the commerce of drugs, while the *Ingushy* bootlegged contraband fine leather to Italy. The list was long and the stage was set in the new Russia with over five-thousand gangs, rarely missing to 'collect' their cut in 'their' area. Even the beggar's intersection at the Kremlin was under somebody's control.

But what Gaidar and Roshin undertook was new and unexpected. The fuel business, uncovering its increasing prosperity, soon found the concern of Moscow's entire mafia, still living in the very primitive of fear not having enough.

But what did all this have to do with the precious metals buried in the sand of Iraq? Well, this is what happened.

---

[5]   Equivalent to an Italian mafia Godfather.

13

On a bright Sunday morning Gaidar received a phone call. The coarse male voice on the other end of the line suggested a meeting between friends.

Potsche mu? Why?

To sort out some minor problems in business before it might become a real issue. *Ty panimaesh?* You understand? Between *drugy*—brothers, so to speak. It would be fine with both of them. They all agreed on a date and the rasping voice verbalized an extraordinary delight on the uncomplicated accordance of both men.

The meeting took place three days later in one of the five-thousand rooms of the Rossiya Hotel on Ulitsa Varvarka.

Mumbled how-are-you-handshakes.

A Yevgeny Smirnov, claiming to be an offspring of the vodka ancestry, introduced both men to a Jury Pasternak (the, rukvodstvo) who affirmed to be a nephew of the Dr. Zhivago author. Some bottles of Stolichnaya appeared on the table. Nobody touched it. Anything else they like? Hot *chai* (tea) would be just fine. Gaidar felt the atmosphere tense and wondered for a moment, what the hell had moved him to get into an encounter like this, and what it was all about anyway. At least they had followed the appointment more out of inquisitiveness. Certain of themselves, they did not bring a bodyguard along. Chai was served. Sips. Followed by tense and forced smiles. The silence with the accessories of false smiles was short-lived.

Pasternak, sitting behind a huge real oak desk, came straight to the point and did not waste time. His company, that's what he named it, intended to take over a chunk of Gaidar's and Pjotor's fuel and otherwise profitable oil business. And how much would they be willing to give up?

Nothing. *Pochemu?* Why?

They shrugged shoulders.

Pasternak suggested, generously smiling, a seventy-thirty split. Both would have still enough to live high, and look, . . . much less headache. Didn't they agree?

They didn't.

Now Gaidar talked in his deep calm Russian voice. Short, sharp and vulgar. He would not mind if Pasternak would care of his own shitty whoring business.

For two minutes no more words were released from the stunned Pasternak's mouth after the well verbally announced disagreement. Only a stony face, as his left pinkish temple, the result of too much liquid proof, got attention by being scratched with his well manicured finger nail of his left small finger.

Nobody. Nobody dared to talk to him like this. Period.

However, being under control of the situation, a big smile cracked Pasternak's face, creating an unaccountable number of wrinkles. It wouldn't be the end of the world. He understood their hesitation and concerns because they worked so hard for their money. How about if they would think it over. At least . . . poshaluysta . . . please.

They wouldn't.

Pasternak shook his head. Almost forgivingly. If they would like to avoid discomfort, well, why not consider it, at least.

The room was soaked up with silence. A minute went by.

"So, ty ponemajesh?"

Yes, they understood. But they would run their own business.

Pasternak used the ultimate Russian malediction—yup fuja mat. Weren't they all Russians? Drugy? Brothers? Yes, they were all brothers. Russians. They agreed on this one. Now, Pasternak with well-absorbed cinema mentality of Marlon Brando's Godfather-mentality floated like a vulture, accusing them of robbing their motherland blind and that they should be branded. On their foreheads. Yes. And off to Siberia. He had lost his nerves and yelled.

Pjotor doubted the well-articulated admonition and cracked into a leery smile, making his face look like a corrugated metal sheet. Gaidar took the threat more stoically, absorbing Pasternak's rigid fixed stare in a more relaxed, but internally sober fashion. He promised himself, forgetting his partner, a short withdrawal and evaporation from the scene of oil commerce in the sometime near future. Pasternak a native Russian, was a chieftain, a thief in power a *vor y zakone.* The 'academy' of the thief-in-power was an old tradition and went back to the time of the Czars, when squads of brigands would establish a community and elect a chief to mediate squabbles and distribute the booty of robberies and thieveries and plot general schemes and tactics. With this tradition in mind Pasternak had solved a lot of problems between the new breed of thugs in government offices and on the street. But he had to admit the negotiation with these self-declared oil merchants had failed. There was no *Dosvidanya*, no hand shake, when Pasternak and his five-hundred-dollars a month bodyguard left (the average earnings in Russia is $60). From then on, both men would watch over their shoulders not to pay a high price for the self-declared rights to run a business that returned four dollars (after costs) for every dollar invested. A summer later in the fuel business, they had to be constantly observant about hired assassins, an increasing threat of nurturing the art-of-trade without being hurt.

*

Meanwhile, Moscow was in competition with New York when it came to violent crime, which was up to 20,000 per year, including an average of 1,350 murders. Not a bad start into the new world order for a country wanting to catch up with the West.

By the love of God, who wanted a French supermarket in the middle of Moscow, where the offer was *foie gras* and Chateau Monton Rothshild Bordeaux for 200 dollars a bottle and frozen dinner of *blanquette de veau an coq au vin?*

The retirees who got paid from the government? Thirty-two dollars a month? The soldiers and officers in their falling-apart barracks and shabby apartments? The military unpaid, unfed, and unhappy? Historically, this was classic fertilizer for a civil war.

While the Zil automobile plant deposited half of its lingering faithful servants of 30 years on exit, just around the corner on Tverskaja Street, some strides away from the Red Square, the ingenious business lodger was Trinity Motors, specializing in Cadillac vending and repair, competing against the nearby dealers of Mercedes, Volvo and Rolls-Royce. The derangement of new money was a sort of a mental disease. Especially since the funds rolled in from the International Monetary Fund into Russia. Ten billion total at a rate of $ 17 million a day, only to be controlled by dubious banks and white-collar mobs and pumped out of the country again. Showing up in private bank accounts in Andorra, Cyprus, Austria and who knows where else. Who were these guys buying the California real estate up by the square mile without being asked by the authorities where the money came from? Let a Mexican buy a piece of land by San Jose, and he would be harassed to the end of his days to show from where the money came. Not so with the Russians. So, crime grew with the growing opulence of a new class.

But all this was not Gaidar's or Pjotor's kind of concern.

*

After the meeting with Pasternak, they never heard a word again. A year went by and nothing happened.

But on a cool evening with some fog lingering over the Moscva River, hesitating to make it onto the streets to dampen the old cobblestones, Pjotor enjoyed the "Krassnaya", Moscow's latest fashion restaurant, a grilled lamb from New Zealand with rice from Pakistan, prepared by an Uzbek chef. It was a very flashy meal, which he washed down with a bottle of Mumm's Champagne from California. The price for this *one* culinary befalling was close to the monthly salary of a blue collar worker. After the opulence, he had in mind to call a hooker to be entertained, what he delicately described as screwing his and her brains out.

While Pjotor tapped his mouth with his napkin, a new guest with large Porsche sunglasses on his face, stepped into the restaurant. He took his glasses off, stopped and looked around. Like searching. He was dressed in a vested light-grey suit, wearing a crisp impeccable white shirt and a tie. Decent and not loud. In short, it was a tasteful, elegant appearance, with courteous fine manners (he apologized when he bounced slightly against a waiter). The new guest also wore a pair of very thin, fine, navy-blue leather gloves. Obviously the man knew what he wanted and what he was looking for.

As the new guest walked across the restaurant to Pjotor's table, his right glove-dressed hand disappeared under his jacket, only to reappear a moment later with a gun in it, a Makarov 9mmSL.

Nothing showy like having chrome, ornaments or such doohickeys on it. The transparency of the grip permitted an optical count of the nine rounds it contained. Simple in its modest elegant shape, it meant business. Not even a silencer was attached to it. Nobody paid attention.

The man stopped for a brief moment, then continued to walk around Pjotor's table and came to a halt behind him. He was well trained and it was sort of a replica rehearsal in what he was doing. He had just returned from Spain, where he had done a similar job. And after this, the same in Italy. He was a professional assassin and would not botch this job. Took one more step, indicated an almost invisible re-positioning of his left leg, and aimed short with an outstretched arm like having a training exercise. Curled his index finger around the trigger.

Pjotor did not realize what was going on because he had just reached for his rim-filled crystal champagne glass. The shot was loud and provocative. Death embraced Pjotor without further delay. The impact of the bullet into his left Sphen loid threw the self-established oil tycoon from his chair and made him crumple to the floor. As he plunged from his seat, he had a sort of reflex motion within his hands by holding onto the fine white damask table cloth, as though he might have been able to take it along on his lengthy cruise to eternity. The gripped fine linen followed Pjotor, taking along with it the delicacies and Meissen porcelain once so well-prepared and placed on the table personally by the chef from Uzbekistan. Blood began to pool around Pjotor, soaked up by the tablecloth, releasing the pigment of the spattered body fluid like the color of spilled good Merlot wine. The dark brown hardwood tiles, once serving nature as two-hundred-year old oak trees in Estonia, didn't act as a display for the hue of blood at all. There was just a dark and swift spreading spot of murky liquid, expanding fast in diameter. The breaking of the Meissen, the crystal glasses and all the fine silver equipment of cultured eating used for the superb meal, absorbed the sound of the second shot.

Just to be sure he finished Pjotor off with two more shots. Pjotor's body jerked twice in a short motion. The hit man bent down and placed the used warm Makarov 9mm pistol beside Pjotor's body almost thoughtfully. This gesture was the calling card of Russia's new aristocracy. The act of putting down the gun beside the dead Pjortor wasn't a performance of imprudence. It was the calling card of the princes, the Dukes of contract killings. With the same calmness the unknown triggerman had walked into the restaurant, he left, putting his sunglasses back onto his face.

Wrote the *Moscow News* once—"real professionals use each gun only once." The man who left the gun behind was a part of the ominous escalation in one distinctive category of crime—gangland murder by contract. After the killer had left, there was, surprisingly, no panic among the guests. Only a stunning silence. It happened too fast and unexpectedly. The Milizia arrived at the scene of the crime forty-five minutes later. It was a really short response time, but it did not help. There had been twenty-five guests in the Krasnaya, including three foreigners.

Had anybody seen anything?

Nyet. No. *Nein.*

Just heard.

What?

A shot?

Yes, a shot.

The man from homicide, police captain Yuri Shishkov consulted in whispering manners his colleague. Back to the guests with an expressionless face.

Maybe two shots?

Possibly. Could be.

Anything else?

Nyet.

The shrugging shoulders were leading to nowhere—*Ya nechevo ne znayu*—I don't know anything and *Ja ne ponemaju*—I don't know. Homicide understood he would not get an answer that evening. But he also had to deal with a lot of anger he could not show. Policemen were only allowed to carry this particular lethal mace. Actually to enjoy the permission of possessing this pistol, the laid down Makarov 9mm needed a special permission from the Internal Affairs Ministry's licensing office in Moscow. From the government. But somehow he had gotten cynical after 1991. Things were out of control. He was not surprised since 70% of all registered guns now flowing around in Russia were stolen army weapons.

*

The next grey-skied morning over Moscow, Gaidar was *not* yet aware about the unnatural extinction of Pjotor's life over lamb and champagne, when a bomb exploded in his brand new Mercedes 600 and blew off his driver's head. Gaidar narrowly escaped with some insignificant damage to his Armani suit and burn marks to his hand, and understanding the message and brush with death, he immediately decided to drop out of sight and leave his beloved Moscow behind. He learned about Pjotor's kismet between the exquisite table clothes, and took off a week later for San Francisco. Pjotor's extinction encouraged Gaidar to take one of his former spetsnaz pal along as a bodyguard, Avi Cotter, an Ukrainian Jew with strong ambitions and overwhelming enthusiasm to call Israel his new homeland.

Avi Cotter had also a weak point in his course of life.

He loved women.

A lot of them. He preferred women with the skin of cafe latte. When more women appeared in one of those high-glossy pictures in a magazine or his Internet screen with glistening perceivable membranes, the more he was happy. He could hardly the real thing in life since the physical distraction he had experienced in Chechnya. Once a woman looked at him, she wanted this good-looking man. When Gaidar turned his face she wanted to get away as fast as she could. So, Avi made peace with himself and he began to like hookers.

Now, Avi was on his way to San Francisco with his boss Gaidar, where he wanted to purchase, in the lush market of real estate, some apartments and perhaps a fine house for himself on Belvedere Island in Marin. A chain of gas stations were on Gaidars mind. And with the help from some higher-ups in Moscow, Gaidar planed to make San Francisco a new international diamond center. Diamonds from Siberia.

Avi Cotter remembered something.

A week before taking off, a minor delay occurred in Gaidar's travel plans. Before he left for sunny California he got a phone call. It was about a deal Gaidar could not resist. It was about a helicopter.

*

The General of the Russian Air Force, Yuri Mirzev, was an unhappy man. He was the commander of the Eighth Air Force transport squadron in Oktember'an in Armenia, just three miles from the most southern outer military post in Armenia to Turkey. General-Major Yuri Mirzev needed money. Dollars. Fast. It hurt his dignity as a soldier that he might have to sell off, without the permission of his government, some assets of his base, not belonging to him. Who the fuck could blame the man! It also hurt his professional feelings how the government in far away Moscow had betrayed its soldiers by not paying a single damn ruble to the faithful sons of the motherland over the last five months, and had reduced the once-so-proud warrior's life to distress and deprivation. The General was considered a hero, having the chest of his uniform plastered with medals. In the late sixties, as a young officer, he personally had advised the Vietnamese in Hanoi in their war against the American imperialists. He had raided, with his MI-24 attack helicopter, valleys of Afghanistan and Chechnya. Was wounded twice, and even went as a United Nation adviser to Kosovo. And now he had to realize, disillusioned, that his own government had let him down and would not appreciate his past devoted service, and that they had run out of money. What the General wouldn't comprehend in his simple and straight forward military mind was why all this money, flowing into the country from the IMF, millions every day, didn't leave some change to feed his own men. On top, he was tired of his wife's constant justified whining and complaints about their meager existence, while obviously around him other officers had prospered from whatever they could sell on military assets in the black market. The most and best senior officers once appraised to be the utmost defenders of the socialist motherland, acted now on different levels of corruption, from arms-vending to selling (or renting) their military equipment out their back door like real capitalists, still with Red Star and other honorable medals on their uniformed chests.

General Mirzev had received his last paycheck three months ago. One hundred-eighty dollars, in form of Rubles. He had had it. So, the high ranking loyal son of the Rodina decided to take matters in his own hands. Why should he, a General, accept thirty thousand rubles every three (perhaps) months, while some businessmen grabbed millions and bled his beloved country dry?

Mirzev took a deep breath, picked up the dark colored phone, and dialed. Ex-sergeant Gaidar lived in Moscow and was now, the General had learned, a successful oil merchant. The General really felt miffed, having to call an ex-sergeant. But the urge for money overruled his dignity. Didn't he once saved sergeant Gaidar's life in a botched mission in some lonesome, nothing-valley by Grozny? And didn't he fly, under intense fire of the Chechens, Gaidar and some of his wounded men (the rest were dead) back to safety, to Buynasks? So this Gaidar owed the General, at least his life, because if caught by the insurgents, he would have been maybe decapitated like the two colonels.

The second ring. Somebody picked up. In a five minute casual how-are-you-talk, they heard each other out until the ex-spetznaz asked the General how he could help. He had something to sell, the General said with a voice in control and demanding respect.

Something big. Military equipment.

Gaidar, recognized the voice and could care less who it was. He knew well how people cave in when they needed money.

What was it he had to sell?

Gaidar used a don't-waste-my-time-voice.

A helicopter.

A very big, very big mother-of-a-helicopter. Carefully tuned, the question rushed down the wire and reached the General's ear. What kind? A MIL Mi-6. The General could hear the short whistle on the other end. Yes, he believed he could help. Gave him an address in Moscow and the location of a restaurant with the name Odessa. There he should wait. Somebody would contact him there. Wished him good luck, and the line went dead.

The next day General-Major Yuri Mirzev changed his uniform for a rigid orthodox suit of Moscow vogue, a hard and uncomfortable dark wool outfit (he, like all military men, did not feel comfortable in civilian clothes), wrote himself a set of travel permissions and took the next flight to Moscow.

The Odessa restaurant, located just up Sverdlovskaya Street, and thus only about two blocks away from the former KGB prison Lubljanka, did not really have a lot of substance to be called a place with class. It was a grim spot where one was forced to stand at small chest-high soiled tables, covered with bread crumbs, overflowing ashtrays, spattered beer, half-eaten cucumbers and Papyrossy buts. Nobody cleaned it. The scent of heavy onioned borshch, served by a gloomy waitress with a stained apron, hung heavily in the air and between the drunks. The General did not like the place at all. But he was here for the sake of private commerce and confessed to himself that he had been in much worse establishments. It was a medium-size restaurant and, at any time of the day, was filled with factory workers and taxi drivers who had just put their work day behind, depending on the shift, and before departing to their homes, had a vodka and some kasha in the steady dim light. There the General hung out, with some worry in his heart that he would be seen by somebody he might know. Three days went by and nothing happened. He was sick of this place.

It was at the beginning of the fourth day.

He had a window seat overlooking the street and watched soldiers begging on the street. Uncertainty had slithered into his senses when some drunks stood at the bar and sang a doleful tune about the Baikal Lake, three thousand miles away. He observed the street and ignored the question of the waitress, which he could not understand anyway because of the noises and her mildly drunken slurry speech. Holy Mother of Kazakhstan, he thought, it was just 10:30 in the morning and she was already plastered. The General decided to get back to his garrison. He was overwhelmed by the very frustration of being slightly fooled by the man whose life he had saved, plus the fear of upcoming whining of his wife. He felt displaced anyway and got up. It was then he saw, in the last perceptible angle of the window, Gaidar approaching the restaurant. A well-muscled man behind him. The dress code of both indicated a very low profile. No apology, why late but a big Russian bear hug between men. Gaidar noticed the General's surprise about the second man.

"This is Avi Cotter," Gaidar smiled," you might remember him?"

Yes, the General remembered. The last living fifteen men were in a very precarious situation. The rest was dead. The *spetsnatz* had just been overrun by the Chechen fighters from the mountains. Brother death was satisfied. The living rest had run out of ammunition. The left side of Avi Cotter's once so very handsome face was badly burned beyond repair. The trauma had also created very bad heart conditions for Cotter. General Mirzev personally landed the gunship between all the heavy shooting. Four medics threw everything into the chopper, of what seemed to be left alive or worth sewing up again. Between the piles of bodies were two young sergeants, Gaidar and Avi Cotter.

"You remember him? We owe you a favor. I understand you have something big to sell," paused," a helicopter."

Yes, a helicopter, the General admitted with a depressed voice. A MIL Mi6. How much? The General named the price. Would he be willing to deliver the chopper to a certain place in Turkey to his client? Personally, of course. Gaidar's eyes had more of a "you-have-to" than a "would-you-please" in it. Yes, he would, the General responded, but the chopper needed a second pilot. This was out of question. Okay, it would be possible to drive the chopper alone. Knowing the border area to Turkey, well nobody was more entitled and qualified to lift literally the chopper from under the Russian Government ass than the General. They had a deal.

Back at his garrison in Oktember'an and with two million dollars in his bank account, the General flew the heavy chopper from his base at an extremely low altitude across the Aras Nehri River into Turkey, setting it down on Turkish soil. And here he took a man onboard. This was Rasit Demirsar. Besides being the middleman and Gaidar's emissary in this region for oil products, Rasit dealt in weapons needed, bought, and sold, keeping the already unstable southern regions of Russia in a constant civil strife. Rasit was a *mabuha*[6], proud of his Jewish connections and possessed excellent ties across the Mediterranean Sea into Beirut and Aman[7], in Tel Aviv. In silence the General flew the MIL Mi6 with Reset further south to Calcite, just a scratch away from Iraq and parked the chopper at an airstrip outside the town next to planes, better for not being checked about the owner's fate and country of origin.

And so the Russian MIL Mi6 had ended up in Turkey.

Not unnoticed. The two movements of the chopper from Armenia into Turkey threw a recognized pattern over the far-off area. Asana Air Force base in Turkey with its enormous listening devices got a short radar glimpse and sent out an Apache helicopter to "paint" the unidentified target with laser. They did not find a thing.

Israeli Intelligence (General Ephraim Katz) got the facts from, yes, Rasit Demisar, the wheeler-dealer. Rasit stripped the chopper of all unnecessary accessories. Made sure all tanks, including the additional tanks in the cabin,

---

6   A non Jewish informer for Mossad.
7   Military intellegence of Israel.

were loaded up with fuel to the rim. Rasit placed two suitcases inside the chopper and installed a GPS (Global Positioning System.) The suitcases contained three sets of camouflage uniforms and weapons. After this Rasit placed a five-second long phone call across the Mediterranean Sea. to Israel.

The phone rang four times. Nobody picked up the receiver from the public phone. After the last ring Ephraim Katz walked away. Rasit smiled when he hung up. Six hundred miles above the earth the Ofek-7 satellite was passing over the Middle East, like it did for months every eighty minutes. Ofek-9 was injected into the orbit by a Jericho rocket just six months ago in Israel. It was the real thing because this satellite intelligence gave the country access to any threatening movements (sometimes even in three-dimensional images) close to their borders and elsewhere. Ephraim Katz was up to date. In Langley, Virginia, DCCI David Meyers had to deal with the Russian who had decided, like in the old days of the Cold War, to announce to the world, the use of nuclear power in a first strike, in case they felt threatened with the new NATO expansion, reaching their doors through Poland and Hungary. Meyers was an old war horse. He had never trusted the Russians in the first place. Being confronted with real priorities, a stolen Russian helicopter was not really on Meyer's mind when he read about it. Besides, the new NATO problem, about the increase of caught smugglers bringing nuclear material into Europe via Bratislava and Vienna, shone more significance into Meyer's professional life. And so his experienced and engaged mind, overflowing with preeminence of new threats to the West, neglected to assimilate the report about a single Russian MIL Mi6 flown into Turkey and disappearing there. He opened the left drawer of his desk and dropped the report into it, what he called his do-it-later-drawer.

14

San Francisco

In her daily life she had a delicious sense of humor and laughter. She was one of those one-thousand-dollar-a-night-hookers. Florence A. Hamilton. That was her name, and she had the crème color of Cafe Latté with a touch too much milk. Sensual lips and ravishing long legs. It was her nature to have her lips slightly open revealing a perfect line of white teeth. No caps. Real. Everything was real on her. Showing sensuality, this normally did not exist in her kind of profession. Her black Anne Klein slacks created the illusion that her legs began somewhere higher than her hips. A high waterfall. On top, originating at the upper part, a mild blue Cashmere sweater signified to her a hedonistic feeling she liked on her braless skin. She knew she was worth the money. Some of her regulars lived eight hours of their daily life in some bone-dry offices along Montgomery and were actually decent executives, who had chosen a profession to accumulate wealth for others on the basis of a modest fee for themselves. Husbands who would return home every evening to more or less small estates north of the Golden Gate Bridge where they would be obtained by their wives of thirty years. No wonder they called her. Not only because of the entertainment and fun she would provide. No. She was also smart and intelligent. A good listener and a good sport. The high heels had raised her elevation and blessed her with an additional three inches. Total six-feet-four. When she was on her tour of duty she casually carried a purse over her left shoulder, holding some Trojan Plus2 condoms of different color with nibbled textures. The condom packaging pledged about a special receptacle end and a spermicidal lubricant, whatever that meant. The purse also contained a toy, a strap-on jelly dildo in a perfect shape, with a sturdy permanently attached soft leather strap system, so she would, in case she a had client with special wishes, gently introduce the lover to their enjoy by being ingresses wherever they yearned to be. Another fine possession of hers was a handmade Rosewood box called the Sensual Lover's Kit containing a seven-inch-long vibrator and a set of seven different latex phallus sleeves. Even she, having seen enough in her horizontal profession, had to admit some looked like they were from outer space. And she knew that some of her regulars would go almost into orbit when she took the toys out of the sex kit. She got the kit at wholesale price from Xandria Collection when a year-end sale was announced in their catalog. One toy was a very serious one. A silver-plated gun. A .38 special. This evening her searching crusade had brought her to the cessation of Union Square only to cross over to Bush. Watching a hare dim Jew, dressed in black, canvassing a young blond. Disappeared with her in a car and drove off. Florence A. Hamilton was hungry. Not for food. For love. She was in an aroused stage of female mind where a women would wreck any man's position. Working freelance, Florence considered this evening as her day off. What made her feel good was the actuality to be independent. No pimp.

The last man, some good looking piece of shit from Guatemala had threatened her, if she would not work for him, he would slash her face. That's what he had done to several young girls in his hometown in Nejapa. When the police caught up with him, he fled his country and invaded California via San Francisco International Airport. Mumbled something about being a freedom fighter who now feared for his life in the country of his habitation, if returned. A worn-out line, but perfect when in use, and so it worked for the pimp from Middle America like a charm. Immigration let him in. And when the high-rise vista of San Francisco had absorbed him, he returned to the only business he understood—pimping. He had some girls working for him. Wanted to have her work for him. If not, he would slash her face.

Florence A. Hamilton obtained twenty four hours from the charmer to think it over and he seriously thought he was a fair man with this kind of bid. It was a mistake to threaten her. She had stared him out like a cat without saying a word afterwards, while he spattered his admonition out in an English which nobody would have even understood in far away Bangladesh or Rwanda. Eight hours later, it was around 0100, he rolled in anguish and agony on a gutter between some rotten and dripping vegetables along Mission Street.

"Honey bun," Florence A. Hamilton said, "you ever come near me again, you'll loose the other one. We got this straight, babe?"

In other words, he would no longer have the proprietorship of his left knee cap if he would show up in her neighborhood. For her it was a matter of precaution, a sort of preventive strike, since she had come from the rough side of Oakland. Had grown up between 51th street and Ashby. Actually she was born in Haiti, with a touch of French, Scottish and somewhere along the line in the past, African. Her brother had been killed in a dimwit fight between some rival gangs. Once Florence believed she was in love. This was the reason she got pregnant when she had reached the honey-eyed eon of sixteen by a man who with his crack-paralyzed mind had killed her brother. He was still in the slammer in San Quentin doing time for another twelve years. It was not easy for her to leave the child behind with her mother. But it was better this way, and she made sure that every month, two thousand dollars went into a trust fund to secure the future and education of young Sam. Her friends from Montgomery, she served so well below their belt line, helped her create a portfolio and watched over it. The money grew. The no-fee situation for the account was a fragmentary benefit for her libidinous charity, so to speak. She did not want handouts from the government and felt responsible that little Sammy would not end up on the street corner fighting a senseless obtuse fray with another pack. She wanted him to have a good education. Florence would look after this. Perhaps two more years and she would leave the fucking-for-money business.

It did not need an immense rule of contemplation to protect herself against the morons on the street. This was the reason she carried a gun. The cellphone she had strictly for her friends from Montgomery. So, that's what she carried in her toolbox. That's what she had labeled her purse.

It was a crazy idea, but she would do it for free tonight. She wanted to be held, loved, kissed and driven to a high of sensuality from where she wouldn't want to come back so easily. Florence could imagine a man who she would like and he would like her. Clean and neat. She sighed deeply, filling her lungs with the remainders of the warm evening air. She stopped at the end of Macy's and waited for some time. Suddenly, she raised her head by instinct, like an animal feeling the upcoming anxiousness of a forthcoming copulation. He walked over to her and her mind melted when she saw the face, so unselfishly provided by nature with good looks. He was tall and younger in his appearance than he might have been, regardless of some premature grey hairs that his full short-cut mane exposed. And voracious he was. She saw it in his dark-grey eyes. He was hungry for love. Physical voluptuous love. The graceful animal in her had found the willing prey she would make love to. She was in no hurry. Time would not exist, since duration was relative to her. Her eyes had meandered over his trim hard body. Strayed over his face. The right side so handsome. The features of his left side were irregular, looked wrecked. A wide scar, badly healed, ran across from his left side of the forehead, across his eyelid down to his chin. Paper-thin skin, showing pink fine arteries. But there was something that made them smile into each other. And she did something what she never had done in her entire career. Took his right hand, almost like trying to prevent the unknown man from leaving her and she began to walk with him. Avi Cotter walked with her another block then they took a taxi. To the Fairmont. It was her day-off.

*

Her playing toes were gripping the cotton bed sheet. She stretched her leg into the air and threw it away with a throaty soft laughter. A comfortable laughter of surprise on how she had been swept away. It had not taken so much time to transfer from the elevator to the king size bed in his room 617. An hour later, her body told her how pleased it was. Very pleased, the way he had made love to her. No, it was not clinical act—it was love-making she had experienced. After the sheet faltered on the floor she sat up and looked down at him. Her slender lean body looked now even more bewitching to Avi in the soft light of the bedroom. Roaming over her tender brown nipples and the triangle smooth curves of her hips.

"Who taught you?" she asked."

"Nobody. That the way I wanted to do it with you when I saw you."

"Why?"

"It should be like this."

Avi Cotter. It was one of the rare carnal occasions in his life where he felt calm and quiet having a woman snuggled up on his shoulder when he fell asleep. Only fate knew that Cotter's life, by wandering with Florence to his room 616, took a surprising twist, a minuscule mortal element to make changes in a human life, components with often a fatal effect attached. When he woke up he moved his right foot across the king size to find her. Empty. She was gone. It had been a long time since Avi Cotter felt so relaxed. He looked at his watch. The O125 indicated a very young night. That's all that it was, time wise. Cotter got restless. His eyes gazed through the room softly lit by light making it from some street lamp through the windows. His eyes caught the piece of paper on the table. He switched the light on.

"Honey bun," the message said, "you feel good. I have some business to take care of. F."

So, here he was. Avi who had taken an exquisite hooker to his place to do the upper-class-game he had heard so much about. Felt nicely bedded and wondered why she hadn't asked him for a check. Avi was also a superb thief by character, with the tendency of being a kleptomaniac. His once-bosses in Moscow, some thieves in power (var y zakone) preferred not to deal with him any longer, when they heard about the complaints from their gang members whining that Avi would break any rules of the guild, endangering the thieves who had already spent a considerably long time of their lives in state penitentiaries with names like Kargopol, Sysran, or Beresneki, to cut trees or even mine gold far north at a Gulag camp called Vorkuta. Cotter was gifted with a strong affinity, turning later to an obsession, of not being able to withstand the temptation to make it behind doors into rooms where he did not belong and to pilfer items which were not his. Actually, the very early morning hour was his time when he would involuntarily alter his sudden yearning from being in an extrinsic room into a solid burglary. Avi also had the mysterious sense whether the rightful owner of the properties, soon in his possession, would be home or not. There was no reasoning for it. So in Moscow, Avi was joining up with the organized thugs, like an executive would on Wall Street. No pendulum, no glass ball. He just knew it. First, the new Godfathers paid for his nearly psychic facilities, just asking him whether a house would be occupied at a certain specific night or not. He was never wrong.

His Great-grandmother had thought him some shaman things while sitting on her lap as a child and listening to her warm voice filled with the old fairytales of past times. She also, like so many nice grannies in this world, preached hate in a whispering tone into little Avi's ear, making young Avi dislike anybody who might have done wrong to *his* people.

When Cotter saw the swags ragged from the houses he had so surely pointed out to the thieves, time had come to his mind like a giant tsunami, to make a major decision. To branch out. Do things on his own. Why use his talent for some mind-and-heartless thugs? The new move contained much more profit. No sharing with anybody. All his. The down-side was he no longer could resist a temporarily vacant house anymore when he got the vibes. Once he had made out a property, his only satisfaction was, he needed the mental confirmation whether or not he was right. It was a must, and burglary followed like a mental chain reaction. This demeanor launched a sort of obsession within him whether he was right or not. Some ego involved. But not much. The or-not-factor was never his concern. He was just right. Cotter, also sensed during his marauding, when to leave the premises he so unlawfully raided.

Cotter sensed the room next to his was vacant but empty of human. He got dressed. Took one of his tools, a pair of thin Italian leather gloves. They fit his hands like a second skin. Waited behind the door for noise fabricating overdue-home-comers. Silence. Cracked the door open and peeked outside. The door's hinges, well greased, cooperated with him, not releasing the slightest stir. Moved his head left, then right. Stepped into the hall and hurried with four long strides to the next door with the pleasantly polished oval brass sign at the upper part of the door frame, telling him he had reached the gates to room 617. Cotter was a pro. Was all smiles when the little green light at the door lock allowed him to enter, after it had just being tickled for ten seconds with Cotter's Visa Gold.

Stepped into 617 and closed the door. Certain of himself, he switched on the light and was ready for the ransacking of the room. When he started, Cotter's eyes couldn't disregard what was on the table. Papers. A lot of them. Document-like. Obviously studied but spread out with no concept. He stepped closer with the well-honed ambition to behold something that just might be significant enough to change the status of ownership. Just papers with some printing on it. Then something caught his attention as he was going to turn away. A map. Bold letters on top, communicating to him the word 'Iraq', delivering the name of it to Cotter's eyes. The Avery Dennison yellow permanent marker was still close by. Like a mysterious symbol, it was laying across this definite most northern province with the name of Dahuk on this Lambert Conformal Projection SP 12NI38N map.

Curiosity took over. He let his hands reach for a blue folder and he opened it. Cotter was also a well educated man and absorbed immediately what he had in his hands. What caught him off guard was the note about a MIL Mi6, flown from Russia to Turkey by Russian General Mirzov personally and parked. Darn, didn't he meet this General in this sleazy 'Odessa' restaurant in Moscow? Flawlessly absorbed the rest of the notes. Numbers, dates, coordinates, timing, flight patterns to and from Turkey into Iraq and such. Stored it all away in his brain. He was stunned what kismet had offered him. He didn't filch a thing. Avi Cotter didn't even look for a wallet. There were some traveler's checks between the papers. Didn't touch them. The room was occupied by a male. He could see this. And he left the room in the same silence as he had entered it. Along he took the idea to steal six-and-a-half tons of gold. He decided to talk to his boss Gaidar over breakfast.

*

The next morning, Berret just caught the elevator when the doors of it began to close. He stepped inside and expressed his appreciation with a short nod and a breathless *thank you* to the man who had kept the impatiently shaking elevator door open. The man only had a short it's-okay-nod while talking to a second male, well-dressed. Conservatively and quite expensive. The other one doing the talking had textiles a bit too much on the loud side. A bit too much polyester. Head angled to the inside. If Cotter would have seen from which room the man had come (room 616) he would have been more careful with his talk. But he didn't care because he spoke Russian. And who speaks Russian in San Francisco. In an elevator? Perhaps a homesick worn out Ukrainian from Marin County.

Berret leaned against the wall of the elevator, covering with his back a plastic-topped poster with a smiling waiter promising the finest at the Tonga restaurant. Berret had no further special regards or attention to the two passengers, like everybody else would have in a lift like this. Shoved the New York Times under his left arm.

Berret affixed his eyes in a well-mannered elevator-behavior at the numbered glass panel above the door, counting the digits of the floors they had already sank to. He glanced briefly at the strangers and his eyes caught, with its first roaming, the left side of the fast-talking chap's face. Badly burned. It seemed like the healing, for whatever reason, would never be really completed. Thin fragile skin, with a lot of fine capillaries visible. A stretched visage like a facelift gone bad. It was then that Berret stiffened slightly when he heard the excited half-loud voice of the fast-talker. Russian. The fine dressed one kept quiet but listened.

"*Ty panymajesh? Iraq!* You understand a map!"

For the first time in his life, Berret blessed his mother for the beating she gave him for his unwillingness to learn this major Slavic language. Russian. Now, after years, Berret heard Russian which contained information to make him think about his survival. Something didn't feel right last evening, when he came back to his room. Now he knew what it was. It set his mental stage for the kill. He took a deep breath, and as if knowing Berret's state of mind, the elevator hesitated for some seconds before going down to the ground floor. And these were the words Berret began to absorb. Words like *soloto* (gold), sarnolet (airplane), bertolet (helicopter), General Mirtzev and Turkey's Cappadocia.

"What should I do?"

Gaidar, with his Moscow illicit greedy mobster mentality, had a straight answer.

"Simple. Kill the person in the room. Bring the paper and the map. And we will see."

Scarred face was surprised.

"Pochemu cuot? (Why kill?) I just will get the paper."

"Because if it's true and worthy, not a stupid question is asked. *Ne swiderem. Ty ponymajesh?*"

No witnesses. Do you understand? Berret understood. At the ground floor, Berret was chilled when the door opened. The two even didn't bother him with a second look or have-a-good-day-smile. He just had stood together with his murderers. The gold was *his*. He would not say a thing about the troubling Russians to the Major or Rosco. He knew what he had to do.

*

Avi Cotter sat on the bed in his Fairmont Hotel standard room. His mind was involved in deep and sad thoughts. This was an assumption that thoughts like this would never come to his cool professional mind. It was a disturbing factor for him. The mills of his intellect attempted to produce the warning signs of a colossal blunder for, say, two hours. No results on his side.

He cleaned his TEC 18 pistol twice, to make sure that the mace would function in a flawless anticipated fashion. His life also depended on it. The whole faculty of his nature was focused on the upcoming kill, which did not make sense to him. A dead body might leave a trail of questions behind. Even Cotter understood San Francisco was not Moscow. Avi Cotter did not like the idea of canceling somebody's life at 0430 in the morning. Nevertheless, it was a precise order from his Russian master. But sometimes a single order did not make sense and did not give him the whole picture. Once in room 616 again, he was certain of it, it would be a clean and quick kill.

Cotter screwed the silencer to the TAC. He was just an all Jewish handyman for some Russian Mafiosi with a big ego. This made him even angrier. He promised himself, after this assignment, he would go to Israel and open a shop with his brother somewhere along Frischmann Street in Tel Aviv. He would get married and have children. Maybe he would even move to a Kibbutz to nurture and harvest citrus and lemons. He smiled. This would be pleasant. He was so tired of this body guard-absurdity and homesick.

Israel. It was his homeland where he belonged to. He sighed deeply and put the gun on the night stand. The sun had escaped behind the Golden Gate Bridge. The horizon and the darkness began to roll out a carpet of lead-grey dark clouds along the skyline.

He switched on the small lamp on the night stand. Distant traffic noises hesitatingly filtered through the tinted double glass window. There it was again. A short shrill sound of uneasiness rushed through his mind. This variety of uneasiness signaling from the sub consciousness that something was not right in his life. It was a repetition from minutes before.

A soft rain started to come down. So soft that the impression could not be distinguished from a cloud. Water, like tears run down outside the window, adding even more depression to his mind. Cotter stared out the window and watched the flashing beam of the Alcatraz lighthouse. The phone rang. He got tense and picked up the receiver.

"Yes?"

"This is the reception. A Mister Gaidar is here and wants to talk to you."

A Mister Gaidar will wait for him in the bar. Immediately Cotter was happy. Gaidar had decided to change the time of the extermination.

"Thank you," he said.

He hung up, pocketed his gun and went for the door.

*

This was the most critical moment for Berret. He put on his thin leather gloves. He saw Cotter disappeared in the elevator. With Cotter out of sight, Berret moved quickly to the door of room 616 and slid the Visa card looking plastic master key into the lock. To borrow the master key had cost him one-hundred dollars and a tongue bending cunnilingus with the Philippine maid in his room. The little flickering green light allowed him to enter. He pulled down the handle with his elbow. The door opened. Invaded the room and pressed his body against the wall for a moment. Nobody in it. Budged across the room in swift strides.

Berret pulled out the lower drawer.

Empty.

Wondered for a moment why hotels have this kind of space—absorbing furniture, nobody would ever fill it with anything. People come to a hotel to do business, watch TV, get plastered or fuck.

He opened a compartment of the navy-blue duffel bag he had brought along. Pulled out a small high powered battery driven Black and Decker saw. A single sheet of plastic foil followed. He unfolded it on the floor. Put the drawer on it and cut with the saw a five by five inches hole out of the drawer's back. The plastic collected the saw's mill. Folded the plastic up and looked at his watch.

He estimated another five minutes. Opened the zipper of the duffel bag and had his thumb and index fingers of his right hand immediately behind the creature's head.

She could not react so quickly. For two reasons.

She knew him. Berret was her master. *And* she had spent the last minutes in the duffel bag on a wet hand towel. The wet towel, folded up, was filled with ice cubes. And as the temperature dropped her body temperature plummeted. She was immobilized. He placed her carefully into the drawer. He looked at her and said mentally good bye, like to a long-term lover. He jammed the drawer's lines with Crazy Glue and closed it. Knowing her long enough, Berret knew what she would do. He moved back to the door. Listened for a moment. Silence. He opened the door and budged for the emergency staircase just four doors away. Two floors down the maid waited. Demanding the master key. He gave it to her, as promised. Saw the entail for another cunnilingus in her hungry eyes.

*

The dark drawer could not be considered to be warm. It was not Coral's favorite temperature. The temperature created a physiological stage of nervousness. The room outside was warm. She sensed the warmth through the five by five inch hole on the floor of the drawer. She slid through it in a long and graceful motion. There, in the room, she rested. Still she felt cold. The snake also had not eaten for quite some time. Her slow metabolism had enabled her to wait for weeks to have the right and perfect meal. Very slowly she moved her head. Knew she was not alone in this room. There was a prey. A warm-blooded one. Somehow the prey moved in its sleep. Absorbing the vibration of its motions with her precious skull bones, she stared with her unblinking 'up and down' eyes covered by a transparent lid, to the sources of the disturbance. Lifted her head slightly further and made some dancing-like flux. The snake was too focused to feel it as a dance. She meant business. It was a motion to hunt the warm-blooded prey.

Coral, the snake, possessed a very specialized pursuing device she now began to inaugurate. A gadget, to sense the body temperature of the quarry. To detect the warm-blooded meal in the darkness of the night, the reptile was armed with heat-sensing devices. Small craters, on either side of her dangerous snout between the nostrils and the eyes of her exquisitely formed head. The craters were sculptured out of the maxillary bone and lined with heat sensor cells, designed to detect changes in radiant heat. It would help to guide the range and direction when the time of the strike would come. Fast and slender. Quick and merciless.

Avi Cotter, the warm-blood, in his deep sleep had never been considered a natural part of any poisonous food strategy of her. Coral had very developed salivary glands. In the course of evolution as a venomous snake, nature had converted the saliva gland into a poison producer. Her poison was a sort of modified saliva and supported from the beginning of its effect the digesting system of the creature. The poison producing gland was just under the lip scales and would send the venom into trenched teeth at the end of the upper jaw. She felt the cold breath of the air conditioner and yearned for warmth.

The snake moved her exquisite slim body across the lush carpet. With the beginning of a deadly movement in perfect silence, she was now closer to the warm-blooded specie and began to activate a second hunting and feeding device. It was called the Jacobson's organ. This particular component in a vertebrate animal contained a pair of cavities that were located inside on each side of her snout with aqueducts leading to an opening in the roof of her mouth. The ends were heavily supplied with nerve endings and used for smell. She smelled the warm-blooded specie but was not fully aware about the size of her prey. Had reached the bed and could now feel the comfortable warmth. She raised her body.

The sleeping man moved and his mind still worked on it, why he had missed Gaidar, the man from Russia. Before he had gone to bed he placed a wake up call by 4:00 a.m.

He had taken his gun from its holster and put the killing instrument back on the night stand, within reach. The reptile froze for a moment and moved her heat sensors. It was in close range. She rose further and slid under the warm cover and felt the warm skin. That's all what Coral wanted. Warmth. The warm-blooded moved again. This motion set her defense mechanism in motion, which, by nature, was to flee. Especially she noticed suddenly that the prey was much bigger than she expected. In defense, she opened her mouth wide to strike.

The very long fangs.

They laid folded flat along the roof of her mouth. When she opened her mouth wide to strike, they swung into a vertical position like two long needles. With a quick motion of her head she plunged her fangs deep into the warm-blooded flesh. Off course there was no conceivable rationality why she should have warned her prey of her poisonous intention. It was a short and violent encounter. She sank her fangs deep into the soft sensitive skin around the Crest of Ilium. Nicked the femoral artery. Since nothing really exiting happened in her life of skilled hunt over the last weeks, she injected half her venom load in a most effective way via the channels in her teeth into the naked human body. The poison of her lethal modified saliva was a neurotoxic one and began to act immediately on the killer's nervous system by beginning to paralyze his breathing system. And the muscles of his heart.

Waking up in screaming fear and horror, Avi wanted to move away from his bed, realizing that he hardly could inhale the suddenly badly needed air while the ability to scream had already diminished. He still was not fully aware what happened. Weakness took over and the beat of his bad heart started to flutter. He crawled away to where the door should be. Confusion had already taken over his mind. But it was the bad heart which could not withstand the stress and horror.

Coral registered with her skilled hunting instinct what the movement of the prey was. To flee. This was her nature, how she was programmed by the creator of all things. In the wilderness her prey often would not, or could not, die after the first lethal injection from her fangs and try to get away from this ultimate hunting machine. She would wait for two or three minutes and follow the doomed poisoned prey, stalking it down, to finish it off with a second bite. Then have the meal. And for this kind of final pursuit the Almighty had contributed to her the Jacobson's organ. She had two potential tools to trail her victim. Remember? She could smell. Her forked tongue would pick up the odorous particles from the fleeing creature and transfer them to the organ, or the air itself would transfer particles to the openings of the Jacobson's organ. It was a stimulating move.

She followed from the warm bed with her feeding instinct the doomed prey and had caught up with the slow crawling prey in no time. She raised her body, opened her jaw wide and like a whip her body shot forward to sink her poison-filled needles a second time into the man's body, hitting the Median of the left upper extremity, close to the heart. A fine vibrating shock wave went through the Avi Cotter's body, signaling the near and absolute end to the reptile. Cotter came awake one more time. He grasp what was attacking him. At that realization his heart gave in to a fatal arrhythmic attack. And Cotter diet.

But once she had attacked, her problem was to find an end and to begin to ingest. Actually the reptile did not have a further problem if the quarry had been a lizard, something small. Or even a rabbit. This prey here was immense. No way she could handle it. But the body was still warm. The snake moved twice around the dead body while the two tips of her forked tongue touched the dead quarry. There was another interesting aspect of her food liturgy. In a boa-like fashion she wrapped herself in coils around the dead man's shoulder and neck. She gave him a last quieting shot of venom. Like it was a sharing.

Morning rose with the fifth wake-up call. Nobody picked up.

Security went up to his room. They found Avi Cotter naked, head pointing at the door and a rattler. The snake was wrapped around his pale neck and shoulders. Regardless rigor mortis had not left the dead body yet the snake still tried to get warm and was wrapped around the dead Avi Cotter like a glamorous scarf.

Mark Berret stood outside on Bush Street, the Fairmont's servant entry, and watched, when a closed green-black body bag, obviously containing a human body, was carried vigilantly to a van. The morgue. Berret drew a long breath and pushed it out, lingering in the fresh morning air. It tamed hidden emotions and with a short smile, he went for his morning run.

The fine rain had not stopped yet.

15

Anataya, Turkey, December

The ride was rough from the moment they took off from Ankara. Upon take-of the pilot took the 737 immediately into a steep climb, close to the tolerance level the plane would take. By nineteen-thousand the plane leveled off, unexpectedly, making the stomach jump upward to the heart.

Tom looked thoughtfully out of the window and studied the layout of the old town of Ankara. He gently squeezed Rachel's hand and wished it was only a vacation. He was tense and had not spoken a word since the take-off in London. Rosco and Berret were in Ankara. Duskin somewhere in a hotel in Central Turkey. Had they stretched themselves to thin? Perhaps they were all too fascinated being treasure hunters. Perhaps they were just lunatics.

"What is it, love?" Rachel asked, "you are being awfully quiet."

Tom answered with a bearish grunt.

"Just checking."

Two hours later the bird made a final adjustment to the left and whistled through some light-soaked clouds, bouncing and romping against the wings and with the landing lights on the jet got closer and closer to the runway. Thunder of reversing engines. The Boeing trundled like a fat bird down the runway, turned around and reeled to the terminal, inching in a gentle movement to the airport's diminutive flat building. The classic warm and damp 'east-Asian' winter weather was fantastic that year and was still holding. Today, for example, the sun tried to shine her best light that she was able to produce. Stubbornly, one single cloud stayed motionless in the blue sky, not allowing the sun to throw any direct light at the airport. The airport was the gate of bringing sufficient numbers of tourists into town. Having the upcoming summer season in mind, some parts of the terminal had been gutted and were ready to receive a new and upgraded interior.

The observation platform.

It was populated by some locals, enjoying the excitement of incoming planes with bellies full of relatives returning from Germany and out of season tourists.

In the crowd stood a man who had watched the graceful landing of the plane and its taxing down the runway, until it came to a halt, with a sort of cool and anticipating curiosity. Actually there was nothing unconventional about him.

First, he had gotten royally paid to watch the landing and to organize matters after the touchdown. He also knew that the man he had to meet and talk to had not arrived yet. So, patience appeared to be a necessary commodity in this last contest of his dubious existence. The man's appearance molded quite well into the image of the locals, dark hair, a mustache. A fairly bronzed skin with a two day unshaved on it. He had dark eyes, sharp and observing. Around them, he had more wrinkles than he should have had for his age. A lace of tiredness only visible to a person who would have a probability to watch his face closely. The corrugations of his face was not only the result of looking into too much bright sun in the mountains of the Balkans, reflected from the snow of high mountain altitude. They were also the visible consequences of the métier he worked in. His hair was covered by a simple grey chapka, covering strong full mane with too much grey in it. In short, he looked older than he was. His clothes were not loud and not overly elegant. He wore a Geoffrey Beene shirt, grey French Valentino jeans and Tod's shoes. The white shirt in its simple cut, the upper part open around his strong neck and powerful shoulders, was covered by a beige *Nautica* wind breaker, some mass market item, and uncomplicated in its style. There was another feature of Rasit Demisar which one could not have overlooked, if only discernible. Snuggled under his left arm was a holster, made from fine thin but strong grey Italian leather, containing a 9mm Glock pistol and two extra magazines. Rasit did not wear the lethal automatic to show off. No, he would use it with precision if necessary. There was a self-promise to use the last bullet on himself, should it ever come to it. He didn't have it anymore (maybe he never had) what it would take to withstand the physical pain created in an unknown prison by members of a state security who would ask him under pressure about things he might know. Having a closer look at his left hand revealed to an observer the fact that Rasit was not in possession of his left thumb anymore. It was the consequence of an interrogation by the Mukhabarat[8] in Damaskus and

---

[8]   Syrias secret police.

a Hamas security man to make somebody talk. The Syrian interrogator, not bound to any law, just clipped the thumb of at its root with a wrench, promising to do the right thumb the next day, should he not decide to talk. Clipping of the thumb was not an act of safety and protection of a country, and certainly did not submit a damn thing to the safety of Damascus. No, this was for the Syrian's man wrongly-programmed ejaculation that he enjoyed so much, especially when breaking a new prisoner.

A guard, disgusted with the Syrian methods, left the door to Rasit's cell open, to let him go. Rasit left. But he could not quit, thought the money was more important than having his thumb. Actually, what had been such an unpleasant experience was the result of the kind of business he was in. Rasit was in the trade of a deadly commerce. It was the world of lethal weapons, the most lucrative and ruthless of all businesses, after drugs. And, not surprisingly, the deep involvement of governments and their high brasses of the military in it. Rasit did not deal in penny ante stuff of military surplus such as clank canteens or old web belts by the dozen. This was something for the close-out sharks, roaming along the isles in a Las Vegas trade show with the sleaze of badly-covered greed on their faces. Rasit had more class. He meant genuine trade. Rasit was a sophisticated peddler and his deals were indeed different: aircraft, weapons and their parts, worth millions of dollars. His inventory list of commodities included attack helicopters, parts for the Stealth fighter, grenade launchers, M-1 tanks and such. He had a whole warehouse full. Rasit was oblivious to nationalities or purpose, as long as the men or "freedom fighters" (Rasit smiled about the characters hiding behind the acronym) came up with the cold cash. For example, Hams had approached him. They wanted to be better equipped for their future fight against Israel. Regardless of what had happened to his hand in Damascus, and his bad experiences with his clients, Rasit made sure the delivery of rocket launchers, mortars and anti-tank missiles was completed. Abbas personally approached him, telling him, that "his" (Abbas') people needed the weapons. Rasit didn't believe it, but he made sure that the transfer of rocket launchers, mortars and antitank missiles they said they might need, was done without a single shortcoming. Rasit even proposed a score of Katyusha rockets which could be fired over a distance of twelve miles. Rasid delivered and they bought it. Since East Germany did not exist anymore in the international weapons bazaar, Rasit had to search for new sources. Rasit once had a good relationship with an East German company named Commercial Coordination Inc. at the Waller Strasse in East Berlin. There was a general by the name of Schalk. And Schalk sold everything what looked like a weapon. Like to the Iraqis in the late 80s, when this maniac (that's what Rasid thought about Sadam Hussein) gassed the Kurds and wanted to kill his Muslim kinsmen across the Euphrates and Tigris rivers. Well, what a larger, more discriminating historical picture revealed to Rasid in the weapon business, a labyrinth of strange alliances and associations, bedfellows of power or functionary significance. It was like having a hooker's "little black book," so to speak. Rasit knew *this.* He had sold weapons to African countries without asking where the money had came from (why should he?) and bought heat-seeking missiles, operated by a guy who could hardly cover his bare ass with a worn out T-shirt. The TV screens were full of pictures of the starving across Africa. But nobody asked where they got their money to buy the expensive toys of killing. Somewhere, somehow, banks had to be involved in this kind of shit. Perhaps they delivered the cash in shoe cartons. Who knows? But how did you get it into an account of this size without establishing skepticism in the world of an IRS?

Rasit could care less. He liked those nasty little wars, the wars without television cover. Wars nobody really knew anything about, but people would die for the sake of the Dow Jones Index and a nervous stock market. War between countries whose names hardly could be pronounced or found on a map. That's what he liked.

For example, Rasit delivered weapons to a little shitty war between Armenia and Azerbaijan over a region called Nagorno-Karabakh. Ever heard about it? It did not even qualify to be mentioned on a map. But there was oil, a lot of oil. More than the Saudis ever had under their sand

But hell, if *they* did not have the money, *who* paid for it? Who? Rasit, like all of his colleagues in the commerce of arms, certainly did not run a charity enterprise and would not have distributed without the understanding that *their* money was already in the account in Liechtenstein, Andorra, Cyprus, London or Caicos Islands. Were did the money come from? Who paid for the weapons he sold? Countries not having a pot to piss in, like Liberia, Rwanda, Angola or Benin?

Rasit sighed. He liked, he confessed to himself, to be a sort of mercenary in the field of the weapons swap. It was hazardous but lucrative. More and more, money was important to him. And it did not matter to him how many people had to die. Since there was no existence of the East Germans anymore where he could he have gone to buy the lethal toys Rasit needed to sell, his new supplier was the Pentagon. The surplus system worked for the Pentagon in a very sufficient way. And so it functioned for Rasit. Within the tightly structured world of the Pentagon the dilemma of precisely disposing of oversupply of weapons, electronic warfare systems and such, wasn't new.

The sales of surplus weapons or weapon parts are under the control of a Pentagon office called the Defense Logistic Agency (DLA). It manages all the military supplies and equipment, and once a decision has been made about the disposal of part of a jet fighter or an M-79 grenade launcher, it is trucked to a warehouse sales lot. The sales operation is then overseen by the Defense Reutilization and Marketing Service in Battle Creek, Michigan. And here, Rasit had friends he visited once a year with his impressive wish list.

In Michigan he bought what he needed for his clients, high-tech surplus military parts, electronic weapons parts, ammunition and machine guns, tanks (declared to be bought for museums or private collectors). Shipped them overseas, hiding the deadly toys in seagoing containers under tons of scrap metal. His major patrons were China, Iran, and Iraq. Oh, yes Rasit knew his way around. His last shipment even included fully operation encryptional devices, submarine propulsion parts and radar systems. Rasit even had picked up the things he needed by E-mail messages from surplus lists of the Pentagon, which had generated (with or without Rasit) 302 million for the DLA. Rasit could have cared less about illegal activities. And so, over the years he had made a fortune. More than he ever could spend in his lifetime. It was not the money which drove him not to retire (yet). Like so many things in life, it can be an addiction, but for Rasit the enslavement was money. He had enough, but he couldn't stop. Money was just pouring into his accounts. Rasit allowed himself one of his rare smiles. Currency meant power, potency, and strength, and more power. Control and ultimate control. This was the trade, the most ruthless and deadly business Rasit was involved in. Beside serving Gaidar privately and different factions of the new Russian Mafia, Rasit also peddled information and news between countries for years. So called "freedom fighters" and the other riff-raff in politics, he assisted and had learned and overheard from his clients, for hard currency, where the French (Sûreté), the British (MI-5), the Germans (BND) and Aman of Israel benefited. CIA knew about Rasit's existence but was not interested to deal with the man directly, since Langley did not have a problem to get the information from Israel anyway. For Rasit, it was not only a matter of prestige not to screw around with small talk clients; it was also a matter of survival. He called himself a drifter between the political farts of history. More than a few people in West and East honestly wondered sometimes how this provider of sensitive intelligence and wanderer kept himself alive. In fact, they did more than just wonder.

Rasit was well aware about the truth and knew that his existence might be short-lived, since the knowledge he had amassed over the years in his brain made him a dangerous time bomb to all he served simply for the return of hard cash. Some, with blood on it. And that had concocted enemies from the past. Interestingly, Rasit did not have an official address nor office. By staying no longer than three days in any one place had certainly saved his life. He only could be reached by a voice mail, returning the calls promptly. And then delivered. No e-mail or cordless. He saw the cordless phone in his business as a sort of tracking device. Had learned his lesson when he heard of the rebellious general in Azarbaijan, who was blown to pieces by a Russian guided missile while using his mobile phone. Or this guy from Hamas, who got his head blown off when he began to dial. It would not happen to him. Rasit was a canny man. His old-fashion communication scheme had outperformed high-tech. There was another aspect in Rasit's life. He was honest. He never had pulled a fast one on anybody. Years ago the word went out about this rare attribute. He admitted to himself he did his best to live up to the Ten Commandments but to no law of the lands he dealt with. Oh no, he certainly did not run an escort service. Such a thought was furthest from the mind of this man standing amidst the expecting crowd. For Rasit, a crowd had a generalized stink. For him, a man had a distinctive scent which his dog could recognize. Being within a crowd always made him a little bit nervous. It should not have really reflected negativity to his mind, but it did. Because he felt he could be too easy a target.

Now, here at the platform, he felt the thing with the Russian helicopter had gotten a little too big for him. It was the first time Rasit was scared shitless, he confessed to himself. After this job he would quit. He was tired of it grab. He was tired of looking over his shoulders. He was tired of not knowing whether he would be still alive the next day. He was tired not having a place what he could call *home*. He would leave Europe and go to Mexico. Get married and have a life. Had heard good things about Mexico (he had his money there anyway).

The obdurate cloud began to relocate a small degree and a glowing beam of the sun caressed his eyes. Squeezed shut for a moment, his strained eyelids. He stood at the railing and looked down at the plane which had just come to a halt. The shrill whining of the two Brat & Whitney engines marred his hearing for a moment. Then the pilot shut the engines down. Stairs were wheeled to the plane's side door.

In the crowd Rasit saw the woman. Unmistakable, her permanent. The shoulder length curled hair. After three more passengers left the plane, her husband appeared. He knew them both well from photos provided to him by General Katz. Rasit had read the poorly—and obviously hastily-made copies of their dossiers to understand them better. The General was very frank about one thing. If word were to leak out, he would not loose his right thumb, Rasit would loose his life.

Rasit had gotten this kind of forewarning from the leader of another new moronic army—the Kosovo Liberation Army. Dreaming about an *Albanien Reich*. Rasit had delivered by mule weapons to the Albanians in Kosovo. Knew their secret trail across the mountain. And all this knowledge kept Rasit in line. What a life.

When he was certain about the woman and the man he turned around, left the observation platform and became just another nobody between the locals. He stopped at a phone booth outside the airport and called a number in Ankara. The phone of the General Consulate of Israel in Ankara. It rang twice.

A click.

"Yes?" an alert husky voice asked.

"Tell him they are here now," Rasit said.

"Good. Don't loose them."

And the line went dead.

16

CIA Headquarters, Langley, Virginia

The season and the color of trees had slowly changed to winter. Dawn had come late as usual at this time of the year, slightly later than the day before, with a soft touch of smoky cold sunlight, still hesitating behind the horizon grey clouds and the small board-like hazes of pollution, whose creators were still on the freeways in their cars, sorting things out on their car phones before they arrived in bad moods at their offices, with minds already used up by the messages they had gotten an hour *before* entering their office.

First frost had laid some icy sugary powder over the grass and trees with the indication how Christmas might look with just some days ahead. Some stubborn red-yellow leaves still wouldn't let go of the tree they were hanging on to show some proud colors of the past autumn. The reason seemed trivial to the man who had just read a three-page report for the fourth time. Deputy Director of Central Intelligence David Meyers picked up the phone and dialed. DDCI Meyers was troubled about the report he had received from the National Reconnaissance Office. Meyers could not remember having read in the NID (National Intelligence Daily) about a summary of any unknown operations in Iraq. Not even, God forbid, an indication of new hostilities. The fact of the matter was that nobody at the CIA had a clue about present activities in this mess between Mosul and the Saudi border. Perhaps the NRO knew something, which had not been filtered through all levels of bureaucracy. Maybe NRO could help out. The NRO was a quiet agency with a low profile, responsible for satellite and other aerial intelligence-gathering. It reported to the Secretary of Defense, but first, any of its activities were to be arranged by David Meyers. Getting information, regardless how vague, estimating its value, and how it might fit in with other previously received data could be a very brittle process. Meyers already sensed that the contents of *this* report did not fit into anything he was aware of. He really did not want to buck Edward.

Edward Rose, Deputy Director for Operations (DDO), was in charge of CIA activities abroad and conducting covert actions, managing human intelligence, and attending to other touchy intelligence. The report was damn irritating and too thin on the other hand. Director Meyers liked Rose for his sharp aptitude and common sense. The phone rang twice.

"Rose," the voice boomed.

He has some information, Meyers said, and he is disturbed about it. And could Rose come over for a moment. Five minutes later Ed Rose walked in. He was tall, six feet something, and had thirty-two years of service under his belt. A pro with a handsome, firm face, plus the indifferent, slightly bored phraseology of a man who had seen too much in his life. Ed Rose had a reputation for adding a cheerful attitude and a lot of humor and fun to any group. Behind the smiling countenance was a personality of strength and merit any good observer recognized immediately. He was also a man of the past Cold War with decent experience of a young field officer in Hungary and Romania during this obscene historical time where he very successfully played the complicated contest of recruiting spies from communist officials, those corrupt preys to be paid off and able to corrupt so quietly. Then he was station officer in Saudi Arabia, Damascus, and Jakarta. His last assignment, before Langley needed his wisdom in-house, was one of a 'declared asset' in Ankara, meaning Washington informed the Turkish government, though none other, that he was a sleuth. Rose had the seasoning and the beat of a street cop together with an extremely quick working mind.

Handshake.

Coffee?

No.

Hypes him up too much. Chose a Perrier. Rose glanced across the room to the William J. Blaeu map from the 17th. century, printed in Amsterdam. Meyers had bought it some days ago in the Old Print Shop in New York. With its saltwater stains and age cracks, it edited some character to the shown lands, when drawing maps was still a guess work, and was now protected by a plastic sealer. Nicely framed, it had found its decorative purpose on Meyers southern office wall above the Saladino Landau sofa (Meyers had brought this private furnishing along since he spent a good part of his life in this office). He took the three-page report from his desk and gave it to Rose. Rose observed Meyer's troubled face, sat down beneath the map, crossed his legs, and began to read. Rubbed his chin.

He stopped reading after two minutes, shrugged his shoulders combined with the betoken of shaking his head, and looked thoughtfully at David Meyers, already with a lot of consideration in his cool eyes. His view roamed restless through the office and focused on the two-by-four print of De Kooning's *Interchange* painting. It should express the bodies of the world. Even if it was so, as the critics of this 1950 painting wrote into it (groins, elbows, bellies, thighs, and all in a death green), Rose did not see it. Another painting was snatched by a collector "Mountain Tortoise" in Japan for a lousy $ 20 million from Sotheby'ls in New York. It stared into Rose's face. Rose was happy to see the print and pushed his reading glasses up into his full grey-indicating hair. His hand ran across his face, rubbing his eyes for a moment.

"Let me get this straight. *This* doesn't happened very often. Somebody flies a huge chopper from Armenia to Turkey. What type of chopper is this anyway?"

"A MIL-Mi6. A Russian"

"How do we know?"

Rose avoided diplomatically an accusing 'you.'

"Then somebody takes off with this crate, as I understand, in Turkey, and it just disappears again. It shows up for some minutes on the radar of Adana and gets lost in the center of Turkey again. Disappears before we can have a look at it. It . . . just disappears before it can be painted*. I don't believe this. Everybody get's pissed because nobody did a thing this time. We have nothing going in this area. At least not to my knowledge."

"What do you think?" Meyers asked. Uneasiness lingered in his voice. If Rose did not know anything, who would?

"I think," Rose continued, "it's better if we let the station in Ankara know. Something doesn't add up. If somebody is planning something, some preventive evaluation might help."

"What do you want to do?" Meyers voice was very quiet.

Seconds of thoughts went by.

"Well, Baral Alok is a personal friend of mine. I will ask him to help out. So, we don't go through official channels."

The truth of the matter was, beside being personal friends, the Interior Secretary of Turkey was on Rose's payroll for the past eight years and a valuable human asset for NOR while the Interior Minister climbed through the ranks in his government to the top. There was something even more interesting which had to be considered between Rose and Alok. One of the advantages, so to speak, in human growth over the period of its evolution was the forming of secret societies—religious cults and political clubs, mirroring a lot of non-existence into ordinary daily life. There was the exclusivity of carefully-selected ancestry and kinship, symbols and rituals, living in the illusion of being elité for the common mental masturbation of some special charm of cream society. The very secrecy of those societies granted on the chosen fellows, a power of mystery over the rest of others—the non-elité, the masses, the peasantry, the riff-ruff. The elitére feeling of belonging to something, of being chosen by men lingering in their self-importance of already granted participation. A no-toll-free permission granted to set foot on the hardwood floor of a country club where it was easy to manipulate the newcomers, to keep them at mental bay from questioning the ones in the higher ranks.

Rose and Artok.

Men from two different cultures. Their exclusive participation in a secret society, was actually one of the most powerful weapons both these men had. Their lodge had special signs, passwords which performed valuable functions of shoulder-rubbing, like in men's establishments everywhere. The brotherhood, the comprehending expertise, the delicious knowledge of exclusivity bound *those* members together in mysticism. Newcomers, the neonates, taken into the league of secrecy increased their knowledge step by step into confidentiality, giving them a special status, what they often longed for in life, where their acceptance was not easily gained because of lack of self-esteem or knowledge. And most fellows in such secret societies would never proceed beyond a point to understand the secret purpose of the leaders, the brightened, the illuminated. It did not matter if it was called P2, Free Mason, Knights of Malta, Knight Templars, Illuminate, Party or Bilderberg Group. Rose understood quite clearly that the goal of the society he and Minister Alok belonged to had to be re-enforced in everyday life without questioning its existence and purpose. Serving the secret society was always in the best interest of the goal of its superior. Leaders were called *adepts.* And Rose and Alok were adepts and they belonged to the *esprit de corp* of the *Illuminate,* representing the *metaphorical* rebirth into life without going through death. The organization they both belonged to had come out of Afghanistan in ancient times and was called the *Roshaniya—illuminated ones.* Denying their existence made them even more powerful, by never referring to it. Strongly believing to have the granted status of being supreme. They also called themselves the *Order.* The new world order. Breaking the code of silence and secrecy meant being ruined, or even death.

So, Rose and Alok were (they believed at least) Supreme beings and an oath bound both men. Alok (CIA cryptonym Tophat) would have the sources to set things in motion in his country. Rose was silent again. Then the landscape of his face assumed a serious expression.

"I don't like this," he said, "whatever it is, we'll find out. Even it doesn't make any sense at the moment."

*

to : htt:\wwwvac. com\residence\field ankara station from: act:\termwwm. com\central urgent . . . immediate attention. central needs a complete list about unusual activities during the last days in ankara and east. areas in or around cukurca and daglari mountains which might be related to air activities or other uncommon actions of land traffic. air activities are related to an uncontrolled low altitude from Armenia to area above. 'topas' has human assets available to assist you. it is recommended to keep this investigation in this present stage to number one, you and Walker. langley\central\rose

17

Ankara, Turkey

Garry Kessler read the e-mail. He decorated his face with a smile, a friendly one with some memories visible. He knew the area around Cukurca very well. They had left from there. Drop point forty-seven . . . shook his head. This Iraqi thing would take a long time before it was declared history. Sometimes he thought about the Major and Rosco. Promised himself to give Rosco a call, one of those how-are-you-just-checking-in calls. Wondered how Duskin was doing in Singapore. Shit, time moves fast. Now he . . .

The phone interrupted his mental note-making about calling sometime. He picked up and listened for five minutes. At the cessation of the listening he only said a clear 'yes, sir' to number one, the Ambassador.

Kessler sat down and began to read the e-mail message again. This time more carefully and slowly. Not missing a single iota of its content. After he finished he went across the room and looked at the map and wasn't quite sure whether Langley knew what they were talking about. It was a solid distance of one thousand miles between Ankara and Cukurca. Hell, where to start first. Leaned back and shook his head. And what was it all about anyway? He had enough instinct to know that there was something in the air. It was just a gut feeling. On his way home he dialed from a public phone booth, the number of the man with the codename "Tophat."

*

Francis D. Walker.

Strolled to the bus station and didn't feel comfortable. He did not dislike the idea of having a car, accepting it as a part of his job. Some sneaky discretion was required this evening. A car at his destination could have drawn some troublesome attention. Francis didn't need the consideration of others of what he might be doing there. He waved a taxi. Like a reflex. He reminded himself that he was not allowed to take a gun along. Walker looked at his watch.

Francis had been raised in Alabama as a good conservative devoted Catholic of Irish and Polish blend, with the soft spoken calm manners and fine attitude of a real southern gentleman. After two years in the Special Forces, Francis D. Walker admitted to himself that he didn't like it and decided that his health was not the best. His group leader was a man with the name of Peter Duskin, a man he loved to hate for his guts and serenity. But eager to serve his country, Francis D. Walker applied at the agency and joined the CIA.

Ankara was his first foreign assignment after he had pushed papers for some year at Langley. He liked it. This life of a foreigner with the flair of secrecy regardless of the fact he had started as a serf by subordinating his office hours to Garry Kessler, the operative of station Ankara. Colorless, congenial and inconspicuous, that's what Walker was. Visibly good material for being a spy. It was late that very same evening, just after eleven, when Walker arrived at the east end of the city, an industrial area with some dubious bars and cafes. Walker stepped into the cool night and a heap of decayed vegetables. At this time of the night Walker had good reason to be nervous, since he had never met this contact before. Scuttled through nearby streets and played it by the learned rule that was called 'surveillance detection run'. Backtracking and studying faces, whether any reappearance would occur. Checking his reflection in store windows to see if he was being followed, and getting used to his environment.

He reached the building, a street cafe with a name written above the entry, 'Habbibi'(My Friend). Nicely lit up in green, that's what a street cafe has to do to lure the guests in. To him, the two men at the entry, pretending to play like real chess players, were a notch too intense to even have a Queen Pawn which should have started with a close P-Q opening and a great barter of maneuvering on the board. Their eyes carefully followed the man entering the place. The bar keeper scanned him over with dark and restless eyes. Eyes, sitting so deep in their sockets, surrounded by dark rings, leaving the impression that the man had spent his entire life on duty in this repugnant place without ever getting any sleep. Those dark eyes then cued toward another man. The next man, leaning casually against a door, did not hide his intention to interrupt any attempt to do something stupid, with his gun. This man came over to Francis D. Walker and addressed him.

"You ugh . . . Gentile?"

The man from the government nodded and said in his soft spoken voice: "Yes, that's me."

"If you would follow me, please?" correcting himself physically, carefully, by walking behind Francis. They walked down a hallway built from strong white sandstone and so small that Walker couldn't turn around anymore in this place. How could he be so stupid to walk into a trap like this? The shadow stopped and made it clear with its view not to move without further notice. Walker stopped in front of a huge brown door with carved unknown insignias. The sentry knocked a certain rhythm, a bolt shot back and somebody drew the door open.

'Hell,' the man from the government thought, 'this is like a bad movie,' watching the guard taking his place immediately behind the desk (standing). The floor with its white and black square tiles appeared like a chess board. The only soft source of light his eyes were able to take in, was a huge candlestick holder made from fine gold with seven arms. Each arm was holding a tall burning shine of flickering light. The candlestick consisted of a shaft rising out of it, with six arms coming out from two different directions of the shaft, with seven luminous sources supplied by the burning energy of pure olive oil. Candle arms decorated with three kinds of carved ornaments of globes and blossoms. Frank D. Walker was surprised to see, painted on the wall in dark letters against a bright background, a sign behind the man he wanted to meet.

"Ordo ab Chao"
(Order out of Chaos)

"I bind myself to perpetual silence and unshaken loyalty and submission to the Order. All humanity which cannot identify itself by our secret sign is our lawful prey."

The wall behind the desk bore a huge board with the signs of the Grand Lodge Jewels, twelve of them. It began in the left upper corner with the sign of the Grand Master and Deputy Grand Master. The man from Alabama, because of his profession and also because his genes, was a sharp observer, noticed that the two first seals contained the precise triangle of the 'Eye of David' that can be found on the one dollar bill, or the Bavarian Infantry flag from 1742 under Emperor Carl VIII. Centered below was the insignia of the Freemasons, always having accommodated in history the ranks of the Illuminates between them. The man from Alabama was mildly confused about the strange place and wondered for a moment what his government, or at least his agency, had to do with this odd location. But he was hiding it well, that's what he had learned to do.

A man rose from behind the desk. He was almost bald and huge. He radiated authority and enormous strength. The skin of his face was pale, ashen as a face could get in a lifetime. One would think he had used a bleach to get that pale. Underlined, was the impression in the diffused light. His face released a joyless smile revealing a line of gold-capped teeth into the room. He obviously had just finished a meal, which might not have been good for him, since the two-hundred-fifty or something pounds revealed an unhealthy eating habit. He tongued the rest out of his teeth and combined it with a mild burp.

"I am 'Tophas," the Interior Minister of Turkey, Baral Atok, introduced himself, "and you are . . . 'Gentile.'

'This is ridiculous,' Walker thought, but then reminded himself that these Levantins liked their mystics.

"I understand . . . ," 'Thopas' said gravely, removing his light framed Rothenbrook 2.0 bifocal glasses, and paused for a long time with closed eyes, like listening for advice from some higher spirits, then exhaled audibly.

"You are looking for some exegesis (yes, which was the word he used) of certain unusual circumstances, which might have occurred during the last days in my country."

He did not say in 'this' country'—no, 'my' country. Expressed it like talking about a private property. Walker's throat was dry. Nothing was offered.

Not even a glass of water. Strictly business. Impersonal. But Francis D. Walker liked it somehow, because this small missing gesture of courtesy avoided any delicate concession on his part.

"We will help you."

What did he mean by *"we"*. Walker was tempted to ask.

"Give us two days," Tophas went on, "perhaps three, to find . . . something," fixing Francis D. Walker with a staring glance, "we have enough contacts. I will mobilize the forces I have available."

He played it like he was the right hand of God. Yes, two days would be fine, Walker agreed. Perhaps some gentle advice. His people should not chase old circumstances, nor make too many waves. Because of the media and such. Perhaps for nothing serious.

And the probe began. A whole structure of Ankara's secret societies and underworld, gangsters, pimps, MIT (counter terrorist department) and the Grey Wolves, collecting the gossips, went systematically for two days and two nights to amass rumors, news and events, to locate them at gas stations, whorehouses, hotels and such, country clubs and travel offices, airports and bars, barber shops and street corners.

Day one. It resulted in the arrest of a child molester on the run, a shootout with members of the Cowardice Red Democratic Faction, killing an innocent bystander at a bus station while everybody else involved escaped, the confiscation of 600 pounds of hashish (without an arrest) brought in from Pakistan, and the solving of a four-year-old murder case. Nothing in the east and nothing really of much interest for the station officer Garry Kessler on the first day.

Day two.

It was a cool one, with a lot of moisture in the air, and offensive winds from the Koroglu Mountains, a Russian was arrested, trying to peddle a sample of weapons-grade nuclear material, containing plutonium enriched to 87 percent. And no other news. Except five days ago somebody had bought an almost brand new *Volvo* eighteen wheeler with a 40 foot refrigerating container from an American woman running a car rental place. It was a cash deal. This was not a subject of further preoccupation either. E-mailed his report as it was requested by Rose and went home. Garry Kessler decided to have good night's sleep.

*

Night.

It was right after the middle of the night. It was the time when thoughts are free and inspirations are at their best. He bolted straight from being deep asleep to being thrown into a stage of being wide awake. He swung his left leg over the right side of the bed and blinked passively. Sat there for a moment, fighting the sleep-comfort away.

The rig. The eighteen wheeler. All cash.

"I'll be darned," he mumbled and hoped he was wrong, but he already had the gut feeling he wouldn't be. Got up and lurched to the kitchen, while he was trying to get into his bathrobe. Switched on his Krups Classic 10 coffeemaker and stared at it until the first drops of Gevalia coffee fell into the glass carafe, releasing the rich aroma of the brew to his nose. He had already filled the water container last evening as usual, to gain some time in the morning. Executed the ritual of filling his mug and had a sip. Gosh, he hoped they wouldn't have done it. Maybe they hadn't. It would be his obligation, a heavy burden, to stop them, expose them. Damn! He, Garry Kessler, CIA Station Officer-Ankara, owed his life to the Major, Rachel, and Rosco.

*

Kessler remembered the last mission with the COES (Columbia's Special Operation Group). Rosco, the Major, and Kessler found out almost too late when the shoot-out with those corrupt scavengers from the Colombian Drug enforcement agency began, that the lab bust was a total botch from the beginning. It happened outside a small town north from Medellin, called Yarumal, on a river named Cauca. They had taken off from a military airstrip north of Cali, and the Bell 212 helicopter flew low, very near the treetops. Rachel swept the chopper over the dark green trees and began to hover over an area where small puffs of smoke came from below, the source obviously between the trees. The clearing was too small to land and get the chopper down onto the ground. The Major, Rosco, and Kessler lowered themselves quickly from the chopper on ropes. Followed by seven Columbian Anti-Narcotics agents. When they had reached the ground they spread out and waited for the shooting to start. But they were only received by silence. One-hundred feet across the clearing was the lab they had come to destroy. There were more buildings than they could handle or they expected.

Kessler made the first move to the lab and raced across the small clearing. He reached the drug lab and dashed into the building. Took a quick look around. Empty. The *lavaperros9* had just dropped their work when they had heard the chopper and fled into the jungle. They had left behind thermometers, presses, and three tons of cocaine, 150 drums of acetone, fifty huge plastic cans filled with mushy cocaine hydrochloride and five hundred jugs of red gasoline. One building after another was torched down. Rosco threw in the hand grenades, adding a ferocious additional fuel of destruction to it. Kessler sped to the last building. The door was locked. He stepped back, popped himself in a wide stance, raised his Uzi and pulled the trigger. Sheet metal gave in to high velocity bullets. Kicked the door in and was confronted with an enormous pile of plastic wrapped bricks. Cocaine. Perhaps five tons, ready to be shipped to mangle souls. Only to end up in a world of denial and lies. Across the pile were sixty jugs of highly flammable ether. This would do the job. He bolted further into the building, snatched some jugs, and emptied them around the pile, hurled the balance into the heap of cocaine, followed by two hand grenades. Raced back to the entry and stepped back. Taken by surprise, he wouldn't believe what his eyes were forced to take in. One of the

---

9   Workers in a drug laboratory.

Colombian narcotics agents pointed a gun at him. He wanted to go for cover when he heard the shot, followed by the numb pain in his right thigh.

In the process of a slow-motion collapse, he saw the Major raising his Uzi, releasing a burst of fire throwing the Colombian agent two feet into the air before hitting the ground. Kessler's mind worked clearly knowing there were only ten seconds left to live before the detonating hand grenades created the upcoming inferno that would absorb him in a drapery of flames. He wanted to crawl away but could not. His fainting mind began to wonder what the heavy shooting was about and hoped to be dead before the lab exploded. He rolled on his back and was ready to perish. He felt lifted up and noticed looking downward from somebody's shoulder, that the ground moved. Away from the lab. He heard the immense blast and felt the heat wave gushing over his body. The ground came closer again, his head hit the ground. He could not feel a thing. Blood ran from his leg like a fountain. Funny, he felt so light, when he fainted again. Actually it was a heavy flesh wound, but the bullet had nicked the long saphenous vein (the doctor later explained it to him this way). He would have bled to death in minutes. While Rosco systematically took out the double-crosser of the government, the Major did his best to stop the bleeding and called the chopper in. But there was nothing to land on with all this rain forest around. The clearance between the trees was uncomfortably small in its diameter.

Kessler still shook his head sipping on his coffee. Rachel had 'squeezed' the Bell into the clearance of thirty-five foot trees and hovered some inches above the ground. The Major threw Kessler over his shoulder and made a dash for the chopper. Rosco backed up with his MAC 10 until the chopper took off. He never would forget the sound when the helicopter's blade chopped off some branches of the trees as they got away. It was Rachel who brought the Bell 212 out from this burning death trap under the trees. By now he would be anesthetized, so to speak. Yes, he owed the two men and Rachel his life.

He looked at the clock. 0100, and picked up the phone and dialed. It was daytime in Petaluma, California. After the fourth ring somebody picked up on the other side of the globe.

"Hola," a voice said with Spanish undertone. Female.

"Can I talk to Mister Dean Rosco, please."

"No here. Meesterr Rrrosco no home."

"Can you leave a message for him? To call me. My number . . ."

"Meeester Rrrosco no here," the voice from California insisted," go to Europe. No come back. Maybe tuumorrow come back. Maybe come back next week."

So much for explanation from the maid. He hung up and swore to himself. Jesus H. Christ. He still hoped he was wrong and they would not have done it. Sleep was now the last thing on his mind. He dialed again. Napa, California. The Major. The second ring.

"Sorry, we can't take your call right now, please leave your name and a . . ."

Kessler hung up. Went to the bathroom and gulped down a glass of water. Back to the living room. Sat down and looked over the lights of Ankara, focusing his straying eyes on the missile like shaped building of the Hilton two miles away. The silence of the night mercifully granted him some time to think, and the more he thought, the more confusion began to occupy his mind. Wondered what morning would sweep into his office and where the Major, Rosco, and Rachel might be. Still, he hoped they were home. Just had gone out for lunch, gone to the beach, or playing with each other's skin. For their own sake. But he doubted it already. Before he went back to bed, he tried California again. Nobody picked up the phone. Kessler's message was to call him. Left a number and location. Sleep did not come easily.

And then his mind channeled information into his consciousness, that the truck had left Ankara already a week ago. Some smile-indication appeared on his face in the dark. Then he remembered about the information, already half asleep, about the Russian MIL MI6 flown into Turkay and dumped somewhere around Mt. Ararat. From there it had been moved to the area of Cukurca. He had not so much on his agenda the next day. He got edgy. He'd better read this report in the morning again. He stashed away in his dead files. The Russian chopper and the truck. There must be a link.

His mind was still in stage of veto, but he knew better. It had something to do with the precious metals in the desert in Iraq. It made sense to him. He did not want to stalk them. He had no false resentments in his profession but, hell, heck, shit, they were once a squad. He only could hope they had not done something stupid. And then a thought jumped into his mind which he did not like. But there was not much space for Garry Kessler to think it over again.

Station Ankara officer Kessler awoke shortly before six o'clock. Morning gazed incredibly serenely through the windows. Over the ritual of his morning coffee he picked up the telephone and called a doctor who worked occasionally for the embassy.

Kessler had a plan.

*

Rosco had listened into his messages four-thousand miles away in Petaluma, California and really didn't feel comfortable. Message number one revealed the desire of some company offering him a new credit with a limit of four-hundred dollars(pre-paid) with low interests and no annual fees. His stockbroker wanted him to call. A new phone company proposed to switch over to their latest superior system and superb(what ever that meant) service. His gardener wanted to get paid. It went on and on. A lot of people had a major in minors, so to speak. Message twelve found Rosco's undivided attention. It was a voice he knew so well. Garry Kessler wanted to talk to him. Wherever he was—just call. The number followed. Rosco overheard the heavy traffic's background noise and the seriousness in Kessler's voice.

Now, as a result of message number twelve Rosco wandered through a snarl of back streets, well served by cool winds, in Ankara to kill time, and get used to the unknown nervous environment. He admitted he was edgy. He looked at his watch. Then another twenty minutes went by. Nothing happened. His inner voice couldn't overcome the warning to be careful. Perhaps it was a mistake to come into this desolate area, where even the moon (if only half of it) hesitated to hurl any light onto it. Damn. Couldn't they just have met in some restaurant or coffee house? He was almost certain that Kessler wanted to know about the precious metals. Somewhere, somehow, something had leaked out. No way to turn the clock back.

While he walked another block along the street he had concluded how he would play the whole thing out with Kessler. He continued down the deserted industrial boulevard, only filled with life during the day, made a left onto another unknown street. Again, forsaken and vacant. On both sides the corrugated rusty walls of the old warehouses bounced off the sound of faraway traffic. Rosco suddenly felt he was not alone and sensed it with the well-trained instinct of a soldier—he was followed.

Hesitated for a moment to set down his left foot. He did. And there it was. The clatter of a step between. They had walked in the same gait as he had. There was silence in and under the obscure street lights he had reached. Now he also had heard the sound of running strides through the dump of moist air towards him. The cryptic silhouettes of two men appeared in the murky yellow street light. His mental alarm bell went off, and he began to increase his strides. And, as life repeats in unaccountable times a day, on the savannas of Africa or in backyard of 'modern, prey is secured, when it is isolated and away from the herd, regardless of its breed. Solitary, distanced from the rest of its kind, and deliciously vulnerable. He looked back and knew he had made a mistake by not getting back to the light-filled street just one block north. Knew he was encircled. But he wondered why they really did not want to follow him. Had they lost their nerve? He heard a noise and turned around. Saw just inches away the shadow of two more characters (from where had they come so suddenly?). He tried to jerk away. He turned to a defense. It was too late. He failed to notice the four hands clutching at him from behind. And it happened too fast. They were pros. Used the men behind him as support for a last desperate attempt to get free. Jumped and kicked the new approaching shadow with both of his feet into the face. Hurled him across the street. Fifteen feet. Rosco could feel through his shoes the fine bone structure of the nose as it gave away to the force of his kick. Rosco spotted one more man in front of him. There was not a second chance for fighting with arms bent behind his back. Felt lifted. In the poorly lit street, he saw the needle of a syringe flashing like an arrow, and before he could react, it went brutally straight through the garment of his sports jacket into his upper arm. He gasped, felt the sting and got the numb feeling of something he could not fathom. He suddenly and at once felt limp and lost the feel of the firm reality—did not know what was going on.

A comfortable sensation of being lost and disintegrating. Caught in a trap he could not examine. He had just received a shot of sodium pentothal—known as "truth medication," injected into his arm. It was a barbiturate anesthetic, and infused into Rosco's body, it created very quickly a pleasant feeling of nothingness and disregard. More important—the chemical reaction in his body created a conscious of unconsciousness. He was awake and had no knowledge where he was, to whom he was talking or what he was talking about. The injection led him to an all-over calmness—sedation in a small dose. It *was* a small dose. The dose of the Pentothal would be cleared from the bloodstream so swiftly that from moment to moment control of the drug was not necessary, while Rosco could be kept in a twilight state of reduced mental and physical control for just a short time without memory for the yore of five minutes.

Rosco noticed the pavement of the street blackened from the nightly moisture and did not realize he was dragged across the street to a car. The only functional similitude he could utilize for this experience (he knew something was terribly wrong) was the one of a slow motion movie in which he was at two places at the same time—viewer and actor. It was like underexposed black and white film to him. Things around him moved in slow, and then again in fast frames with the sound track of rap and violins. Still, it kept him calm and clearheaded, and so responsive to reality that he willingly gave answers to the questions, which did not relate to his answers. He was outside of himself and watched with curiosity, loosing the path of time.

Before this performance took place, station officer Garry Kessler had called a certain doctor in Ankara, who had been on the payroll of the institution for fifteen years. They provided the doctor every month with a decent payment in exchange for knowledge, plus forwarding everything about his colleagues in the medical community. An intellectual merchant, feeling safe while selling his colleagues off and out. Kessler had consulted the doctor, clarifying without giving away any further details his needs and the urgency of a fast working drug.

"I need", Kessler said to the doctor, examining the tip of his mild Davidoff cigar, "something to make a man tell me the truth in five minutes without hurting him. And more important, I need the man's lack of memory for seven minutes out of his life."

The doctor was reluctant and looked with a sympathetic distaste at this American from the embassy. But he gave it to him, with the remark that the firm did not work this way anymore, indicating that he was doing him a favor. The aversion of the medicine man was audible. The company did not work anymore this way, the doctor repeated, to be sure Kessler understood the meaning of the repulsing voice. So the doctor justified it to himself there must have been a reason for the hasty urgency. Some extraordinary peculiar measures.

Now Rosco was in the car. Kessler released the men from the TNSS[10] who had carried out the attack, with a short motion of his hand, filled with impatience. Shame overtook Kessler. Inside the car, Kessler slapped Rosco's face, bringing him into a state of semi-consciousness. The questions he shot swiftly to Rosco didn't make much sense and were evidently not related to each other.

"What is your name?"

"What is your opinion about Glenn Miller and Oppenheimer?" "Do you like San Francisco?"

Kessler did not wait for an answer.

Then Kessler suddenly went sharply off on a tangent. "Why are you in Turkey?"

"Are Tom and Rachel here?"

"Who else is here? Berret, Duskin?"

---

10   Turkish National Security Service.

"Why you are here?"

"When do you want to pick up the gold in Iraq?"

"Tell me everything. Now."

At this point Rosco's mind wandered down a tunnel to track the planned logistics. Kessler listened with increasing amazement for another three minutes to Rosco while already making up his mind. Examined his *Pulsar* wristwatch carefully. Now he knew it all. He always had sensed and now was afraid of, to carry it as confirmed knowledge. Kessler was suddenly scared.

He saw Rosco was on his way to consciousness. Rosco looked somehow surprised at Kessler with still not really clear eyes. They were alone in the car. Kessler had folded his hands like a priest praying as he looked at Rosco.

"You almost got fucking mugged," Kessler smiled, "this is a bad area. We should have met somewhere else."

Rosco still felt puzzled. But that's all what it was. His logic was intact and there was no evidence that anything else had ever happened. Kessler gave him the posthypnotic illusion that he was perfectly all right. Rosco had no recollection of what had appeared over the last minutes and had no doubt he was okay.

"What's up?" Rosco asked, "you wanted to talk to me."

"You really want to pull this off. Don't you," Kessler said with an open smile.

"What?"

"Don't give me this shit. You are after the metal."

"Yes," Rosco answered, trusting his instinct not to withhold the truth. Was there any other possible reason that Kessler wanted to talk to him.?

Rosco listened for thirty long minutes.

"Is there anything I can do for you?" Kessler asked.

Rosco shook his head.

"Now what?"

"Leaving tomorrow."

"Going home?"

Roscos's silence did not need further clarification.

18

Ankara, Turkey, November

She had a small two-room office above a truck repair shops in the older part of the city of Ankara. Close to the whorehouses and bars. Midday had arrived with some clouds as companions, but preferred for the moment to twinkle its bright light into the run-down grey business district of human meat and artificial lust, which would come to light and color only after darkness would take over its shift. The hookers and pimps, the bouncers and musicians and, most important, the buffoons. These were the suckers of daily life, coming from their offices, gas stations, ships, to waste their money and would bring to existence a psychedelic scene into the red light district, almost never remain brothels and bars. The street sweepers had not entered the scene yet to remove the littered trash, the beer cans, the today's papers with yesterday's news, the cardboard boxes saturated with the grease of dubious fast food, and the soaked rotten vegetables thrown out from backdoor kitchens, the makers of debatable substance. Some forlorn clouds migrated across the sky, covering the sun, and painting immediately the surroundings in a sleazy color. Light had to give in to grey as a half-bright moment through closed lids.

According to the annals and tradition of Turkey each alley or courtyard of a bazaar was specialized in craft or trade agreeing to the old societies. The cities of the old Ottoman Empire were established in surroundings formed along religious and godly lines. The seasoned municipality's midpoint, with its places of worship, trade and amusement was where the natives merged, maintaining their culture and way of life. The architectural scene of churches, synagogues and mosques, the mission schools could be found side by side in the old city's center without interfering in different beliefs. It was a clean conscious heritage.

The balance of a cultured tradition could not be found here in *this* rundown area. It was a sort of prison sentence to live and to work here. No substance. In short, the place stank like the gutters of Hades.

*

There she had her office and did reasonable transactions buying, selling and renting cars and trucks. Although in her very late fifties she was still exceptionally attractive. She had undertaken everything and had done everything for the past twenty years to fight time. The whole nine yards of whatever the plastic surgeons had up their sleeve. Paring, peeling, lifting, sucking and stretching. The whole arena of narcissism. She had her breasts done twice, they were now firm and ideal in size and in classic Grecian form. It made her *believe* to *be* thirty-five and in her prime. Great attention had been paid to the details, by having her nipples colored into a lush dark pink, standing up. Permanently. Those little attention-getters pressed against the texture of the coal-black silk of her turtleneck.

Blepharoplastic was done twice and fat and excess skin on the upper and lower eyelid had been a five-thousand dollar removal some time ago. She had some unhealthy obsession about her body and appearance, explaining also her practiced yet imitated youthful movement (like a softened up walk on a Dior's runway). Despite her brightness and intelligence, some grotesque mental-psychotic obstacles did not allow her to grow or to accept aging with grace and as a fact of life. All the bodily remodeling she underwent in the past had been successful and had contributed to a fine slim, tall body, which anyone in her presence, man or woman, could not disregard. A body she still *insisted* she had to "call in" badly needed attention from the past: show girl (that's what she once was in Las Vegas), hooker (what she never intended to be, but was), model (what she never would be) and such. That's what it was she narrated to herself. Years ago grey had taken over her full mane of hair and she artfully understood to shade the tress close to the roots of her scalp every two weeks, avoiding the no-class appearance of different colors close to her scalp. It was beautiful strong hair, naturally curled and shoulder length. Actually she would have looked much better in grey. Real bright, honestly earned grey.

The teeth were a touch too white and flawless to convince believability of the age she made herself to believe she was. The years had persisted to alter the alignment of the gums to her teeth she had achieved; they would not fit the gum anymore. For example. She had some difficulties to pronounce certain words in a proper way. She lisped, especially articulations ending with 's'. Her tongue, restricted in its movement, couldn't master its performance and bounced its pink tip against the back of the upper elongated capped incisors, creating a slight hiss when a 's' wished to express the demanded articulation at the end of a word. Her beauty was changed by the lisping like sounds released by her pouting mouth.

Her eyes. Those eyes with its almost anemic transparency. The color of hot bitumen with a satiny touch of dusty blue, only visible to somebody physically very close to her. Good eyes, seldom mirroring the scale of wanted or unwanted emotions to others. Today, five years after the last "lift", she still did not want to look into the mirror.

She went to the small window and lit a thin Van Houten cigar. The sudden disappearance of the sun contributed even more depression to her already sullen state of mind. Inhaled deeply, and when exhaling she sighed with the appearance of blue smoke around her mouth. Business had not been bad over the last weeks, especially the rig, this almost brand new *Volvo* eighteen-wheeler she had sold some days ago, brought an unexpected filling to her business coffers. It was all paid in cash. Soon, she would move her office away from this sewer pipe environment of human trash.

When she exhaled she saw the man walking across the street. His body movement was a very self-confident one. From his unhesitating strides, she noticed, he knew what he was looking for, because he knew already where it was. Her mind radioed into her consciousness that something was not right. Then the consciousness signaled an uneasy premonition that the man on the street, for whatever reason, was searching for her and her office. She brushed it aside. Nevertheless, her mind maintained persistence that something was unbalanced from the moment she saw the man.

Why was she still in this dirty country anyway? She had nothing to hide. Actually, five years ago she had shot a man. This act of ultimate violence did not take place in *this* country. When the slam of the door downstairs reached her hearing she turned away from the window, moved quickly to her desk and sat down.

It was heavy.

This huge beat-up chunk of wood, six feet wide, four feet deep, without the charm of a certain fashion trend in the luke-warm pisspot industry of interior design, was lacquered some unknown years ago, with a characterless brown paint like a stain from a gas station urinal. It appeared to be useless beside the actuality that it carried an inconceivable, for the eyes annoying, distorted pile of financial annals filled with invoices dated at a time and made out to payees, who might be dead already. The real purpose of the desk was to provide the woman with a protecting shield, invisible to the visitor. The vertical front fascia of the desk was re-enforced from behind with two inch thick Teflon panels to withstand the impact of armor piercing bullets, should somebody, for whatever reason, squeeze off a few shots. It was not the best socially accepted neighborhood. The old Turkish adage, 'Don't buy a house, buy a neighbor' had no meaning in this district of town.

She sat behind the desk in a youthful motion and allowed her right hand to slide under her skirt to touch gently the soft warm skin of her inner thigh. Close to her crotch, her hand loosened a short black stretchable velcro, holding the Beretta automatic snug in a holster, placed firmly where nobody would suspect it. The index finger shifted the safety lever down. Securing herself against the anticipated, the pistol was ready to be fired. The close touch to her vagina had aroused her for a moment. Gosh, she needed to get laid, flashed into her mind.

At precisely 3:47 p.m. her hearing system digested the short demanding knock on the door, and before she could vocalize an 'enter please', the man, the one she had noticed a minute ago on the street, invaded her office with his strong appearance. The receptionist had gone for the day. In an instant when he walked into the office she regarded him as a threat. He was tall. A man in his late-twenties, perhaps early thirties. His face was pleasingly outlined with a straight nose and cheekbones, emphasizing the vitality of the intruder. Dark blond short hair with no indication of grey harmonized with a nice touch of a suntan and blue expressionless eyes. His cool stare was a good section of a threatening influence on her. Nothing extraordinary about his dress. A brownish leather jacket. A stone-washed blue Levis shirt with open bottom, French jeans and Niki shoes.

"Yes," she said, meaning it more as a question while trying to swallow away her suddenly hard to manage uneasiness.

Hands against his back, the unknown trespasser just walked slowly around for a moment, judging, without any recognizable enthusiasm, a shabby print of the *Ayasofya* (Hagia Sophia), this master piece of Byzantine architecture above the Bosporus, here covered with some fly shit in the left lower edge and faded colors by the daily impact of light. The office did not have any elegance. Tacky. Beat up, unpadded, dirt-encrusted carpeting the cleaner had given up years ago to maintain. Walls covered with cheap panels of imitation wood, suffering from the weight of some more fake paintings, looking like specials in his home town of Billingsley, County Autauga, Alabama, USA. He opened the door to the next room and had a look into it.

"Yes," she asked nervously. Now her voice was a pitch too high for being appraised to be relaxed. This was also the second time she moved her right hand between her thighs in the attempt to get to it in a most casual way for the sake of her safety. Something filled her head with ice.

"Put your hands on the table. Don't touch yourself. We know where you wear the gun."

The 'we' calmed her, why, she had no idea, and she gave this received recommendation the slightest and agreeable possible nod. And, like promised with her nod, her hand appeared on the desk again. Silence hung between the man and the woman. She looked him carefully over and would not regard him being a trucker on his route into the Mid-East, asking for a TIR address along the way.

The man had noticed her agreeing nod with a short pleased glance. He pulled a crummy looking, once white, vinyl chair close to her desk, turned it around so that he could drape his arms over the back. It changed the ambience immediately to an interrogative situation. He sat down and looked intolerantly at her. She also saw that his perimeter for permissiveness was thin. He sat down and his jacket bulked exposing his 9mm Glock pistol, embraced by the soft dark-grey leather of the holster under his arm. Brought out a blue pack of Dunhill, took one from the pack with his mouth and used a silver plated Dupont lighter to light it. 'He has done this on purpose,' she thought.

"How are you, Amanda?" he asked in a soft spoken manner, having her within the reach of exhaling cigarette smoke, consciously blown into her face.

She frowned. How and from where did this stranger know her name?

"Who are you?"

And would he mind introducing himself?

Yes, he would mind.

"I come from the government, Amanda. I have some questions to ask."

Frank D. Walker did not even leave some space to be questioned about caring for a glass of water, coffee or such, which would have taken out the tension of an upcoming and (perhaps) unpleasant meeting. He watched the cracking silence of her discomfort and observed with professional inquisitiveness her initial slip of vigorous self-control. It was this first indication of disposition. This tiny little slip signaled the first self-betrayal expressed by her body language. The sudden, almost not observable dipping of her shoulders creating the sort of submissive arrogance of a real estate agent when showing a house to be sold. Displayed concealed apprehension.

Implement fear in an individual. That's what they had taught him at this secret CIA school at Camp Peary, Viginia (the Farm). He remembered well the words he could say in his sleep from page 124 of the agency's 'Human Resources Handbook':

> *A threat is basically a means for establishing bargaining position by inducing fear in the subject. A threat should never be made unless it is a part of the plan and the "questioner" has the approval to carry out the threat. When a threat is used, it should always be implied that the subject himself is to blame by using the word such as, "You leave me no other choice but to . . . He/she should never be told to comply "or else!"*

Now Amanda had less poise-radiating less self-confident. She swallowed one time too much. That's what the man was waiting for and was pleased how quickly it happened. His inquiry would be easy. He had her approval. Maybe he would throw in some threat at the end. He knew in an instant this slut here in this office would perform well. When Amanda first heard and focused on the southern accent it seemed to be the past returning. An uncontrollable twitching of some muscles in her face occurred. This histrionic spasm always happened when she got too excited.

*

Amanda Maltas.

It was something of a mystery to her friends why the life of a woman with so many undoubted proficiencies should have gone so wrong at the peak of her career. Especially since she possessed in the past, a ravishing appearance of a beautiful and exquisite woman with the talent of running one of the best trucking companies in Nevada, after a fine career on the stage with Siegfried and Roy at the Mirage had come to an end. She was a quick learner.

Curious about life she was married twice and had an estate outside Las Vegas she had inherited from her grandmother. Amanda mothered a child with a passion-filled stranger. She desired to have and raised it on her own. One daughter. Along the course of life she decided to take on, in the name of vanity, the risk of an unnecessary facelift. It was not a discount job. It was uttered all over town that this doctor was the best. The doctor had suggested a laser treatment but she could not imagine a controlled burning in her face. She was afraid of it.

To achieve a perfected high required an ever increasing amount of pills and pot. Dr. Ference Bogy had smoked marijuana since his freshman years and for him, pot was no longer just a social drug, sometimes casually inhaled to "feel good." In his case the use of pot had reached a level where the interaction of delta 9-etrahydrocannabinol(THC) with his brain receptors had led to a tolerance for the drug, forcing him to smoke more pot to get high. He had reached a stage where the chemistry of his body had to rely on the shit. In other words he was an addict. It had become a one-thousand-dollar-a-day enslavement. Most of the time his hands were cold and unpleasantly sweaty. A short, sometimes a second long shake appeared, only noticeable to him. The night before the surgery, he had experimented with a variety of mind-altering trash like LSD, hashish and mescaline. On the morning after, his memory bank of necessary data about his clients in his brain was hampered. Amanda wondered for a moment when he looked down at her why his pupils were extremely dilated. Even his intellect was in a hazed stage and his sense of sight, touch and hearing was distorted. His mind wandered and he began to imagine as well—working over such exquisite beauty.

And he began.

He did not know what he was doing. His right hand, containing the scalpel, moved along in one elegant cut from the superiorpost suriater connective tissue behind the ear for a fine line. He was behind the other ear when he had to pause, for his view was suddenly indistinct and his hand clenched. As he looked down at her, he attempted to wink away a mild fog from the cornea of his right eye. He had to restore the urgently needed visibility. The cornea refused to do so when it happened.

It was just a tiny move.

The scalpel.

Sharp in its appearance and for its created purpose it did, what it was asked by the hand to do.

Cut.

This one tiny move of the scalpel. The unknown and unfelt damage was permanent and happened to the newest tissue at its exit from the stylo-mastoid foramen. When the hands jerked unexpected, the scalpel had cut through the dura of the Seventh (facial) nerve, the motor nerve for all muscles of expression in the face. Actually it was not so much, more a nick. From a point of distance, a nothing. There were twenty muscles in her face to change the appearance. But this cut would affect most of the muscles of expression in the future by being paralyzed. The postoperative recovery created the usual soreness and discomfort, controlled easily by medication. But being so heavily bandaged and supported by gauze, wraps, oils and such, it went unnoticed for weeks until she observed she could feel but not move those desired expressions of coyness, philanderering and fluttering eyelids. When the swellings and bruises were gone and the lengthily healing time of cold compresses and slightly elevated head was over, the devastating chain reaction via the remodeling of her face was fully visible and understood suddenly (she had promised everybody that she would look younger than her daughter).

She had no idea (nor the doctor) that she would not be able to close her upper eyelid while the lower lid slouched. The punctum was no longer in contact with the globe and tears would run involuntarily. The worst part, her mouth had been drawn to one side and food would collect between the cheek and gum from paralysis of the buccinator, the fine thin muscle between the jaw at the side of the face and creating (once set in) a horrifying fetor to others. If she would not watch it, the food would rot in her mouth. There would never be another chance to sip from the surgical fountain of everlasting youth.

*

"Somebody bought a truck from you. A *Volvo*. An 18-wheeler?" the man from the government said very calmly, allowing the fact to appear as a question.

"A reefer. Is this right?"

She would not put up with this nonsense, she said. Would not talk about her business and clients, Amanda replied. Rebellion was audible in Amanda's voice. Then she picked up the phone to place a fake call. And, by the way, she would call the police. A fraction of a non-readable smile appeared around Francis Walker's well-formed mouth as he bent over and his left hand took the receiver gently from her hand, putting it back at the cradle. He went back into his vinyl chair. His calm friendliness was the creator of fear and began to threaten her again.

"This is not very wise. I am just asking you about a particular truck and show you some pictures of some men," he paused for better effect, "and you just tell me which one bought it. Fair enough?"

Silence.

Then she promulgated she did not know what he was talking about. And it would be better if he would leave now. The man got up from the chair and as he walked to the window, he touched Amanda's shoulder with the tip of his right thumb converting at the same time the move of this particular finger into an order.

"Come," he said, "come here. I want to show you something."

Standing beside him she looked down on the street. There was a car parked across the street, one of these invisible pieces of non-existent shit. A little bit banged up here and there with a dirty brown color. A car nobody would remember. It was this kind of car which only would find public recognition in traffic when it had hit somebody because of its failing brakes or other lewd malfunctioning. But under its hood was a perfect running engine and it had perfect tires. While putting his hands into his pockets Walker pointed down with a small motion of his head.

"They are from the Turkish government. See, if you don't tell me who bought the reefer," he shrug his shoulders in an apologetic gesture, "we'll leave it to them to ask you."

She jerked her head back when he suddenly was about to touch her face with his left index finger. He had tilted his head back and looked down at her.

"The plastic surgeon did a lousy job. Didn't he? Fucked up your pretty face. Didn't he? See, we understand why you shot this creep in Las Vegas. You shot off his face. No pretty woman wants to see her face messed up. Perhaps you did a service to mankind. But we still call it murder at home. Look, you're still a very attractive woman. But I am telling you, once you're in a Turkish jail, you're done. Perhaps you don't know what happened to Lawrence of Arabia," again a long pause, "they raped him for days. See, and he was a man. *You leave me no other choice,* if you don't tell me." (The picture book text from the 'Handbook' he thought).

'What did he say just now? She is still an attractive woman?'

Amanda couldn't give a shit about what happened to Lawrence in a Turkish jail. She bathed in his words and it did her in, the man from Alabama saw it. 'Poor harpy,' he thought and felt for a moment, honestly sorry for her.

"We could, or would disregard this profane incident in Nevada and you are off the hook. But we want to know who bought the truck. And when."

"How can I trust you?" she asked with a hoarse voice.

"You don't have to."

He waited as the silence began to be thickening with its feel of enmity. Reached into the pocket of his leather jacket, pulled out an envelope and placed the first picture like a set of gambling cards on her desk and watched her. No reaction. The next picture. Watched and saw her body softened up when she recognized this devilish good looking man in the picture. He waited patiently knowing she would surrender to his plea.

"Is it him?"

She nodded.

"Did he come alone?"

She shook her head.

Next picture.

He looked at her.

She nodded.

"See how simple it was," as he pocketed the pictures, "you remember his name?"

"Bryan Iscander," she said tonelessly.

How about the second man's name.

He did not talk at all, she said, but he drove the rig away. Francis Walker believed her. How about the rig? A long description of the truck followed. The tractor was red. Burgundy red. The usual chrome around. The tires? Goodyear NX 23-087 she conceded. She walked to the file cabinet and pulled out a folder. It was a cash deal. As is. Yes, a whole 23x24x12 inches Vitton briefcase filled with one-hundred dollar bills. Yes, and she remembered the Teakwood corners around the Vitton briefcase. He got up and took the folder with its contents.

"Thank you Amanda, you have been of an absolute inestimable service to your country."

"H'bout your promise," she asked with underlined desperation in her voice.

"You can come home now anytime, "he said.

She believed him.

The end-of-conversation-threat came.

"But there is one more thing. If you talk to anybody about the truck we'll be back and kill you. Do I make myself clear?"

Amanda got ashen and wondered in irrational thinking how he would manage this if she would talk. She believed him, observing he was serious.

*

Amanda Maltas left her office around 19:00. She was halfway across the sidewalk when she got some strange sensations. She sensed something was not right. Amanda stopped, watched the traffic around her, allowing her eyes to take everything in. She saw a car. It was the car she had seen before.

The same, passing her twice, when she crossed the street. Being in the middle of the road it did not feel right. Suddenly Amanda was panic-stricken and puzzled when she could see clearly the contour of the car very close. Too close. But again the car passed by. She turned into Ala Turk Avenue which ended into the wide open Kurtulas Park surrounded at the periphery with palm trees and benches. She calmed down and stopped for a moment. Then the same car came veering around the corner. This time it made a straight dash for her. Paralyzed and with horror-filled eyes she looked at the fast closing car. Then came the realization telling her where she had seen the car before. Across her office and she . . . there was a sick stomach-turning sound, followed by a short painful outcry of a female voice. The trunk contained two bags of sand creating an additional weight of 200 pounds to the vehicle.

Amanda Maltas was already dead when the left rear tire crushed her chest. The silicon implants that had composed her perfect breasts she was so self-admiring about and whiter than the color of her bones, burst through her squeezed flesh and was forced from under the tire to the surface of the street. The fifth rib of her Vertebro-sternal, broken, pierced through her left lung and heart.

*

The next day.
from: htt:/wwwvac.com/field ankara station to : act:/terwwm.com/central mal individual who bought truck accepted under the Name of brian iscander. definitely identified as dean rosco. Second subject has been identified as mark berret. description would be misleading. Whereabout unknown. it can be assumed with certainty, above mentioned individuals iskander / rosco is with the purchase on turkish territory. the whereabouts of the other four individuals is not known at the moment. signed kessler

Garry Kessler had no idea at the moment where to find them. But this would be his taskmaster's problem to provide.

19

It was dark and windless.

A dim blue laced with good visibility.

Rasit sat in his car. He leaned forward and looked at his watch. 20:05. Leaned back again and continued the waiting. He fathomed, like so many times, he had to be patient in his kind of business. He felt isolated and uncomfortable. There were some trees between where he was and the fence. The trees looked like skeletons in the dark with their decorated frostiness. He wished suddenly, but just for a moment, to have a cordless and to call the whole thing off. The sky presented overcast with high clouds, leaving some holes, allowing some dim lights of the stars come through. Where he parked, the airfield was in sight, the best darkness was willing to reveal to him. Two hundred yards ahead he could see the grey straight band of the airstrip. He even could make out the profile of some mountain not so far away through the thin layers of frosty mist. But further above another thin steam-like looking haze made the clouds appearance waning, creating an indication of a rainbow ring around the invisible moon. It was cold. He shivered and rubbed his shoulders with crossed arms. He had nothing to do but watch and listen, nothing to see as the navy blue nightfall mixed with hidden moonlight behind the scattered clouds. Nothing to hear other than the silence. The rend in the clouds above began to increase in its diameter. More stars flashed mild sparkling light. The moon was still hidden, close to the split of the hazes far above. Once more he moved without any comfort in his seat and decided to take his gun out of his holster to place it beside him. Then decided to sit with half of his ass on it to have it warm. He did not trust ice-cold weapons. They could stall easily. Checked it, so it would function properly as it was anticipated.

More dim light now took over and across the open area he could make out the edges and profile of the warehouses he knew so well. Rasit was not nervous, but tense. It was too close to the Iraq border, just two miles, to feel comfortable. He felt captured and forced to do something he never had to do in his profession. Never had he personally to hand over the goods he had sold.

But this time. The friggin Russian chopper. He could even see the contours of this stupendous monster. Rasit had to admit it was a fine piece of machinery. Like a crane. The thing could ferry anything. From guns, trucks, any freight, to troops. Before Rasit agreed to arrange the transfer, he did his homework. This chopper had been flown by the Algerians, the Peruvian Army, the Iraqis, and the Vietnam Air Force. He wondered for a moment, where the chopper really was headed for. A wave of uneasiness splashed over him. Should have disqualified himself from the whole doohickey by saying 'no'. Shook his head about his foolhardy decision to make this deal. Once he had agreed, he couldn't get out of it anymore. This General Katz had put a lot of pressure on him. The road coming here, alone, would have been enough to have refused, in good terms, the whole thing at the beginning. Dear God, the road alone! It was not even sanctioned on any local or tourist map, this washed out, pot whole rich, rough path.

The truth was the path was actually created by the daily use over the last years. A new turnpike for men in the smuggling business on their way into or out of Iraq or Persia. The smuggling was done in the old-fashion way, by using the human back, or mules to transport smuggle-worthy accessories of life. Rasit also saw it this way while he appreciated God's everlasting wisdom. He did not have to fly another mile in the chopper. Whoever would fly the chopper away, better make damn sure that he knew what he was doing.

Rasit looked into the rearview mirror hoping to see some headlights bouncing up and down coming closer to his car. Nothing. He wondered for a moment why Rosco had not arrived yet with the other two. Rasit's eyes strained into the darkness ahead. He had the overwhelming desire to smoke but knew he couldn't since just two-hundred yards in front of him was the fence. The clouds didn't allow the moon to release any more light. There was no need for light. Rasit valued it and he hoped it would hold up. He sighed again and shook his head.

It was not a little war this time where he delivered the goods needed to kill. No, it was something bigger this time. Something considerably immense. Something power-damned big, where the greed had fed upon itself, until the immense good might had become the superiority of evil. Rasit was not driven this time by cold ambitions for money. He moved his damaged hand across his face and felt some perspiration on his forehead.

The General had made it quite clear—if he bungled this, or even worse, double-cross him, the General had assured him that he would die. He, nervously, masticated on his right thumb when he began to feel somehow heavy, like not being in possession of his own will anymore. Dazing and not clear minded. No, he was simply tired, he concluded. He could not tame his emotions any longer. Could hardly hold his eyes open. He shouldn't't sleep. Sleep was the brother of death. Just a sort of a recess for a moment. He tried to open his eyes and it was like seeing an over-dimensional portrait of a Chinese man with a ponytail painted into the nightly air. Tense dark eyes staring at him. Rasit felt a chill and then he began to loose control of his environment. Gosh, was he tired! Rasit closed his eyes and leaned his head against the head support of his seat. Just a short nap. He was sure he would hear them when they came.

At some point in time, he heard the sounds of metal knocking against the window. Immediately he was wide awake, saw the shadow and his right hand reached for the gun. It was gone. The right door was open. He heard the sound of garment rubbing against his shoulder and felt the firm pressure of the pistol against his right temple. Somebody sat beside him. A pressure, demanding him to stay where he was. He felt the cool metal of a gun barrel and he knew it was too late for a response. Surprise was in their favor, whoever they were. The door on the driver's side (his side) began to open.

"Get out," a voice said.

It was Rosco's gentle and calm voice. The gun on the right side of his head pushed him gently out of the car. It was difficult for him to soften himself since he noticed something inside. Panic and fear of death. He wanted to live so badly, wanted to already be in Mexico and spending his money with women and booze. He had no greater ambitions at the moment.

"Well, I think . . ."

"Just get out."

Rasit did as requested. A long and almost palpable pause followed. His eyes began to adjust to the night, and he noticed three more shadows.

"Now what . . . and why? I have done everything they wanted me to do," he said, feeling the anger rising up inside him and his straight back, but still scared. The fear began to fade a bit. Rasit experienced defenselessness. Did they think he would double-cross them? He had ripped out everything of no real use in the chopper. Things which might create perhaps unnecessary dead-weight. Eleven internal tanks filled up. Additional barrels of fuel, sixteen of them, anchored and installed in the cargo bay and linked into the fuel system. Not only had cost him *this* a bundle, Rasit also had to pay off some guards. The electro-thermal anti-icing system running for hours. Engines warming up. All a go. And now this. For his good work? A gun on his head?

"Just wanted to make sure you were alone."

Rosco had too much dispassion in his voice to depict further danger to Rasit. It was like the moon placed himself in the middle of a cloud-hole for a moment. Now he saw it. The man beside Rosco had infra-red night goggles around his neck (he couldn't make out the face.) Rasit understood. Smart. No wonder he had not seen the car coming. They had driven the damned vehicle up to him without lights, in the dark. The moon disappeared again.

"You have the pilot?" Rasit asked rebelliously, but still frightened. He did not believe what he saw when Rosco pointed at another shadow. Rasit, typical mid-eastern with a well developed and macho comprehension about women's limited position in life. As, for example, to bear children, run a kitchen, and please her spouse and, for God sakes, not driving a convertible fell apart. It was a *woman* Rosco had pointed to. How in the hell could they . . . well it was not his business.

"It is all warmed up. Just take off."

He looked nervously at his watch.

"You have another twenty minutes to take off. Remember after I have closed the gate you're on your own. That was the deal."

The constant changing of the dim moonlight made Rasit nervous. Now some moon began to show over the edge of a cloud. It gave some light and made it easier to make out the chopper. Rosco had a closer look at Rasit and identified something in the man's face. Pure fear. The face of a man who wanted to get away from all of this as fast as he could. He saw that the lines descending from his nose down to the corners of his mouth were quite deep, deeper than when he had seen the man the last time in Ankara. The two lines, the two vertical above his nose bridge on his forehead. The same. Rasit motioned with his head, telling them to follow. A slightly metallic sound was released from a chain wrapped around the center of the mesh wire gate, holding it together. Now open, just enough to let the three in. Rachel, Tom, and Rosco stepped into no-man's-land.

*

Inside the chopper.

Rachel got immediately into the seat. She had her head up and her eyes followed the line of little lights, green and red and blue along the overhead dashboard. In the dark, flicking over switches like she never had done anything else in her life. Rachel had gotten through thirty five different switches when she turned to Tom. He could see she was thoroughly absorbed with what she was doing. She ran down the specifications Tom had to take care of during the flight. Then a heavy hum and whining set in. Multiplying and spiraling, gearing and helixin. Shrill, screeching, penetrating sound waves of the two 5,500 hp Soloviev turbo shaft engines.

Eleven thousand horsepower came to life and began to rotate the main shaft of the 114 foot wide rotor. Lift and forward maneuver began.

20

December, Iraq

Some lead-grey clouds invisible low in their altitude were not ready for snow yet. Both the timing and the weather seemed to be the impeccable collaborators for what they had in mind since the casual meeting in Mendocino. The hazy night seemed to be holding a gentle clench around the moving chopper, like a concerned alien giving cover. Actually Rachel and the two men lived now in a stage of a flawless and intact loneliness without any back-up. It was the perfect freedom. Rachel, Tom and Roso. Relying only on something beyond their understanding, they were willing to be aware and to accept.

Nature was patient and would let the winter wait for some more days before the gale would blow its heavy breath across the mountain, helping, in a follow-up by nature, to cover the mountains with snow, bringing the visibility down to nothing with the whirling snow.

*

Some leaden-grey clouds, low in their altitude ware not ready for rain yet and invisible. Both the weather and the timing seemed to be impeccable collaborators for what they had in mind since the casual meeting in Mendocino. The hazy night seemed to be holding a gentle clench around the moving chopper, like a concerned ally giving cover. Actually, Rachel and the two men lived now in a stage of a flawless and intact loneliness without any back-up. The perfect freedom. To live or to die. They only relied on something beyond their own understanding; they were willing to be aware and acceptance of it. The *Shamal,* the sandstorm, was still off season.

Nature was patient and could let the gales wait before they would begin to blow their heavy breath across the desert, bringing the visibility of the whirling dust down to zero. The cosmos would change the desert into a place were men and animals would retreat from life to a bare minimum. Like they had lived through for thousands of years.

They had gotten the chopper out of the fenced airfield without obstacles. In no time the MIL MI6 had crossed the border of Turkey into Iraq two miles south from Cukurka at an altitude of only ten feet, leaving behind a trail of dust invisible in the darkness. For the next twenty five miles Rachel used the slow flowing Zap Suyo river for an even lower altitude until she reached the Semdinli Cayi delta. There she broke off. When she reached the stabilized road to Zebar, she stopped for a moment, hovering. There was no traffic to be seen at all. No searching headlights of trucks on their way to Saudi Arabia. She crossed with the metal brute the well-paved highway and moved straight south-east with full power. It was hilly dune land. It was easy to fly during the day, but this was a solid pitch-dark night. The men were tense, but they trusted Rachel, regardless they thought, it was almost fool hearted how she flew the bird. Wild and bold. The altitude was critical and it required an electronic sensor to produce pictures from the terrain ahead. Actually they had no idea whether some hindrance had been built over the last year such as bridges over a dry wadi, power lines, or any structure that would have brought this flight to a fire-balling standstill. At least they would die together.

The Russian helicopter was equipped with two important electronic devices. But *when* had it been maintained or calibrated the last time? There was a forward-looking infrared sensor (FLIR), which could pick up temperatures from an object ahead from a digital camera into a video-like image to a monitor on the dashboard, observed by Tom. It would warn them when to pull up and fly over or under an obstacle. It was backed up by a moving display that constantly showed where they were on their projected flight path. The radar altimeter presentation displayed a constant altitude of five meters by measuring in a split second the radar impulse required to reach the ground. Bouncing back and producing the signal that held the chopper at the favored elevation in the twisting valleys and hillsides of the region. Assimilating the signal from the radar altimeter, the hover coupler sent the message to the rotor control, regulating the pitch of the rotor blades to soothe up or down draft.

Still Tom had the feeling they flew blind.

*

He woke up in his tent because his herd of cattle roamed and had gotten restless. Got up from his humble sack and moved outside to check the livestock. His name was Alimut and he was a Bedouin. The herd of goats was agitated and he could hear why. He was a man of the desert and he also could see in the darkness. It was just a remote distance away where he noticed the thundering popping sound of a helicopter. Saw even a fog-like trail of a huge plume of sand dust, like a ghostly caterpillar. He did not see very clear the source of his interrupted sleep, but he could hear it. Oh, he knew the sound so well. This harsh popping sound of those ox-like looking flying machines. For Alimut the sound meant war and trouble and he hoped that there would not be another war on its way. With a soft utterance he spoke to his animals. He moved between them. Padding them and hearing the sound of his voice, they calmed down. He went back into the house. Turned down the wick of the petroleum lamp, blew out the small flame, swung his legs off the floor and pushed further into the cot and snuggled against the generous ass of his wife. He needed rest. Alimut had enough of his own problems and did not need a new war. In a protective motion, he put his arm around her. She smiled in the dark. Before dawn (after he would kiss her cheek) she and her Alimut would have to milk the cows.

*

The crew of tree was calm and quiet when the MIL hovered three feet above the ground like a searching bird to land on the right place. The giant rotating blades whirled the dust into the dark chilly night. Gently Rachel inched the chopper forward, hovered it again, turned it slowly and waited for Rosco's command.

"Here," he said. She budged the chopper around the high dunes and adjusted its direction with the simple help of the compass. She set chopper down on the small clearance.

"How far off?" Tom wanted to know.

"We're right at the bull's eye. Just two seconds of target time," Rachel answered.

It was 2200. When the dust began to settle and some indication of the stars appeared again on the black-blue silk blanket of the nightly sky, Tom and Rosco left the chopper and began to climb up the hill. The rear end of the chopper faced the point where the crashed German Messerschmitt 264 rested undetected for now over fifty years. The chopper also had two clamshell doors and folding ramps which represented an easy loading of freight. Rachel began to operate the hydraulic to open the rear doors. The ramp began to extend outward the same time. The system moved and opened, representing the engineering lord minds with their masterly composed light-weight structures and the way the designers wanted it to function. It opened as ordered and was ready to receive. Rachel killed the engine. The silence of sylvan solitude took over, covered by the blue-black silk blanket of the nightly sky. Tom and Rosco left the chopper and climbed up the fifty feet to the convex bend on the slope.

There was another of the standard equipments of the MIL, which came in quite handy. It was an electric winch with the capacity to move (or drag) 1,765 pounds into the cargo bay, right through the open clamshell doors with ease and time-saving speed.

Tom and Rosco took along a cargo net with fine openings, normally used for loading ships. They also took along their weapons, shouldered utensils of a deadly trade, only 12.8 inches long. The diminutive Heckler & Koch MP5K submachine gun would get off a shredding nine-hundred-rounds-per minute in full automatic mode. Tom wondered for a moment how the weapon had come onboard of the MIL. To conserve ammunition the MP5K could set off a lever to fire one shot at the time or baggy a three-round smash with each pull of the trigger.

Tom looked at his watch. The glowing hands of his slim profiled *Swiss Field* watch suggested 22:15 by now. Ten minutes later both men were inside the buried Messerschmitt. Nothing had changed inside the plane they had left behind four years ago. The same bone-headed smile from the dead pilot, watching over the treasure, with its Knight's Cross around his neck, like a mysterious unreachable creature. The same skeletons in the same position. The same desert, same dune. The same precious metal—just laying around, waiting to be picked up.

*

NATO's reporting name for the Russian MIL MI6 is 'Hook A.' 'Hook A' is a twin-turbine all-metal heavy duty transport helicopter and the world's largest of its kind. Attached to its fuselage are two small detachable shoulder wings, off loading some twenty percent of the total lift in a cruising flight. 'Hook A' has eleven internal fuel tanks and two external tanks on each side of the cabin and storage for two extra tanks inside the cabin with a capacity of an additional 7,695 pounds of fuel. The chopper has a total fuel capacity of a decent 29,312 pounds.

The extra tanks in its cargo bay, the maximum ferry range is close to a thousand miles with a great payload of twelve tons.

And they began.

*

Desert. The ocean of sand and earth.

Forms of land are here anything but eternal. A surface assaulted and shaped since the beginning of time by the powerful actions of torching heat and paralyzing cold. Mountains of the most solid rock, impossible to date the time of their creation, once proudly raising their solid stones sky high, had been wasted away during the never-ending immense earth process of shaping and reshaping in timelessness and re-creation. Mountains like towers, of once vomited out by the inner core and forces volcanoes in form of lava, made in solidity and strength had to give in to the will of the elements. Once strong in their mature stage and glorious days, young, arrogant and wild, they used to withstand the sharpest of the repeating cycles of the never-ending higher rules of creation. They thought, like mortals, they would forever impose and dictate this part of terra firma. But the gods had new arrangements in mind by employing the winds and the weather. The heat and the cold, the water of the rivers and the storm-driven rains. They had not yet completed the creation. They had a new order in mind employing the force of the wind and disintegration and such. Rain was crashing down in drops, only to be rejected.

The first crack appeared. Just a thin almost invisible crack, a tiny microscopic one. Nothing to be really exited about. Nothing serious at the beginning. But the decline began. From the top. Fragments broke away only to be wasted and to be minimized further when they fell hundreds of feet down into the valleys. Worn down from above, worn down from the side. The mountains began to choke on their own debris and it was only a question of time before the once-solid and conceited rock was decimated to sand.

Still, there was no rest. The wind, the *Kabsurs,* never stopped to move sand, building and frolicsomely created the dune. Some new and strange, like other-world topography. The moving of millions of tons of sand and dust. The wind never stopped to move the sand, building and rebuilding playfully the dunes, Shaping and reshaping. Nothing was solid, nothing permanent. The wind-borne sand and grain skidded along the ground, colliding with each other in harsh but flawless irregularities, modeling and contouring the grains again and again. The prowess of the gales were the fastest form to profile the cereals of sand. When the wind left them alone for some hours the grain were seeds for new profiles and forms in just hours. A solid topographical display. Detailing it in a map was just not possible. Not the finest and most sophisticated computer arrangement was able to map out a precise direction or guidance.

For God's sake, how five highly educated men and a woman could would do such a stupid thing! Going into the desert of Iraq after years to find a crashed German plane of World War II a second time in a landscape which was not solid, just constantly in motion like a slow moving ocean.

21

The soft winds, the furious sandstorms play their own games and rules. *Four* solid laws of shaping dunes and their character were exercised in the maelstrom of deserts.

There was . . . well, from above they looked like frozen ocean waves. They were a product of an uneven tempered and middling wind which moved only light sand. The tumbling air swirled the massive grains aside, originating ridges which would change their shape and forms with the next wind entirely. They were named the

Traverse Dunes.

When the stronger one-way wind began to blow, it would move the more fine granular sand, cutting along through parallels with the path of the breeze. No solidity. Would flirt away with the next wind like a young mare chase by a stallion. And they were named the *Longitudinal Dunes.*

Where the sand was relatively insignificant, a wind blowing in a constant direction created the crescent profile of dunes by painting the sand more readily over the dune's low edge than its core. Only a change of the wind direction would allow the half moon-like shaped dunes to execute a reverse in the crescent shape. This new shape would be wiped out with the next gust. And they were named the *Barchan Dunes.*

So, everything the Almighty played in the desert was a constant mobility. So simple was that. But was it so simple?

The dune under which the crashed German plane with the loot rested was a different one. Unlike the other categories of dunes, dancing in the direction of the conquering wind, this one remained solid, permanent and stable. This kind of dune would *not* move and keep its incorruptible and lasting shape because the wind breathed from *all* directions and sides and just nurtured the dune's delicate form by taking some sand away, only to build it up in the *same* form immediately. And they were called the *Star Dunes.*

The men of the desert, the Bedouins, also called it the *rhourd—the starshaped.* Looking down, let's say from an airplane, the dune would rest there with a radial buttress, stretching in many directions. Just like a star. This dunes were *permanent landmarks* in the ever-shifting ocean of sand around and therefore they were the guidance for caravans since the Silk Road existed and the men of the desert, the Tuaregs, the Kurds or Chaambas had began to cross the desert. The *rhourd* was once a part of a relative small area called the desert pavement. Its surface was composed of small rocks fitting together like a mosaic. That was all that the heat, cold and rain had left from the once so proud rocks and mountains.

But the center of the rock still stood like a sand-blasted totem of a stone pillar, eighty feet high. There it had started one day. The strong winds of the storms did not allow the driven sand to slow down on this abrasion and oxidation high polished low stone plateau, with its stone pillar in the center. Just letting the grains of sand skid over the surface, the *erg.* But every time the winds stopped, some sand settled back down, where over the years the sand began to accumulate. When the wind came back, it would pick up some of the grains to move them in a linear way, they bounced back on the harder surface. Then would encounter a patch of sand collected behind the eighty feet stone pillar and the crashed plane. Here, the restless sand ricocheted less and settled down, increasing the heap of sand. This, of course, in much earlier times. And as long the wind was willing to bring sand, like a child on a beach, building his little sand castle, the dune grew until it had reached the high of seventee feet. There, and into this built up sand, the German Messerschmitt had crashed and was buried. Ten feet of rock column were still visible on top of the stippled sand. This was an additional mark.

And that was what drop point '47' was. A star dune. A star dune with six and a half tons of gold and precious metal. They just had landed on it.

Tom and Rosco stood for a moment inside the plane so they would get the feel of what they wanted to do. First they laid out the ten-by-ten-feet strong canvas. Six inches away from each corner of it was a four inches in diameter steel catch securing a hook connected to the four steel cables which at the end were united through a strong oval crampon. One of the men would hook the crampon of the chopper's winch cable. Regardless that the winch could pull 1,765 pounds, they would not overload it, by using only fifty-two percent of the drag capacity. When Tom and Rosco put forty gold bars (a thousand pounds)on the canvas Rachel received the order by short distance walkie-talkie to operate the winch and pull the loot through the open hatch of the plane. The first forty bars were towed from the plane by

23:11, sliding down the slope forced by the momentum of its own weight. The winch dragged the spoil straight through the open clamshell doors into the chopper. Rachel had splashed two gallons of liquid soap onto the ramps surface, increasing the slippery to make it easier for the battery power. Both men follow to unload the canvas in the chopper. The winch and the soap made it virtually effortless to move the metal.

Tom and Rosco worked quick and methodically to set the bars on the canvas and slipped the crampon over the hook of the winch's cable. Back into the chopper loading the heavy bars on the canvas, back to the plane, dragging along the winch cable and the canvas. After the fourth haul gravity let both men experience the first heaviness in their arms. It was a slow down which they could not afford at all. Time was now their only and most valuable asset. Both worked like obsessed. They were getting tired and pearls of sweat run down their faces, crackled between their teeth and made their skin itchy, especially around their crotches. By 0520 Tom and Rosco tumbled away from the emptied plane with the last tow, sliding down into the chopper. They both had not a fiber and strength left. With a soft whining of the hydraulic the clamshell doors closed.

Daylight was coming with a streak of grey along the line were the land and sky once had created the word horizons in the human understanding of describing something. They now would rest for some hours and sleep took over immediately. Rachel watched over them like a wolf over her cubs. Suddenly she felt impulsively restless and sensed something was not really right.

Tamar, my beloved sister
there is danger. the hill
protects you. don't be careless.
Remember, you are in charge. Watch
and warn.

She couldn't fathom what her mind wanted to tell her. Definitely something didn't feel right. Maybe the nerves combined with the emptiness of the desert. Then suddenly while early afternoon had arrived with vigor and vibration of heat, she woke them up. Rachel looked at Tom with badly concealed seriousness. Even Rosco saw it. Mentally both men shrug their shoulders. Everything had gone well and they would take off any time and fly into the day when Rachel was ready. Daylight was their best protection to fly. It would not look suspicious with the Iraqi flag on the fuselage. Deep hanging grey clouds, added to the biting frostiness. A harsh cold wind had come up and blew from the south-west filling the air with an additional chill.

"Have to go for a leak," Tom said and left the chopper. He walked around the hill slightly with his head down, still having on his mind Rachel's mood scale. Something forced him to look up. His body movement froze instantly. Cautiously and without making any hasty move he went slowly, very slowly, down to the ground. There was something.

They hadn't noticed him.

Just one-hundred yards away.

Four men squatted around a bone fire beside a BIT-60PU using the lee side to stay out of the chilly wind. The air carried the sound waves of two idling GAZ-498 engines to his ears. It was a special Russian armored personal carrier with an Iraq insignia on each side. The men warmed their hands over the fire and obviously cooked something. Sitting on a carpet in the shade of the armored carrier, rolling rice with their left hand, were four Iraqis. The carrier's front faced the hill. If the carrier would have parked during the night only fifty feet closer they would have been already detected, perhaps finished off, or worse. The 12.7mm gun pointed aimless into the air. Only thick groups of bushes were between the carrier and the helicopter. Tom could make out with his bare eyes the special antenna on top of it. This meant inside was a generator to power an extra communication system.

This was deadly serious. So, that was on Rachels mind. Bone-cold hungry men do not pay so much attention to their environment and Job as they are supposed to do. Tom opened his zipper and relieved himself by laying on his left side with a close eye on the Iraqis. The winter camouflage protected him well. He pressed his body against the cold ground while he held both his cupped hands like an eye shade over his forehead and soaked the picture in. Was it a good place to have an armed confrontation? The momentum of surprise would be on his and Rosco's side. He heard a noise behind him.

"Rosco," Tom said, without turning around to reduce motions, "don't move. We have five visitors at ten o'clock and an APS." he paused; "we might have to kill 'em."

"No", Rosco said with a firm voice," we will not. Let me handle them. You stay with Rachel. Something goes wrong, take off and proceed. Get your binoculars."

For the first time Tom realized Rosco had taken over the operation somehow. But he felt comfortable with the change. He pulled his binoculars from his left pocket. And Rosco took off. Tom saw Rosco's face and understood the passionate tension in it. It was the face of a man who had to carry out the following movement with the greatest rectitude and swift as possible because the life of others depended on it. It was the dignity of a man who carried out what was unknown to him. Tom saw also the coverage and earnest strength of Rosco's eyes which were full of knowledge and confidence to survive. There was also a sort of noticeable unsteadiness that the upcoming short event might kill him. Before he left Rosco had a last look at his watch. He made a wide circle, moving with the sound of the idling engine. Rosco moved slowly and carefully. It took him ten minutes to reach the carrier. He leaned exhausted against the wheel of the ARP with the heavy Browning 9mm in his both hands. Rosco had his mouth wide open so he would not release the sound of his breathing to the eating soldiers.

He wanted to take his first sip of hot tea to wash the rice down. But Lt. Sahid Malhul put his cup down. He had no idea how to handle this. His chin dropped, leaving the expression of something unthinkable in his face, when he suddenly looked into the visage of a dark haired man with bright blue eye pointing a heavy Browning at him. Attached to the Browning was a silencer. The Iraqi also understood the gesture to go down to his knees and raise his hands. He heard in his own language in a clear but low voice: "*Tecon nakor* (Don't move)". The Iraqi officer wanted to reach for his gun. Then Rosco added on very calmly: "*Tofangeto bendaz zamin Modar sag.*" Which meant in plain English—drop your gun, you son of a bitch. Facing the heavy pistol made the Iraqi think twice. His four men followed his display of concede. He went with his men down on his knees and waited. Fighting was not on the men's mind. Rosco fired a shot into the radio equipment of the carrier, letting some sparks fly. He pulled out his survival skinner knife which was combined with an all-in-one nut wrench. Cutting and wrenching through all the wires and cables he could see inside the ARE, he took the ignition key. Still pointing the Browning at the soldiers he opened the motor compartment and let the blade cuttingly wander through some more cables, well bedded around the motor block. It was a sure thing that this ARE would not move or communicate for a long time. Rosco collected the weapons and left the stunned Iraqis. He seldom had killed in any assignment in the past. He hadn't done it now because immobilizing was much more for effective for its essence. They had two hours lost in their timing.

"Let's get moving," Rosco said with a thin smile when he came back.

Minutes later Rachel started the engines.

22

Invisible in the whirling dust Rachel mindfully raised the chopper to a loftiness of only five feet. The low altitude and the just thrown-in bars of different precious metals made the chopper unstable for a moment because what had happened during the last hours didn't need a qualified pay-load officer. Rachel turned the MI Mil6 slowly around by pointing the nose of the chopper north-west. She handled the sluggishly responding chopper like riding a dinosaur, taking off with six and a half tons of gold and precious metals in its guts.

After a mile or so Rachel shifted the chopper forward with more power. Ten minutes later she reached a river by the name of Hezilsut. Here, at full power, she whirled the chopper for ten minutes along within a cloud of a sort of water-smoke, sucked up from the river's grey undisturbed surface. The river was also the border dividing Turkey from Iraq. She crossed into Turkey and had to scrape along the international boundary to Syria for ten agonizing minutes. But this way Rachel shaved off ten minutes of her total flying time. She flew the helicopter in a nap-of-the-earth technique by skimming the ground, helping her to conceal the MI6 most of the time from radar and perhaps from approaching aircraft. To Tom this flying 'attitude' was an unacceptable hazard. Before the Syrians air defenses got alert, Rachel let the chopper disappear into the valleys of the so-called north-western plateau of Turkey. It was just high ground—spacious swelling steps with some small breaking-up mountains of just eight hundred meters with nothing to grow on. She changed the pitch of the rotor blades and flew now the chopper on silent mode. The thunderous popping sound faded out. The two men and the woman did not let their guard down. Another thirty minutes went by. They could not believe how their luck was holding up and difficulties did not exist. Then Rachel saw the silver strings and lines of the Euphrates river and behind, like an indestructible citadel, the never-ending chain of the Taurus mountains. She winged the chopper closer to the water and got away from the radar side of the Turkish Second Tactical Air Force of Diyarbakir just five miles away.

Later she maneuvered the chopper out of the wadi and let it vanish into coulees of the appearing mountain after they had left the Marmara Sea behind. From now on the chopper would guzzle fuel, moving over mountains sinking into the valleys and raising again over the top of another obstacle of rocky magnitude. The darkness of the ending day had taken over most of the light when they reached the unpaved road north from Siverek. Checking the clock on the dashboard, she saw they made up one hour of the missing time. Tom put the nylon head gear of his MPN-150 night-vision goggle set over his head and scanned the ground. This optical masterpiece was once made in the Soviet Union (top secret) and was now sold to everybody in the world who could afford to spend six-hundred-ninety-nine dollars for this system developed for hunting, boating, and other wide ranges of "professional uses," Odd world.

"See anything?" Rosco asked, hardly hiding his tense nerves.

"Negative," Tom mumbled.

Scanning again.

"Wait," he saw the agreeing blue light flashing somewhere on the ground. "That's it. Rosco, you're ready?" The chopper hovered.

Rosco didn't need a further clarification and swung his Baja waterproof bag over his shoulder. Rachel carefully lowered the chopper another three feet and with a touch of her right hand unlocked the jetisonable door at the port side.

"Now," she yelled," move. Now."

Dust gyrated into the open door.

"Get the fuck out of here. Now!"

Rachel had no seconds or kindness to spare. Rosco hardly saw the ground three feet below. He raised his hand like a short greeting and disappeared by rolling over his left shoulder into the darkness. The whole structure of the chopper shuddered when the metal beast sharply ascended. Rachel moved away and let this flying machine climb immediately over the next four-thousand feet of Taurus Mountains. It was also the first time she looked at the fuel gauge and raised her left eyebrow slightly. Still one hundred miles to meet Berret. This did not include the ups and downs. He saw it. If they . . . . Tom brushed the thought aside.

*

Rosco hit the ground and rolled away. The sound impact of the two Soloviev engines just fourteen feet above had made him nearly deaf for some minutes. He tumbled over small rocks and pebbles to the small blue flashing light. When he reached the car he threw up.

"It's okay pal," Duskin uttered holding the shaking Rosco for a moment, "better we get moving now. Sorry, I couldn't do more. Just relax, man, relax."

He patted Rosco's shoulder.

Both men got into the car and drove into the chilly night. South. By 04:00 they rolled into the small town of Payas at the Gulf of Iskenderun. What Duskin did not know was that the last hours of his life had emerged with the young fresh day. He stopped the car a half mile from the pier. Night still managed the darkness. With an obscure-blue string of promise, upcoming daylight along the horizon was willing to take over the shift of time. Fishermen had already completed their preparation to set forth their boats into the sea for the catch of the day. The lapping soft sound of waves, bouncing against the pier, could be heard between the light chilly morning winds and let the bows of the tied up small fishing vessels perform a gentle dance, releasing crackles of different rubbings against fenders, mooring lines, wood and such. A thousand years ago the fishermen had used the right winds and currents to find the blessings of the sea. Now it was the power of diesel engines, the radar, assisting the over-fishing of the sea for less money they had made years ago. It was a heavy black painted trawler Rosco walked to. He got onboard. Some obscure vibes that were not identifiable went through Duskin. Vibes that he might not see Rosco again. For a moment he had the hallucination that the man was literally absorbed by the dark hull of the trawler, like being soaked up by the shadowy surface.

Actually his mission was completed. As he walked back, a medium-sized but battered car squealed to a halt twenty yards away. Four men got out and as they approached, Duskin got alert and froze. At this early morning there was no traffic at all in both directions. Not so far away was the sound of the sea.

They were all in their twenties, wearing attractive but simple and inoffensive designer clothes. They approached Duskin and pretended to be polite and uninterested. Duskin responded intuitively in the strange environment by being defensive. The whole muscle system of his body tensed involuntarily. He did not know from where they had suddenly come. The first blow over his head echoed through his skull and made him stumble. He collected himself quickly and used the constrained forward momentum of his body to roll over his left shoulder away from the assailants and returned to his feet in a horse stance position. He raised his right knee to his solar plexus to protect the center line of his body. Executed at the same time a right, upper-level knife hand, a *shuto*, which was an inward strike to the jugular vein of his close attacker with the left hand supporting the right elbow. Peter stepped back and created a three-arm-length distance between himself and the second attacker. He saw from his right side the shadow of a man approaching him, when another blow to his head knocked him down again. As he lay on the wet cobble stone, he pulled both his arms behind his neck. His hands reached the handle of the knife positioned between his shoulder blades. He rolled further away (there was no time to get up this interval), and while rolling, he threw the knife.

It flew. Precisely as ever, on its way to hit. The hurled and accelerating dirk went without hesitation through the omo-hyoid of the attacker, slicing, in one cut, through the Thyroid Cartilup and found its first resistance, the tip of knife broke away under the impact, in the second vertebra were the spine ended inside the skull. The attacker stopped in his movement while both hands went up to the handle of the knife, trying to remove this unexpected strange object so suddenly placed into him, from his throat in a cotillion-like movement. His right hand had a waving-like flux into the cool morning air and, hesitating for a moment, caught in a surprise, he fell. The man did two tap dance-like steps, not forward, but left and right, like not being quite certain in which direction he would have to dance. But cousin death had already taken over. The strange thing about the ongoing destruction was that it happened all in silence. The second knife. In an almost casual motion Duskin's right hand felt the bedded blade on his left lower arm and threw it in a short and hard motion at the second attacker when he saw from the side of his right eye an unexpected motion, a silhouette. It was a kick of a foot garbed in soft Italian leather with a steel rim around its sole. The steel rim revealed its dangerous and justified existence in the reflection of some dirty streetlight sending it's blinking, intimidating light to Duskin. He had the feel his head exploded again. Before he went out he noticed with a certain satisfaction that the second attacker was holding his face. He had fallen onto his side and curled up, by holding his destructed face with both hands. The second thrown knife had made a clean and elegant cut across his face making the attacker swallow the blood of his own slashed visage. The man couldn't comprehend the sudden cut through his cheek as his tongue followed the rip, smutty and vulgar, through the wide slash, dangling through the unforeseen crack of his face. For a fresh moment, the attacker looked from one second to the next like a clown with an over-extended smiling mouth. then tumbled away by holding his destructed face. The blood dripped through his cupped hands on his face, slipped on the moist cobblestone, went down to his knees and collapsed. Duskin pulled the third knife (and it would have saved him.) Out of the side of his right eye he glimpsed a shadow. In the last fraction of awareness, Peter Duskin was grateful, that Rosco had already left the port with the dark trawler.

The metals, Duskin thought, the precious metals, for what? Why did he get into it in the first place? The next two heavy blows, one across his face, the other one against his left temple, knocked him out. A third kick threw the knife out of his hand. Duskin did not feel the handcuffs that someone clasped around his wrists. He did not see, nor feel somebody remove his last knife from his right lower arm. He was unconscious when the two men dragged him along the still-dark street and dumped him into the trunk of an old beaten-up car. A piece of invisible shit with a perfect running engine and almost brand new tires. Some days earlier, a similar car had run over a lady by the name of Amanda Maltas in Ankara. The last blow against his left temple had also created a medical problem to all involved. A dilemma nobody had in mind, because they needed his words of admittance.

*

His head, he noticed it was the left side, released a painful pounding. Each single cell of his body signaled agonizing to his brain. Carefully he attempted to open his eyes. He felt they were bruised and swollen. He began to fathom that he with his face on a cold concrete floor. He sensed it was a cell. The chamber delivered only darkness into his mind. The worst thing to him was he did not know where he was. The surroundings were a smell of sweat, urine, human excrement, stale air and the fragrance of seasoned human vomit.

The last frozen screams lingered in the unlit, created by senseless beating, often followed by extinction, had been absorbed by the old wet sand stone walls already days ago. Fear and suffering reeked around this place. He was in a weird stage of being hypersensitive to pick up on it and knew that he was in a room where souls would be broken and raped. No windows. As far as he could see with his half-open eyes, red lines were smudging past him as he tried to gather the stimulus of surviving. He thought he was laying on a dark edge of the cell he was in, to fall over it into an abyss any second. It was a bulky darkness. His mouth felt dry. He moved the tip of his tongue around his lips. Split, dry and swollen. His mind observed in an ambience of curiosity that they were crusted with blood.

He was occupied with himself exploring the damages done to him, when a naked brutal light with two-hundred watts came painfully into existence. The strong beam of light was released from a simple office lamp, turned and aimed in the direction were his face was. Pain shot up from every direction. The abrupt brightness hurt his harmed eyes. He moaned and rolled in a protective motion on his stomach. Four powerful hands raised him from the floor and slammed him into a chair. Duskin counted the four pressures. The light beam did not stop hurting his eyes. He turned his head a bit. It was just five feet away. The brightness felt so flaming on him that everything around was a total darkness. The sharp pain in his head returned, pounding in the same cadence as his heart. He felt something was broken in his head and he passed out. The first thing he realized when he woke up again was that he could not move, because his body was strapped with heavy leather strings against the chair. He trembled because it was cold and dark. He still felt his mouth was dry, and the pounding headache made him unable to focus on where he was. He could hear someone stepped over to legs. Fingers pressed behind his ears and unconsciously he opened his mouth. Somebody forced water into it. He had to swallow not to be suffocated by the forced fluid. He could feel the soft tickling of some sweat running down his forehead and swallowed desperately, sucking air at the same time to survive. Then it stopped. A long energy—sucking silence appeared on the door steps of his soul, belonging to nobody. First he thought he was dead. *It* was just there (*what ever it was)* in this dark and bright room, waiting to be lifted or to put down. The lethargic calmness was interrupted by the sudden short clack of a cigarette lighter to inflame something. Smell followed. It was the scent of an aromatic cigarette smoke. Serenity again.

"I come from the Government," a very calm voice with a heavy southern accent said, "how are you Mister Duskin?"

The speaking appeared in a flat mechanical tone. It was a voice which was expressionless. A voice saying nothing. It was a voice with a shapeless face containing nothing. A voice which was not being comprehended for what it was saying.

Peter Duskin listened, but he could not hear. When he heard he could not listen. The man in possession of this accent had used the I-come-from-the-government threat successfully some days earlier when he had a conversation with a lady by the name of Amanda Maltas. Francis Walkers assumed the intimidation would work also this time. Like always and with the same easiness. Duskin raised his head like a deaf animal and tried to open his bruised eyes. *Now* he noticed he was tied up to the chair.

"You know," the southern dialect went on; "you have killed one of their men with a knife. The other guy's face is gone. You are good with knives. We know that." Duskin heard an understanding pretending sighing.

"They called *us*. Listen, and listen very carefully what I have to say. They gave me thirty minutes to talk to you to find out what is going on. You know why?" There was a pause for affection, "They like to keep a low profile."

An audible smoke-exhaling pause came up, created by Walker's invisible curled lips.

"Let me untangle something. You are in the hands of JITEM, the Gendarme Intelligence and Counter Terrorism of Turkey. See, not even their own legislature knows about them and *we*" (Walkers liked the 'we' as a tool of threat) "did not have a clue either that they existed, until now. You see, there seems to be a problem in this country and you might be a part of it. You might. So, please," southern slang had now the tone of a first grade teacher's voice, "you just answer some questions I have on my mind and you go home. Ciao. Sayonara. Dosvidanya. Auf Wiedersehen. Free. Okay?"

Walker waited for a response. There was none from the man tied up in the chair.

"Or you can have it the other way. The hard one. *They* will talk to you. And this, I can assure you, will be very unpleasant. They know how to create pain. They are masters. Now, here are my questions. What were you doing in Iskenderun at the Mediterranean this very early morning? Where are Tom Peters and Rachel? Why did you and Rosco come to Turkey?"

Again, the long pause, filled with questions, was only interrupted by gentle exhaling, disengaging the inhaled aromatic smoke from Walker's lungs, sinking blue-grayish into the beam of light. There was a long, almost palpable, pause.

Duskin listened very carefully (he considered now his maimed face as a blessing because it was not readable any longer) and had noticed the orator of the southern accent's give-away without knowing it. Duskin knew the voice and knew who he was! But important to him—they had not seen Rosco in the harbor entering the black painted trawler.

"What do you think?" southern dialect asked. Then Walker was stunned when he heard his name.

"What are you saying, Francis?" Duskin asked through his split lips.

"I am telling you not to be a hero, Peter," Walker, doing his best to keep things in balance, because of his sudden disclosure, countered and hoped for a moment it would make now things easier.

"What do you want from me, for God's sake?"

Duskin began to lose the first stratum of outer reality. "Look, I am here as a tourist and some motherfuckers walk up to me and I was mugged. Ask yourself whether I had the right to defend myself. I don't know what YOU are talking about."

Walker inhaled deeply the next drag from his Dunhill Blue.

Somehow the man was right, when he heard, "there is nothing more I can say, not until somebody has a court order and I get a lawyer. And you bet it is better you tell me my rights to contact the embassy."

"Christ, you might not understand something. There will be no lawyer or embassy. We (the 'we' again) just want to know. Talk, man."

The Turkish interrogator got uneasy observing that both men might know each other. He interrupted with his heavily accented English.

"Weee just want to know, whyyy you weeere in Iskenderun."

Walker looked at his watch. Five more minutes were left before he had to leave Duskin. His mind was crowded suddenly. The power of silence returned. Minutes went by. Unused on both sides. Walker felt a tap on his shoulder.

"We take it from here," somebody else said. Francis Walker hesitated in his movement when he had to leave the room. And before the door closed behind him he could hear the first sickening blow. The new interrogator was lost in his ego-driven power and created a scenario of questions AND answers that moved away from reality, and the pain-created perjury was accepted as truth on both sides. The beating did not help. What bothered Duskin was, and it frightened him, he could hear the beating, but he could not feel it. It was not painful—it was like he could see the punishment he received, but not being a part off it. He could hear the crunchy sound of the soft bones splitting in his head. Somewhere in his body fragmented bones moved in different directions. And in a flourishing throb of his blood he heard, Duskin fainted and then emerged again. It was a painless pain in his head. His mind and sensors were far beyond recognizing pain.

All in a few crystalline seconds, he wondered how long his body could go on like this. His temples vibrated in numbness while his intellect reeled between being awake and deferred. And the compensated time of his now outrunning life flew by with all the beauty from the past and somehow he was grateful that his torturers did not know this and could not realize the grace of his upcoming death, which began to wrap kindly and compassionated around him. The final countdown of his soul's escape from earth began. It surprised

Peter Duskin somehow when he heard a faint whirring sound indicating to him and he only understood it in this stage of life, to start again. Then he awoke from the dream momentarily for a brief relief from the dread that he felt he was in. Immediately, he fell back into a drowsy dream. He heard himself saying in the dream that there was no need to finish the dream to see the end of the tale, because he could escape it if he wanted to. He felt a clear comprehending that the choice to die was his. It was up to him. And Peter Duskin wanted to die. His left hand moved along the cool concrete floor. He felt the moisture and was not absolutely certain whether it was his own blood or the dampness of the floor. He felt relaxed because he knew his life was coming to an end. Carefully he relocated his body to a new cool spot on the floor and in a more comfortable site, like a feeble, shot animal in the wilderness. The last blow to his head had expanded the crack he had in his skull since he was carried away in Iskenderun. But his consciousness functioned clearly and he knew it was a question of seconds before he would move on to eternity. The treasure. Was it a curse? Was it worth it? Somehow he was not surprised about the outcome. His face grimaced into a sort of smile. Gosh, was he tired. He felt nauseated and dizzy. If he would try to move, he would feel paralyzed und moved his body again. He was Flustered by his response to the upcoming death. A small gush of pain rushed from his head through his body, down to his toes. He felt some hot sweat running down his forehead.

Man is a political animal. He had seen the agony on the visages of human beings disciplined to war and senseless fighting, despotism of parties, and therefore the denial of human basic ethics. Peter smiled ever so slightly, vaguely victorious, and then mechanically shrug his shoulder. The coolness of the concrete floor nurtured gently his neck like the gods had decided to ease his progressing demise. All the years Peter Dusking knew that an intense death could have been a very genuine choice to retirement in his line of work. Security. For whom? For some beings concerned about their material possessions and importance? He moved his body again and moaned, but it interfered with his thinking only for a vanishing moment. By facing death he was now honest with himself. To die, he had envisioned pain, perhaps even fear. Possibly, a sort of self-pity, when it would come to his end. A sort of dignity accompanied him on his way out. He opened his eyes as best he could and stared unfocused into the darkness while his mind brought him to the edge of perpetualness. How long had he been there on this cool concrete floor? A cozy loneliness of his death overcame him. But it did not matter anymore. He was on his way to separate his body from his soul and any fear and pain retreated from his being. The soul part really mattered to him somehow. He finally began to reject his survival and his death was just a temporary continuation of his chemical body household. His vanishing mind began to signal in an unceremoniously way the supreme and perfect end. Perhaps there was still some time left he could figure out who he really was and what he really wanted from life. In the last fractions of life Dusking's thoughts still worked surprisingly sharp and rational. He thought about that his character in his own dream was hidden in the background of his mind and . . . extinction took over his body in serene and delicate swells. He felt a light nobody could see and take away from him. Where was mother at the moment? Peter Duskin felt that his last physical strength began to leave him. Also his willingness to live began to suffocate his system. Born alone. And he died. He escaped into the gyrating shaft of light nobody could see.

23

Anatolia, Turkey, December

Slowly, steady and carefully, the puzzles of time were falling into place. Traffic along E-49 east was thinning out. Relaxation intercepted the country, preparing for the upcoming holidays. *After* Saturday and Sunday, a three-day national holiday, the *Seker Bayrami* began. Flexible holidays with dates moving forward by twelve days each year on the Gregorian Calendar. Actually it was three days of Muslim holiday series of sorts, and was called the Candy Festival. During these days, special sweets were eaten to honor the end of Ramadan's fast. It even got better. This year the Gregorian Calendar and tradition had moved the Candy Festival immediately behind another holiday, New Year. Shops were closed up, so there was no service. A country in slow motion for five long days.

It was cold.

Two-hundred-fifty miles southeast from Ankara, Berret shifted the reefer in question into the fifth gear and accelerated. He took the exit into E-88 east and turned into the main asphalt road *(ana asfalt yollar, according to the map of the Turkey Directorate of Information)*, and that is all he had, to Kirsehir. He slowed to fifty-five, reached the six-mile stretch of the highway along the town and made an elegant east turn to Mucur. The reefer moved for twelve miles through the rolling, snow-covered hills, passing some villagers with their mule-drawn wagons painted and laced with decorations of garlands in red and pink, on this crisp early evening. The sky's color was a smell of snow, filled with the promise to deliver.

After the twelve miles he slowed to thirty-five making a straight dash along the panoramic unpaved road to Nevsehir. Empty land, covered with a thin envelope of previous snowing. No traffic. The land began to change into stone wilderness. There, where he wanted to be, and had to be.

In the stone tundra. The evening released the remainders of daylight very quickly from its liability, changing its colors rapidly to a touch of being darker. Sharp blankets of cold air wrestled with the arrival of evening. Five-foot cushions of low icy fog flowed along the valley and disappeared along the road. Nevertheless, the merciless drive and the search began to take its toll on Berret and the lateness of the hour did not feed him with enough energy to take in the beauty of the surroundings.

*

Cappadocia.

Highlands of Anatolia.

It was a surreal tableau stretching through canyons and elevations along in velvety tones of ashen-gray, terra-cotta pink and dark yellow. Tuff, made from soft volcanic rock. The winds and rains of the millennia had sculptured the tuff into columns like obelisks and cone-shaped figures, all along the wild horizons. Soft huge lumps and swellings mixed up with curving ribs of soft smooth stone.

Time, the impression could not be ignored, had come to an unabridged standstill here. With no trees in sight, the voluptuous topography of the terra incognita made the sphere naked, rustic, and untamed shameless. Rocks, soft wild rocks had come to live here, when three million years ago, the volcano Mount Erciyes had erupted at once and the ashes were transformed into a stratum of soft porous rocks, also called tufa. Magma filled with huge gas bubbles froze in bizarre forms, leaving it also with immense chambers and stretches.

There were no trees or shade to hide the reefer in the light of the sure-coming next morning, maybe telling Berret—*hey, you idiot, you lonesome loony—what are you doing here in this cold uninhabited land? And why did you bring this witless rig along?*

He did his best not to listen to the chant of discouragement.

In the light, left still workable for the eyes, crests and cliffs began to show up in a series of cathedral-like sculptured minarets.

Five minutes later, the last indication of light disappeared. The land began to look shadowy. The cold wind blew from the north and delivered dark clouds. Looking darker than the overtaking night, pregnant with snow, letting everybody know, the final but cold part of the year had arrived and the really harsh part of the season was on its way and just around the corner.

Five miles down the road, the sky decided to let some snowflakes fall for the night, just warming up for the cold season to come, and began waving another gentle blanket of white over the area. He liked it. His luck was holding up. No traffic. Blessed be the holy days. It was a wild and strange stony land. History here was old and wise.

Cappadocia.

Being located on the crossroads between east and west in the highlands of Anatolia, it functioned since men began to trade outside their own status quo, as a stop-over for the caravans with their precious goods from Arabia along the Silk Road to Persia, India and China two thousand years ago. So, the inhabitants of Cappadocia had prospered but they also had to wait, to a great extent, with the looting and greed of foreign political overlords and armies of the Assyrians, Persians, the Greeks from Macedonia, and, yes, Rome didn't want to miss out with its legions. Then the Crusaders came with their swords, pretending to free the land and make it holy.

Nobody ever got a nickel. Not a square inch of silk, or an ounce of precious metal. Gold, silver, or such. None. Zip. Zero. The soldiers of so many foreign armies only stood there and rested in the valley, gazing stunned up to the cities so close to be taken and yet never reachable. In the rocks far up, stone carved houses beamed down in their timeless strong formula of survival, high up, just sitting there. Not even the skilled engineers of the Roman legions with their splendid knowledge of war technique, who had broken the gates of many lands, could come up with a concept how to conquer those soft rocks, the tuff, which actually, would not have withstood the swat of a battle axe or iron-covered club.

To be safe, the people of Cappadocia had carved and hacked their houses, comfortable, fine warm dwellings, far up in the very soft rocks (a single skilled man could chop out a 3,000-cubic-feet room in just a month). They only could be reached by ladders that could be quickly drawn up, when armed hordes of a foreign country showed came to their gates for ransacking and what politicians already loved to call at this time, pacifying. The domes and strange chapel-like sculptured rocks had allowed the beings living here to carve their shelters into the protective boulder, like untouchable pariahs.

But they did not stop there and went to an even more spacious shielding system. Cities were dug underground.

First, they excavated downward until the life-important water was hit. From then on, they started to expand horizontally. These secret cities in the valley of Goreme were cleverly masterminded to support up to twenty-thousand people, *including* warehouses for food, herds of cattle, water wells, and even air cavities, also to be used as speaking pipes between the underground assemblies. Some of the underground cities even had two storage layouts. The upper level would shelter community kitchens with areas to eat, with wine cellars, stables, rest rooms and such. The lower story was the real hide-out. There were the armories and the chapels, the prisons, and the burial places, the meeting halls and churches, the size of huge cathedrals.

Some stretches of natural caves with incredible lengths of 5 miles, only slightly reshaped by human hands, had been smoothed and functioned as underground streets, or escape routes. The first chapels, churches, and monasteries were already carved during the fourth and eleventh century. In short, invisible towns were carried in the mountain's gut, acting like a mother-animal. What had made these underground cities so comfortable was that no bats, lizards or insects could live there.

Another aspect.

All these once-secret places were abandoned in the course of history, presenting to amazed tourists centuries later the life and survival skills of the past.

And as the last millennium had come to an end, only *thirty-six* of such underground cities were known to the world and more would be discovered in the years to come.

*

Snow was falling more intense as he drove another five miles. He passed Urgup and went south for precisely fifteen miles when he saw for the first time in the last light the day was willing to deplete, the mountain. The rock. He counted mentally to thirty as requested and left the street with a sharp right turn. Here the surface of the street was lowered to a point of having no embankment. It was the only sixty-five-feet stretch without it. A gentle blanket of snow would cover soon the tire prints of the rig.

Berret saw the huge plateau with its bizarre formed towers of cathedral weathered edges, mixed with wind-carved forms, guarding. He stopped, cut the light and strapped over his head an MPK 35k-I infra-red goggles. Started the engine and rumbled for another twenty minutes or so, first gear in place, for several miles.

Navigated the rig uphill to where the rock's foundation began. Berret felt like being on another planet with the green appearing infra-red picture taken in by his eyes. He had the map memorized.

Here his driveway ended.

Some master masons of the past had built an aerie from stones, which blended their work sumptuous with the rock. The aerie had made things behind it invisible for centuries. It covered completely a hole in the rock to the outside world. It was the beginning *of a cave.* He moved again and the reefer provided him willingly with a sharp left turn, stopped for a moment and took a deep breath. He did not feel the beat of his heart anymore. Then he drove on into a grim darkness.

The green visibility of the goggles made it like a move into non-existence. After one mile or so, it was scraped and carved by humans. It was a tunnel. From somewhere, from a long time ago, then forgotten and not discovered *yet* to the world to come. His thinking acted abstractly as the walls of the tunnel in their enormity moved along (he came to see it this way). He felt the gentle slope downward. Minutes went by and the right wall disappeared. He stopped and cut the engine, listening and waited. Took the *Lorcin* pistol from the underside of his seat and pocketed the two spare clips, shoving the pistol in his belt.

When the sounds and cracking of the cooling-down engine had disappeared into the darkness, impeccable silence took over. He listened until his ears adjusted to a not so far echoing noise of water drops falling into a pond. Soft waves of fear appeared on his mental doorstep and he wished almost to be dead. Or at least he would be back somewhere on Highway 10 in Arizona. He did not know were he was or what his environment looked like. Looked senseless at his time releasing watch. But it was like his mind was detached and executed two different performances the same time. The two glowing hands of the watch got only as far as his eyes. It was eleven anyway. Night. There were symptoms of a sort of jetlag inside him. But his body system could not regulate the pulse, involving his sleep-wake cycle. He had been right on time. He had to wait for another two days, perhaps three. But work had to be done the next morning (would he recognize it as a day)? He shivered a bit pretending he was cold.

The invisible dropping water got a bit on his nerves (like a Chinese water torture) as he listened for another hour into the silence of darkness for strange noises, perhaps indicating approach and hostility. There was none. He pulled out two wool blankets and prepared his bed in the cabin. The fear as an expression of loneliness and being buried wavered around him. He crawled under the blankets and hugged himself as he curled up in a fetal position. Sleep would not come easily. He dawdled off.

24

Fon Yun woke up from his meditation and his eyes viewed the new date on a calendar across the wall. Two more days. He could hear the sound of the relaxing, murmuring waves of the Mediterranean.

*

General Ephraim Katz was deeply asleep when the telephone rang. The message was short and no name referred to it. All was right on schedule.

*

The next morning. In disbelief, carefully angling his head back, Mark Berret looked at the opening in the 80-feet-high ceiling, shaped like a dome. It was the natural grace and elegance of a Gothic cathedral exquisitely stretching its proportions with striking simplicity of a Bruno Leask, the Italians master architect of the 15th century. The opening in the ceiling in its diameter of 138 feet was the beginning of enormous shaft straight up to the outside world 150 feet above, allowing the glittering sunlight to stream down like cascades of bright light into the cave, creating a radiant dance of it, reflected back from the walls with a soft light brown glow. Now he understood. Rachel would sink the chopper through this shaft. Berret was numb for a moment.

"My God," he mumbled, battling against some upcoming apprehension, as he looked up. His eyes roamed through the cave. Along the floor and back to the walls the corneas of his eyeballs did their best to soak the place in, trying to introduce him to his odd environment. Along the wall were long tables and benches carved out from the stone, as the enormous room itself rose from the floor. Water dripped from a small overhang of the wall into a pond filled with clear water (suddenly he understood the sound of the night). The dimensions and construction of this unknown place was beyond his comprehension. His eyes just took it in to let him deal with it later.

He went back to the rig and maneuvered it out of sight. He brought out a toolbox. Again he looked up to the ceiling and the shaft of light. Still in disbelief he shook his head. Opened the back doors of the refrigerating container. Slowly and methodically he began.

The reefer had a 'flow-through-air-distribution" structure. When normally traveling along the road with meat, fruits or such, things would to be cooled down by five fans installed on each side of the ceiling. The fans would pick up the warm air from the outside at ceiling level, push it down and guided it inside the airspace between the guard wall and the outer wall of the reef. The air would then flow across some evaporation coils cooling the air down. Continuing its flow along the side walls being squeezed into an airspace 1 ? inch wide, to be discharged at the floor level where the gutter was. The floor, having its own space, was cross-ventilated and allowed the air to gush away from the sidewalls to the center.

Berret began to mark the internal panels with a Sanford Sharpie fine point permanent marker at the upper left corner, so he would know later their precise positioning. Opening the toolbox he took out a Makita 3/8 inche Corellers operated with a keyless chuck. Took the four slotted three Phillips screwdriver and inserted it into the fling. He had three sets of twelve-volt power batteries as spares. Wrapped the Makita into a piece of high density foam to reduce the noise. Each single 1/8 inch Phillips screw undone was mindfully placed into a the two-by-three compartment of the dark blue toolbox. After each unscrewing he paused and listened. The noise would absorb hostile incoming sound. There was none. He only heard the pounding of his heart and the dripping of the water.

He removed the unscrewed floor panels, took them outside the reefer and lined them up against the rocky wall, according to the numbers he had written on it. The removed panels revealed the ventilation space created by the framing of the trailer with its galvanized evaporator coils, connected to the pipe system. The pipe system allowed the compressed ammonia to flow and to be (in its compressed form) cooled off in the system. Berret loosened the fittings on both sides between the coils and pipe with a wrench and removed them, took a heavy cutter and clipped the ?-inch copper pipes away just above the framing of the reefer and down at the gutter. He had three inches of space now, all the way around. All needed. All available. Suddenly the light was gone and with it the day was over . . .

*

The third day. He had nothing to do in the darkness and silence. This pure-cave-silence with its water dripping had gotten more and more on his nervous system. It was about time that night appeared again. Or as he saw it, the big hand of his watch had circled eight times to signal rest. Berret's entire system, still intact, was stretched while he listened into the dark calmness. The worst part was that his eyes had not seen for days the first rosy clouds and rays of bluish dawn, nurturing him with the beauty of a new day.

The light.

He had always seen it in Arizona, this never-ending blue sky with a patch of a cloud here and there. He missed the intense light of the sun. The constant change between the dim light (during the day from the shaft) and darkness had interrupted the flow of his biological schedule.

For example, a drop of Melatonin in his system would have told him that morning had arrived, and his body chemistry would not have to struggle with the adjustment to the timelessness of the cave and his mental stand still. He sat on the floor with his head leaning against the wall, the gun beside him on the floor. The bleakness and constant tranquility with its water-dropping background worked steadily, like it wanted to deteriorate his mind set.

Mark Berret thought about his wealth.

He was a rich man now. It astonished him somehow. He envisioned the next step, after Rachel and Tom would arrive, loading the treasure onboard, almost casually, knowing that with his chunk of the treasure he would be free to go anywhere and whenever he was pleased to. He would not feel inadequate any more. He would stand above the rest. The hoards, the rabble, the riffraff. Fame would be now the name of his life. From now on he would wine and dine with the world of splendid. He would be interviewed. Perhaps he would be invited by kings. Or he would invite them and would marry a Duchess. Or at least have a write-up in *Vanity Fair* about his wealth.

He would settle down. He, Mark Berret, had reached the final crossroad of his life. Never being really home because of the lost years of childhood plus the assignments when he was with the Special Forces, or something he could call home—this form of life had not assisted him to create this kind of personal geography inside him, what most people have.

It didn't matter anymore because noble fine living waited for him. The future? Wide open. The sky would be his. *They should be here by now.*

He was afraid his mind could be overrun by an unknown force inside him.

Something inside him prodded his mind to look in the direction where the truck was parked in the dark. Mark Berret took his strong flashlight and sent the beam of light across to the truck. It told him it was not positioned right. The position was *wrong*. He took the flashlight and went over to check.

It was not right.

It did not feel right.
Got into the truck and started the engine.

Inched it away from where it was placed and now strongly felt, that it should not be there for whatever reasons. Maneuvered forward and reverse again. Forward and reverse again. The air brakes were hissing in disagreement. Had to be careful with the air. Jackknifed a little bit. After five minutes he had the truck at the opposite of the cave, straightened it out with the tractor facing the exit. Then he moved the panels.

Rachel, Tom and the chopper.
Where the hell were they anyway!
They should be here by now!!

His rage began to ripen. He just lay there with a festering soul in the rising spiral of disbelief. His mind poured out more irrational thoughts and uncontrollable anger intercepted his logical thinking.

Perhaps they all cheated you out of your wealth, his mind whispered. Those bastards. Those greedy unreliable scavengers. Or they just simply screwed up somewhere along the line. They really had thought this through to cut him out from his part of the deal. Or they just screwed up. He called them all the names available in the dictionary of obscenity. Like Linda, his wife. Couldn't wait to get laid by the ass-tattooed neighbor. Perhaps she had laughed her head off about his stupidity to fight some other country's stupid drug war. The beam of his mind's radar searched the past. Who else to blame for the full barrel of shit he was sitting in? He went over his mental notebook. His thoughts became blurred and incoherent.

Oh yes, here. Like his mother.

She had not moved her butt for years to find a job. Just hanging around the welfare office with her whining voice to get food stamps and the vouchers to get vegetables in a Farmers Market. Who did she think she was? Taking the little money he made as a busboy in some penurious Mexican restaurant in Galt, California. This three-pack-a-day smoking fat-assed bitch, started drinking the cheap and on sale wines in the afternoon.

His anger, bubbling inside him, was irrational and contaminated his clearheaded thinking and reasoning. The loneliness had now gotten to him.

It might be better to get out of the whole thing right now. All the give-up reasons he could imagine, initiated to intercept his mind.

Too bad, he was here in this cave. He had to make it back somehow. He just was getting started with the plan of how to leave the cave and this whole area without too much endeavor and without the rig. Sure, he might have to walk a couple of miles through the snow and the cold. It would be in his best interest to get out. His passport was okay and he had a ticket and . . .

Suddenly.

A something-from-far-away sound.

Hollow.

It had wandered down the shaft for a moment and disappeared.

Then it came back. Making his membrana tympani digest some sound vibrations, forwarding the message to his brain. First he wouldn't accept it. He couldn't believe it. This indisputable clatter combined with the popping clear sound was the signature of fast milling rotor blades. The sound he knew so well from missions he had completed and survived in some countries along the equator. The second round of sound waves bounced against the walls, grasped greedily by his nerve syllabus. Making his drums quiver, signaling the sound of something he had waited for so long and desperately.

No qualm. A helicopter.

First he grinned. Then he began to chuckle.

Actually, Linda was always a good sport. His mother was not that bad after all. Yes, she smoked like a chimney and drank herself stupid. But what the heck, she was his mother, he admitted. Tom and Rachel were great people. He knew it all along. They would not let him down. They were too good to screw things up.

Berret got out of his giving-up state of mind and moved fast to the center of the cave. It was also the midpoint, extending the invisible line, of the ray. He ignited the eight red flares, as he was supposed to do, and set them around crosswise and in a circle on the floor bellow the shaft. The gentle red little fires began to glow. Seen from far above they created the visual impression of a red glowing hole in the mountains. He had done his part. Nothing else that he could add anymore.

*

Daylight was now completely gone and handed time over to night. Rachel navigated the chopper between the mountains and valleys in the pitch-dark night keeping the gross weight of flying forty-five tons close to the ground, masking the moving chopper from radar detection. She drove the chopper into the Urfa Plateau by using the profile of the Guneydogu mountain and was leading the metal beast into the valley where the Yeniu river was stirring south. They were close. She would not miss the 3919 feet Eriygas Dagi rising sharp and proud there. She knew wearing night-vision goggles made the piloting more difficult since the goggles made things closer than they were, because they restricted the peripheral vision. She moved the helicopter another ten miles between the mountains. Snuggled it against the slopes of the rocky terra incognita.

The forward-looking infra-red sensor projected on the moving displays map the position precisely. The rock was now only four miles away. The slightest mistake and it would all be over in fire-balling seconds. She consulted the instruments and had a very thoughtful look at the fuel gauge. Enough to keep the MIL Mi6 for another fifteen minutes or so in the air.

"One more click," Tom said without believing it, watching the display map of the rock they approached. Rachel eased the control stick back to reduce the velocity. Her right hand reached over to Tom. They hovered for a moment five feet above the ground. She squeezed his hand gently and did her best not to look at him, focusing on the flight pattern. He glanced at her and when he saw the fine contour of her face in the reflection of the greenish instrument lights, he was aware of how much he loved her. Both felt the dance-like exchange of the energy between them. They would go together to the end. He wished they would die in the same instant.

Softly and carefully she withdraw her hand but stayed with him emotionally. The energy of her love just spilled over to him. Being with her was like resting in each other.

"I love you too, paramour," she said as she removed her hand from the seconds of tenderness. The unspoken understanding that they would carry it along to new dimensions in case something would go wrong.

And even if . . . it would have meant their time here on earth was up. They both did not believe in 'luck.' For them this statement was the lazy and handy way of avoiding the confidence of being guided, an area most beings were not willing to accept or explore. Rachel and Tom were explorers. Searching life together had taken away from both of them some time ago the belief of chance, luck and so-called accidents, and therefore concerns were replaced with whatever phenomena had removed them, with the joy of living the moment. In their growth together Rachel, the Indian, had taught him to understand that death was just a visitation of some sort in the everlasting life-survival concept. And it wouldn't't stop afterward. He began to believe it.

The infra-red sensor painted the image of an unknown heat source on top of the rock closely shown on the display map. Tom reached for the 'Magellan,' and switched on the GPS. Knowing the precise location was an essential part of their operation. The edge-mounted antenna rotated skyward and by pressing the POS button the cellular phone-like unit started the position-finding procedure. It took only seconds and the receiver displayed the precise location where they were. It began to update the reading every second. Tom pressed the WPT button, allowing him to read the coordinates for the waypoints, the checkpoints en route to the destination they had in mind. He got the reading.

Next he pressed TARGET, followed by the distance he read in combination of the laser range finder. Missing the preferred pinpoint in the rocky landscape by only a few yards could leave him and Rachel with the chopper not only stranded—even worse.

GPS was a panacea, an arrangement of navigation satellites that told Tom the precise location through this hand-held receiver. It pinpointed its target and precise coordinates. He pushed SETUP to adjust the unit for the new territory. They were right on target.

"There it is," Tom said, looking at her again. But it was from one second to the next like he looked at a strange appearance of one of her ancestors advised with something by something through something. Rachel felt the shift and tried to understand her senses being suddenly directed in a way she had no influence or control over it. Any tense muscle in her body, any high-strung thought began to vanish. She pulled up the collective control and let the MIL Mi6 climb in a slow and cautious move to the top of the rock just keeping ten feet of distance from the slope of it.

The time of venerable bareness had come. Minimizing radar detection by training she kept the chopper close the shape of the rock. The chopper reached the top.

The crater.

The beginning of the shaft.

It began with a wide opening. The crater was formed like a cone. From the top to the shaft reducing its diameter. Some remote indication of a matt weak red was released from down somewhere. She let the chopper slip over the edge into the shaft, like she had done it years ago during a NATO maneuver, and sank it twenty feet into it. Eased the collective control down.

Gently, very gently. Hovered. Switch. Bargained a move of her left hand for the two powerful search lights to be turned on. One of the adjusted lights of bright controlling supremacy shone downward. The second light shot its radiation straight against the wall of the shaft narrating the assumed crude visible distance left between them and the wall.

Not much space to play with, you two weirdos, that's what was reflected back to Tom and Rachel. She calibrated carefully the pedals to set the pitch of the tail rotor blades generating enough thrust to hold the one-hundred-eight feet long fuselage steady. Meager sixteen feet on each side of the one-hundred-fourteen foot wide rotor. Adjusted the rotor blades to some negative pitch. The descent, the final approach of a gross weight of thirty-three and a quarter tons began. For Tom, a monstrosity of time-stretch launched in his mind. Seconds bombarded his mind, culminating each of this measure of time into hours. He did not dare to look outside or even down. The lightened wall in front of him did not stop rising and he could not imagine where Rachel took the energy and coolness.

He was sweating all over his body. His face was wet and a drop of sweat dangled on his left eyebrow. He wiped it off with his left hand. The chopper shook when the strong upward chimney effect of the shaft and the rotor blades as a streaming force responded to it.

A twinkle of a frolic. Not much.

But it threw the chopper out of its descent course and rotor blade number five came in touch with the rock. Screeching along and leaving scars in the soft stone accompanied by a shower of sparks. Adding on additional high decibels to the sound inferno of the two Soloviev turbines and the rotors. The MIL tumbled and rotor blade one banged against the wall. Sparks flew. A hard rock, like granite, would have finished the chopper already off. Time began to be meaningless to both of them. Rachel looked at the fuel gauge. Zero. Try tanks. When would the engine stop? The never-ending wall of the shaft disappeared. They had reached the cave. After twenty more feet downward they saw the eight red flares absorbed by the burning eyes, acting like a signal from heavens. Another now easy sixty feet to go.

Tom thoughts just began to formulate it when the engines began to stutter. Rachel switched quickly to battery power to keep the lights going. Then the engines flamed out. She let it go. Nothing left to do. It seemed like the momentum of the still-spinning rotor softened the beginning free fall.

*

Berret watched in astonishment the appearance of the huge stumbling chopper into the cave. Than the engine went dead.

Shit, not now. Please.

No.

NO!!!.

Berret believed even as he had screamed the 'no' because the abyss of sound chaos was just too overwhelming, increased by the reflection of the walls. He absorbed the shade of the dark slow whirling blades mirrored in the red light of the flares as a millionth-of-a-second-flash of light. Like in a stroboscope, lines of pictures of a periodical event could be observed at the same time from different corners.

He screamed again without hearing himself. It was a mental survival struggle for him. He screamed (he didn't even know why anymore) and five torturing seconds later thirty-three tons of gross-weight helicopter impacted with the floor, computing to the Hades around him additional senselessness. It collided heavily with the ground were the truck had been fifteen minutes earlier. The extremely strong landing gears collapsed like matchsticks. Shorn off was the once-so-supportive left wing like a piece of cardboard. The searchlights went dead.

Knowing his environment well, Berret raced through the darkness for the tunnel and for safety. Sound of breaking away segments of fuselage and metal yowled. He remembered he had once listened to a tape of a submarine breaking up. Exactly the same. The still pivoting rotor blades, three of them, hit the ground, lifting in a slow motion the enormous fuselage up again like a huge dying animal. Then it fell back slowly and skittered across the cave in a phlegmatic motion and came to a screeching rest, bending heavily to the left against the wall. The two rear clamshell doors broke open and splattered bars of gold, platinum, iridium, and all those other metals with such fine names over the ground. The resulting silence was unreal. Only cracking little break-up noises from the hot engine avoided a dead silence. Berret backed up further, expecting every second that the whole chopper would blow up. But nothing happened. It was all too much.

He went down on his knees and began to cry. He couldn't synchronizes his mind. Holding his face with both hands and moaning. He crawled into a corner. They were dead. Tom and Rachel were dead.

It was all over. He whimpered uncontrollably because the silence had returned without sympathy to him. How much time had gone by?

"Berret!"

Echo bounced back his name.

Somebody had called him by his name.

"Berret!" a female voice shouted.

He moved his head in the darkness like a chased animal and listened with wide open mouth. If seen, his eyes would have shown the beginning of a deranged mind.

'Did somebody call my name?'

He raised his head like a stressed-out animal hearing its master's voice.

"Berret, where the hell are you?"

"Here," he whispered.

"Here," his voice got louder and stronger.

"Here!" he screamed and got up to his knees. He got up to his feet and stumbled across the cave towards the voice. In the dim light of the red flares he saw the shadow of a human being approaching him. Then he felt arms around him, holding him. It was female. The gentle touch took his fears of loneliness away.

"It's okay. It's okay now," Rachel said with a soft shaking articulation. After all the silence and the broken down hopes, the voice was like music. Like an uncomposed chant he had heard once from an Indian warrior in New Mexico, a sage. How strong she was. She had just survived a crash and nurtured him already. Only a woman, a strong woman, could do this.

The Major followed Rachel and swept his eyes in the faded light over Berret's face. He saw that the man had reached his limits. A day longer and Berret would have gone insane in the darkness. Tom had seen eyes with this kind jaggedness in men before when they were picked up after a mission.

Rachel still stroked gently Berret's arm. The Major waited four-hundred heartbeats, an appraised five minutes, before he said something at all.

*

One hundred fifty miles south the radar search of the Adana Air Force base had caught for a fraction of a second a reading on the far reaching radar. It was declared an unauthorized flying object without any further identification. A routine report went straight to Langley and ended up on the desk of David Meyer. The report reached David Meyers at the same time as an internal paper about a plagiarized (so it was expressed in the report) MIL Mi6 helicopter from an airfield in Turkey. The airfield was under supervision of UN soldiers. In this particular night, when the helicopter took off unauthorized (a more elegant word for being 'stolen') the airstrip was under guard of an UN unit from Nigeria. African soldiers are notorious about their traditional fear of darkness and therefore not at their best at night. There was no point to have them there in the first place since they also have the annoying habit of closing their eyes when they fire.

On top, commander Bobo Makimba had gained possession of three?—gallon bottles of Jim Beam for his fellow's soldiers and five-hundred dollars cash for himself from a man he only knew by the name Rasit. Later one it was impossible to realize from the report that the whole operation to get the chopper out had lasted less than three minutes

25

Langley, Virginia

After lunch hour Rose appeared in David Meyer's office. He had brought along a simple blue folder, which he, shrugging his shoulders, tossed with raised eyebrows on David Meyer's desk.

"And?" Meyers asked.

"Nothing", absolutely nothing," Rose sighted.

Some silence went by.

"Are you telling me that this whole Russian chopper just disappeared in Turkey and we don't know where it might be, the Turks don't know, after we had it twice on the radar? Adana does not know.

Who knows, hey? God knows."

"I don't think this is the issue. Remember, when this weirdo pilot crashed his A-10 here in Colorado and we had to make up all these stories to the press *why* the Air Force lost the plane on radar? And why they couldn't find the bloody plane for two weeks with the best men and equipment. And this was in the middle of *our* country! And winter time."

Meyers leaned back from his desk taking along with his left hand his coffee mug. Had a sip and thought for a moment about how Rose had explained his point well. Meyers took the blue folder and read the report again. Attached this time were two satellite photos, revealing nothing of interest about this particular chopper situation. He was certain the chopper had not crashed and he said so to Rose. Rose agreed.

"Look," Meyers went on,(his mind as a former field officer worked precise) "we caught the chopper on four occasions on radar for only a fraction of time. It was never caught by a satellite. Why?"

"This is an easy one. Whoever flew the chopper knew the window timing of our KH-11 satellite covering Europe and Central of Asia. But something

Jürgen Dallüge

does not compute. I wish we would have some *real* intelligence from *real* people about this shit," he sighed unconventionally.

"Why don't we call MIT[11], perhaps they know something."

Rose shook his head.

"Checked this one out already. The only person we could talk to is on vacation. They have a five-day string of holidays coming up. You know. like we almost close down everything around the Fourth of July. Nothing is moving'."

"Well, then . . . wait a moment . . . yes, that's it. Rose, that's it." Meyers got exited.

"What?"

"Did you say they have five days of holiday??"

Rose frowned and felt suddenly a great chill as soon as he had mentally identified the message Meyers had just revealed to him. Israel had been overrun by the Egyptian army in 1973 because of some holiday. Hell, five days. This was enough some dimwit would do something nuclear moronic with impacts not to be overseen or understood at the moment on the scale of world politics. Meyers decided to have a word with Station Ankara, Garry Kessler in private about the series of incidents. He picked up the phone and dialed.

---

[11]   Turkish Intelligence Organization.

26

Ankara, Turkey, U.S. Embassy

He was still in the office and had spent hours not moving from his chair. It was late evening in Ankara when Station Officer Garry Kessler picked up the phone, because the fifth ring demanded now his attention. For whatever reasons he could not explain to himself, he knew it was Langley. One of the Gods.

"Yes, Kessler," he articulated into the scrambled line. The puddle of light from his desk lamp was soaked up by the gloomy top of his desk, which was always neat and orderly at the end of the day. Kessler had enough instinct to know there was something in the air with the last ring.

David Meyer's call from Langley, Virginia reached him at 22:05.

It was also at that precise moment when Rachel began to sink the helicopter into the crater some three-hundred miles away. Actually it was because of this hairy maneuver somewhere in the center of Turkey that Kessler was still in the office. Because he knew.

After two minutes Kessler hung up without having said a word, because there was really nothing he could chip in. His mind didn't stop working independently. In cultivated and friendly words he just had received the order to appear at home and to report directly to the DDCI about something which came to the surface and was not acceptable in Turkey. Kessler would have to take the first plane out of Ankara.

Kessler put the phone back into the cradle and went to the window. Looked at the cotillion of lights from Ankara and took a deep breath. He went back to his desk and pulled out a bottle of Dimple. Broke the paper seal and poured himself a full heavy crystal tumbler (he had too much class to use a plastic container). Inhaled the smoky scent for a moment and gulped it down in one straight shot.

He swallowed two times before it reached his stomach. Filled it up again and put the glass down on his desk. Had a sip. One between a big swig and a gulp, a chaser. He felt the rush of the first shot. Sat down and waited. Dimmed the light. He did not know for what and why. Admitted he was just breathing. Francis Walker was still in his office after he had returned from his trip. Kessler looked at his watch. Time did not make sense to him. He waited while arranging the terms to have it out with Francis Walker. One hour or two had gone by when Walker suddenly stood in front of Kessler's desk, his left arm hanging loose while throwing with his right arm three pages on Kessler's clean desk top.

"I am sorry," he said with a muffled voice, "this Duskin guy's dead. I think," adding it like an apology, "they didn't want it. It was a sort of mishap."

Kessler felt an abruptly chill and a deep exhaustion took over. He pressed his eyes together and released a deep sigh. He felt sick.

"Francis," he said, pretending calmness and avoided looking at Walker so as not to show how angry he was, "Duskin was a very fine man and my friend. And didn't I ask you to see me, before you left? Damn. What did *you* do there?"

"Where?"

"Don't give me this shit. I'm talking about this fuckin' JITEM prison, man. Couldn't you intervene, man. Somehow. Stay with the man so he would not have been killed."

Kessler rose both arms and his voice sounded louder than life to Francis.

"So what did you want me to do? Hold hands?"

Kessler walked around in silence. He stopped in front of Walker and stared coldly at him. Anger rose inside him like a fever. He grabbed Walker unexpectedly by the collar of his jacket and slammed him against the wall. It took Walker by surprise.

"Now," Kessler said, in an uncontrollable anger, his voice low and filled with an almost hissing softness, "listen to me you arrogant son of a bitch. You really think the dead man is not your business, don't you?"

He banged Walker again against the wall and let him go.

"There are four people in a very severe situation between here and who knows where. They are my friends. Three of them have saved my life. You understand? And if this is beyond your intellectual understanding, you'd better go back to dull Alabama."

Walker struggled desperately to maintain an air of indifference for a moment.

"Sweet Jesus," Francis Walker uttered and began to collect his body in the chair across the desk.

"Why didn't you tell me what was *really* going on. Why didn't you tell *me* the *truth*? If something *was* on I should have known it in details, damn."

Francis Walker had never seen Garry Kessler furious about anything. Always calm. Now he saw it for the first time and he got alarmed.

"The truth? For Christ sakes." Kessler raised both hands, "The truth. Think. You know what truth is?"

The first shot of Dimple had loosened his tongue and he forgot to wait for Walker's answers.

"Truth!? You know why you are with the firm? You see if a man has been killed out there, an American, you and I, the institution needs a clean record. We have nothing to do with it. Even if you were there. Anybody from the media gonna have a field day questioning everything for a couple of days. And any American will watch it on TV over lasagna. They shouldn't have a chance to find out anything. No files, no paper trail. Forget this."

Kessler crumpled up the three pages on his desk, leaving them like two snowballs.

"You are with the institution to keep your country out of real trouble. Somebody has to do the dirty work. You understand? You are here to *invent* the truth, should it be necessary. That's the concept of facts in politics."

Kessler took another sip.

"To your government it does not matter *what* you believe. They give a shit about your loyalty to the country. Just let them think you work for them. But you're doing more. You know where truth is?"

Kessler touched with the middle finger of his right hand his forehead.

"Here. You see truth is now monopolized to suit the power need. Ever watched this obtuse television? You want to shovel shit in a congressional hearing? Want to be fried? Go ahead. Any other truth that contradicts their's is called 'anti-government.' No exception of somebody else mind. The outer reality has no truth, only millions of individual opinions. Cheap commodities, those opinions. You know why you are here?"

Another sip.

"You do things in private. You don't want those congressmen to know what you are doing for this great country they have lost touch with. And they don't *want* to know it in reality."

He took another swig and went on. With some well covered amusement Walker noticed that Kessler was on his way to getting drunk.

"We work so close and in private that nobody knows what we're doing. Understand? The government calls you to notarize them and abandon your own visions. They want you to believe in their emotionalism, their love for the country and the globe. Folktale behavior of twelfth-century jongleur with the ostentatious hunger and craving for more power to feed their over-inflated egos. They don't have passion. Passion means commitment for it. Look at them. You even don't want to be with them in an elevator."

He wave with his hand and lit a cigarette.

"This is opiate hogwash. This children-first crap the congressmen and congresswomen use. You know why? This is their only excuse for their failure and it lets them accomplish even less or nothing. Selling the country out by talking. You know what gets to me? When those politicians use the same story about kids. Always the kids. Have you seen those kids with their blown-away legs from land mines on television? Here we are, so dressed and so civilized. But we say 'no' when it comes to ban them. Nothing you can do about it. You see, and if you fall for . . . for . . . this rubbishes, their priesthood, your own vision will be reduced to rubble. We work in private to protect them from their lack of competence and their own moronic appraises. It never happened with Duskin. You understand? You are with the institution to weigh the consequences of your doings. We have to backhoe the shit for those nice old neat families and power players, CEOs and all those other titles on the East Coast and West

Coast for their decent lives in their noble country clubs and on their sailboats in Maine and their mellow horses in California.

Kessler lit another cigarette.

"Could you imagine what happened? Think for a moment. Your smiling, bored congressman walks over to you and would say—hey, Walker," Kessler burped, "excuse me. I heard about this thing in Turkey. What happen to this Duskin fellow there? We heard he was involved in hauling a six ton treasure out of Iraq and we are ready to roll in. Do *you* want to justify this? And if yes, tell me how, Sir, *how*," Kessler raised both hands in a dramatically gesture and paused like a good Shakespeare actor about to speak the play's last line, "you know, confrontation can be a mean trap and you should avoid it at all costs."

Duskin looked with a fixed stare out of the window reflecting the city of Ankara in his eyes.

"Jesus. What? What are you talking about?" Francis Walker's questions rang like shots through the office. Now he paid full attention. He jumped up from his chair. He had never heard about gold and such. Until now he had no idea what it had been about over the last days.

"You're not attending to your own will, brother."

Next sip. Some slurp sounds were audible.

"You're living," he interrupted his sermon with a hick-up, "to the will of others. Did you ever notice? Every day you meet some asshole with a degree who wants to tell you how to live and how to run your own life to *their* specification to make you fit in?"

Kessler's unsteady hand grabbed the bottle and filled both glasses up again. The bottle was empty. He laughed when he lifted his tumbler: "Drunk guys and children tell you the truth. Don't they?."

Walker was stunned about Kessler's outburst and took a long swell from his glass.

"So, you want to know what happened? Okay. Listen."

And Kessler began to talk.

27

Cappadocia, Central Turkey

With the rising humble and cool sunlight penetrating the icy fog of daybreak, the late bright morning crawled down the shaft. Colorless, it painted a clear surrealistic depiction of a Dali painting about this history forgotten cave with a crashed helicopter, an eighteen wheeler truck in it, and spread bars of gold. The front of the truck was focused ahead at the cave's outlet now—the beginning of a dark cupped tunnel, the two miles long exit to liberty and (for Berret) daylight. All three had slept well and were rested. Without disturbing each other, one by one they woke up, got out from under the blankets, stretched and run a bit in circles to loosen up.

Berret took one of the spattered gold bricks and dropped his arm, surprised again at how heavy the small piece of metal was. He could not remember this kind of weight he had experienced in the desert of Iraq so many moons ago. It didn't even enter his mind that he was holding three-hundred-sixty-eight ounces of gold in his hands. A cool one-hundred-eighteen-thousand-three-hundred-seventy-four dollars. He was honest to himself because for a moment he suddenly did not understand what was all the fuss about it, except you called yourself rich and you had "made it".

"Well," Tom said, feeling that Berret was now in control of himself again, "shall we?"

Berret started the reefer and maneuvered it so it would be parked with its open back as close as possible to the shattered chopper. The reefer was now parked backward, close up the open clamshell doors. The day provided enough light. The loading began. And this would take some doing since the once-so-useful winch with its 1,765 lb capacity was no help at all this time. First, they had to collect and load the bars splattered across the cave. They

worked like maniacs to collect the scattered treasure from all over. They
found the one-hundred-thirty gold bars. One hundred ten times bending
down, lifting twenty-five pounds and carrying it to the reefer. The first hour
went by easy. The four crates, totaling six hundred pounds of Colombian
emeralds had survived the crash. Two smaller boxes with ten pounds rough
Burmese rubies (without rival in value) was build between the front wall
and its panels, but only after the seven cut diamonds larger than 110 carats
had been mixed between their dark-red brothers. The rubies glowed like
hot coals when the ray of the flashlight fell on them. The muscle and bone
strain showed up three hours later. Eight backbreaking hours, the MIL Mi6
chopper, which never would see the daylight again, had been emptied. The
gold bars were now systematically laid out on the floor of the reefer. Like a
bright glowing mosaic, showing its yellow hue in the forbearing reflection
of the filtered daylight from above. But the gold had almost its own glow.
They had done it all without any long rest. The floor panels. Hauled across
the cave and laid out on the reefer's floor and screwed back into position.
Tom threw the MPK Russian infra-red night goggles across the floor where
the chopper rested.

Russian chopper.

Russian night vision equipment.

Armenian dealer.

All three got into the cabin. Berret started the engine and turned on the
headlights. Got his bearings while he shifted into the first gear. The Major
looked at his watch. It was 22:00. Three hundred miles to drive. Twenty four
hours left to safety. The reefer began to move.

*

Ankara, Turkey

It was still dark and quiet when the doorbell rang, twice and demanding.
Garry Kessler nurtured his mild hangover with a salted coffee. He interrupted
packing his suitcase (had to be on the first plane out of Frankfurt) walked
to the door, opened it and looked down the street. Nobody. Looked left and
right. Empty. Took a deep breath of fresh air. When he wanted to close the
door he saw the bag.

First it stared at him like the bag of a cleaning company, delivering his
clothes. Kessler had a closer look and bent down.

At first it did not make sense to him when his eyes took in the small portion of a human hand. He wanted to blink it off.

Thought it was a hallucination.

"Sweet Jesus," Garry Kessler mumbled and pulled the bag into his house. He tried to collect his thoughts. When he bent down and opened the plastic zipper further he was certain that the body bag had been purposely delivered to his doorsteps. His jaw started to tremble in short tiny vibrations.

"Oh you foolish man. For gold?" was his whispering question recognizing the handsome face of Peter Duskin with a dark blue spot at the left temple. He almost repented it that he had opened the body bag. It felt like he had disturbed the man's sleep. Rigor mortis had left the body already some hours ago. The face looked so serene. There was an indication of a smile like he was already seeing a more refined world.

And after years in the precarious service for his country it was the first time that Garry Kessler broke out in tears. A huge sob left Kessler's mouth. Another followed like it was sitting there for a long times. The sudden encounter facing his dead friend and over twenty years in a trade were a human life didn't mean so much, or nothing, brought him to a stage of disassociation from where he thought he could not return emotionally. Kessler felt, from one second to the next, burned up and used. He hadn't prayed for years and there was suddenly the overwhelming urge to do something for this so proud and now propelled into a senseless death, man. This deep, touching motion, a gesture of life since humans began to live in self-inflicted dissensions and destruction, preserved his balance and let the cool professional thinking return to take over. He picked up the telephone and dialed.

*

Lufthansa 0123 to New York was just three minutes from take-off time when the Boeing 747 left the side path to migrate onto the main runway. Twenty minutes before take-off, a last cargo had come onboard. It was a carefully sealed box of six and a half feet by two feet. The height was only eighteen inches. The relative small height avoided the image of looking like a coffin. But indeed it was.

Lift off and climb was easy. All the way across Europe and the Atlantic clear weather. A man, sitting in row D9, stared out of the window at the fast-disappearing Europe and listen to the grumbling sound of the wheels being pulled into the bay.

He tried to figure out how to explain the death of Peter Duskin, the odd inquire to come: "What happened in Ankara?" And *how* (and he hoped it never had to do this), for God's sake, would somebody explain it to Duskin's mother? He was the only child she had. What a lukewarm job. Station officer Garry Kessler leaned back in his chair and closed his eyes. The path of his life had brought him to a new crossroad. He wanted out.

28

New York

Jetlag had not caught up with Kessler. Meyers filled two glasses with Corbel, reached over and handed one to Kessler. Somehow, both men liked each other in their professional quietness. And it was David Meyers who had recommended Kessler for the position in Ankara. From Meyers point of view, Kessler was one of the last of the old kind from the time of before computer and Internet existed. He was from the days when CIA operations had more to do with getting the information from human assets, real life agents, than being involved to amass evidence about congressmen's or even higher, financial and sexual unevenness, so to speak.

"Cheers," Meyers said by taking a small sip and with a disappearing smile. His tense blue eyes half closed as he gazed at Kessler and being a sharp observer, he noticed the change in his Ankara man. The concentrated energy which Meyers always noticed in Kessler's face in the past, an energy which was necessary to carry out action for the sake of his fellow men or his country, existed only in a thin layer, now almost gone. Meyers had the ability to read even blank faces, and what he saw was a man who had been burned up and out overnight. Kessler managed himself quit well by staying calm and controlled. He turned to the window and looked down at Lexington.

"How are we doing in Ankara? I read your action report."

"Good . . . we are doing well," Kessler said without any great enthusiasm.

"For God's sake, what happened to this Duskin you brought home?"

Audibly, Meyers sucked his teeth. Kessler didn't answer for several moments.

"As I recall it from the report, Sir, he was a tourist. The police protocol confirms this somehow. What we know is he was mugged by some thugs,"

Kessler said with the indication of a brittle voice and felt uncomfortable with his lukewarm rhetorical presentation.

"I suppose this was a very good definition to resolve the problem."

Meyers didn't buy it, but the following long silence disconnected the precarious subject from any subsequent further close examination. Meyers did not conquer his disbelief and Kessler saw Meyer's jaws tighten, repressing a sigh. They both were pros and could cut through all the bull of formalities. Meyers stepped even closer to the window and a long pause followed.

> "I need your help," Meyers said still looking down at Lexington, with a tone beginning to be crisp. "What's going on there in Turkey? Tell me. What do you know about this Russian chopper? This MIL Mi6 coming in from Serbia or Albania or Turkey. *What do you know, I don't know.* Tell me everything you know. Let's work it out right here. It's still private. Very private. Talk."

Kessler was confused for a moment by Meyers' explicit personal demand.

"I don't want to see you in front of the security council. So, don't give me bullshit. You understand?"

Meyers' tone had changed to a slow and quiet timbre with a clear background of warning, not allowing the assumption of a verbal escape. The tone had gotten too quiet to be considered as comfortable, monotone and rigid. He still had not turned around. It was a fair gesture to give Kessler time to collect himself. Meyers had gone in a foreseeing silence, a stillness lingering in the room for six seconds while Kessler had listened with a sort of curious expectation. The sudden vacuum prompted him to respond. In his life he always had to clear his throat when he had something important to say. Kessler cleared his throat.

"Yes, there is something I should mention, Sir. I don't know whether it will help."

And Kessler began to talk about the mission in Iraq before the air attacks began, their covering on this desert, the crashed German plane they had found with the all the gold, platinum and gem stones. He talked about the shelter it has given them, the dead Luftwaffe colonel. The two dead SS men with their Schmeisser machine guns still intact. And how they had talked about how they wanted to pick up the trinket after the Golf War crisis. Kessler talked about the drug he had used with force on Rosco to find out the truth in disbelieve.

" . . . to be frank, I always thought it was just a sort of boy scout talk. Who in his right mind would go back into something like this anyway?"

Meyers raised his upper lip, inhaled through his teeth, and still had this fixed look down at the taxi-packed pavement of Lexington, digesting what he had just learned. Then he asked in a slow tone: "Are *you* serious?" believing Kessler already, resulting in another long pause, "do you think they are still there?"

Kessler's silence was an unspoken confirmation. Suddenly Meyers remembered the four men and the woman in Mendocino again.

"Sir, I don't know where they are. But I am sure they are in Turkey."

"Why wasn't I informed about this at the beginning, or at least in a very early stage of this mess?" Meyers asked irritated.

"I didn't have any proof about anything, sir. Not a single iota.

And to be frank, sir, the first inquiry about all this came from your office. Or I wouldn't even have known about it. You and I would not even be here."

Meyers admitted that Kessler had a point. The urge for hurry shot up in Meyers. He knew Kessler was burned out but he was the only man he could send back to convince them all to go home.

"I want you on the next plane back, Mr. Kessler. Find them. Turn everything upside down. Just find them and tell them to get the heck out there. If this thing goes public, if I might say so, any thug or service will be after them. And after all, what do we want to report to the President if he gets wind of it. This is close to be a politicum. Who else knows?"

"Walker."

"I hope he knows what is at stake . . . for the sake of his health."

DDCI Meyers called his secretary, once a field officer in West Berlin during the heyday of the Cold War, covering the section of the resident Berlin-East. Meyers wanted to know everything about a *Luftwaffe* bomber, a Messerschmitt 264 IV flown out of Budapest in the spring of 1945. The evening news of CNN and ABC divulged the death of an American tourist, male, who had been attacked and killed in Turkey while resisting a robbery in a small town at the Eastern Mediterranean. The State Department had launched a protest and requested a full investigation from the Turkish Government. The Turkish government regretted the incident and promised to investigate. The Dow went up four points. In Namibia Prime Minister Mugabe claimed his country was poor, regardless of the diamond production increased of 185%, and South Africa's Mrs. Mandela insisted again to have nothing to do with some Zuzu ritual killing. In London a conference took place behind closed doors about the gold of holocaust victims.

*

Epraim Katz

In the last daylight a sharp observer's eyes could only take in the picture of a lonely man with his head bent down. A picture of a man deep in thought. Ephraim Katz leaned against the railing and stared down into the spiraling luminous light of salty foam, hissing along the moving hull of the ship. He raised his head and looked at the first humble glow of the diamond-like evening star. General Katz suddenly felt burned out and lonely regardless of all the power he was holding with his rank and had accomplished over the years. A power even to make decisions over life and death, without justifying it to others.

Was this the achievements of the years? Suddenly in the oneness of the perfect sea and the silk-blue gentle sky he remembered how much he had given to the country once so young, desperate and innocent. He never had a family. His wife, his beloved Ruth, highly pregnant, had been blown to pieces in a bus by a bomb in one of those so senseless attacks long time ago, somewhere in the West Bank. Never had he felt the smooth sweet touch of his own offspring. From then on he had no geography of his intellect to feel home. Or was it the past that he could not let go of? Ephraim felt like a man without a country. He knew there was a life inside him, like a comfortable cottage he never had lived in. A life which was always available to him but he always rejected. He had sacrificed his life to the country whose struggle did not go away. The treasure? The six-and-a-half tons he had reclaimed from the dark past to serve his people? He was not quite certain anymore. Would it help to change human minds? He moaned. He did not feel satisfaction, as he once expected he would, of having completed the assignment of a (his) lifetime. Ephraim looked over the sea manned thoughts migrated into the past.

His mind was silent, now awed by the desert beauty of the last day rising so abruptly from the darkened eastern horizons. It was a sort of timbre of calm and peace. He chuckled when he remembered the time when he and his men stole five missile boats from under the ass (and with the help) of the French government in Cherbourg to bring them home to Israel. He recalled Entebbe and all the other stunts he used to be a part of, from the beginning when he walked as a very young man into building eight-five in Tel Aviv.

Now after all those years later and the accomplishments for his country, Ephraim Katz was not so convinced anymore whether it had been worth it at all. The cultural developments of possessing power and massive regulating people's simplest rights of privacy away in this world had made Ephraim Katz aware that civilization, as he knew it, had come to a certain end and would go in a sudden crash overnight of economical, spiritual and human values. When? He did not know. But it would come. The beast of greed for material things. He looked down at his right arm where his tattooed number was still visible after all the years. How long will it agonize free human minds? For years, life had given him carte blanche to look deep into the darkness of political and therefore human demeanor. At the end of his career he was fully aware that nations had already entered the gigantic struggle between nationalistic militarism, terrorism and industrialism (oh, this ism's had gotten to him). He did not want to be apart of all this any longer. He did not want to be a part off all this any longer. He did not want to deal with the mentalities of militaries and the arrogant patois of politicians. Katz had seen history, the one they did not teach in school, nor dare to make known, so that the men in their grey power suits could save face. And in many ways Ephraim Katz drew his own conclusion. The conclusion of his life, there had not been any difference between the age-long conflict between herd-hunters and farmers, bankers and such in "modern" societies. Katz had his doubts whether the industries would ever triumph over militarism because they would need each other to survive. Men never would accept peace and harmony as a normal mode of living amongst themselves, because men had never been willing to accept the fact that peace and *respect* would be the best for their welfare. And like in the early ages when men danced around the golden calf, each tribe was surrounded by circles of increasing fear and suspicion. Like nation's (tribes) leaders today creating the phantom enemy, searching and nurturing the future conflict for the sake of power with artfully kept-alive hate from the past. Never forgiven. Wounds synthetically kept open with the salt of the past. Just dragging along the same old same for the ego. It was their only satisfaction in their forlorn lives of greed.

General Ephraim Katz pressed his eyes together and shook his head. He understood, now at the end of his last assignment and his career that the worship of wealth-power would lead to the total disorientation of values of ethic, integrity, dignity and discipline, if not thought anymore. Freedom without discipline did not present what it was supposed to be. Over the last fifty years he was a part of finding the enemy. Now he knew better.

Enemies were not born.

Enemies were made.

His long suffering journey was coming to an end. He had walked the path of obligation, of faith, to perform the duty he had conditioned himself for fifty years earlier. His path for justice was not over yet. He would write. Knew this already. Perhaps poems. Would write about the life he might have lived. A life wearing faded out jeans on a desk, and writing. A day beginning with the warm hug of a wife, a mate. The late summer was his. He was ready for it.

29

Berret drove the reefer for miles over an unpaved, road. Later they turned into a twisting mountain highway. It was a day of a color inflamed sky with rich blue Mediterranean waters, stretched to an invisible horizon and placid enough for the bottom to be seen along the shores.

The sun began to settle for her break, like a yellow disc in the west, still adding to the daydream of giving the water's surface the brilliance of a golden radiation. Some parts of the north-eastern sky indicated some darker blue, where the sun had already lost control over the graceful past day already. The end of the day announced its tender coming and created its own strange early evening light in the East.

Actually, looking into the generous color entertainment of nature gave the woman and the two men the needed distraction from the tension of the last days. When they started to drive away from the cave in Cappadocia they were full with jabber about what they had accomplished and the wealth ahead. It had changed to silence now, to thoughts that each hour in life maims and the last hour would kill. It was serenity with a touch of uneasiness what would be next, awed by the desolate panorama of the mountains rising again from the valley's image to featureless geometric shapes.

Rachel wanted to ask Berret what his decision would be concerning his new wealth and what he wanted from life after all this was done, when her attention was captured by the still far approach of a car swinging carefully between the trucks behind them to pass. Well, it was just a car. Rachel took the road map from the dashboard, folded it up to make it more manageable. The tip of her index finger with dark half moons behind the nails moved along E-90. They had just passed Gazi Antep.

"We go northwest and then we get onto the Highway. Forty-eight clicks."

Berret had another glance into the mirror checking the traffic behind him. It was the third time Berret noticed the car continued to close the distance in daring maneuvers until it was just two trucks behind. It was a Mercedes. Nothing special. An older model, a 280 SE. Dusty matt-grey silver. The sun had burned up some paint on the hood and had made it shabby looking. Hardly to be noticed with its colored skin. It was snuggled among the eighteen-wheelers. He would keep a close eye on it for another ten minutes before he might say something.

The asphalt road through the mountain, marked in the legend of the Freytag & Berndt map as a 'main road' with a firm embankment, suffered from heavy traffic.

Eight miles later the silhouette of the mountain gave way to the broad plain of the Mediterranean coast. His foot pressed down the gas pedal, adding five-mile acceleration to the rig. He shifted up again until he had reached the speed limit. The road eased back into the mountains and the Tarsus Pass. He checked the mirror. The grey car was still there. Berret thought he was clear, until he caught up with a mixed convoy of dry bulk tankers and some dump trailers. The trailer in front of Berret was a tank-truck combination and its elliptical tank was to haul chemical liquids.

The configuration of the rig did not look trustworthy, perhaps welded together in some iron shop in Bursa. For the next hour Berret stared at a huge sign on the tanker's back. *Dikkat, Tehlikeli Madde.* In plain English—Danger, Explosives. There, where the license plate should be was another sign—*Allah Korushum,* suggesting that Allah would protect the driver. Now, that was faith! The rig was trapped between the tanker and a tailgating Volvo truck. He could not refrain from letting his eyes go back further. Still, it was there. Berret became uneasy and nervous.

"I think we have company," he mumbled.

"I know," Rachel chipped in.

"Pull over at the next turn-out. See what happens," the Major agreed.

Berret set the emergency blinker, eased to the embankment and stopped to let the car pass. The Major got out. Rachel looked at Berret. She read his face and assumed he wanted to stay where he was. She saw his poorly disguised greed in his face. Uneasiness washed over her. Standing at the rear of the truck, Tom had a much better view of the traffic flow. His eyes scanned the movement of the trucks and finally, twelve trucks back, his eyes caught up with the 280SE, slowly coming closer. First he saw the chromed grille and the tinted windows. The window went down, inviting Tom to have a peek. Four men were in it. Their complexions clearly specified Chinese. He began to relax. What do Chinese have to do in Turkey?

Rachel stood at the truck's left front wheel when the car passed. She looked at the 280 SE and experienced a flash of hypnotic captivation. She *saw* the car passing in extremely slow motion. She *saw* the pleasant face with its strong qualities. First it was irritating, but she felt very calm as her mind stepped out from under the clouds of the previous past. It was incredible. She doubted what she had seen and closed her eyes to re-synchronize them and to organize her thoughts. When she opened her eyes, the car was gone.

*

Berret shifted down. As they crept along, the traffic was heavy against them. He looked at the temperature gauge. It was okay. Daylight was going fast now. Ten more miles.

Darkness arrived and the traffic had died out completely. Any trucker on the country road had by now retired from driving. It was not worth to be robbed by some Yazidis Kurds. The first stars began to throw their humble lights.

Berret wanted a cigarette, but decided against it and rolled the window down. There was only the shadowy company of the embracing night and the headlights, cutting a pillar of light through the darkness.

The turn-off.

It was an impromptu road. Not an adequate surface for a seasoned 18-wheeler to be on. It was an infirm path with a 17 degree downward slope and of unknown age. The surface was soft and washed out from the seasons of rain and barely wide enough to assume the weight. Berret swung slowly the steering wheel and edged the rig into a wide turn, attempting to avoid the soft shoulder. After the third cut Berret could not offer the trailer a wider swing to avert the dangerous off-track. The rear of the trailer followed now in a substantially shorter path. The path, beginning to absorb the pressure of the rig's rear axle, became life important. Berret stopped the rig at an outcropping of a pile of loose dirt and set the handbrake. Tom opened the door and left the rig. Rachel followed him. Loosening the brake again, Berret moved the big eighteen wheeler over the edge and onto the crumbling path with his knees shaking. His left foot braced against the floorboard, preparing himself for the shock of loosing touch with the road and being hurled down the embankment. The king pin gave a cracking sound. The trailer frame moaned abusing. Close to a jackknife. Then the tractor straightened out, while half the trailer still inched in a wide turn over the embankment. They faced the real challenge, the steep down-slope, and an extreme downgrade. Berret cut the light and killed the engine again. He took from the glove compartment a 'Moonlight NV-100', a night vision system with close-focus efficiency. He pulled the string system over his head. The 40-degree field of view gave him the full picture that was ahead in absolute darkness. The night vision system amplified any ray of light pollution 60,000 times and could spot things 1,000 feet away. Berret saw Tom through the bright green image raising his hand.

Ready.

He pushed the starter bottom. Still warm, the engine fired up. Had a last look at the air pressure gauge for the brake's system. Full. Hopefully he would not have to use too much air. In this kind of maneuver the air compressor would not keep up with the air they might need.

Clutch down.

First gear.

Kicked in the differential lock, engaging the front and rear differentials. The wheel system of the tractor would have the same grip on the poor hill's surface.

Released the air brake. Slowly and never out of the low gear, the rig drove down the steep path. No left embankment. Just a rocky wall raised straight into the darkness. On the right side was the embankment with its 340 feet drop. The slope began just seven inches away from the right tire. It was nearly two miles of rutted unstable surface.

Precisely twenty-five minutes later the rig ended with a last left turn on a small beach and came to a halt parallel with a natural seawall of rocks. Once they had reached this small piece of strand it was clear to them they would never have a chance to get out again with the rig. He cut the engine. From somewhere they could hear the sound of breaking waves.

The sea.

*

In the age-long strife between land and water, for many seasons the sea had been successful in shaping new designs from the lands left and separated from the sea. For millions of years the waters of the Mediterranean Sea had patiently cut, serene and firm, through an eighty-foot thick wall of soft rocks, that secluded a small sandy stretch of beach from the waters of the sea. The result was an eight feet wide rift. Nature's construction of it had started long before on earth, when time had not yet been invented by destructive mortals. The water's excavating of this cleft was the result of an originating spirit to donate something for shaping matters and intervals for the future inhabitants.

Homos sapiens were not even an idea on the blueprints of creation. This sandy stretch was just one hundred feet long, a width of forty feet, and bedded deep inside a crater. Nevertheless, the remarkable section of this terra firma portion was, nature had enveloped it in a way, it made this place invisible from the seaside and the land. Nature vetoed the notion to make this place known to the world and so a mortal had never set his foot on this unseen segment of earth.

If the storytellers of time and space could be trusted, the rift had even survived the sinking of Atlantis, this natural Waterloo, from where any Levantines claimed that his country, being the cradle of civilization, had been a part of it. If Atlantis had been located where it was claimed to be, the tunnel sank with the land into the gushing floods of the rising Mediterranean Sea.

It was said that the reason for the sudden rise of the sea level was the broken natural barrier between Gibraltar and the North African Coast, separating the vulnerable grace of the sea from the harshness of the higher elevated Atlantic Ocean. With the breakdown of this barrier, the waters of the Atlantic Ocean gushed into the Mediterranean and raised the water level.

When Atlantis disappeared, nature included with this new reshape of the planet earthquakes. Flames shot from the surface of the earth and soared sky-high. Massive black clouds of muddy substance soon rose, blackening out the sun and it seemed to be the end of days had come. So it was said. Volcanic matter, called lapilli and maroon-hot scoriae rained down, covering the land with a deadly torrent of ashes. Darkness governed the planet's veneer and the panorama was made even more prophetic by lightning, the rumbling of earthquakes, and tidal waves. The stretch sank into the sea, only to be hoisted by a volcanic gush on to a cushion of molten magma, creating this embraceable barrier of boulders around the sandy spot on the shores of southern Turkey. And there it remained, undisturbed and unknown.

In the sixteenth century the merchants of the Republic of Venice discovered it first, when they were sent out under the order of the Doge to examine the worlds and shores of the Eastern Mediterranean for expansion and domination to the honor and tribute of the ruler (the Doge). The merchants sailed through the crack, using the lofty waves of the high tide, and landed on this beach in the heart of the Ottoman Empire. And the coast was theirs. Unknown and unseen, they dug a path through the rocks up to the plateau, where a thousand years earlier the legions of Rome had built a road eastward to the borders of Persia. Now, one thousand years after Rome, the embankment had changed to Highway E-90 to carry the heavy traffic of 18-wheelers from and to the Middle East.

*

Like a huge yellow disc, the moon stood on top of the rock, the invisible line of the horizon's edge, reflecting its yellow disc back to the surface of a small water pool, left behind when the high tide had reached its peak hours ago. Berret checked the position. No good. Started the engine again, maneuvered the truck so it stood inches away and close to the rocky wall, facing the crack. He cut the engine. At once Tom and Berret pulled out from underneath the seat a camouflage net and began to mask the rig. Five minutes later the rig was invisible. By then it was 0140. Some more hours to wait.

The Mediterranean Sea had a kind night and the breeze had not gotten drowsy yet, still constructing large waves with crests on it, propelling, only to be exhausted in their momentum, with a hiss onto the velvety sand.

It was an old pier.

A jetty.

The uniqueness of it was that it appeared and was only visible during low tide. Its 200 feet long steel structure looked worn and unstable. The appearance of the pier did not reveal the real strength of it. The oxidizing beating of the *Akdeniz* (Mediterranean) had not weakened considerably the potential of the structure to hold anything.

And this was the jetty's story.

*

It was 1945. April. In just three weeks and in rush, it was at the end of World War Two, the steel structure had been sunk into the shallow sandy ground on the shores between Bozyazi and the historical side of Anemurium in southern Turkey during the last months of this war. Its existence was planned for the landing of British troops in a sort of a Mediterranean D-day. The pier never got the veneration of being a real part of the war. In short, the purpose discontinued its planned use for military intention and was immediately forgotten, because with its completion, the cessation of World War Two had taken place. From the year of its closing nothing out of the extraordinary happened to it.

Except the Office of Naval Intelligence (ONI) had, as a main responsibility, to keep naval planners informed of the war-making capabilities (and intentions) of the Soviets during the Cold War and supplied the information needed for plans and operations. The ONI had built up bulky, but precise files on ports, harbors and beaches from around the world and on potential targets for amphibious operations. Considering the amount of money and effort expended since World War II, it would have been inexcusable for the Navy and NATO to be confronted with problems similar to them posed during the preparation for the landing in North Africa or the D-day at Omaha Beach. In the course of mapping it all out around the world, the jetty's existence was acknowledged in the maps of ONI and classified as strategically not important.

*

Being just sixty miles north from the shores of the island of Cyprus, it found the interest of a Greek Orthodox priest with political ambitions by the name of Makarios. The priest was nurtured by the help of the Soviets to smuggle weapons and ammunition by boats to Cyprus to land on the shores of Alsancak, located at the 34th latitude, to topple the Turkish government. Makarious was basically a trouble maker and grateful that his tabernacle rank provided him with the badly needed immunity. After losing the second weapon shipment to the Turks, and being a man with plenty of resolve, the priest did not surrender to the feeble circumstances of his movement and shifted his political desires to more comfort in his life—the U.N. This was a political home run. In short, Makarios abandoned the idea of being a freedom fighter.

Just a political talker.

The jetty served only another time, its planned design.

A last NATO maneuver took place in 1998 in southern Turkey and a group of the U.S. Special Forces used the structure to land in secrecy in "enemy" territory. This time the jetty was classified also as unsafe. The team leader was a young captain with the name Tom Peters. Since this NATO event the pier was just there looking to be used. Overall the weather-beaten steel structure was another loss of human inventiveness. Now here they stood and gazed over the rippled surface of the sea. The monotone sound of the waves created a relaxing mood. Rosco would be here with the boat soon. They walked back. They went for the bunk and fell asleep.

Rachel took the first watch. She walked to be closer to the water and took some time to cherish the never-ending sound of the incoming waves and the peace and the reflecting moon which filled a section of the sea with its light. She sat on a stone and looked over the nervous sea. Waves were rising while the crests lashed, like white horses of the sea would waive their pearly manes.

A kind of comfortable sensation seemed to fill her head. Hearing was suddenly seeing, and seeing began to be hearing. She leaned against the rocky wall. Soon . . . The boat . . . *She was aware,* something had taken over her mind, like hypnotizing eyes like warning her.

> *do not resist. tamar. sister.*
> *why do you do this to me*
> *brother? I don't want you to*
> *die again. your knowledge is*
> *no match for me. don't resist.*
> *whatever happened, don't. but I*
> *love tom. I know and you should.*
> *be on my side . . . tamar . . .*
> *sister. only then you all will*
> *survive.*

She wanted to shake off the force embracing her with paralyzing power. Rachel tried to open her eyes again.

30

Cool morning dawn ignited in a red-blue soft flame and began to light up the horizons, helping to identify the dark wild profile of the graceful Bolkar Daglari Mountain. The daybreak had shown up, like a messenger of a neutral bulletin, suggesting a memorandum of a final decision to be made.

An hour before dawn light Tom's thoughts drifted off. He thought about Rachel and tried to imagine what his life would be without her. She was self-sufficient and had boldness, preventing her from failing whatever she undertook. A woman who knew how to use all her potentials. When this all was over, he would take her to . . . decided to resolve this minor subject of life later.

He looked at his watch. It told him 0615. The boat would be there in another hour or so. Took the powerful small binoculars and got out. Rachel was asleep, curled up under her mohair blanket; he had bought her two weeks ago in a bazaar in Istanbul. He did not bother to wake her and walked to the open beach. Tom leaned against the rocks and scanned the horizon. No boat in sight. His body itched, demanding a shower. He sat down on a rock.

It was 0640 when Tom spotted the boat. His eyes, locked to the glasses, scanned the horizon and water. No, two boats. A wave of uneasiness washed over him. The two boats moved through the choppy sea swiftly and without being disturbed by the rolling and bouncing waves, sailing above the erratic waters like the Flying Dutchman. Not even leaving a low curtain of white foam in the waves behind. Making a straight line for the pier. Tom kept the binoculars on them.

He decided to get back and alert Berret and Rachel about the boats. He suddenly sensed something was not right. His mind could not decide what it was (was it just simply too much suddenly?). He paused for a moment and gazed for a second over to Rachel. She had gotten up.

And than he saw it.

First Tom closed his eyes and shook his head slowly, hoping to correct what his eyes had just taken in. But when he opened his eyes, it was still there. No, actually it moved. Like a shadow. Casual, but strong. It was a Chinese. He was tall and good looking. The ageless face was blessed with a generous handsomeness. His black hair combed straight back. The ponytail was held with a small golden silk band. The features of his body were strong and elastic and clothed in black garments. He wore a black leather vest with pockets containing visibly four hand grenades and at least ten speed loaders. With some casual authority a Heckler and Koch MP5 dangled down on his hand, a blackened silencer case attached to it. It was a delayed blowback with selective fire. 9mm Parabellum. Just 8.8 inches long and had a cyclic rate to fire six hundred-fifty rounds per minute. An extra short version of a submachine gun which could be concealed easily on a person. It would even fit into a glove compartment. He had the index finger around the trigger. Snuggled under his left armpit was a leather holster containing noticeably a knife. A kris. The whole physical appearance was the lethalness of an expert. Tom moved two steps.

"No, Mister Peters, this is not such a good idea."

The voice was calm and friendly as the left arm raised the HK.

Berret got out of the truck and froze.

"You see," the Chinese continued, having a gentle combat smile on his face and while ignoring Berret, he moved his right arm in a generous magnetizing gesture like being on stage, "you have to confess you are dealing with some disadvantages."

Tom followed the Chinese' arm gesture in a tense body motion. Another trim tall Chinese raised gently a Valmet M76 Rifle. Tom had seen this kind of rifle and had respect for it. The face was motionless with a stern warning in it not to do anything stupid. He knew these kind of men. They were trained to wait only for the slightest indication of aggressiveness. Tom had to overcome his astonishment. Who were these guys?! Who were they?? *And* from where had they had come so suddenly.

"I assume," the ageless Chinese went on, apologetic, reading Tom's thoughts, "you want to know who I am."

He pointed in an unexpected gesture at Rachel.

"My name is Fon Yun. I helped this young lady to find Mister Duskin in Singapore."

Rachel was like in a trance and her mind declined to follow the situation around her.

tamar, come over to me.
will you harm them? no,
we will not. but I need
you with your words. you
are using me, brother?
no, I will need you, so
you all will live, sister.

The inner mind dialogue had taken place in a fraction of a second.

"The way things are for you right now, you might not have so many choices." He went on.

"All this gold, the platinum, iridium, emeralds, diamonds and rubies" he pointed at the camouflaged rig," will kill you. Nobody will have the chance to deal with this amount of money. Nobody. Where do you want to sell it? You are all amateurs."

Then he added with a strong voice: "It does not belong to you. You understand. It has to go back where it belong."

Fon Yun shook his head again.

"Being dead would be better for you all, instead of ending in a Turkish jail for the rest of your life."

The lecture went on.

"Ten thousand Americans live at the Adana airbase. Just sixty miles east from here. It is a front line operation since a new worthless encounter with this Saddam Hussein is coming up again. You Americans and the British will not be able to finish them off. Because they are weak. The complexity of this giant radar system in Adana, and allow me to remind you, your NSA has quit its stake in it too, will certainly get you all."

He paused for a moment, bent his head down and shook it before he went on.

"You see, the human's level in its ability to observe is very limited. It is almost pathetic. When humans keep on amplifying and exaggerating things they think they have reached the top. All they find are new circumstances they had not expected or wanted. That makes them unhappy and does not let them live in the now. And that is where you are. You expected something else. What is your choice?"

He shrugged his shoulders.

"Tell me, do you truly believe you can unload in a bank 654 million dollars treasure and gems with unrivaled value. You're not so naive, are you?"

Tom stepped forward.

Another henchman, pointing his Colt Commando at Tom. Looked more like a Malay. A very beautiful face with an expressionless but warning smile. In an instant, Tom noticed the Malay's inconceivable intention of shooting him point blank in the merest fraction of time.

"Don't, Mister Peters. This man there has seen more corpses in one small skirmish than any of you have seen in a cemetery. A few more lives . . ."

Fon Yun shrugged his shoulders again.

"What do you want from us?"

"The key. The truck"

Tom gestured at Berret.

"Give it to him," Tom said.

Berret stepped forward with his left hand stretched out. He maneuvered the impetus of his movement slightly behind Fon Yun. The man from Singapore did not even look at him when his leg went straight up in a sidekick, hitting Berret's jaw with a tremendous force. Berret dropped the key, went down to his knees and collapsed. Fon Yun caught the key from the falling man and smiled, shaking his head forgivingly.

"He is not well trained. You know, he is too ambitious and greedy. Any decent fighter could sense what he had in mind."

Fon turned with an inviting gesture to the open sea. One could see that the boats were very close and maneuvered close to the pier, reversing their engines like in a cotillion only twice. Bumpers impacted with the jetty. The men at the wheels steadied and worked the throttle forward and reverse to keep the boats steady and close to it. One Chinese jumped from the first vessel and secured the aft and stern with mooring lines. The same parade with the second vessel. Now Tom could see it. They were *Pchela Class* hydrofoil boats.

Russians. Not the latest technique, but still very impressive.

The *Pchela* boat was a transport hydrofoil boat with four 'skis'. Using the shallow-depth effect it was even able to run over extremely low inland waterways at high speed. This kind of craft used the surface piercing system and adapted even better when running through a choppy sea. Here was the logic why they had sailed so smoothly and swiftly to the pier.

A Pchela was just 82 feet long and with two 2,400 hp diesels on two shafts, and could reach a speed of 50 knots. The former owner of the two Pchela boats was once the KGB and were operated by the KGB only. But there was no KGB anymore in this world. If not the Russians or organized crime, who had come, for God's sake?

Rosco appeared on the deck. He looked tired and did not move away from the boat.

"Tamar, come here," Fon Yun said gentle.

To his astonishment Tom observed it like glancing through an uneven glass panel. Rachel walked over to Fon Yun, like in catalepsy. She stood in front of Fon Yun and looked at him. In a friendly gesture, the Chinese put his right hand on her shoulder and looked at her.

> *you all will be free and*
> *alive. what makes you think?*
> *so, brother? trust me. you*
> *have to tell them it's over.*
> *why don't you? tamar, be*
> *the voice of peace. men can*
> *do disastrous things to*
> *themselves when they theorize*
> *they have lost.*

Rachel turned away and walked with rigid steps to Tom.

"Paramour," she said with a firm and stable voice, "let them have it. It's over. It's not worth it. Let's all go home as long as we can. I love you. I will die with you, but I will not be separated from you and be in prison. Look, there is so much to see. Will you go home with me?"

And with so little that she had said he understood her while the question was still expressed in her eyes. He looked at the mountain with their opulent green. There was the raving blue of the sea and the impossible blue sky. He saw a white contrail, painted in an elegant stroke along the sky by an anonymous plane.

Fon Yun was right. They would never find rest. The treasure would kill them, ruin their lives and along with that, their personalities. Rachel was right. There was so much to see and to read, so much to expand. How many days had they left from life anyway? He pulled her close and held her. Even through the sweat of the last few days he could smell the sweetness of her skin.

"Yes, let's go home."

She turned to Fon and nodded.

Nobody had watched Berret being on his knees, holding his jaw. He jumped up and went for another attack on Fon Yun when his back suddenly showed an ugly dark spot. It was like the impact of the slug picked Berret up and threw him into the air before the bullet crashed the Lumbar vertebrae. Like a tap dancer, Berret landed on his feet as the force of the bullet caused his right arm to spring out from his shoulder. He stumbled and set his left foot in a way down like he had stepped on something. Again, and for the last time in his life he went down to his knees. He had a child-like sorrow expression in his face, inhaled in short convulsing motion and exhaled the same way. The painful grimace in his face formed the impression of a smile. He opened his mouth wide, like drunks do when they have to throw up, gasping for air. The exhaling sounded like a loud laughter until the chuckle began to mix up with a bubbling noise of a toilet being flashed. He vomited blood and raised his arms like he wanted to pray, gasped and fell forward. His body contracted and arched for a moment as if the soul fought to encounter the sudden disengagement from the lethally maimed body. Tom watched the dying Berret in a paralyzed horror and his body felt numb. The shooter jumped from the ten foot high rock. The elevation did not exist for him at all. Elastically he landed on his feet. Now the Valmet rifle was pointed at Tom. With a generous motion Fon Yun threw the key to the sentry. The guard lowered the weapon and caught the key in the same dance-like fashion as Fon had thrown it and went for the truck. Fon shook his head without showing remorse.

"Fool. So senseless. This is exactly what I wanted to avoid. Greedy men are unpredictable and obtuse in their action. Let's move."

They had lost.

"What makes you so sure you can pull it off?" Tom screamed, suddenly in anger about the dead Berret.

Fon's face did not show any expression.

"Mister Peters, in *this* world of primitive egocentrical interest of power it is important to understand *that greed is a person's fall.* People do not talk about *who* they are but *what* they have. Once you know how greedy humans can be, you can step on them. Disgusting this kind of human element, isn't it? I bought ten hours of freedom for all of you from the Turks. The rest," he smiled, "I don't know. And about these two boats. These days Russia sells off its assets. Yes, even the noble heroes of the past, the KGB. You would not have gotten very far with a cutter anyway. Now let's move."

"What do you want to do with us, kill us?"

"If you want to be a hero and do something obtuse, the answer is yes. Take your passport and tickets from the truck."

Adding with the smiling tone of a real gentleman: "I also appreciate your assistance, loading the boats."

It was nearly day now. They walked in silence with Fon onto the pier. Behind them the guard threw the dead Berret into the sleeping cabin of the tractor and then the Chinese started the engine. The truck rolled through the underpass of nature onto the jetty. It was maneuvered and positioned parallel with the steel pier, the wheels on the edge of it. One of the Chinese guards moved to the back and turned the latches of the empty trailer. The doors opened. From the boat closer to the rig they brought powerful Black and Decker tools. They unscrewed the eight aluminum guards and two front walls inside the reefer. It exposed the careful, like a gold brick wall and the tremendous wealth in the five-inch airspace and gutters around the trailer.

The loading of the Pchelas began. The first bullions were packed on the obviously recently installed wooden floor in the cargo bay. It was back-braking work. By noon the two Pchela were ready to move.

31

Inside the boats.

Invisible.

The most powerful explosive ever invented.

Semtex. Tweny-five pounds of it. (It's inventor, Bohumil Sole, blew up himself with his own invention in 1997).

The explosive was artfully wired to a radio receiver. Fon had the oscillator in his pocket. If he would press the switch, a high frequency was transmitted. Once the frequency was absorbed by the receiver, a tone would escalate registering the amplify. At a certain point a fuse would burn through and break the circuit. This short then activated a timed signal which could not be stopped anymore, once set off.

*

The last seconds off the truck.

One of the Singaporean started the engine and moved the truck down the jetty, shifting and speeding up. The *Volvo* rolled in high acceleration to distribute with its last assignment to the irrevocable conclusion of the whole operation. To vanish. At the end of the pier the rig had reached a speed of 45mph. The guard-driver opened the door and in an elegant jump dove from the moving carriage into the water, separating himself from the deadly momentum of the forward movement. Actually the rig budged another ten food through the air before it descended into the sea with the extinct Berret in it.

Fon Yun made a sharp gesture to the first Pchela, underlining his order with a short motion of his HK. A flux which nobody could disregard in its unquestionable dominion. They unhitched the mooring lines and pulled the fenders aboard. One of Fon's henchmen started the engines.

A loud and introductory rumble gave in to murmurs of the powerful engines as the bodyguard kept it moving from the pier, as swiftly as possible. Reversed only twice before moving forward. The second boat followed with the same sumptuous and quick maneuver. After five hundred yards the boats had reached the open waters. The exhaust system gurgled for some more seconds beneath the waterline. The drivers, almost simultaneously, pushed the throttle forward and brought the vessels up to full speed in seconds. The Pchelas appreciated the sudden freedom, raised their hulls above the water queue on their 'skis' and leaped forward. Picking up the fifty knots easily they almost flew above the surface. The men on the helm showed nerves like steel, driving their boats exactly eight feet from each other. They were so close together that they would appeared on any radar screen in the area as only one single scratch. Tom knew it was not over yet.

*

The rushing wind of the high speed and the noises of the engine would have changed talk into an absurd screeching. They went for seventy minutes at fifty-five knots. South, in the dazed light the coast of Cyprus appeared. The men at the helm kept the hydro foils south-southwest for another thirty miles. When there was no land to see anymore, they cut the engine abruptly. The water piercing surface system stopped acting and the Pchea's hulls sank from its five feet high into the water and rested. The men threw one mooring line aft and stern and tied the boats loosely together.

There was silence between the boats, men, water and the nebula of the day, the sun. The sea's companion, the wind, normally swirling around playfully with the surface, had disappeared like waiting behind the horizons to find out what would happen next.

Tom looked at Rosco. He did not know what to make out of it. He expected that they would be tossed any second overboard. He did not wanted to die. He did not want to be thrown into the sea. He wanted to live and be with Rachel. He would plead with all reasons in the world. All this reasons would be Rachel. To his surprise he noticed how calm she was. Wondered for a moment what thoughts went through her mind.

"You will live," Fon Yun said and clutched his hand behind his back. He read Tom's fear.

"How can we trust you?"

The Chinese brought out a light smile.

"You do not have to, but let me . . ."

At the same moment the door to the wheelhouse opened and the handsome Malay, who was at the helm, pointed to the western blue-grey horizon. Fon took a binocular and skimmed the skyline above the water.

His face lost its softness.

"We have some disturbance off the starboard bow. Coming to us," he said.

To Tom's surprise Fon gave the binoculars to Rosco. He scanned the horizon and caught it in an instant.

"Holly shit," he mumbled.

"What is it?" Tom asked.

Tom took the glasses and crossed the skyline twice with them. He spotted the dot slightly above the horizon. Ugly moving particle, like a smear at the blue sky's cathedral ceiling. The spot stopped. It just sat there. Tom kept the glasses on his eyes and watched when it started budging again. The dot made a circle and came in their direction. Straight for the Pchelas. Low, uncomfortably low. The chopper passed straight over them with its thunder popping noise and whining jet engine. Three-hundred feet away the helicopter executed a banking pivot, circled around the boats four more times and made another close pass over them for a final stern-to-aft look, rose sharply, leveled and was soon in the distance and small as it used to be when Tom saw it the first time on the horizon. Then it disappeared completely. The grey-blue matt skin had an insignia. A black circle with a white star imbedded. Three stripes left and right on a white star in the center.

It was a SH-2F Sea Sprite.

U.S. Navy.

*

It begun with a radar contact out of the ordinary and needed to be checked out. One hundred ten miles east, the aircraft carrier *U.S.S. Enterprise* lingered in the Mediterranean Sea.

The request had come from the Adana NSA station. The agency intercepted signals intelligence and conducted eavesdropping operations into this part of the world, using the finest listening equipment and satellites. They also kept track of what was going on in this part of the Mediterranean. One speck on the huge plotting screen, moving, after charting it out, with a speed of fifty-five knots south-west, raised the interest of the Adana station. The coded message was forwarded to the aircraft carrier *Enterprise* and the Sea Sprite took off for a check-up.

The crew detected nothing for the first twenty minutes into the flight and hovered for several minutes over the water to search the wide skyline. Co-pilot Hawking detected something. But he was not quite sure. Far out and north-east. The Sea Sprite began to move again and made a direct run for what they assumed they had seen. Two minutes later the chopper circled around the two small boats they just had detected.

"That's interesting. Two Pchela boats. See anything?"

The co-pilot pressed his binoculars against his eyes and adjusted it.

"Negative. Wait . . . this is . . . well . . . I see a lonely Chinese on one boat."

"You see . . . a what?? A . . . let's see it."

The co-pilot handed the glasses over.

It *was* a Chinese. How the hell would anybody believe this one? In the middle of the Mediterranean. A lonely Chinese on a Russian Pchela boat. He moved the binoculars to the second drifting boat. Nobody on it.

They flew four more circles before they went back to the *Enterprise*. Since it was close to the waters of Turkey it might be better if the Turkish Navy had a look into the matter.

*

Twenty minutes later a MEKO-200 frigate, the *Izar Celik*, changed course and began to search for two crafts. Pchelas. The Captain shook his head in silence. It was said that only one man, a man of Asian descent had been spotted on board.

*

Fon knew they had run out of time. The four Asians and the three American appeared from the wheelhouse where they had been hiding during the chopper's approach. He turned to the Malay guard and said something in Mandarin. It sounded like a sharp command. His men got ashen.

"You all will leave now," Fon said in a tone which would not allow any resistance.

Tom was stunned and began somehow to sense the depth of this man.

"Yes, but . . ."

"Go! Now! Or we all will die. Go. My men have precise order to serve you. You have shown enough courage."

The swiping gesture of Fon's hand followed. He stepped close to Rachel and looked at her, raised his hand and gently touched her face.

"Tamar," he said, "sister."

She narrowed her eyes and her mind fought desperately against this ultimate separation. They looked at each other and she tried to smile in understanding.

> you have to let me go now.
> i'll wait for you. somewhere,
> . . . out there.

Fon made a gentle motion with his head to the sky. Without looking back he went to the wheelhouse. Tom found himself staring at Rachel, trying to understand this strange closeness between Fong and her.

They jumped on the deck of the second Pchela. With a soft gurgling sound the single craft went slowly into a southerly course. Rachel looked back and saw the lonely man on the other boat, disappearing in the brightness of the lowering sun.

The warning came in form of a sound wave.

Just a distance of five miles (the sea is a good sound transmitter) across the sea one could hear the humming thundering sound of powerful diesel engines. Demise signaled his arrival.

Fon threw in a mighty motion the HK overboard. The vest with the hand grenades followed. There was no use for it anymore. But he kept his knife. The kris. The one with the oxidized dark spots on the blade. He had the oscillorator in the right pocket of his trousers.

He went into the wheelhouse. There he completed the ritual of the upcoming death by starting the engine. Slowly the boat moved west, into the direction of the approaching upcoming death. With this movement he also made sure that once the searching frigate would surface from out of the mist, the many eyes on board would be lured away from the second boat. It was a gamble. Fon, the pilgrim of time and space, had made himself the target. He stopped and let the craft drift in some unknown current. The engines idled. His last hunt had began. He closed his eyes and waited.

*

Captain Emin Hakarar of the frigate *Iza Celik* ordered a one-third from full ahead. The frigate slowed down. He took a binocular and searched the still sea. Five miles away he noticed the drifting boat. The Americans were right. It was a Pchela. But there should be two. He had seen them sometimes in the Black Sea during the Cold War. But here? In the Mediterranean? Strange, nobody was on board. He had to have a closer look. Than the Pchela moved again. West.

Leading the hunter away from the real prey.

*

Fon Yun increased the speed slightly, when the frigate appeared in the hazy sunlight, giving it a chance to close in on him slowly. He turned the Pchela onto a course to have the frigate behind him. And the sun in forepart. He had nothing else to do but keeping his course west. The frigate followed. It was the kind of inaudibility that one might imagine in outer space. The low thundering sound of the frigate was a part of it.

*

"Any radio contact?", Captain Hakarar asked, noticing that it became increasingly difficult to close in on the Pchela and stop it.

"Mad man," he mumbled, "he knows we are behind him. He needs a reminder."

The *Iza Celik* launched a 2.75-inch rocket at a range of one thousand feet. The Swiss made *Oerlikon* rocket hit the water and exploded thirty feet away from the bow of the Pchela, letting the water shoot a one-hundred impressive feet into the air with the intimidating sound of the explosion. The port side mounted 20mm Gatling gun fired and the slugs laid a string of pearls like looking impacts on the water surface. It was a clear message and not a seductive invitation for any other boat in a situation like this. Stop or be sunk.

Not so the Pchela.

*

The two 2,400 hp engines sprang to full life and rose the hull from the water surface as it leaped forward insect-like on its hydrofoils. Fon Yun had his eyes half closed when he moved the wheel swinging the racing boat around in a wide circle. His time to let life go had come.

For years he had lived with the sense of guilt in his awareness and the assumed disloyalty to beauty and goodness. His mind switched back to the burned down house in his hometown in Malaysia, the knowledge of the cruel death of his mother and father. To Tamar, his twin sister. The so senseless death of his young brothers and the funeral of his whole family, the scream he wanted to scream for over forty years and never did. Suffocating almost his soul. Tamar was alive and he had saved her and his men.

*

Fon Yun completed the nearly two-hundred-seventy degree sharp circle, facing the frigate. His consciousness was in a very precise and highly, but uncomplicated, stage of alertness. He pushed the lever down and asked the Pchela for everything she had. The boat rose another three inches out of the water and went for the frigate.

*

Captain Hakarar was pleased to see the effect of his rocket launch. The Pchela turned around and came back. He pressed his eyes against his binoculars and followed the course of this fast boat, which would now certainly slow down any second and stop. Everybody on the bridge was focused on the racing Pchela.

*

Fon Yun approached the forward moving frigate's bow at an angle of ten degree. The high speed and the last seconds of his life turned everything into a slow-motion performance, a trick of the mind. Something broke down inside him. It began with a great, deeply rooted chill in Fon Yun. An immense cold wave of a scream he had suppressed for so long. The act of suppression might have saved his sanity during the course of his life. The scream he brought up from inside where the soul might be, but never articulated. In that moment it was there. This scream had once turned inward to move to the deepest corner of his soul, where it waited for a long time to be released.

He screamed with a wide open mouth and screamed out the pain of years of destruction he also had created for himself and lived through. His death was now his moral choice to secure the survival of the seven people on the second boat and secured that at least, half of the treasure would reach the right owners. Fon Yun experienced with his adopted death the supreme test at the end of his outrunning life.

*

Blinded by ignorance and with a cold inquisitiveness Captain Emin Hakarar could see through binoculars into the wheelhouse of the Pchela. What he saw surprised him somehow. He saw the grimaced face of a Chinese. Like in screaming pain. The captain also noticed with horror that the Pchela would ram the frigate. Emir Hakarar shook his head, understanding as an expert of the sea, that the Pchela was no match for the frigate. People do strange things when they want to die. That was his thinking.

*

Fon had passed the stage where he would surrender to live. With the first touch of both vessels Fon Yun depressed the button of the oscillorator in his pocket. Twenty-five pounds of Semtex explosive erupted. The Pchela vaporized in an orb of fire.

*

Captain Emin Hakarar was thrown against the steel wall.

The last thing what he saw was a sheet of a bright fire moving in his direction. Then it absorbed his body in an orange glowing flash. The crew of the *Izar Celik* never knew what hit them. First the frigate's bow seemed to be hurled upward in her two-thirds-forward move. Than it crashed back. The force of the explosion peeled away the skin of the hull like opening a can of tuna. The momentum of the forward moving frigate's maneuver through the water funneled ten-thousand of gallons of water into the frigate at once, taking her down in an immediate nose-dive to the bottom of the sea in only seconds.

*

The force of the explosion concocted a striking mushroom of water. Raising almost two-hundred feet into the air, a sharp observer would have seen in the raising cloud of water, yellow bright sparks and flashes, reflecting the sunlight from solid matters. Stars of glimmers flew into different directions. Each spark was a bullion of gold. A lot of them. Worth nothing while sailing away and plunging back into the water of a salty sea.

The sound wave of a growling thunder rolled across the sea and reached the seven mortals on their boat. Rachel's head bend forward like she did not have any physical strength left.

32

Considering her age of only fifty-four, her skin was grey and brittle and her outer appearance was the one of a sloppy bitch. She was slow and had a sort of clumsy elegance. The scent she wore was the one of blue waters and salty winds.

Once when she was bright-eyed and energetic she had traveled three times with convoys from the coast of Maine to Murmansk during World War Two and delivered the sinews of hostilities. Tanks, airplanes, full bellies of ammunition, trucks, food and such. Following the most historical error of the United States, it went to the Soviet Union. Oh, this Land-Lease Agreement.

Her design was very simple. She was powered by one 2,500 horse-power three cylinder recipro-steam engines, developed in *1879*. Two-thousand seven-hundred-forty-two had been built in eighteen shipyards during the wartime program. This one's keel was laid at the Kaiser yard in Portland, on November 8, 1942, and was operational four days later, the record ever set for building a 10,000 toner. Now she was one of the last ships from World War Two. Her name was *Bell Rose* and she was a Liberty ship.

The summer of 1944 was her last run during World War Two. She carried fearful young men in uniforms from the shores of Boston across the Atlantic Ocean to Sicily to land with General Patton on European ground.

In Sicily the men in the earth-brown to-die-costumes left her behind. She was abandoned and soon forgotten like a woman a man had made love to for one night. And so the Mediterranean became her new home. Somebody bought her who did not deserve her. Some slimy merchant from Morocco. She did some dashes in the not really honorable swap of smuggling between Tangier and Italy. She bootlegged everything. From weapons, cigarettes, booze and silk. Whores from Tangier to Naples. You name it. She was caught with drugs at the island of Malta. It had something to do with a 'French

Connection' in Marseille. While the owner did time in the slammer, and there he was killed, because he had talked too much to his interrogators, she was chained in the port of Valetta, never to sail again. Nobody wanted her anymore. It seemed to be her fate was final and she was destined for a scrap yard. It was a close call for her.

But she was bought 'as is'. The new owner was a ship broker with the unique combination of names, Gerry Papadopulous from Brooklyn. The deal was closed in a rat hole of an office in the Empire State Building between stale air and the 'General Consulate of Israel' at the end of the floor. The new buyer did not even dare to think about taking out an insurance against a major repair, which might have been necessary after the usual inspection.

Her new country of registration was Panama, regardless of the fact that the new owner did not have the sincere intention of ever getting closer than ten-thousand miles to the 'Middle Americas', except paying the yearly registration fees. And she never made it to Panama either.

But she sailed again. Delivered some used machinery from Odessa(Russia) to Michigan. After this big trip, she did some piddling voyages of timber and wine from Spain, scrap metal from Germany, between the local shores of North Africa and the rest around.

She ended up in Haifa with a broken down engine and underwent a major overhaul. This included a rebuild 16,900 hp Sulzer engine from Winterthur in Switzerland and a new name. She also received a new skin of several layers of fresh paint of different color. The facelift helped but she still kept the relict of an old steamship and was accepted with her new name, *Nimrod*. She knew all the ports around the Mediterranean Sea. Still she was considered to be a tramp, shuttling from port to port in the Eastern Mediterranean, delivering commodities and taking merchandises along. That was her official job.

What nobody assumed was that the real new owner was the Israel Navy Intelligence. The crew—Mossad and AMAN[12] men in a joint venture operation—highly trained no-nonsense-men. Inside her was a hatch in number two hold, separating the smelly commercial part of the ship from a newly installed room with no window. The room itself contained the best electronic gears money could buy with Israel's own new reconnaissance outfit. In short, she had changed her profession and was now a spy ship.

*

---

[12]   Military Intelligence of Israel.

During the last two days something had gone wrong with her. Her speed was slow and she was limping through the calm sea along the thirty-second longitude. North. The disappearing Cape Arnauti, Cyprus' most western point was the last reference point for Captain Gerry Steinberger. And here he received the coded radio message from AMAN he had waited so long for.

The search for the two Pchelas began.

Five minutes later a correction was radioed in. One Pchela only. Steinberger made some last calculations and bent over the charts. His right index finger went along the course, then looked at another map. They would meet the boat in less than one hour. Captain Steinberger ordered the new course.

Among the men on the bridge was a tall man with the slight appearance of Burt Lancaster. Being dressed casually in jeans and a white T-shirt, the man did not conceal the obviously strong military training. The short dark hair did not hide the gray in it. General Ephraim Katz looked in thought down at the map and followed mentally the Captain's calculations.

"Where are we?", the General asked in a calm voice. He was hiding his personal excitement behind a cool professional mask, being so close to the goal he had worked for all these years.

"We are . . . here," the Captain pointed with his sharp pencil at the extended map, indicating a light cross on it.

"And what is the position of the boat?"

"They are here," the Captain replied and showed the General the Pchela's position on the map.

"So, we're right on schedule?"

Captain Steinberger nodded, "yes, another twenty minutes."

The clock read 15:35.

The Nimrod's engine came roaring to life. A wisp of black oily smoke appeared for a second at the top of the funnel and she went into a north-northwest course with at seventeen knots.

*

Exactly at 15:35 the Pchela changed course and went straight south at forty knots. Tom noticed that Rosco was somehow restless and looked at his watch several times. He then scanned with two Singaporeans constantly with their binoculars the southern horizon. As far as Tom understood, there was something wrong. Rosco was aware about something he, Tom, did not know. The confusion rose in Tom. Why this consistent scanning? He stood silently beside Rosco and was tempted to say something when he saw the winner-smile in Rosco's face.

"There you are," he heard.

Rosco lowered the binoculars and said something to the helmsman in a language Tom did not understand (it was Hebrew). The boat increased its speed for five minutes to thirty knots, until it was only one-hundred feet away from a ship. A Liberty ship with the name, clearly to read in white large bold letters, *Nimrod.* The Pchela circled around the freighter in closing spirals as Rosco scanned the ship through the binoculars. The whole thing did not make sense, until Tom read the letters on the aft. The freighter was even from Panama. It hit Tom and a chilling cold grabbed his neck. Anger shot up in him.

"You double-crossing two timers. You bastard. You motherfu . . . , you . . ."

He lunged at Rosco and felt at the same time a blow on his head, making everything spin in front of him. Tom's eyes recorded the entire scene in a fast slow motion picture formulation. He saw Rachel leaping for the Chinese like a Cheetah would rough up any enemy to protect her cubs. But she was no match. The last that Tom saw, to his surprise, the Chinese did not hurt Rachel. He dropped his fingertip in a sort of a very domesticated move behind Rachel's right ear. Just slightly behind, were the Pneumogastric Nerve with its most far-reaching share of nerves passed through the neck, is. Normally the blow could have killed her. But placed with skill it would not do any harm. Rachel had a child-like surprised face before she went down.

Tom heard a second explosive-like sound, created by the Malay's open-handed whack. It was a well calculated slap against a certain point of his head. Used by an expert the blow would not have left a mark but would have killed Tom. This kind of killing would have been undetectable in an autopsy. To use this kind of sensitive "touch" to whack somebody out meant not to have the willingness to kill. While fainting somehow Tom admired in a rush of irrational thinking the efficiency of the man who knocked him out. They did not want to kill him. He really had never considered that this kind of violence would be the end of what had began (how long ago?) with the charm of a saloon conversation in Napa, California. The impact had thrown him against the wall. He bounced back and the ceiling of the bridge circled around him. He saw a flash of bright sunlight through the window and felt sick. For a fraction of a second he saw Rosco's face. 'Traitor' he wanted to yell. Wondered were Rachel was and he should not look into the sun when the window would appear the next time. Because it would not be good for the eyes. No window showed up anymore. The floor came closer and circled around him. He gave in to the embracing darkness and was surprised how easy it was to die. Didn't feel Rosco's arms holding him gentle to soften his collapse.

Artfully the man at the helm brought the Pchela in a short maneuver along the freighter. One hundred men began to unload the Pchela in a way they had trained for this operation, in absolute secrecy in an emptied and closely guarded hangar of the Israel Air Force by Be'er Yaakov. It took only thirty minutes. The board crane had moved between the Pchela and the freighter just four times. In her adventurous life of war, smuggling and surveillance the Nimrod never had carried precious metal. Not an ounce. Now she had three tons of it in her guts.

Tom wanted to wake up. Mental clouds covered him and did not really let him awaken. The name 'Rosco' burst into his mind, demanding his intellectual response. It was pointless for Tom to speculate about why Rosco had betrayed them all and people had died. He was a spy. Rosco had been sleuthed all along. Slowly Tom raised his hands and massaged his eyes with the tips of his left and right thumbs. The worst part for him was, he liked Rosco as a friend. It was like an emotional amputation.

He opened his eyes and somehow he was not surprised to see Rosco sitting on a chair beside the bed he was laying on it. Rosco's face was calm and he had a thin smile carved into the landscape of his tired face. Turning his head for a moment, he saw Rachel. Christ, she still wore the same jeans. She slept with her shoes on, but somebody had loosened the laces. Rosco had obviously watched him since Tom had been brought into this bunk.

"Why?" he asked.

"Well, we had to silence you for some minutes. You might have been in the way."

"That's not what I mean. Why?"

"I am not a traitor, you think I am."

"Yes, you are. I should have killed you."

"You wouldn't. Because you are not a killer. You okay?"

"Ohh . . . screw you. Yes."

"Now I know, you're okay," Rosco smiled, "come".

"Alright."

Tom got up from the bed and stood for a moment on unsteady feet and tried to assess the whole situation he was in. It still did not make sense. Rosco did not make sense. The ship did not make sense. The bed did not make sense. He looked at the sleeping Rachel. She did not make sense to him either.

"Let her sleep. Come."

*

Left-over daylight rested across the western horizon. An explosive expert had rewired the Pchela with its twenty pounds of explosives. The explosives had been shaped like a hallow-out hemisphere that directed its destructive force downward.

When the *Nimrod* was clear, the expert pulled a lever on his radio ignition. It was a dull and short thunder, and the boat seemed to sag in the middle immediately. The ex-KGB craft began to sink, lethargically first, like a living being, not understanding the lack of loyalty, after she had saved the men's and the woman's life. Why wanted they to kill her? The bow went under. Her hull rolled to the right side, like a wounded whale, and then she was gone.

Captain Garry Steinberg did not like to sink ships. But it was a necessity. Before he set the new course the radio man sent out a message announcing that two persons, American tourists, a man and a woman, had been rescued from a sailboat which had taken on too much water through its leaking hull, and sank. Their names were Tom and Rachel Peters. A third person, male, a Mark Berret, had drowned (which was true to a certain extent). The Captain ordered full speed ahead.

Haifa. Israel.

*

Tom sat silently on a coil of manila ropes and watched the blue sky, still trying to assimilate what had happened in the last hours. He sat there with hanging shoulders and helplessly, rubbing his hands. Somebody sat down beside him. He did not have to look. It was Rosco.

"It was not your gold . . . not ours," he heard Rosco's calm voice, "you see," he sighted deeply, "when we were at this drop point 47. Remember? I picked up one of these gold bricks. Somebody had engraved words. Gold teeth had been broken out from people's mouth."

He shook his head.

"You see, it all had been stolen, Tom, it came from the camps, from all over Europe. The gold had been melted down together with rings and gold watches. Can you imagine as much as 72 pounds of gold was wrestled every day from the mouths of people. You understand?"

It began to dawn on Tom. They had used him and Rachel.

"Is this the reason—Israel?"

"Yes."

A shadow bent down over Tom and Rosco got up.

Tom paused, not having a chance to collect his thoughts.

"General, this is Tom Peters."

General Ephraim Katz reached out his right hand with a warm smile.

"I'm glad to meet you," the General said," you're a fearless soldier. And I want to apologize, we have used you."

"You cannot live with blood gold. Can you?"

Tom became angry.

"H'bout Berret. He is dead."

The silence was heavy between the three veterans when Rachel came. She sat down beside Tom and began to rub his shoulder in gentle motions.

"I know, and there is nothing I can say," the General replied, "but you have to admit it was your superb logistics we used to be successful. And you wanted the gold too. Didn't you? Sounds hard but the . . . well, the thing with your friend Berret, I understand that was his name, would have happened anyway . . ."

"Why didn't you do it yourself? You . . . you with your prestigious Mossad, AMAN, Unit 131 or whatever the you have in store."

"Well, young man, there is the factor of politics, you see. Should *we* have operated inside Iraq and Turkey? Think about the consequences for a moment. Would you excuse me now?"

The General walked back to the accommodation section of the ship.

"What about this Fon . . . or whatever his name was. And how did you come together with him?"

Rosco's took a deep breath.

"Fon? I met him in the Jaffe Center for Strategic Studies at the Tel-Aviv University. He thought two courses about prevention of terrorism in Asia. Don't ask me how he got there. I don't know. But I think it began when General Poran served as defense adviser to the Singapore Government."

"Who is Poran?"

"Former Adviser to Prime Minister Begin and the connection between Israel and Singapore. You see, Israel's relationship with Singapore goes back to 1969. The Singaporeans bought from Israel fifty used AMX-13 tanks and later thirty-six Gabrial missiles. Singapore was vulnerable at this time like Israel. They even had a military mission in Singapore with forty-five military mentors. Until 1974. But now it is the main Mossad station in Asia."

"Where does this Fon Yun fit in?"

"Fon designed the over-all security logistics for Singapore. In 1976 a bomb exploded in the Israeli embassy. Fon's son was there in a meeting when it happened. He died without a face. By 1985 somebody tried to place another bomb. Fon was sick of the violence and an angry man. So he offered his help. Then he learned about the loot, the stolen metals, and the stolen art. He had lost his family in only one night. But this was a long time ago."

"So, you all used me?"

"Yes, we did."

"Where do you fit in, Rosco? Did you work for them?"

"No, I did not work for them. I worked *with* them."

Rosco moved his head to look at Ephraim Katz.

*

Napa, California

A cool but brilliant sun rose and left the Napa Valley still in hazy white velvet of transparent fog. It would soon burn off in the rising sun. Rachel took a deep breath and glanced up at the sky. She was home.

"I love you. Seeing you is like coming home."

She smiled and wished Tom would say it again, write it down. Those wonderful words. But she let it sink into her memory, knowing they only had the 'Now.'

*

The envelope was a simple one, and arrived with the normal mail. Nothing fancy. The left upper corner revealed in bold font size, courier new twelve, the sender.

Cooper, Shagan & Yun, with law offices in San Francisco, Hong Kong, Singapore and Tel Aviv. The off-white legal size message to Mr. and Mrs. Peters was to visit the office in San Francisco at their earliest convenience to finalize a matter, which was not verbalized any further in writing.

*

Helen Berret, mother of Mark Berret, received a phone call from a bank in Eureka, California, she had never heard of, letting her know that the current bank balance of her account was now two-hundred thousand and the taxes on it were paid. According to the letter, the money was inherited from some relative who had died in South Africa. It could not be proven otherwise. She never heard from her son again.

Cherryl Duskin, in San Diego, signed for a certified letter, accompanying a certified check made out by the Hong Kong Shanghai Banking Corporation in Singapore. She had inherited two-hundred-thousand dollars and never saw her son again.

*

On page seven of the *Washington Post*, on this day and month, in the left lower corner, was a three-by-two-inch short column.

"Divers of the Turkish Navy, investigating the fate of the frigate *Iza Celik*, discovered four deformed gold bullions in the engine room of the sunken vessel. The investigation is still underway. No one had an explanation for the tragedy. Smuggling and foul play had not been ruled out.

*

Tourists discovered an entirely unknown underground city in Anatolia, Turkey. Nobody understood why a huge crashed Russian helicopter sat almost in the middle of the cave. On a weekend, DDCI David Meyers read about the chopper and the Turkish unknown cave in his Daily Briefings.

He raised his head and looked out the window at his home in snow covered Connecticut. Stared into the soft falling white flakes of snow and shook his head. Then he chuckled, smiled, and shook his head: "I'll be darned."

He kept the assumption to himself.

*

The new station officer in Ankara, Francis B. Walker oversees certain activities in the Middle East.

Garry Kessler resigned from the service and studies theology. It is said he will be a minister of a congregation in a small town somewhere in Oregon.

*

What about Gaidar? Gaidar dealt with stolen diamonds from Russia's state treasure. Gaidar could not have done it on his own.

London would not allow this.

Warned the conglomerate's three-hundred wholesalers with the given license of the Central Selling Organization in London to tell the dealer and stealers about the dumping of Russian diamonds.

They cautioned Gaidar.

Gaidar didn't listen.

Gaidar didn't believe it.

It happened one early morning. Gaidar stepped out from the elevator on his third floor office. He glanced at the three men in their high-priced suits and briefcases, standing there in front of the opening sliding doors, waiting for Gaidar. The three entered the elevator. Gaidar had heard how matters were handled by the cartel, when an alien would deal with "outside goods", try to sell the flash without their blessings.

At this time of the day the floor was empty. He wanted to leave the elevator. They didn't let him. Pushed him against the back wall. One of them even apologized. Gaidar granted his mind permission to understand the seriousness of the moment. A thin wire, daylight reflected from it, falling through the front windows where the elevator had landed, on its angular surface. Looked like a guitar string. The one who did it was a short stocky fellow. Gaidar recognized him clearly as his murderer. The wire looped around Gaidar's neck. Ten seconds later, Gaidar was dead. De Beers does business as usual. Moscow sells its diamonds to De Beers again.

*

Rachel and Tom moved away. They went on an extended vacation. It was their second honeymoon. A year later Rachel gave birth to a girl. She was named Tamar Y. The last letter stands for Yun.

THE END